The Exile of Nicholas Misterton

Acknowledgements

I would like to thank Ricky, Debi and Ian at Ellipsis,
and Andrew at Clays for their generous support in the production of this book,
and I am eternally grateful to those who inspired me, in different ways, to write the story.

First published in the UK 2014 by Vance Wood
www.vancewoodnovelist.co.uk

ISBN 978-0-992-96130-5

Copyright © Vance Wood 2014

The right of Vance Wood to be identified as the
author of this work has been asserted by him in accordance
with the Copyright, Designs and Patents Act 1988.

All rights reserved. No part of this publication may be reproduced,
stored in or introduced into a retrieval system, or transmitted, in any form,
or by any means (electronic, mechanical, photocopying, recording or otherwise)
without the prior written permission of the publisher. Any person who
does any unauthorized act in relation to this publication may be
liable to criminal prosecution and civil claims for damages.

This novel is entirely a work of fiction. The names, characters,
with the exception of a few historical figures, and incidents portrayed in it
are the work of the author's imagination.

1 3 5 7 9 8 6 4 2

Typeset by Ellipsis Digital Limited, Glasgow
Jacket design by Ian Cardwell, Ellipsis Digital Limited, Glasgow
Printed and bound in Great Britain by Clays Ltd, St Ives plc

This book is sold subject to the condition that it shall not, by way
of trade or otherwise, be lent, re-sold, hired out, or otherwise circulated
without the publisher's prior consent in any form of binding or cover other than
that in which it is published and without a similar condition including
this condition being imposed on the subsequent purchaser.

For all those I love

The Exile of Nicholas Misterton

Vance Wood

With best wishes.

Vance Wood

03 December 2015

CONJUROR

Chapter One

On a fine day, you can see two dishes of grey sea but no human being on or between the coastal hills as smooth as ducks' eggs. Gifford's Farm stares out over Marshwood Vale towards them, as if trying to spot any tell-tale sign, such as a plume of smoke or cart as high with hay as the trees, that the landscape has not been abandoned by farmers and labourers. At twilight, it feels almost deserted. Distant barking drifts across fields, the only replies the complaints of sheep, cows, and crows.

No one but birds could see Nicholas Misterton making his reluctant way from Pilsdon Pen to see Farmer Stockwood; the hedgerows, bubbling with black brambles, hid him. He dragged his feet, thinking about the message sent to him, late in the day, as he and Wilfred Sedgecroft had been stacking stooks of reeds into golden barrows in the top field.

"Best to do as the master says, Nicholas. He's a proper temper on him, these days," Wilfred had advised, wiping his sweating brow on his sleeve.

"Just when we've nearly done for the day!" Nicholas had lamented. "All in good time, though. I shall see him, but he'll have to wait. I shan't be rushing for anybody after a day's hard cutting."

Wilfred had watched him amble out of the field.

"And don't you get answering him back now as you do me, or you and he'll part company as quickly as a hare leaps across this field. It don't do any good to go a-sticking up to our masters," he had muttered, as if reminding himself that work and a straw bed in the barn were hard to come by in those parts.

Zachariah Stockwood fidgeted by the window, unused to being kept waiting. George Ludwell, the messenger, had been back in the farmyard twenty minutes. The grandfather clock, standing sentry by the door, struck solemnly. On the last chime, Nicholas came into view, his pace unhurried, surveying the scene, admiring the green amphitheatre in which he took centre stage, stretched his arms upwards as if casting off the day's aches and pains, and yawned exaggeratedly.

"What is it, Father?" asked Victoria, who had entered the room to inform him that bread, cheese, pickled onions, and cider were on the kitchen table.

Stockwood turned mechanically, abstractedly.

"Nothing. Just watching the sun go down over yonder. I like this time of day. It's supernatural."

Victoria recognised the signs that he was lying: his half-glance at her, the quickness of his reply, and the broken smile. She edged towards him, and he backed to block the window with his square, wide shoulders.

"Are you expecting anyone?" she asked. "I can move the victuals."

"No, you run along, and I'll be in, in a minute. Go on now, my pretty chicken."

His feeble endearment did not deceive her, but she left the room, he then free to intercept Nicholas Misterton before she could catch sight of him.

"You took your time!" accused Stockwood. "Ludwell's been back ages."

They were now hidden from the farmhouse; artfully, Stockwood had guided Misterton behind a hedge.

"We just had those last few stooks to bind and stack. Couldn't leave Wilfred on his own. I came as soon as I could."

"Well, that's as may be, though you didn't appear to be busting to get here when I spies you a-coming down from Pilsdon."

Misterton looked away, the shrug of his shoulders barely perceptible.

"I came as soon as I could."

After a pause in which Stockwood tried to control his anger, he said, "So you say, so we shall leave that one alone. Now, what I've got to say to you aint to do with scything, herding, or lambing, but everything to do with you and your secret ways."

"My ways? I don't rightly know what you're on about. Since you set me on, a year ago, I've strained every muscle in my body for you, all hours God sends," Misterton reminded him.

"As I just said, it aint to do with your work. My Victoria, see, she . . . well, I know she's taken a shine to you, but you're a grown man, nearly, and it's not right you turning her head, behind my back. I rue the day I ever hired you, I do!"

"Well, your daughter's a grown woman, nearly, and knows her own mind. As for turning her head, I can't help the way she feels."

Stockwood clenched his fists till they were like knots on tree bark.

"When I set you on in Bridport, it was to work in the fields, and mind your own business, not polish your silver tongue on Victoria. Oh, I'll admit, it don't matter in the milking parlour; brightens up their day, no doubt, but you'll not mess with me and mine. So, you can collect your things from the loft and be off. I don't want you hanging around these parts, either. If I catch you anywhere near Gifford's Farm, I'll shoot you!"

"Why, it aint your land anyway. Does Mr. Gifford know one of his tenants is evicting a worker without just reason?"

"He does, and he said he'd shoot you rather than look at you."

Misterton's face drained of colour, his black, wavy hair accentuating his pallor. He had not been expecting dismissal, just the usual reprimand for something trivial, and he wondered who had told Stockwood about his trysts with Victoria at Shave Cross.

"No harm's done. I respect your daughter, but she's her own woman, and though she's as pretty as Marshwood Vale, it's not for the likes of a common man like me to go thinking above his station. Why would I take the risk and be back to knocking on doors, a-begging, eh?"

Above, frenzied martins slashed the sky as they sped from the house to nearby trees, distracting the men. Then Megan, the farmyard collie, slunk round the corner and pricked up her ears, sensing her master's antagonism towards Misterton.

Anxious to have the final say, Stockwood produced coins from his pocket, and offered them.

"Go now and be gone for good. You'll know what to expect if I see you," he warned.

Without hesitation or further argument, Misterton took his week's wages early, having gone without money too many times to stand on his pride.

"Am I allowed to say goodbye to the girls in the parlour?"

Stockwood nodded grudgingly.

"They're be just in the middle of milking, so don't keep them long. They've work to do."

Then he clicked his tongue to Megan to follow him back to the house.

As Misterton made his way to the milking parlour, he saw, out of the corner of his eye, white mist tumbling down Pilsdon Pen. In the air was the scent of burning oak. The sun slipped behind the hills, making the vale darker, and shadows stretched across fields.

Outside the parlour, he could hear Edna, Mabel, and Edith, singing their favourite song:

"When he loves her no more,
when her kisses him bore,
then back he will come
through the open barn door."

The door was half-open, and he watched them leaning their cheeks against the gleaming flanks of the cows, the milk drumming against the inside of the pails. Tiny, big-handed Edna squeezed hard and quickly; Mabel, full-cheeked and dimpled, sang out of tune; and Edith, tall and slim, milked blindly, her blond, wavy hair flopping over her blue eyes.

Misterton stole into the barn, just as he had done on his first day, when he had made love with his smile to all three of them, and stood near them but out of sight till they had finished their song with a giggle and sigh.

"I've come to say goodbye," he stated matter-of-factly.

They started, unsettling the cows, which rocked as they turned their heads inquisitively.

"Goodbye?" echoed Edna.

"Why?" asked Mabel.

"Master's had enough of me, so I've to go right away as soon as I've packed my bag."

Edith could not bring herself to look at him, and moved to another cow, so that she was hidden. The other two watched her slide out of sight, then turned to Misterton.

"Where will you go, this time of night? Can't he let you stay till the morning?" suggested Edna.

Misterton shook his head, stepped forward, and invited her into his arms, his sleeves rolled up, revealing his golden skin and muscles of rope. She wiped her hands on her smock. Her body shook against him, and he kissed the top of her head, as a father a child. Mabel watched them, knowing it was her turn next. As he drew her to him, she glanced up at him, wondering if he would kiss her on the lips, as he had done impulsively after drinking cider at Beaminster Fair. This time, he pecked her on the cheek, his lips less rough than before, she thought, the perfume of apples again on his breath. Edith knew what was coming, but stiffened and stopped milking.

"Edith," called Mabel, "Nicholas is going now. Aint you a-going to see him off with us?"

Edith pretended she had not heard and resumed milking. Nicholas looked at Edna, who shrugged. Mabel shook her head.

"I'll be off, then," decided Misterton, leaving to collect his belongings.

When he was out of sight, Edna went round to Edith and snapped, "There was no call for that!"

Edith kept her back to her, to hide her tears.

"Leave her be, Edna," called Mabel. "It's up to her."

At Shave Cross, by the signpost, waited Victoria. Her father was used to her taking an evening stroll. She loved the stillness of the end of the day, when the hedgerows fluttered, and rabbits limped into the lanes. In the pale, blue sky, the opaque half-moon was a scythe, and Misterton was late.

When he came round the corner, she moved towards him, but halted when she noticed his bag slung across his shoulder. Usually, there was a porcupine of wheat, his good luck omen, he said, behind his ear. Instead, he wore only his green, felt hat.

"I'm surprised you're here," he began.

She held back from kissing him when she felt his tension. His bag bulged. It was still too warm to wear a coat, but he did so.

"What's the matter?" she asked, her skin pimpling with anticipation of bad news.

His sigh was long and hopeless.

"He knows, and now I'm to go with a few pennies in my pocket. Somebody's seen us."

"Who? How could they?"

"Who don't matter. I'm going to be shot dead if he catches me hanging around."

Her heart thumped, reminding her of the beat of the breast of the baby rabbit she had prised from Megan's mouth, earlier, that day.

"I'll come with you. I won't give you up, Nicholas. We'll get by. We could get married. I have a little money of my own. Come. I'm ready." Misterton looked at her hand stretching towards him, and she saw he was tempted. "I'm old enough to do as I please."

Misterton enclosed her fingertips, at arm's length, and shook his head.

"We can't get married. He thinks you can do better for yourself, that you'd be better off with a rich farmer or land-owner, and he's probably right. I have no money, no house, no prospects. You'd despise me after a while, and that would be worse than me going away."

She bit her lip, and a gunshot cracked in the distance. They both jumped, fearing Stockwood was trying to carry out his threat. Mischievously, Misterton theatrically felt his torso for wounds, but Victoria was not impressed with his ill-judged humour.

"You jest as you walk away from me?"

Misterton put his finger to his lips.

"Someone might hear us, and the next gunshot might be your father's," he pointed out.

His bag stayed round his neck, and she sensed that their tryst would not last much longer. In the fading light, his eyes, which had fixed hers whenever they had met, disappeared. He was becoming part of the hedge.

"Is this the last time I shall see you?" she cried, leaping forward and grabbing him round the waist. Her chin, buried in his chest, hurt him. "Will you send word to me? You know, when you've found another job?"

Her desperation reminded him of their good times together:

when he had pressed her against a haystack, and how pieces of straw had stuck in her hair; the declarations of her undying love for him; when she, scented by yeast and flour, brought him loaves she had baked. These were worth a lie.

"Yes, I will. Of course, I will. It's just that tonight we wouldn't get a room together, round these parts. You know what folk are like. But I'll write, just as soon as I'm set up and working again."

"When will that be? Say it'll be soon!"

That was the best and worst about her: her need of him. His going made her feel as empty as a field ploughed into bare, rough rills, on a wintry day.

"I can't say. Wilfred says wages is dropping all over Dorset. Farmers is getting greedier. Say a word, he reckons, and you're gone before the sentence is out. But I'm a good worker."

Then she had an idea, which excited her as much as the discovery of a nest with a sleepy-eyed blackbird in it.

"Let me speak to Father. If he knew we loved each other, he'd change his mind. I can be stubborn as him when I put my mind to it."

Misterton momentarily considered this, then slowly shook his head.

"No, he's taken against me. It's not just that we've gone behind his back. It's because of what I am as well as who I am."

"How do you know? You're a decent man, a good worker," she argued.

"Thank you, my sweet, but he has a lot to lose with me, and much to gain by marrying you off to some rich fellow. But I shall write, and, in the meantime, don't fret."

He kissed her decisively on the mouth, drew away, and soon was out of sight.

She stopped crying and turned up the lane towards Gifford's Farm. Her decision not to show her wretchedness to her father was taken when she remembered Misterton's promise to write. Should she help finish the milking? But the prospect of the three maids being stiff towards her sent her straight to her room to wash her face.

The road to Bridport was long and meandering. The moon was scored by branches, and sat on the top of the high hedgerow. In front of him, a barn owl flapped noisily, looked at him as if to say, "What are you doing here?" He strode quickly, wanting to be back in town, have contact with people again. His hunger grew, and the coins in his coat pockets reassured him that they would buy food and a bed in one of the inns, for one night only.

In Bridport, he walked up the hill. The moonlight laved the dome of the bell-tower, at the top. Down the hill clop-clopped a horse and a ghostly carriage, squeaking and creaking as it bumped over holes in the road.

He turned right onto the road to West Bay, a long, straight, silver avenue, inns and shops at the top, terraced cottages at the bottom. Outside The Thatcher's Rest, he hesitated, then continued determinedly. His heart began to race, and his mouth dried. It had been a long time since he had last walked along that road, and it had been in the opposite direction. All the doors looked similar. The one for which he was looking had once faced the Quakers' Meeting House. That must be the one, he decided.

The curtains were closed. No sound came from within. It had been ages: three harvests, and winters cruel enough to lay him up with a chest infection. A barn, he knew now from experience, was no place to sleep when the ice sets in swirls and whorls on the farmhouse's windows. He had forfeited the right to knock now, to turn up unannounced, but that was what life was: never knowing when you might knock on a door, or have to open one to someone you guessed would come, but not know when.

"Was that eight striking?" called an old man, across the road.

"Nine," replied Misterton.

"Oh."

Misterton waited for him to be out of earshot. The man was wheezing and tapping his stick like a blind man, and his face was ghastly.

The bolt banged back, and the door opened to reveal a man, holding a candle.

Misterton looked at his face. Was it the right house? The man waited for him to state his business.

"Sorry to disturb you at this hour, but does a girl by the name of Ruth Abbas live here?"

He felt the man examining him.

"Who's asking?"

Misterton thought quickly.

"One who lost contact with her and wondered whether she fared well or what in these difficult times."

"Been gone ages. We've been here since June. Place was empty."

"Did you ever see her?"

Then, behind him, appeared a woman, a blanket round her shoulders.

"What is it?" she asked.

"Fellow here wants to know if a Ruth Abbas lives here. Don't know the name myself."

The woman stepped forward, interrogated Misterton's expression, and knew instinctively who he was.

"Yes, you do, Christopher. She used to live here, but now she don't."

"Where did she go?"

Christopher turned to look at his wife.

"Well, I didn't want you to know because you'd have turned down a perfectly good house on the back of a bit of superstition, but the fact is, she went to Heaven, or Hell, where some folk believe you go when you do what she went and done."

Misterton had no patience for riddles.

"For God's sake, woman, speak plainly, will you?"

"Now don't you go taking the Lord's name in vain, coming here and a-knocking, at this time of night!" defended Christopher.

"All I want's a straight answer to a straight question."

The woman took a deep breath before giving her visitor satisfaction.

"Well, the truth is – at least, it's what folk said at the time, though the landlord didn't want folk knowing case it put them off coming here – that she jumped off the cliff at West Bay, on purpose. Folk who saw her do it said it was deliberate."

Misterton turned his back on them, and, without an expression of gratitude for this information, walked back up the street, bereft of appetite for food, and crumbling, like the cliffs at West Bay, with guilt at having pushed his wife to her death, in a manner of speaking.

Chapter Two

"He aint dead by the sound of it," observed the landlady of The Mariner's Cutlass to her husband. "Snores like a stuck pig."

"It's a blessed wonder he aint gone after drinking what he did, last night. Paid for it, though. Probably gave me too much, if truth be told, the state he was in, though I don't rightly recollect, what with my head a-banging and a-clanging, and my stomach feeling like an anchor's being dragged around it," confessed the landlord. "He could have handed over a treasure chest and neither of us would have been the wiser."

"Well, it's time he was up and off after a bit of breakfast. I must admit I didn't like the look of him. 'I'm a Bridport man,' he says. 'Which street?' I asks. And did you see him robbed of his tongue when I asks that? Goes all coy and jumpety. No, I want him on his way, and on his way he will go."

She knocked on the door, and Misterton remained silent, like a sculpture on a horizontal tombstone.

"He can't hear you."

"You go in, then. Tell him to pay his dues, and be on his way."

The landlord opened the door. There on the bed, fully clothed, was Misterton, mouth open, his bag still across his shoulder, in case anyone had a mind to steal it. The reek of stale sweat and foul breath revolted his visitors. Holding his nose, the landlord shook Misterton's shoulder, disturbing the rhythm of the snoring.

"Time to be going, sir. The sun's up, and there's a bit of bacon and bread for you if you make haste."

Misterton opened one encrusted eye, then the other. His mouth was as dry as a field of sharp stubble, and a sudden urge to relieve himself made him sit up.

"Do you have a pot?" he croaked.

The landlord handed him the one under the bed, and withdrew.

Misterton rested his head against the wall as he peed, and swayed like barley in a breeze, trying to maintain his balance and guide his stream.

The night before was now a fading tapestry: Ruth falling through the air like a dislodged rock; the fire in the inn's hearth thawing his blood frozen by the realisation that his chance to apologise, beg one more night, perhaps more, under her, *their* roof, had disappeared, as he had done, without explanation; and the pennies he had generously passed to the landlord for ale to soothe the gash of guilt. Oh that he could pay pennies for penance! he wished.

And now he had to go, without knowing but suspecting why she did it: he had all but pushed her, the wife who had turned as cold as the frozen pump at Gifford's Farm had, last winter, when the snow reached the windows of the farmhouse. He had left her, angry that she had turned her back on him in bed, had denied him, night after night, without explanation. His wife had changed into a stone hedgehog at his touch.

"Going anywhere in particular?" the landlord wondered, picking up the empty plate. Misterton had scraped the crumbs with his fingertips, and wiped up the fat from the bacon.

"Dorchester," he burped.

"Any particular reason?"

Misterton looked at him with suffering, bloodshot eyes.

"Work," he burped again.

"Long way on foot. You might get lucky on the main road.

Market day today, see. Folk'll be on their carts now, some even earlier."

"Thanks."

Misterton felt for his money, but it was gone.

"Paid me last night," explained the landlord.

Misterton half-smiled. On went the green, felt hat, and, with a nod, he shuffled out.

Already, merchants and farmers were heading for Dorchester, some in their working smocks, others in their best clothes, out to turn a head or two. It was an ideal time to secure a ride, but Misterton made his way to the churchyard. The gate clanged noisily behind him, and he winced. Below his feet, some inscriptions had almost worn away, and others had been splattered with gull excrement. Away from the eyes of the road, he was gripped by nausea, and he expelled his breakfast onto a bunch of pink carnations left at the foot of an angel with only one wing.

Feeling a bit better, he said, after looking at the grave he had offended, "I'm sorry for that, dear, I truly am, and one day I will make it up to you."

He wiped his sleeve across his chin, and then on the grass. His whiskers scraped the back of his hand like a whetstone.

Headstones leaned at odd angles, pushed by years of wind. Flakes of sandstone had fallen off, robbing the dead of their identity. She would be here if anywhere, not alongside her family, who had lived and died in Sidmouth. Her headstone, if she had one, would be small; he had left her with no money. A pauper's grave, then, for her, in some corner, a plot of shame.

Then it caught his eye, her resting-place, in the sunlight. Unable to read himself, he recognised her name, which she had written out for him, so that he could begin to learn his letters. Those nine letters, in that combination, were the only ones he had mastered. On the grass was a blackbird, a worm in its mouth. He approached it, and it flew away with its breakfast. The inscription read: Here lies Ruth Abbas, last of that name, whose life ended in misery.

The words blurred. Buried in the churchyard in which they had strolled, arm in arm, after their wedding, she had kept her name. "There are no more Abbases. If I take Misterton, we are wiped out," she had explained, and he had understood. His own name was not of his choosing; he could take it or leave it. Now there were no more Abbases.

"Did you know her?" came a voice from behind him.

The vicar was not a Dorset man, not the one who had joined them in holy matrimony. That one had been younger, with golden curls, angelic.

"No, I was looking at the blackbird, that's all."

"A sad case. A sad case, indeed. She was found at the foot of the cliffs at West Bay. Seems she couldn't bear to take her baby with her. A hardy walker saw her on the edge but could not prevent her jumping. At least, that is the story. He saved her child, though."

Misterton barely concealed his shock at the news of the infant.

"And the child? Is it still living in Bridport?"

The vicar was sensitive to Misterton's urgent tone, and became more circumspect.

"Its circumstances are unknown to me, as is the name of the man who arrived just too late. The parish workhouse keeps records, and I believe that is where Mrs. Abbas spent her last days. Whether any charitable organisation looked after the baby for her, after her death, I do not know."

Misterton dropped his head, knowing the vicar had seen the effect the existence of an abandoned baby had had on him.

"Workhouse?"

"I believe so. Her husband had left her, apparently, without means of support."

Misterton's hat hid his eyes, which dared not look at the vicar's. Above, a buzzard patrolled. The vicar produced a big, iron key from under his cassock.

"The poor child," croaked Misterton. "Was it a boy?"

"A girl, if I remember correctly. There is an odd smell around here. Most unusual. Now I must open up the church for morning prayers. The Lord must not be kept waiting!"

Misterton touched his hat, and made for the Dorchester Road. He could not remember when she had begun to refuse him, and when he had decided to leave. The child had a father, if no mother. Was he himself the father? he wondered.

The very last time, he had forced himself upon her, said she had to, as his wife. He never touched her again.

The cart passed him slowly.

"Going far?" called the man with the reins. In wooden crates, between the gaps, chickens stared and clucked at Misterton.

"Dorchester."

"Climb up, then. Going that way myself, to market."

Without a word, Misterton accepted the offer. The man made small-talk, but Misterton was too preoccupied with the thought that a child, possibly his, was being looked after by a stranger.

The journey was uncomfortable. Only the undulating hills and barrows, and the occasional glimpse of the sea bejewelled by stars on the surface as the sun caught its currents, ripples and waves, relieved the tedium of listening to Zed, who was going to sell thirty chickens. Their incessant babble irritated Misterton, whose monosyllabic replies to Zed's rather pointed, personal questions did little to pass the time.

Soon Dorchester appeared, like a mirage, in the distance.

"There be our destination. Ever been before?" asked Zed.

"No."

"You coming back tomorrow? I'll be staying overnight and coming back in the morning if you want a ride."

Misterton felt weak and nauseous again. The jolting and lurching of the cart made him retch, several times, but his stomach was empty.

"No."

"Just after a bit of merriment?"

"No. Looking for work."

Zed went quiet. Misterton saw him shake his head.

"You might be lucky, you might not. Harvesting's all but done. 'Less you got a grinder or press, there's not much you can call on. Got your own tools?" Misterton shook his head. "Make or mend furniture?"

Misterton stared ahead, silently.

"Stop here, if you would."

Zed said, "Whoa!" to his horse, then, "You walking the rest?" But Misterton was already on his way.

"Thanks," he croaked, as the cart overtook him, Zed staring straight ahead.

In the town, streets were clogged. People had come from their villages to buy, sell, meet. Men looking for work gathered in gangs, the emblem of their trade on their smocks or hats. A few women, posies in outstretched hands, begged. One barred Misterton's way, and he barged past her, exhausted.

On his right, he saw Maumbury Rings, a massive horse-shoe of earth covered in grass. With superhuman effort, he struggled to the top, where he lay down, away from the bustle of the market, and fell into a deep sleep.

His arms crossed over his bag on his chest, and his hat shading his eyes, he was eventually woken by the strange sensation of being licked on his hands. He lashed out, and the dog, which had taken a special interest in him, jumped backwards and barked.

"Go away!" ordered Misterton.

Its master, if it had one, was not in the vicinity; the dog had become curious, had liked the salty tang of dried sweat on Misterton's skin.

The sun was in a different place. Misterton could hear the joyous romp of a fiddle or two and the rhythmic clapping which accompanied country dancing. His lips had split, and he tasted blood. How refreshed! he felt. Reborn, almost. Food and drink would set him up, civilise him again, so he headed towards the merriment.

The dog followed him down the ancient monument before finding an alternative scent. A flock of sheep was being driven out of town by two shepherds with sticks and a dog. The music grew louder, and there was the fair, adjacent to the livestock pens.

Misterton approached the throng, conscious that he had not washed, was dusty. From the back of the crowd, he could see the circle of maidens in white dresses, holding hands as they plaited themselves by intricately weaving, ducking under raised arms, all admired by the young men picking out their favourite, hoping to walk her home, perhaps beg a kiss.

A man was selling frumenty. Misterton felt in his empty pocket. Not far away, a hog was roasting on a spit. Its heat haze distorted people as they passed behind it, until they emerged whole again. In his bag, there was nothing to sell, and he was too proud to beg again, the memory of people's fear of him as painful as a pitch-fork stabbed carelessly in the foot. He had disgusted himself that he had stooped to it.

The music was balm to his hunger, and he felt more hopeful when he saw how happy people were. It was possible, he was sure, to start again, be as good as Victoria, do the right thing, rid himself of the guilt that caked him as mud his boots after a deluge of rain in Gifford's farmyard.

He saw his chance at a table, where two youths were arm-wrestling, their faces red as ripe strawberries, each encouraged by a crowd of all-comers wanting to chance their arm. The pile of pennies at the champion's elbow drew him closer. The next challenger put down his coin, and gripped his opponent's hand. He must be tiring, guessed Misterton, yet I have no money. Misterton's arms were used to lifting bales of hay, and chopping logs for Stockwood's fire, were thick branches of oak.

Then he remembered the silver pocket-watch in his bag. It would fetch a shilling, maybe, in the town, but there was more than that on the table, and a man in his labourer's attire would arouse suspicion if he tried to sell it in a shop. It was something he had not wanted to do, but had resorted to when he was younger: stealing. In the cart, Zed had taken off his frockcoat and left it between them. The cart had lurched, and Misterton had placed his hand on the garment to steady himself. The round object had fitted into his palm perfectly. He had then removed his own coat, placed it over Zed's, taken the watch, and placed it in his own pocket. Soon after that, he had nonchalantly and prematurely stepped down from the cart. In the crunching of the wheels and clucking of the hens, he had stealthily sinned.

"Will you take this instead?" he asked the champion.

"Is it silver?"

Misterton nodded and pointed to the hallmark, and the man gestured to the empty seat in front of him.

Misterton slipped his bag over his head, and covered it with his coat. The sleeve he rolled up had been torn, the day before, on hawthorns, the cherry spots of blood now brown as mulch.

The unofficial umpire placed the contestants' elbows together, and they grabbed each other's hand, wriggling to find the best hold. The champion's palm was moist after so many bouts; Misterton's was as dry as his mouth.

"Take the strain, best of one," cried the umpire.

"All right with you?" asked the champion.

Misterton stared through him, disconcerting him, the slightest of nods his answer.

"Ready? May the best man win."

With that, the umpire dropped the square of linen on the table, and the champion attacked. Misterton withstood the force, gauging its strength, but not revealing yet his own. Like condensation on the kitchen window, when a pan is boiling on a cold day, perspiration formed a film in pinheads on the champion's forehead. He glanced nervously at the two piles of coins. At that moment, when his concentration was lost, he felt an irresistible push from his challenger, and there was a cracking sound, like that of a rabbit being necked. Misterton held the man's hand to the table until the umpire declared the bout over, heedless of the damage done.

Misterton glanced up at the crowd. There were few plaudits. A stranger has no right taking a local man's money. As soon as the coins were in his bag, Misterton felt relieved, lucky. The sleep on Maumbury Rings had done the trick.

"You've forgotten your watch," the umpire called as he moved away.

Misterton turned and looked at it lying on the table. The crowd was now silent, waiting for a reply. Again, the two men's eyes met.

"Keep it," decided Misterton.

The bowl of frumenty energised him. His wrist felt slightly sprained. He ate with his back to the crowd, licked his lips, and handed the bowl back to the woman.

"You eat quick," she remarked good-naturedly.

He stared at her breasts, then asked, "The King's Arms still going?"

"Was last night when I was a-serving." He lifted his hat and walked away. "Will I see you there tonight?"

"You might, but then again . . . "

He dropped down into Dorchester, passing the market, nimble-footed between the flat loaves of dung. Young lads were shovelling it into piles for the market officers. Stalls selling potatoes and flour, and women spinning wool, their skeins expertly wound and bound with quick fingers, lined the main street leading to The King's Arms.

Misterton squeezed his bag, knew he had enough for a room, a bath, and a good night's rest, but was unsure whether they would want the likes of him there. From the other side of the road, he saw gentlemen in gleaming riding boots enter, their wives and lady friends on their arms, and in bonnets to keep out the sun. Not a place for me at the moment, he decided, but it will be, one day. There'll come a time when my honest money will be as good as anyone's in Dorset.

He looked up the road ahead. Sunset would not beat him to Higher Bockhampton. When he had passed the last house, he bent to brambles. There had been hardly any rain, that summer, and the berries' juices were not sweet when he crushed them in his mouth. The odd one was to savour, save the pips, which he spat before they lodged in his teeth.

Behind him, he heard the rattle and clopping of a horse and trap. He kept tightly to the hedge to let it pass, but it slowed to his pace.

"Glad you took him down a peg or two," came a friendly, youthful voice.

Misterton glanced sideways, nodded, and confessed, "Needed the money."

"You employed?"

"Used to be."

"Where?"

Misterton hesitated. Why did everyone want to rake over the cinders of the past? They are worth nothing, ashes.

"Crewkerne way."

The questioner interpreted his hesitation as a lie.

"I need someone with your muscles. Mend fences, help with the building. I'm having my old manor house repaired. Needs bringing up to scratch. My builder's a man called Hardy. He's short, too. Lives at Higher Bockhampton. Call by. Tell him I sent you. It's a family business."

Misterton's heart quickened, and he raised his hat. The offer tasted sweeter than plums.

"Much obliged." The young man clicked his tongue, flicked his rein, and was soon out of sight. "So Hardy's is still a-going, eh? Big job, by the sound of it."

The journey to Higher Bockhampton was broken by a short sleep in a field. He trudged towards the heath. On his right was a thatched cottage. In the garden sat Jemima, on a chair. Between her legs was a bucket, and she was peeling potatoes, watching red, purple and white butterflies dancing around the flowers.

Under Misterton's feet, heather, broom and ferns spread like paint on an artist's palette. The landscape seemed different.

He knocked timidly. No one came, so he peered through the window, but the light made it difficult to see inside. Above, a window rattled.

"Nicholas?" called a girl.

"Yes, Emily."

The window shut, and, in seconds, the front door opened.

"Who is it, dear?" called a concerned voice.

"Come and see for yourself!" cried Emily, stepping outside.

"Nicholas?" gasped Mary Misterton. "Is it you?"

"Yes, mother, it's me."

"Then praise the Lord!"

"Is father at home?"

Mary hung her head.

Emily took her brother's arm.

"Father's been gone since lambing. He was tekken sudden."

"What? Left you here alone?"

His voice reminded the women of how quickly he could turn angry, hostile, even. Emily's tears were dew in the sunlight.

"Not gone like that. Tekken from us by the good Lord. Father's buried in Stinsford. He's behind the church, to the left."

Then the words I've rehearsed will be lost in the wind howling round the headstones, he realised. But I must mend my ways, for, one day, I'll meet him again, when I'll be stripped bare by His angels. I must atone.

"Come in, my son. This is your home, whatever happened all that time ago, and it always will be."

Inside, he stood in the place whence he was expelled by his father, despite the protestations of his mother and sister. How they had begged Jacob Misterton to forgive his son! But the head of the house had been unyielding. And the house had felt emptier to the women after Nicholas had gone. They had kept his bed made, and they would now light a fire so that he could once again sleep in it.

"Are you hungry?" asked Emily.

He nodded, and all that evening he watched the cottage door.

"He won't be coming back. Not now nor never," said his mother.

"Then I'm sorry for what I did, mother. I truly am."

Outside, the fading, blue sky nuzzled up to the land, and bats flashed black in the windows. Nicholas stepped outside and saw the ponies, silhouetted on the horizon, at prayer. Once, his father used to bring back an armful of wood, at this time of day. Nicholas used to smell the heath on him when he came close.

"In the morning, I will visit Mr. Hardy, mother," he said before going to bed.

"Are you sure?"

"Yes, I am sure," he replied.

Chapter Three

His back to the cottage, he peed into the ferns in the early mist. A pony was just visible, and then it vanished, as if it had been an apparition. Neither the sun nor the need to pee had woken him; just the urgency to catch Thomas Hardy before he went to the manor house.

The creaking stairs, under Misterton's weight, had woken his mother, who watched him through the window. His father's build, she recognised: wide, square shoulders and upright as a birch. Then she fed the warm ashes with kindling, and soon there was hot water for the oats.

"Any bacon?" asked Misterton, his dewy footprints varnishing the uneven flagstones.

"Not till our Emily gets paid," said his mother. "You used to like porridge."

He took the stairs two at a time to get properly dressed. His fingers raked his hair, and he went outside and dipped his face in the water tub.

"I'll have it when I get back," he informed her.

"Wherever are you off to, this time in the morning?"

He knew that she feared him going again, perhaps for good, that she could not bear a second parting.

At the garden fence loitered a pony.

"Where's Emily?" called Misterton, dropping a windfall apple, drilled by wasps, over the fence for it.

"Work."

Misterton pictured the seraphic young man who had asked him to see Thomas Hardy.

Much earlier, Emily had risen in the dark, felt her way down the lane lit still by a swollen moon, and had smiled to herself that her brother had returned. How she would throw herself into her chores, later, that day! And she would hasten home so that the three of them could be round the fire, on which she would cook thick potato and turnip soup. Her mother would have made bread to go with it. The day would be perfect.

The Hardys' cottage door was ajar. Jemima was fussing over her son, adjusting his collar, by the gate. He had been a young boy when Misterton had left. Books under his arm, young Tom saw him. Jemima noticed Tom's hesitation, and glanced up the lane.

Misterton took off his hat. Tom remained where he was, protectively. A morose fox tip-toed across the lane and passed through a hedge.

"I was wondering if I might have a quiet word with your husband about some work at the manor house."

Tom said, "I'll see you later, mother. Oh, is father practising in the church tonight? The choir will be there, I think."

Misterton did not like this delay in his business, and his lips thinned.

"Sure he said they were at a dance, Tolpuddle way. Or is that tomorrow? No, it's the church tonight."

"Good," said Tom, nodding to their visitor before setting off. "Then I shall go with him."

"I'll fetch him if you care to come through," Jemima said to Misterton.

She could not put a name to the face. He had changed, as had her son. The years had stretched them both, filled out Misterton's frame.

Thomas Hardy emerged, put out that whom he thought was yet

another mediocre journeyman had disturbed their domestic privacy.

Misterton, however, seized the initiative. The sooner he showed willing, the better. There had to be bacon in the house. Porridge clagged his throat, made him gag.

"Master up at the manor said to come see you about work. Said I might be what you're looking for."

Thomas smiled and asked, "And what trade might you be?"

Misterton knew this was his first test: tell the truth.

"Farm labourer really, but master said you might be able to make use of my strength."

"'Tis true I need a man to fetch and carry. Can't all be architects and stonemasons, I suppose. Truth is, there's a lot like you comes this way, but then they goes, which is about as much use to me as a rainy day. But let's see what you're made of. See that axe over there? See if you can chop up that tree that's lying over there. Go well in my fire-place."

Misterton set about it, letting his swing provide the power. The blade bit into the bark, and soon there was a rhythm to the chopping. Sparks of wood shot into the air, and Misterton rested the blade in the final piece. It was a sort of flourish under his signature.

"Never seen a man handle an axe like that. Tell you what I'll do: give you a job fetching and carrying. You any good up ladders?"

Misterton recalled the one up which he had followed Edith onto his straw bed, and laughed.

"In a manner of speaking."

"Then come with me and start today. Got a son helps out, too."

Jemima came out, grinning, in her hand a piece of paper. She saw the men at ease with each other, and waited till they had finished.

"I'll be in the lane," said Misterton diplomatically.

"Look at this," enthused Jemima, showing Thomas the poem. "*Domi—*"

"*Domicilium*, it's called. Our Tom wrote it!"

Her husband tripped over the words, but Jemima snatched it, and proudly read it aloud.

"Well, he do love his books and writing, I'll say that," admitted Thomas, "but that won't pay no bills at all. I'd best be off. You recognise the man I set on?"

"No, though there's something about him."

"I shan't tell him, but I knew him the moment I seed him."

"Who is it?"

"Misterton's lad. Been gone a few years now. Come home, by the looks of it. Strong resemblance. Just like his father. Chopped you some logs, see? Never seed a man chop wood like that."

The work was hard. Misterton's callused hands were rougher, by the end of the day, his blood mixed with sandstone into an ochre paste where the edges of stone blocks had cut him.

Through one of the windows of the manor house, a woman watched him move relentlessly, and saw Thomas stand back to admire his willingness. She hid behind the damask curtains, breathing suspended, almost, as he placed his feet carefully on the rungs. She had not seen him before, and he was younger than others who had laboured.

"Look up, will you?" she whispered, but he would not. It was as if he dared not lift up his eyes in case someone saw who he was; if he did not look at people, he would be invisible.

Then she saw a woman walk over to him, and give him something from her tray. He leaned forward and quickly kissed her forehead. The woman glanced back towards the house to see if they had been caught. Thomas came to fetch his cup, and Misterton stepped back in case, by taking the first one, he had not shown due deference to his master.

The woman behind the curtain rushed down to the kitchen, her cheeks the shade of a robin's breast.

"Emily, may I have a word, in private, please?"

"Yes, Miss. Palfreyman."

Her mistress' voice sounded menacing. Never before had Emily heard this tone. Cook shook her head, and the other girls looked down into their bowls and sinks, lest it be their turn next.

"Emily, this is not easy for me, especially as your work here has been exemplary since you came, but I cannot condone my staff mixing with the men working on the repairs to the house."

So that was it: the fraternal kiss on discovery that they were working at the same place.

"No, Miss."

"Do you know the man's name?"

Emily bowed her head to buy time. Any answer might condemn him. He would hate her for that.

"He meant no harm, Miss. I met him at Dorchester Fair. We're nothing to each other. What you saw was on friendly account of our brief acquaintance. Nothing more. It won't happen again. Sorry, Miss."

During her explanation, her eyes remained fixed on the floor, in mock shame.

Florence Palfreyman became less stiff, but ended the admonition with a reminder of what was at stake.

"This family has a reputation to uphold, Emily. Remember that we are all privileged to be at Palfreyman Manor."

"Yes, Miss. Sorry, Miss."

Emily curtseyed, satisfying Florence.

"You may return to your work."

Outside, later, Thomas called. The sky was pink. Bread and cheese packed by Jemima and shared with Misterton was the only food to have passed their lips. Misterton took the flagon of cider, and Thomas watched the rippling of his throat as he swallowed.

"Need to be off now to fetch my fiddle for practice over in Stinsford church. Take you back?"

"You going back the same way?" Thomas nodded as he drank

greedily; Misterton had left him half. "Glad of a ride to the church."

"You sing?"

Misterton's eyes did, as he laughed.

"Not so's you'd call it that!"

On his cart, Thomas said, "Choir could do with a second bass. Your voice be like a regimental Sergeant Major!"

Misterton could not look at the church as they came into the lane.

"Here?"

Misterton jumped down, reducing the impact with a bend at the knees.

"Thanks."

"Here," offered Thomas. The coins had been warmed in his pocket. "Stop off at the gate tomorrow. I've been looking for someone like you."

"Thanks. I will."

Thomas was in no hurry, and saw the vicar walking towards them from the rectory.

"Ah, Thomas! You will be here tonight, won't you? I've fixed the date for the Harvest Service, and we need to make sure you practise the hymns in time. You know what happened, last year, and we don't want a repetition!"

Thomas looked self-consciously at the empty flagon. Misterton turned away to give them space.

"I'm off to fetch my fiddle now, Reverend."

"Splendid!"

The vicar took quick steps into the church.

"Your father be behind the church, on the left, in the corner, in case you're wondering. Small, square, granite headstone. Gold letters," said Thomas, flicking the horse's reins and exhorting him to move with a clicking of his tongue.

Misterton clung to the churchyard gate.

He knows, and yet he wants me back tomorrow? he puzzled.

He found his father's grave, approached it slowly, in awe.

His fear receded, and he smelt the grass cuttings.

Later, Jemima smiled at him from the garden, and he removed his hat, not stopping but waving self-consciously.

At home, Emily greeted him, one hand on her hip, like a teapot.

"Don't ever do that again!" she warned, out of earshot of her mother.

And he kissed her again on the forehead.

Head down, as a pig with its snout in a trough, he slurped his steaming soup, and ripped off mouthfuls of warm bread from the loaf with his teeth. Eating alone for so long had blunted his table manners, and the day's efforts had given him a wolf's appetite.

"Don't suck so," chided Emily. "It goes through me."

"And aren't you a lady now you do for them at the manor!" chortled her mother.

Misterton theatrically licked his wooden bowl to provoke his sister, and sighed contentedly.

"I'm disgusted!" she cried, snatching his bowl and putting it in the hearth with a clatter.

"There's a baked apple if you'd like one. Might be a bit of honey left. Here, my daughter, you took the last from the hive?"

"In the cupboard."

Emily pulled off her boots and socks and massaged her aching feet. Misterton sniffed the air. His wages had put him in a good mood, a strong position.

"There be nothing else to go with it? No cream? Baked apple with no cream don't sound right."

Emily warned him.

"You push things. You should think yourself lucky."

It took a second to scald his mouth on the soft, steaming flesh of the apple, but he hid the pain. Then he buried his hand in his right pocket, and shared the coins between them, one-for-you, and one-for-you-fashion.

"Mr. Hardy pleased with you?" asked his mother.

He stood up, put on his jacket, and licked his lips, imagining the cream.

"So far."

"You going out?"

He moved to the door, pretending he had not heard; circumstances had made him an accomplished actor.

"She wants to know things, Nicholas, 'bout where you been and what you done. We both do, and you owe it to us. We don't know anything," pressed Emily.

"Just going for a walk on the heath, that's all."

He lit the wick in the oil lamp, and the drowsy flame grew bigger as it woke up.

"Mind them adders!" called his mother. "You'd best not forget them. Tread on one, and they bites nasty."

The ribbon of pathway for which he searched was no longer there. Up the hill and down, out of sight, it used to go, till it reached a small cottage standing alone, as if shunned by Bockhampton, like an outcast leper. Its thatch had been in disrepair, Misterton recalled, its eaves like a boy's fringe hacked by his mother.

And now the thatch was an eerie mirror reflecting the moonlight.

He could see a faint, amber glow of lamplight through the window, so he knocked three times, not hard enough to alarm the person he had come to see.

"Who be there?" called an old man.

"Someone looking for Conjuror Sayer. I lived these parts. You'd remember me if you be he."

The door creaked open. Conjuror Sayer squinted at his visitor in the weak light of the lamp Misterton held shoulder high.

"What you want, this time night?"

"To know something. You still got the knowledge of things?"

Conjuror Sayer let him in and closed the door. In the middle of the room was a table and two chairs. Sleepy, big, black flies clung to the chimney breast. On the table was a stuffed crow balancing on a small log. Misterton did not recall the bird's name.

"Sit."

At the table, Misterton began.

"Wasn't sure if you were—"

"Dead?" Conjuror Sayer guffawed, revealing blackened teeth. "Oh no, sir, I don't being dead. Not me. I know when my time be, as does Percival here, and it be a long way off yet-a-while."

"But you still got the knowledge of things as you used to?"

Conjuror Sayer had confirmed nothing.

"People don't come so much, these days. I still gets one or two, usually from afar, but not so many. Had the vicar from over Stinsford way once. Said I was filling his prishners with the Devil's deeds, and that God would strike me dead if I didn't repent me. I told him, the way I look at it, there's room for both me and God. Fact is, vicar can't explain what I do, and he don't like that because he wants all the power and glory."

Misterton placed two coins he had held back from his day's wages on the table.

"What you see?"

Conjuror Sayer poured a liquid into a cup and passed it to him. Misterton smelt it, but it was odourless. Hesitantly, he raised it to his lips.

"Go on. It baint going to harm you. Elder and whortle, mainly, and a special 'lixir. Drink it, and close your eyes."

Misterton obeyed. The room shifted and froze, just as it had done when he had last visited. Next, he heard the sound of a scraping chair, and Conjuror Sayer was arranging something on the table. The egg wobbled. Percival rose from the log, and perched on

Misterton's shoulder. Feathers brushed his cheek, and Misterton cried in horror.

"It's only Percival."

"I can hear him breathing!"

Conjuror Sayer chuckled and picked up the egg.

"Hold out your hand," he instructed. Misterton hesitated, so Conjuror Sayer took it, and placed the egg in it. "Careful now. Don't drop it."

Misterton's arm began to ache and tremble in its horizontal position. Conjuror Sayer watched the egg for a movement, a wobble, a roll.

"You feel anything?"

"It's alive."

"What says Percival?"

The old man, wiry hair forming a halo of briars, leaned towards his stuffed pet, and placed his ear to the beak. To Misterton, the wait seemed endless.

"What is it?"

"Percival says beware the woman, and seek the child."

"A girl?"

"A boy."

"And the woman?"

But the egg rolled out of his hand and onto the stone floor. Misterton lowered his arm, his elbow burning. The yolk had split.

Conjuror Sayer helped Percival back onto his log.

"It's time you must go. I'm sleepy."

"A boy, you say?"

"You doubt me?"

As Misterton was about to leave, Conjuror Sayer called, "You're not the bad man you once were."

"How you know?"

"Percival says."

"The words of a crow?"

Meanwhile, the choir practice for the Harvest Service had come to an end in Stinsford church. Thomas Hardy was about to leave when the vicar called, "A moment of your time, Thomas?"

Thomas passed his fiddle to his son, and motioned towards the exit.

"Don't 'ee worry, Reverend. We'll sort these hymns out good and proper. Old William was not himself tonight, 'twas plain. He don't usually miss his notes."

"A delicate matter, Thomas. It concerns the man you dropped off, this afternoon. Work for you?"

"First day. He's a good worker."

"Then take care, Thomas, for I found him talking to a headstone after you'd gone, and what he was saying was most disturbing."

Thomas frowned, nodded, and joined his son.

"Up and down the ladder like a squirrel, though," he told Tom. "Not many like him, these parts."

Chapter Four

The work at Palfreyman Manor was completed just before the first snow. Misterton guessed it was coming before he saw it. The icy wind locked his jaw and burnt his fingers, and he felt no pain when he stabbed his hand with a chisel. The sky darkened, and the white petals rocked as they fell to the ground, marking the advent of winter.

For the first time, Florence invited Misterton into the house. Thomas was warming himself guiltily in front of a blazing fire in the library. The hot aches in his hands were a small price to pay for being safe indoors. Robert Palfreyman generously splashed his best brandy into two glasses.

"You prefer cash or a banker's order?" he asked.

In the hall, Misterton instinctively shook himself as a dog fresh from a stream. Florence saw the flames from the fire wriggle in his eyes, which caught her looking.

"Come closer and dry out," she invited, moving to the marble fire-place. There she swept her hand in an extravagant gesture.

Misterton looked up at the vaulted, wooden ceiling, and at the family portraits on the walls. His cottage would fit easily into this hall, he estimated.

Florence saw his interest, and shook her head.

"All dead, I'm afraid. Robert and I are the only ones left. All that land for just two of us!"

Misterton approached the hearth. The heat was no favour, on her part. This was her last chance to speak to him.

"Thank 'ee."

From his stiff beard dripped liquid beads. Florence squirmed with tension. Misterton did not know that she had watched him all through autumn, that she had manufactured occasions when she had spoken to him, usually making polite enquiries about the progress of the work. In the early days, he had answered briefly, kept moving, but had not wanted to appear rude, so had smiled, commented upon the beauty of the house, the landscape, till she was satisfied that he was, as she suspected, an interesting man. Now proud of his contribution to the repairs, he was confident that she saw him as important to Thomas.

"Why didn't you tell me you were Emily's sister?" she eventually asked.

He shrugged, and water ran down his neck, shocking him.

"Don't make any difference, do it?"

Voices were approaching, and she had something else to ask.

"I, *we*, need a man here. You'd do a variety of things: fields, stables, odd jobs. You'd live in, of course, and you'd take your meals in the kitchen with the staff."

Thomas had said nothing about the future, and Misterton had not asked in case it was the end. Florence could see he was flattered, that he was trying not to appear tempted.

"I works for Mr. Hardy," he said flatly.

"I know, but if—"

She was cut short by the entrance of her brother and Thomas. Robert offered his hand to Misterton, and looked at his sister. The cold, wet flesh cut short the shake.

"Thank you, Misterton. Hardy tells me he'd still be here next Christmas if it hadn't been for you."

"Glad you passed me on the way from Dorchester Fair."

Florence gasped and laughed.

"Robert? Dorchester Fair? Whatever next?"

"Went for a stockman. Wish all the labourers were like you, Misterton: hard-working, uncomplaining, and never clamouring for more, all the time."

"Will we take Emily with us?" Misterton asked. "She won't make it on foot in this."

"She's needed here still. It's only two," explained Florence. "But in the circumstances . . ."

"Thank you."

"We shall see her tomorrow, of course?"

"She could stay here tonight," suggested Palfreyman.

"I'll ask her. There'll be extra money, of course."

Money don't buy everything, Misterton said to himself.

Florence found Emily at the sink.

"But my clothes, Miss. Palfreyman."

"There are plenty spare. Shall I pass word to your brother?" Emily trembled with trepidation at the honour. "There'll be extra in your money."

"'Taint the money, Miss."

"Shall I tell him, then?"

Emily nodded, and Florence returned quickly, so that Hardy could be away.

The snow plastered the men on the cart. At times, it seemed only the instinct of the horse kept the cart on the track. Misterton held his hat in place, and Thomas' teeth chattered.

"Your lad be able to get back?" yelled Misterton.

"Got any sense he probly stay in town. Hicks'll keep him at it. Hope Jemima's stoked up with dry afore all this."

Misterton inched towards the next job, if it existed. Twice the question became shy, and retreated.

"That be it for now, then?" it was, when it came.

"Got a job to see about a price to do a chimbley over Tolpuddle way, but see how we goes with all this weather. Can't say, at the moment, but you only up on the heath, so if there is anything, I'll let you know."

In Higher Bockhampton, the snow had drifted into banks so big that Thomas left the cart at the bottom of the hill. The horse's fetlocks were compacted with balls of ice, like decorative bells on show day.

"Looks like she made up with dry," remarked Misterton, at the gate, spotting the fat, yellow genie squeezing out the chimney.

"A clever girl, Jemima. Here. Don't be off beout it." Misterton looked at the money. There had to be a mistake. Thomas saw what he was thinking, and checked him. "Take it. Never did see a man wield an axe like you, nor up a ladder like a squirrel."

Neither felt the other's hand in the cold. Fingers were like frozen carrots.

Thomas struggled up his path and went inside.

Misterton's legs were so cold they would hardly bend to take him up to the heath. He plodded as if following a plough.

His mother's fire rested timidly in the grate.

"Dorset weather!" Misterton cursed.

"Thank the Lord you be back safe!"

"Be His doing! Emily's staying over tonight. Extra pay. You have to dance when our betters snap their fingers."

Misterton took off his sodden clothes, and his mother tried to dry his hair, but he shrugged her away.

"Mother hen! Baint there be snap for a snowman?"

Upstairs, he removed his under-garments. The warm floorboards began to thaw his feet. Dry again, he put on his father's clothes, which fitted him well.

"I'm coming down in father's apparel!" he warned.

The last thing he wanted was to see his mother faint.

She held her hand to her mouth, then her son to her body. She felt better, having both husband and son again under her roof.

"Soup's on."

"Something to show you."

He rummaged in his bag.

"Where you get all that?"

"Honest labour."

And she laughed with him, her notes becoming more joyous as she realised just how much Thomas had paid him.

By the following morning, the snow had stopped, the heath was covered in a glittering, white crust, and the trails of birds', foxes', and rabbits' footprints were the only blemishes. Misterton shielded his eyes. The sun would melt the snow in a day or two. Then he would go to Dorchester, perhaps buy a pig. There was still no bacon in the house. There would be other people to talk to, and new clothes. He would not be his father for much longer.

The church spire marked the top of the hill. The road was muddy. There were signs that life was returning to normal after the snow. Gaudy pheasants hung by their necks, and rabbits by their feet, in shop doorways. Two coaches stood outside The King's Arms, and men in long coats and tall hats went in and out of buildings.

I could look like a gentleman, but not at the moment, what with me having to save up and earn respect, he thought. No one would hand over a child to a man in rags.

He turned left at the top of the hill. His feet were frozen; his soles were through. So he went to the cobbler.

"Can't mend this beout changing the shape, they so far gone. Best buy a new pair. Cost you a few pennies, mind. Make you a pair to collect at three, this afternoon."

"Tough? Good looking ones?"

The cobbler laughed.

"Like these," he demonstrated, lifting the flap in the counter, and stepping through.

"Tell you been a sojer!" quipped Misterton, after the cobbler had stood to attention, heels together. "Pair like yours, then."

"Got some wooden soles for you to stand on, see which fits best."

Misterton smiled, and felt good when the sun came through the window and warmed his back.

From the cobbler, he went up to the market. A pen of pigs pushed noses through bars to rid their nostrils of the stench of impending death.

"Buy that middling one?"

"Dead or alive?" asked the swineherd.

"I lives at Bockhampton. Ring its nose for me?"

"Can do. One that size is a shilling. He be a big bugger soon. Keep you months, smoked up a chimney."

"Better have it, then. Collect it 'bout three."

"No later. Gets dark just after four, and we usually washed up by then."

Misterton handed over the money.

A child with a tin barred his way.

"Save me, sir. Just a penny, sir."

Misterton knew there were other urchins like him, some still sleeping in shop doorways. In Bridport, they were in every place where there was commerce, until they starved, or were driven from the cobbles of angry shop-keepers.

The penny clanged in the tin. Misterton was mute. The boy ran away.

Further up the street, a man with wild eyes was waving his arms. The Bible's pages flapped like pigeons.

"And we are sinners, all of us. And unless we repent, the sins will be revisited upon us. Repent now, all ye sinners, for the Lord God is merciful to those who seek forgiveness."

Misterton changed direction. Down an alley, he heard a window opening, and dodged out the way of a chamberpot full of piss. The window banged shut, and several daggers of ice fell and shattered like glass on the floor.

A woman was waiting at the end of the street. Her lips and cheeks were crudely rouged, emphasising her pallor. As he neared her, she smiled, revealing crooked teeth. Her coat parted down the middle to tempt him, and he looked, unashamedly.

"Cold it be today," she began. "Warm you up a bit?"

Thomas' generosity hung heavily in his pocket, despite the purchase of a pig and boots.

The woman looked at the penny in her bony hand as he walked away.

"God bless you, sir!" she called after him, but he did not turn.

Instead he made his way to a shop. They would know where to acquire them even if they did not sell them themselves. A bell rang as if being strangled. The walls were lined with books, hundreds of them, and precarious obelisks of them were on the floor, so that one had to move carefully to avoid knocking them over.

At the far side was a writing desk, and on it a lamp, illuminating some tomes about the history of the world, and great military campaigns. There was the smell of dust, parchment, and thinking trapped in a soundless bubble. Misterton had never been in a bookshop before, but automatically removed his hat, as if in respect for the effort expended to produce the books.

Footsteps came, one-two, followed by a pause, suggesting a limp or a wooden leg. The door by the desk opened, and in hobbled an old man, an owl, his spectacles doubling the size of his eyes, and his eyebrows defying gravity by adopting a height of permanent surprise. He leaned on his cane; one leg was shorter than the other, and the stick mitigated his list to his right, actually prevented him falling right over, onto a pyramid at the top of which was a book of fine drawings of the flora and fauna of Dorset.

"Didn't expect to see anyone today, this weather. You anything particular in mind?" he asked.

"Quill and ink. I seed the books and thought you might sell pens and ink," answered Misterton, embarrassed by his own ignorance in these matters.

"I have my own, see," pointed the book-seller, "but I'm not looking to sell them."

Just then, the shop door opened, the bell gave a muffled cry, and in came a customer.

"Ah, you got the note I left at your office, then," welcomed the book-seller.

"Yes, that was very good of you. I've been after these Latin verses for some time. How much do I owe you?"

The book-seller pointed out a stain on the back cover.

"A shilling, Master Tom, seeing as there's that tiddy mark, which, by my eyes, is a drop of red wine. Soaked in quick, it did, by the looks of it."

Misterton stood shoulder to shoulder with the customer. The book-seller insisted on the purchase being bound with string for ease of handling, and, during this time, Misterton waited patiently to enquire where he might avail himself of pen and ink.

"It's a better day today," remarked the customer, turning to Misterton.

"Toes are ready to drop off."

Each man recognised the other, and it was the customer who acknowledged the acquaintance.

"Am I right in thinking you work for my father?" asked Tom Hardy.

"Used to. Job's finished up at the manor. Then the snow. Last I heard, there might be work at Tolpuddle."

"You're a good worker, I hear."

"There we are, Master Tom," interrupted the book-seller, holding aloft the book.

"Perfect!" exclaimed Tom. "You after anything in particular?"

Misterton said, " No book. Not a reader myself, though I wished I could learn. No, I'm after pen and ink."

"How can you write if you can't read?"

Misterton withheld his intention, and said, "It's for Emily, my sister. She's learning up at the manor. Miss. Palfreyman's teaching her some letters."

"She'll need all of them!" joked Tom. "Come. I have plenty of what you want over at Mr. Hicks' office. Your sister - and you – must learn to read and write. Our words are the beacons of civilisation. Without them, we are in perpetual darkness."

"It be Providence, one way or another."

The book-seller chuckled.

"You mind Master Tom. He's a way with words. Wonder he baint a writer 'stead of all that drawing of buildings at Hicks'."

"It's not that bad there!" protested Tom. "Come, Mr. Misterton – I hope I've your name correct – and I'll provide you with the necessary apparatus. It's no trouble at all." Then, to the book-seller: "Good day, sir, and thank you for your perseverance with the book."

At Hicks', Misterton tried in vain to press a coin into Tom's hand. The ink was in a small, corked bottle, and the quills were cut by Tom with a pocket knife before his very eyes.

"That all there be to it?"

"Yes!" laughed Tom. "Just catch a goose or pheasant, and you have a handy supply."

"I'm much obliged, Master Hardy. I'll never forget this."

Tom watched him fight unexpected tears.

"That's all right. Think nothing of it. Keep the bottle upright, and make sure the cork is pressed in tightly."

With time to kill, Misterton went into an inn, down a backstreet. The King's Arms would not countenance the awful appearance of his boots, he was sure. Then he ate slices of mutton and mash, and when no one was looking, he licked the gravy off his plate.

There had to be something for his mother, and Emily, when she returned again. The pig would take time to hang, so he bought a pheasant and two rabbits. He smelt them before handing over the money, but their eyes were still bright, and the fur and feathers still had the scent of soil and ferns.

The new boots fitted perfectly, and the pig was compliant enough on its leash. On its nose and cheeks were spots of bright blood.

Misterton had his hands full as he made his way out of Dorchester. The light was fading, and the woman lurching in his direction he thought might have been drunk. She reached out to maintain her balance. Her long coat had no belt, and she wore no hat, her hair tangled and matted like a sheep's. It seemed that the closer she got, the more likely it was that he would not be able to catch her, both his hands being in use.

Anticipating her collapse, he tied the pig to a sapling, and laid the pheasant and rabbits at a safe distance from it. Her words were slurred, indistinct, but when she was upon him, she pleaded, "Help me, sir, or I will die, this night."

Then her knees gave way, and he caught her under her arms, so that she would break no bones. He sniffed, but there was no whiff of alcohol. The ground was crisping as the temperature fell, and there was a rustic seat nearby, the last on the Bockhampton Road, so he carried her to it, and, using his bag as a pillow – he removed the bottle of ink lest it break, or the cork fall out – he laid her down. She groaned with relief.

"Need any help?" called a man, quickening his pace.

"This woman needs help. She be exhausted to the point of near-death."

"Can you carry her to Bockhampton? I'll take the pig," offered Tom.

"Can try. She's light as a sparrow."

He looked for the pheasant and rabbits, but a fox had stolen them, stealthily, and dragged them through the hedge.

Misterton picked her up, and she opened her eyes.

"Come, you!" Tom ordered the pig.

"Nicholas," she whispered.

"Edith? Is it you?"

"Yes, 'tis me."

He put his cheek next to hers.

"You're safe now. Don't worry. I'll take care of you."

Tom heard, and said nothing, except to the pig, which snorted and squealed. From time to time, they took a brief rest, and the moon lit their way. The temperature fell even further, and Misterton wrapped his coat around Edith.

Soon they reached the heath.

"Thank 'ee, Master Hardy. I shall never forget what you have done for me today."

In his arms, Edith was sleeping.

Chapter Five

He thought he ought to do it among the trees, but not too far away as he would need to drag it back to the house so that it could hang in the outbuilding used to store logs and tools. His father had once shown him how to do it, and had warned him that the pig always senses the blade is about to slit its throat, and puts up a squealing fight. A pig with a ring in its nose is easier to control; the rope can be tied tightly round a tree, preventing it moving freely, so that the lethal slash can be administered accurately.

He had been made to stand near his father, and had watched the swift death-cut, and now he had to do it himself, so that there would be, once again, bacon in the house.

It was just light, and the pig was still. The blade had been sharpened in the outhouse, not in the cottage; his mother must not know what was coming. For two days, the pig had been tethered to one of the fence-posts, and, at dawn, had its throat cut on the heath. He remembered to slice the side of the neck away from him, so that the blood would not spurt on him. Stepping back, he hated himself for taking its life, and turned away so that he could not see it gradually weaken, fall on the ground, and die in its own blood. "We kill the pig so that we may live," his father had explained. "The first time is always the hardest."

"The pig is dead and will hang for a few days. Then we can smoke it in the chimney," Misterton informed his mother and Emily, matter-of-factly. "I did it how my father showed me."

His mother said, "I will take the porridge up to Edith. She needs her strength."

Misterton had put Edith in his own bed, and had slept on the floor, downstairs, in front of the fire. He had told his mother and Emily how he had found her on the verge of collapse, on the road, and that Tom Hardy had brought back the pig for him. Now he must tell them that he knew her, and they would wonder.

His mother gave him the chance when he returned.

"She is sitting up. She asks for you, Nicholas."

Misterton knew his mother wanted to know the reason, but he had no idea why Edith was on the Bockhampton Road.

"Worked on the same farm as me."

"She follow you?" asked his mother. "She sweet on you?"

"No one knew where I was a-going."

"You tell no one? Not even the farmer?"

"Didn't really know myself, truth be known."

She frowned, remembered when he used to live there before being expelled by his father, and the awful feeling returned to the pit of her stomach. Her Nicholas had not been easy to live with.

"Strange she be here, then, when you were passing. Don't add up right. Nothing add up right, Nicholas. Don't know where you went. Don't know what you did. Don't even know why you came back. And now there's Edith under our roof, and we don't know how she come so."

"I'll go and see her."

He knocked on her door. She was sitting up in Emily's spare nightgown, her hair no longer matted but washed and combed by Emily. The porridge was all gone.

"Edith," he began.

She pulled the blanket up under her armpits.

He wondered whether to sit on the edge of the bed, but too much time had passed since he had left her at Gifford's Farm to take such a liberty.

"Thank you for helping me."

"Couldn't leave you there."

Weakly, she smiled ironically. He had left her milking a cow and all a-tremble in the parlour.

"Why didn't you tell me?"

"I came to say goodbye, didn't I? You went and hid."

Her sigh was long and exasperated, like air being exhaled from a blacksmith's bellows.

"I mean about you and Miss. Victoria."

Misterton tried to take a step forward, but her gaunt, accusatory face stopped him.

"Was it you who told Stockwood?"

"Wrote him a note, the day after I saw you with her. Wanted him to stop her so that *I* could have you. You were with me first."

There was a long silence. How had he failed to notice her love for him? He had lifted her skirt in the straw, whispered promises as sweet as ripe plums. She had gone to him, night after night, risking her reputation, her security, and he was, at the same time, selfishly deceiving her.

He turned in silence, but stopped at the door.

"You can write?"

"Tolerably."

"Stay as long as you like."

"Her father sent me packing, a couple of days after you. Only one of us three write, see. Miss. Victoria comes into the parlour and grabs my hair so hard I kicks over the pail. All that milk wasted! She was a-screaming at me. I said nothing. Farmer Stockwood pulls her off me, and tells me to go, no money, no nothing."

"For what it's worth, I'm truly sorry," he said, before going downstairs. "Really sorry."

The pens and ink were in a safe place. He would ask Edith when the time was right.

Emily guessed. When she returned from the manor, she sat with

Edith, who could not deny what had passed between herself and Misterton, though she withheld his deceit, believing it would have been scant reward for the Mistertons' kindness in giving her refuge. But she named the farm and its location near Bridport.

"Bridport? That be miles away! How he got there?" cried Mrs. Misterton. "It's a small wonder when he don't tell us a thing, and we have to learn all about him from a stranger!"

"Keep your voice down, mother, or she'll hear you. Nicholas must have his reasons," said Emily. "She'll be on her way in a day or two. She told me. No use raking up the past. What's happened, when all's said and done, is what do please God."

Misterton chose to stay out of the cottage as much as possible to avoid proximity to Edith. The thought of her lying in his bed tortured him, but he would not hurt her again. He asked only one more thing of her: that she write for him a letter to the Western Mail, asking anyone knowing of the whereabouts of the young child whose mother fell from the cliff at West Bay to contact him.

He asked Tom Hardy if he could spare an envelope sheet, and used the occasion to enquire if Thomas had found work in Tolpuddle.

"Indeed, I have," he said, "though it baint much. I aint forgotten you, Nicholas, but you might be better asking up at the manor, see if they've anything going."

Misterton grimaced. He had turned down work there on the expectation of more with Thomas. Besides, he would have to live in, be at the beck and call of Florence. That was no life for him.

Edith eventually came downstairs. Her clothes were now clean and mended. The bread and soup had strengthened her, and she was ready to write for Misterton, who waited for his mother to take a stroll down the lane before he placed the pen and ink on the table.

She wrote slowly, carefully, wanting to make a good impression. His message did not alter her expression, though she speculated about its meaning. When she had finished, she looked into his face, frankly, inviting an explanation, but he offered none. Instead he melted wax over a candle, and sealed the envelope.

"Stay as long as you like," he reminded her.

She shook her head.

"Got used to begging and starving. Besides, you and me: it would be difficult."

"How?"

She hung her head, then told him.

"You betrayed me, Nicholas. Have you forgotten that? I loved you, and thought you loved me. I was a milkmaid, and Farmer Stockwood threw me out. I've picked turnips from the ground since then, and slept as if dead, so tired it made me. And for what? A few pennies. What little work there is out there don't pay to feed a mouse."

The scars of not knowing if she would wake up alive were etched on her forehead and round her mouth, and yet the beauty of her youth flashed in her pale blue eyes like spinning, silver coins of sun on the sea.

"Who you work for?"

"A vile bully, a horrible man called Wareham, a farmer on the Palfreyman estate. I ran away, the morning you found me. Ran till I had no breath left."

Misterton examined her wide eyes, and asked, "What he do?" Edith's bottom lip quivered; she was mute. She wiped her eyes on her sleeve, and could not face him. "It's all right," he reassured, holding her tightly in his arms. "He won't hurt you again. Wareham, you say?" She nodded and snorted against his pounding chest. "Stay with my mother and Emily. I will leave for Bridport soon, but you're safe here."

Her silence he took to be serious contemplation of his suggestion, and he allowed her to step backwards and compose herself.

"He took advantage of me, Nicholas," she stated.

"Then he will pay for it."

"If I stay here, it will be till I'm strong again, but I cannot stay long. I'm bound for Weymouth, maybe work a passage to London, where there will be more work. Perhaps, I can become a maid, or a companion to a fine lady."

"Stay till you're strong again."

She nodded, at last.

Misterton turned to leave the bedroom, only to be addressed again.

"Have you heard from Miss. Victoria?"

He shook his head. Victoria was now a distant memory. He had been flattered by her attention. She had looked over her shoulder at him, one day, a basket of eggs across her arm. He had nodded, leaned on the handle of his rake, appreciating her glance. Any diversion from work in the fields had been welcome to him.

"No. Didn't expect to."

"You heard from her father?"

Misterton wondered where her questions were leading. They were a fox's footprints leading to and from a fan of chicken feathers.

"Threatened to shoot me if I showed up at Gifford again."

Downstairs, the door opened; it was his mother, flushed as a poppy, returning from her walk. Edith understood and lowered her voice.

"Then there is something you need to know, Nicholas."

He stepped back into the bedroom.

"For God's sake, Edith, you should have been a conjuror! What should I know?"

She sat on her bed. The dilemma her insinuation caused scared her. She had said too much but so little that he screwed up his face as if he had driven a fork into his foot.

"I don't know if it be true or not. Rumour, or mischief-making, more like. You knew Mabel, that she once had a child before it died, so she knew the signs, and swore Miss. Victoria was a-carrying. Said her face was swelling like bread in the oven, which be a certain sign, and that her body was a-plumping up like a goose being readied for Christmas, which be a bigger sign."

Misterton merely said, " Aint going to get my head blown off on account of Mabel's gossiping," and went downstairs.

His mother was sitting down at the table. In the air was the sweet smell of smoked pork. Two hams dangled in the chimney.

"She say what her intentions are?"

She showed her hands to the snoozing fire, knowing that hot-aches would soon be throbbing.

"Staying for a bit."

"She fit to come down and lend a hand for her keep?"

He shrugged, but eventually said, "She be on the mend."

He wished that she had not told him about Mabel's speculation. Perhaps, it was Edith's revenge, her way of punishing him for his duplicity. Her words were nettle leaves.

Emily arrived home, exhausted. She had been asked to stay over again by Palfreyman. There was a dinner party, that evening, but she had declined, using the excuse that her cousin was paying them a long-awaited visit.

"Miss. Florence says job's still there, you want it," remembered Emily.

Misterton snorted.

"Don't want it."

"You've nothing with Mr. Hardy, have you?"

"Not yet, but I prefer to wait."

"Think Miss. Florence's taken a shine to you," laughed Emily.

Edith stopped sweeping the hearth.

Misterton pretended he had not heard, and went outside.

The next morning, he woke up early. This was the day he would go into Dorchester to post his letter to Bridport. He had kept it in his bag, and had checked the seal regularly. Still Edith had not asked for an explanation.

As he passed Thomas Hardy's cottage, Thomas was digging up some vegetables he had buried in a box, in summer. He fancied fried potatoes, and remembered the last of his crop. His thumbs pushed off the damp earth from their skins, and he washed them in the water tub, after he had smashed the ice with a stick, firstly into a spider's web, and then into shards, which he dropped quickly onto the floor as if they had been hot coals.

Misterton's head slid along the skeletal hedgerow top. He had seen Thomas busy, and did not want to speak first, but Thomas called, "Might have something for you Portland way soon. Big job if I gets it."

Misterton stopped; he had been thinking why he himself had not noticed the fuller cheeks, the plumper breasts.

"Thank you."

"You off somewhere?"

"Dorchester."

"I hears they may be looking for a murderer, these parts." Misterton raised his eyebrows. "You hear anything?" Misterton shook his head, preoccupied by a different focus. Conjuror Sayer's knowledge: the child. A boy, not a girl. Did Thomas say murderer?

"Never heard nothing."

"A farmer, name of Wareham, on Palfreyman's farm. Found dead, a few days ago, in his barn. Been covered with straw. Knife went right into his heart, they say. Best keep an eye out. Told Jemima to keep the door locked while I be's out. Man going about like that needs hanging!"

Misterton posted his letter in Dorchester. He would settle the bill for the advertisement when advised of the cost by return.

On the way home, he quickened his pace. Thomas' news had made him anxious about the women.

The house was as quiet as midnight. His mother was dozing in the firelight.

"Edith upstairs?"

His mother stretched and yawned.

"Nope."

"Where is she, then?"

"Gone. Left without a word. Made your bed up, though."

Chapter Six

The farmyard, once a marsh of mud, straw, and cow cakes, was now a hazardous, frozen pattern of wheel ruts and animals' footprints. The house occupied by Wareham until he had been killed, as Misterton's pig, in his own blood, was locked. In the barn, a few labourers remained; others, crippled scarecrows staring into the distance, had moved on stiffly. Their master's untimely death had frightened rather than liberated them.

"Here are the keys." Palfreyman jangled them before Misterton, as if teasing him as a jailer a prisoner. "Place'll need airing and cleaning. Wareham never did pay much attention to cleanliness. You'll find one or two workers have stayed on. Nowhere else to go, I expect. Take on as many as you need, but don't spoil them. They won't thank you for being soft. Others come, odd days."

There was no reaction from Misterton. He simply entered the house, and shut the door.

Those who had stayed watched, shivering, from the darkness of the barn. They looked at each other and shrugged.

Maisie Poole cut the silence.

"Must be the new master. He be young."

"Can't be worse than Wareham. That Edith, she—"

"Hush, Simon Beer. We say nothing. She was never here, see. That's what we said, and that's what we must stick to."

Maisie then began to cough uncontrollably. There were strawberry flecks of blood in her cupped hand.

"You need some honey," advised Katy Cerne.

"Where she going to get honey, this time of year, beout money, of which we don't have a sou? You a-talking like that's only going to build up her hopes, and they all but gone by cold and hunger a-pecking," admonished William Seaton.

Maisie sat down and shook her head. She had daubed the blood onto the back of her ragged coat, to hide the seriousness of it.

"This cough be the death of me."

Her words were punctuated by desperate wheezes as she struggled to speak.

Inside the farmhouse were few domestic comforts: a table scabbed with candle wax, a chair, a chest of drawers, a bed. The hearth was bare. The air was so cold that Misterton's breath formed clouds. There was an atmosphere of desolation, as if the previous occupant had fled, had neglected to make his abode habitable. It was as hospitable as a crypt.

Me, a farmer! he mused. If Stockwood could see me now, he'd shoot me on the spot.

The offer of the job as farmer had surprised him. The money from working for Thomas had almost gone. Living on Emily's pittance, as he thought of it, was unmanly. He had to find work, so he had let it be known, via Emily, that if Miss. Palfreyman still needed him, he was available, but he had not expected to take Wareham's place.

"You'll have to live in the farmhouse," Florence had informed him, "though it's not a suitable place for women. Your mother and sister are comfortable in their cottage, Emily says."

"Lived there years. Own it. Every beam, every spider," he had told her proudly.

"There is one other thing: Wareham. They hated him, but he got results. They'll take advantage if they can."

Behind her, on the wall, was a portrait bearing an uncanny

resemblance to her. She had seen Misterton's eyeline veer over her shoulder to it.

"That you?"

"Yes. You noticed? Do you like art?"

"Only when it's beautiful, like that."

Florence's eyelids had fluttered; she had been too embarrassed to look at him. She had interlocked her fingers to control her hands.

"Sometimes," she had said, anxious to change the subject, "I'll need you to drive me places."

He had nodded; he could nod as much as she liked if she was paying him. And he needed to go places himself while she attended to her own business.

The knock on the farmhouse door was timely. He was on his way to fetch wood. The house needed warmth and light. There stood Simon Beer, slightly breathless, agitated.

"Come quickly, please, master. That is if you be our new master, after our last one unfort—"

"What is it?"

"It's Maisie, master. She's taken badly, and I think you'd best come and see her."

Simon put his hat back on, and both men made haste to the barn, heedless of the treacherous ice on the ground.

"Have you no lamp?"

Misterton was angry. At Gifford's Farm, Stockwood had been a tough master, but there had always been light for the sleeping quarters, and beds crudely made with straw mattresses.

"Here she be," called Katy, stroking Maisie's lank hair.

Maisie's head rested in Katy's lap.

"She been a-hacking and a-wheezing for days now. Her breathing's nearly gone," informed Simon.

The nearest doctor was in Dorchester. There was no time to summon him. Her fingers were icicles in Misterton's hands.

"Anyone at the manor told?"

"Master Palfreyman, when we finds Master Wareham with a knife a-flopping in his ribs. Maisie been ill for a long time."

"What he say?"

"Nothing. Just walks on as if he's deaf and dumb. Said no more because of all the worry about Master Wareham, I expect."

Misterton listened to her breathing. By the time he harnessed a horse to the cart, she would be dead, he calculated. The wheeze was shallow, and in the gloom he saw life draining from her eyes. One more paroxysm of coughing, and she was still. Misterton saw the blood, and she closed her eyes gently, though her chest still rose and fell.

"She might have the 'sumption," he speculated. "We'll have to report it to Master Palfreyman. The 'sumption spreads like bineweed. Let's get her over to the house. All of you, come, warm yourselves. Bring an armful of straw, as much as you can hold."

He bent his knees, and lifted her as if she were a tied stook of hay. Her ribs pressed against his forearms, and her left arm dangled like a branch snapped at its joining with the tree.

The fire soon took with dry straw underneath it. They laid her on the table, covered her in straw, and moved her closer to the fire, which threw its arms in the air wildly, as if hysterical at the injustice of Maisie's condition. And Misterton thought of the cost of the stones he had hauled up ladders for Thomas, and of the kitchen in which Emily prepared meals for the Palfreymans, and ordered, through gritted teeth, more straw to be fetched.

"It will warm her. We must all keep warm, this weather. And one day it will be spring, and we will be less cold. And when it is summer, it will be warm again."

The others caught each other's eye, and smiled. This master won't die like Wareham, their glances said. New master be a good man.

"She a-going to make it through?" asked Katy.

"Not up to me. She got the 'sumption, I reckon."

"She got it, *we* all got it, including you," pointed out Simon.

"Stay here. I'm going over to the big house to send for a doctor."

The other two stood open-mouthed.

"No doctor ever came here to see anyone dying before. The sick be there, one day, fall ill, and leave, packed off by the old master. Said if we can't work, we should go. Some make it, some don't, and the dead get thrown on the cart and go. Paupers' graves, all of them, corner of Stinsford, tucked away, so no one's too embarrassed of a Sunday. Most lose the will. A body can only go on for so long," explained Simon. "A body needs rest." Moved, Misterton put his hand on Simon's shoulder, and felt the protruding bones under his palm. "You're a good man, master."

"Nicholas. Call me Nicholas."

Palfreyman met with him, reluctantly.

"The farm baint right. Run down, be my judgement. Turnips need raising, but no day-men have showed their face on account of what they been hearing about Wareham. They scattered like hens with a fox a-licking his lips at their coop. Bound to be folk a-looking for work in Dorchester, though. Come market day, you or me could go and hire one or two. Won't get the crop in otherwise."

Palfreyman sighed; other things on his mind made the farm unimportant.

"Sort it, then. Look, Misterton, I pay you to run the farm and do it well. How you do it's up to you. Just don't come running to me, all the time."

So Misterton began to organise: he counted the pigs; moved Katy, Simon, Maisie, and William out of the freezing barn, and into the unused butt of the farmhouse, where there was a fire and curtains of dusty cobwebs like lace; chopped up logs and planks abandoned in the farmyard; and walked the boundaries to assess how many other workers he needed to hire. It would be a few weeks before Maisie was fit for work. The honey smuggled out of the kitchen by Emily gave the patient strength, and the improvement in her condition was so marked that the likelihood of her being consumptive receded.

Simon learned how to kill, hang and butcher a pig, and Misterton fetched his own mother to show Maisie and Katy how to make bread.

"Secret be in the knuckles," revealed Mrs. Misterton. "Here, turn them over." The two young women showed the backs of their hands. Scratches, cuts, dirt in split nails were stigmata of suffering under Wareham's tyranny. "Used to hard work, I see, so you both be well suited. Bury the knuckles in the dough and then fold back. Do this till the dough be the shape of a boulder but soft as a plump cushion."

Misterton cleaned and sharpened axes, scythes, and long knives. The turnips should have been lifted a few weeks ago.

"Poor man's food, but grows easy," he remarked to William.

"Never thought of them that way."

"Weather backing off now so we starts first light. Three others a-coming. When Wareham pay you?"

"When he felt like it. Wanted to leave but not while he owed us," interjected Katy.

"You still owed?" They all nodded, reminding Misterton of the horses, which sidled up to the fence for windfall apples. "Much?"

"Tolerable."

The next day, they had bacon and bread for breakfast. Outside, hoes, knives, spades and boxes were ready for collection. A deep frost had blanched the landscape. Just what we didn't want, Misterton said to himself. But the sun was loitering, out of sight, just over the horizon, like a labourer who is still deciding whether to go to work, but knows that he must, as others depend on him.

"Ground's hard so use the spade and not the hoe. Like this."

Misterton used his foot, and the blade bit into the earth as a guillotine into the muscles, bones, and gristle of a condemned man's neck. In the golden soil sat a purple and white orb, like a precious stone. Misterton rubbed off the earth, and showed it to them.

"Take off the leaves."

Three downward slashes of his knife, and the turnip could go in the box.

"What we do when the box be full?" asked Simon.

"You show me, and I'll empty it into the cart. Keep an honest tally of your boxes. When the others come, let us make them welcome."

"Yes, master," they chorused.

Misterton worked alongside them, and when the three newcomers arrived, one of them began to sing, and the others joined in:

> "When the sun has gone down,
> and the corn's cut with scythe,
> then cider we'll drink,
> and we'll dance and be blithe."

They moved forward together, as if searching for a precious heirloom dropped by accident. There grew a rhythm to their harvesting, and the sun rubbed between their shoulder blades. Soon they were sweating, so they removed their coats. Simon steamed like a horse fresh from a gallop.

Misterton peered over his shoulder. The rumble of a horse's hooves exploded over the brow of the hill. They all turned, and soon they could see Florence, urging her mount to a faster pace. Her hair was a veil fluttering behind her. Misterton did not recognise her till she smiled and singled him out, and he ordered the others to continue. He walked a few paces away, so that she would not be inhibited by their proximity.

"Good morning," she panted, pulling her horse to a halt.

"Morning."

He waited for her to state her business. She usually had her hair up severely, but liked to let it down when riding, loved the light fingers of the wind lifting her waves and combing through them like a lover.

"You've made a good start," she praised.

The cart was filling up. She noticed their method: the line, the boxes, the cart, their togetherness.

"Needed lifting, weeks ago."

"Never mind. They look good."

The horse snorted irritably. Misterton waited for Florence to begin. There followed a few awkward seconds, in which she was assembling her next words in the right order, and rehearsing them nervously.

"Get on, then. Horse don't like this idling, by the look of him."

Florence bridled at the insinuation that they both had more important things to do.

"Actually, I came to let you know that I have to go to Lyme Regis, next week. I'll need you to take me in the coach. We shall be there for four days. There will be a room for you, and all your meals will be paid for."

Misterton stared at the boxes. This was what he had been dreading. He was just like the pig: ring through his nose, following where she led. But she would not slice his neck, would hold no sway over his life. Then he realised there would be more money, a rest from back-breaking bending in the endless fields, a soft bed to lie on. Besides, he had never been to Lyme Regis. Mabel had told him about it: how the fine parasols twirled on the shoulders of beautiful, young women, and how children scrambled over rock-falls, searching for fossils they could clean, polish, and sell to visitors.

"And the farm. Will you pay them?"

"Ask Robert. Can you trust them if you're not there?"

He looked at them. They were crouching and chopping, oblivious of her presence.

"Need lifting, or they'll spoil."

"Then let them work. You're responsible for them."

He didn't like her tone now. There was no need to remind him what his job was.

"Then I'll set out where to get to for them. They won't let me down."

She smiled, but he was not looking at her.

"What makes you so sure?"

He shrugged. In the rills, gulls and crows scavenged, waved worms in the air before swallowing them.

"I need to buy wood."

"Then see Robert. The farm's *his* domain." Her knees squeezed her horse's flanks, and it nodded as it took a step or two. "You'll need clothes for Lyme. Call at the house, tomorrow morning." And her heels prompted the horse into a canter, and she bounced up and down like a fervent lover.

At mid-day, he heard his name called. It was Emily, waving to him, and she sang the three syllables of his name.

"They let you out?" he laughed, kissing her.

She looked towards the others, embarrassed. Would they think her his woman? she wondered.

"Asked Miss. Palfreyman if I could bring you this which come to the cottage. Got to make the time up later. Told her it was important. Well, it is, isn't it? You never had a letter before."

The letter trembled in her hand. He took it, and slid it carefully into his pocket.

"Thank you," he croaked. "You run along."

She hesitated, and he knew why.

"You want me to read it?"

Her offer was tempting, but she would know about his advertisement. The reply could be encouraging or devastating. He was at work. If only Edith were there! She had written his request, and had

63

not asked difficult questions. She would have read without interrogating him.

He shook his head. Emily hugged him, and went back to her kitchen. Her delivery would make the day long.

The next day, he called on Florence, who asked Robert's butler, Colyton, to fit him out with the appropriate attire for a coachman.

"If you could just leave these clothes on for the moment," Colyton requested, ringing a bell.

Florence arrived and burst into laughter, cupping her mouth to minimise Misterton's humiliation. He looked down, and understood: the tight trousers, the gleaming, leather boots, the white gloves, and the tall hat. They made him feel ridiculous, an actor playing a minor role in a stage drama. Colyton bit his lip to inflict sufficient pain to stifle a chuckle, but Misterton guffawed, realising that indignation would have looked worse.

"Perfect!" cried Florence. "You'll turn heads in Lyme, without doubt."

"I thought I was supposed to run the farm for you."

His self-pity reduced her to tears, until her only escape was to leave the room. She had not laughed like that for years.

"You've made quite an impression on her," observed Colyton.

They worked till dusk on Saturday. The field was empty bar leaves hacked off turnips. Misterton knew his workers needed a day's rest; he himself ached from head to toe. There was another field to clear, a bigger one, which did not daunt them. To them, each turnip lifted meant wages, a meal, a guzzling or two of cider, life and limb intact a bit longer.

"Work tomorrow," offered Simon. "Baint anything else to do."

Misterton advised them all.

"Go to church."

"What use be that? Vicar don't feed us. He puts out his hand and begs from us. What do God care?" questioned William.

"He blessed the crops. Who else you think raised these?"

William followed the direction of Misterton's nod to the laden cart.

"'Tis Nature and God, " opined Katy.

"Go to church. The work will be here on Monday," reassured Misterton. "Here," he added, fishing from his pocket a handful of coins, and sharing them out.

The following day, he went to see his mother. He rode there, saving his legs; he also needed to be as fresh as a snowdrop on Monday. Again, the sky was blue, and the air cold, but there was no wind, and he knew his visit would please his mother.

He looked over the hedge, into the Hardys' garden. Down the path strode Tom, whistling. Thomas had gone to church earlier, to practise a hymn causing the orchestra a few difficulties. The vicar had thought that the unfortunate sounds they had been producing had been due to over-fortification of their spirits by mulled wine, and had called for an early rehearsal, so that the parishioners would not be disappointed, later.

"You've a horse now?" called Tom.

There would not be a better time, so Misterton dismounted, and waited for Tom to reach the gate. In his bag, Misterton felt the letter Emily had brought him.

"Farmer has to have a horse," he smiled.

"You're taking great strides in the world, I hear," remarked Tom sincerely.

"Sooner toil for your father, but baint enough work."

"Jobs come like geese, but then you don't see them for months. There's a flapping of wings, followed by an empty sky."

Misterton liked that expression, and would remember it, might use it himself, in the future, when the situation begged it.

"You got a moment to spare?"

He took out the letter, so that Tom would see it. The bookshop, the kind donation towards his first step to literacy, Hicks' office.

Misterton hoped Tom would now connect them with what was being drawn to his attention.

"You been putting the ink and pen to good use?"

"Would you read this to me?" asked Misterton.

Tom's smile slipped.

"You sure?"

Misterton thrust it eagerly towards him, and Tom opened it, and read. Behind him, Jemima opened the cottage door, looked at them, and closed it again.

Misterton listened, eyes on the floor. When Tom had finished, Misterton looked away, then back at Tom. Tom watched Misterton's Adam's apple protrude and relax as it swallowed on the message.

"Thank you."

"I'm sorry. I imagine—"

"Thank you. I appreciate your time."

"I could teach you. You know, to read. That is, if you want."

Then Jemima emerged in her coat. She was ready to catch up with Tom. The Church expected obedience. And there were people to see, talk to. Worship enabled her to meet others, though she was wary of the vicar, who wanted everything just so. She saw him as a farmer's dog, rather than a shepherd, rounding up his flock, letting no one stray.

Before she reached them, Tom said, "Australia is a long way. Ask folk at Tolpuddle. New world, big spaces, sheep, a fresh start. Such a long way."

Misterton crushed the letter into his bag.

"Thank you. Mrs. Hardy," he nodded.

Jemima's smile was a sunflower.

Misterton mounted his horse, and resumed his journey up the hill.

"What he want?" asked Jemima.

"Nothing."

On his return from church, Tom picked up a pen and dipped it in ink. Words followed, wrung from the memory of the bad news in Misterton's letter. Within an hour, the poem was finished.

Mrs. Misterton clung to her son as if he had been away years and not days. But his mind was fixed on the fact that his child was now on the other side of the world, and, consequently, neither his mother nor his sister felt that he shared their joy at his visit.

Misterton peeked up the chimney. The hams were ready, cured, could be carved, eaten with bread and butter. He sliced one precisely, feeding his sister and mother a tit-bit with a rim of fat on. His father had taught him well.

In the solitude of his bedroom, Tom read aloud his poem.

> "In their empty bed she cried,
> her child slept in its cot;
> her man had dug a chasm wide,
> he'd left her there, his heart had dried,
> and though her own had not yet died,
> it had begun to rot.
>
> Upon the cliff-top, she looked down,
> her child slept on the grass;
> her mother fell in billowed gown,
> her chestnut hair and eyes of brown
> will ne'er be seen in Bridport town,
> so pity, all, this lass."

He cocked his head, read it again, but still the melancholy was too great for him to bear, so he screwed up the poem and tossed it onto the fire.

"Too much," he sighed, "too much."

Chapter Seven

Bridport. A warmer day than of late. The buds on the trees on the road to West Bay were beginning to overcome their shyness. Misterton could not be sure, but he thought the stonemason's yard was behind the houses facing Ruth's. It was. He heard noises from it before he saw it. The metallic ping of hammer on chisel on stone grew louder as he drew nearer. He watched the mason mark the marble, chip out the letters of the deceased's name. The fragments of stone flew as the sharp edge of the tool bit. There was a rhythm to the hammer blows: little taps to follow a line, and a heavier strike to start a new letter. Misterton watched him, fascinated, held his breath so that he would not disturb the craftsman and spoil the work of art. The right moment would come.

The mason wiped the dust from the now complete word, *Beloved*, and stepped back, not to admire but to assess his effort. Misterton coughed.

"Come in," invited the mason, still examining the headstone. "Baint perfect, but no one'll notice. Only *I* know when it's perfect, and the graveyard's more imperfect than perfect. That be a fact."

"Don't much matter, seeing as we're all more bad than good."

The mason turned to his visitor.

"Now that be telling it plain. Not many of us be as honest as that. World be full of hypocrites, especially them as asks me to write one thing on marble when they never had a decent word to say to the deceased when they were alive!"

Misterton edged forward, noticed the barely disguised inspection of his coachman's outfit, in which he felt ridiculous. He looked around the yard. There were no angels with two wings.

"You do angels? You know, with two wings? A girl angel?"

The mason threw his head back and laughed so heartily that he began to wheeze.

"Not much call for them with just one! Impossible to fly with just one, at least in a straight line."

Misterton laughed, too. His request, though sincere, was not explicit enough.

"You mend angels' wings? See, there be an angel in the graveyard got a wing broken off. Fact is, I promised I'd make it up to her, even though I never broke it off in the first place, and time is when I must do it. If you can fix an angel's wings in three days, I'd be glad. To see two wings on my way back would mean I'd kept my word."

The mason looked thoughtful.

"Done a wing or two in my time. What be the name on the grave?"

"Don't know. Can't read. I mean, letters are nearly gone."

The mason scratched his head. This was not a conventional request, and he was puzzled by the fact that the visitor did not even know to whom the angel belonged. The possibility that Misterton was suffering an affliction of the mind made the mason ask a question or two more.

"Why you so keen to mend the angel if you don't know the person buried underneath it?"

Misterton wanted to tell the truth but felt that a confession would not be believed. The headache, the nausea, the shaking, did not show him in a positive light, yet part of the cleansing of his soul was an acknowledgement of his sin.

"Truth be, my wife be buried in the churchyard. Jumped off West Bay cliff, they say, and now our child be adopted and living in Australia. I saw the angel by chance, when I was visiting, and vowed to fix it. You do it in three days?"

The mason scratched his chin. He had other stones to engrave. An angel was difficult. The symmetry of the wings was a challenge. It would take time. To jump the queue would cost money.

"Can be done. Expensive, though."

"Whatever it costs."

The mason turned and beckoned to Misterton to follow him.

"Ten pounds, including erection on a pedestal. Angel have a pedestal?"

He could not remember.

"Maybe, maybe not. I be off to Lyme within the hour, and would be glad to see a proper angel when I return on Thursday. No pedestal, put one in and stand the angel on it." The mason offered his hand, which was dusty and scarred with chisel cuts. "It means a lot to me. It's the least I can do."

The mason picked up his pen, and asked, "Name?" Still staring at his order book, he added, "Yours, I mean."

"Palfreyman. Robert Palfreyman."

"Address?"

"Palfreyman Manor, Palfreyman Estate."

The mason turned and eyed him from top to bottom. The uniform was fascinating, but it did not suit the wearer, he decided.

"You travelling alone?"

"Taking my sister. Coming back Thursday, so I'll call in the churchyard then. Soon as I receive your account, I'll bring the money. Don't carry that amount on the road. See a coach, and the cut-throats'll have your purse if you're stupid enough to carry one."

"How I know you'll pay? What you pay with in Lyme?"

Without a flicker of an eyelid, Misterton said, "You doubt the word of a gentleman? Our accounts are paid in full within fourteen days wherever we go. You never heard of the Palfreymans?" The mason nodded. "Ask anyone in Bridport. Our word be as good as payment." They shook hands again, and Misterton left, muttering, "Ten pounds is too much for the likes of me, but his sins be Pilsdon Pen to my knoll up the heath. He must pay something for Maisie's chest rattle."

They arrived late in the afternoon in Lyme Regis. The hotel sat smugly, overlooking the sea. Misterton had lit the coach's oil lamps, and followed lights in windows down into the town. In the distance, he could hear the rumble of the tumbling tide, and the swishing of the waves as they withdrew through the shingle shoved into a bank up the beach.

On the way from Bridport, Florence had sat behind him, her gloved hand resting on her new box, as if incubating the hat inside, which she hoped her friends would envy. Occasionally, she had made polite conversation, seeking his opinion on matters relating to the farm, but sometimes mentioning Emily in a positive light: how reliable she was, how expertly she ironed and folded linen. Sometimes, Misterton had turned and answered, as a natural response, but more often than not he had looked ahead, had felt her staring at his back, and when that sensation was heightened, he had focused on a feature of the landscape – perhaps a barrow, or a cleft in the hill-side – so that he would not be seduced, would not enter the larder of temptation.

"Will you have some food delivered to your room?" she asked. "After breakfast, I shall spend the day with friends. We have much to catch up on."

"I'll sort myself out."

"Thank you. Lyme has so much to amuse one."

That night, he lay in bed. In another room, in the same building, slept his employer. My, but I be going up in the world! he laughed. Father would never believe his eyes.

The next day, he dressed in comfortable clothes. The ostler was feeding the two horses, and murmuring words of encouragement. Misterton told them it was a rest day; Florence had not said that he was required.

When he returned to his room, there was a knock at the door. He had to meet Florence at nine in the vestibule. The boy waited for a coin, but Misterton shut the door in his face, guessing that Florence would have rewarded him already.

In her hat, she looked a fine lady. The feathers were pheasants', if he were not mistaken. She turned heads as people came and went.

"I shall be meeting friends for refreshments at Sebastiano's Tea Rooms. I shan't need the coach, but the day is fine, a good deal warmer than yesterday. Perhaps, you could escort me there, and then the day is yours."

He did not look at the money she passed him, but inclined his head, and nodded.

There was an awkwardness in his movement as he moderated his stride to hers, which was relaxed yet purposeful. There was a moment when he nearly offered his arm to her, but he knew he must not touch her.

"We meet from time to time," she told him, on the hotel's steps. "Tell each other our news. You know, who's engaged to whom, who is the latest beau to turn heads. Women are rather good at gossiping, you know, but not nearly as good as men. When Robert meets his friends in The King's Arms, they're a match for any of us. The things he tells me about Dorchester!"

"It be the drink with men. It loosens tongues, and turns the truth into exaggeration."

She cocked her head to one side, impressed.

"Quite a philosopher!"

"What I sees, anyway. The liquor is sweet to start with, but leaves the nasty taste of jumbled words in the mouth."

"I'm sure you're right. Will you join me for dinner at seven tonight? You can tell me more interesting things to amuse me then."

"Just as you say."

"A charming turn of phrase," she laughed, before disappearing into the tearooms.

He walked down to the Cobb, watched barrels and boxes being lifted from boats, and lined up ready for the Harbour Master to examine. Landing taxes had to be paid. Up the coast, Golden Cap pointed to Heaven, and tree-tops frothed. Grand, white houses fanned out across the hills, and fishermen lugged boxes of mackerel around the Cobb, which curved and turned its back on the jostling waves. And there they were, on the promenade, the women who twirled their parasols, as Mabel had told him. Misterton thought them elegant, beautiful, self-conscious.

They've never milked a cow or churned the cream into butter. Arms too thin, he noticed.

He had his mid-day meal at an inn, and could not help smiling. Why, here I be in Lyme, lackey to a lady who's taken a bit of a fancy to me. But I baint the sort to be at the beck and call of those who would sooner bury a worker than save her from the worms. Mistress Palfreyman must eat without me tonight.

"But a woman can't eat alone in public!" she protested, when he had explained his wish not to dine with her. "I'd be the talk of Lyme!"

"What you done other times? I'd be awkward. Never ate in a hotel before. Tongues'd wag anyway. You and me baint married. I got my reputation to protect!" he joked.

"Well, I must say I'm disappointed. I had hoped to discuss plans for the estate. Robert wants to groom you. He thinks you're honest and reliable. Heaven knows they are qualities in short supply, these days. Wareham was a reprobate, an alcoholic. I'm not surprised someone took against him. However, if you've made your mind up. Perhaps, on another occasion."

"A lady mustn't be seen eating with her coachman," he called as she fled the room, seething.

In the inn, the fiddlers tapped their clogs, and scraped their bows across the strings as if possessed by a demon spirit. The dancers skipped, spun, ducked under arms, and bowed exaggeratedly when the song had finished. Misterton watched from his table, his face blotchy from the ale and fire. He had eaten meat and vegetables earlier, had congratulated himself on telling Florence the truth: that he would not be patronised, would not make the effort to entertain her. And she was an attractive woman who might lead him to perdition. There was a better, more dignified way of earning his return from exile.

And what if he were invited to join the dance, feel again the waist of a woman, know the brush of her breast against his chest, capture her eyes with his? The yeasty smell of Edith was still in his nose, even though he had walked away from her. And Victoria. He would, therefore, watch only. There had to come a day when he stopped walking away from people.

"Sitting there all alone!" scoffed the young woman, who seized his arm, and attempted to drag him from his seat. "Don't harm a man to whoop and dance with a Dorset girl, do it? And you on your own and not from Lyme, I judge."

Her plumpish forearms were bare, and she had hot, strong hands, like Mabel's, used to squeezing teats in the parlour. If he had had one pot of ale fewer, he would have anchored himself in his seat, but he was too merry, could not refuse without drawing attention to himself. She turned, and theatrically hauling him by trailing his arm, as a rope, over her shoulder, she established their place among the dancers.

"I never danced before," he confessed.

"Don't matter a spickle. Put your right arm round my waist, and take my left with your left. Go where I push, pull or throw you, and no one'll know that you have two left feet!"

The room changed, spun, rushed to and from him, as she guided him, dragging, pushing, rubbing her hip against him, so that he pulled her to him more tightly.

"I'm Nicholas," he told her.

"Maggie!" she yelled back.

"No, *Nicholas*," he laughed.

And with her left hand, she struck his buttock, sharply.

"Don't get many word-jugglers round these parts. You looking to marry a girl in Lyme, you best not try your funny word-tricks on her. Better to learn to dance and sing a shanty and kiss her sweetly."

Maggie offered her cheek, a velvet, ripe peach, as one who knows it will not be refused. And he remembered Edith, how she turned her head, exposing her neck, so that he could kiss it, and Victoria, whose lips were as giving and moist as two segments of orange. Maggie was spontaneous, had singled him out.

He was not a morose man by inclination but had become so when exiled by his father. He had suffered when he had changed into someone else, as if under a malevolent spell, so that he lost himself, hurt others as he searched for the man he knew he had to be, for his family's, and his own, sake.

"Will you walk me home now?" Maggie asked, when the fiddles had run out of steam.

"I can't."

"Why not? You spoken for?"

He shook his head. There was too much to explain.

"Are *you*?"

"Might be. Might not. Depends, don't it?"

Misterton wiped his brow on his sleeve.

"I only came for food and drink. Told you I can't dance."

"That's why you need a good woman."

Misterton put on his hat. The music and dancing had been unexpected. He had not known he had had it in him to be so spontaneous, uninhibited.

"Must be off now."

"You're cruel, Nicholas, letting a woman down, this way."

"Better now than later, Maggie."

"You got another name?" she called after him, as he was nearly through the door.

"Stockwood. Nicholas Stockwood. Farmer at Gifford's Farm, Pilsdon way, just up from Bridport."

"Come see you, one day, then. Give you another dancing lesson."

"Do that, Maggie."

The doorman at the hotel eyed him suspiciously, almost blocked his entrance.

"A guest, sir?"

"Miss. Palfreyman's coachman. Room three, I think."

The doorman stood aside, allowing Misterton access, and smelt ale in the air.

Misterton collected his key from the reception. On his pillow was a note. The hieroglyphics were a foreign tongue. At the top of the paper was the hotel's crest. Misterton remembered it hanging above the entrance, swinging, squeaking in the breeze. He crammed the note into his bag, took off his clothes, and crawled into bed. Allowing himself a chuckle at the thought of Stockwood having to convince Victoria, one day, that he had never set eyes on Maggie, he fell into a deep, dreamless sleep.

The girl who delivered his breakfast could not rouse him. When he eventually awoke, his mouth felt as dry as a haystack in August. He held his head in his hands. What was happening to the turnip-pickers? No self-respecting farmer would be found in a hotel bedroom when he should be in the fields. His labourers had a different idea of him. He glanced over his shoulder at the bed. Maggie was not there.

The cold water in the bowl brought him back to life. He was not sure what the day held for him.

Down in the vestibule, he sat in an armchair, watching people coming and going, ignoring him.

"Is there any message from Miss. Palfreyman?" he asked the man behind the counter.

The receptionist pressed his monocle to his eye, and scrutinised him as a scientist an insect under a microscope, only to discover

76

that the specimen was a common beetle, the sort one might crush under one's foot without a moment's hesitation.

"None of which I am aware."

"I'm her coachman. If she returns, tell her I asked after her."

As he left the hotel to check on his horses, he heard the receptionist mutter something under his breath. Misterton stopped, stood long enough to let the man know that he had heard him, and went out into the fresh air.

He ran his hands down the horses' glossy necks and flanks.

"Full of beans today," remarked the ostler. "Rested up nicely."

"Off in the morning. Early be my guess."

"Make the most of today, then."

Misterton ate mussels and bread near the Cobb. If Maggie saw him, he would speak. There was nothing he would run away from again.

The sky darkened. The sea was made of pewter. His limbs were heavy. Fatigue persuaded him to return to the hotel.

"Will you join me for afternoon tea?" came a voice behind him. "I thought you'd abandoned me."

Her tone was light-hearted, conciliatory, not what he had expected; he had been prepared for trouble."

"I looked for you, this morning."

"I was off at the crack of dawn. I enjoy a walk along the promenade when the sun comes up. I like looking at beautiful things. There is so much ugliness in the world that one should seek out beauty."

"Like your portrait at the manor. Your face be lit up as if there be a lantern under your skin."

Florence's cheeks were pink carnations. She sought different places to look, but knew she would have to meet his eyes again.

Misterton knew she liked compliments, but little else about her, such as why she had chosen him, in particular, to drive her coach when there were others on the estate she knew better.

"Four, in the conservatory?"

He had never heard the word before.

"And where be that?"

If only he did not talk like that, like Dorset country folk, she wished.

"The conservatory is through that door. It looks out onto the garden."

He slept till four. The red, velvet curtains had not been drawn, and the rapidly fading light fell between them like a grey slab of stone.

Florence had changed into a clean dress, and had let down her hair, as she did when riding. She was waiting for him in the vestibule, and he surprised himself by offering his arm, which she took. He had watched other couples, seen how the men held themselves erect, and how the women rested their hand on the men's forearm.

"Will you take a piece of cake?" she asked.

"Don't normally eat it."

"Then a slice won't harm you. I use my trips to Lyme to do something different. I feel so cut off at the manor. Sometimes I am bored with running the house. There are lots of people to supervise, and Robert's not exactly company, even though he is my brother."

"And did you ask me to bring you here because you're bored with the others who have brought you here in the past?"

This stung her. She had been planning this moment since she had seen him climb up and down Thomas Hardy's ladder. Misterton was different to the men to whom Robert had introduced her. They were more interested in themselves than her, were more inclined to go to balls than work the land. And she had steered clear of Wareham after he had smiled at her lasciviously. Misterton was so self-contained, and she wanted to know what had made him so.

"I brought you because I want to know a bit more about you.

It's not often Robert recommends a new worker. He said you beat the champion at Dorchester Fair, that you broke the young man's arm, you were so strong."

"I needed the money. I was starving. 'Twas nothing."

"You are too modest. Here comes the waitress."

The girl came between them.

"A pot of tea for two, and two pieces of Madeira cake, please."

"Certainly, Madam."

Misterton looked up, just as the waitress glanced down.

"Why, Mr. Stockwood! I never expected to see you here!" exclaimed Maggie, gaily. "I must say, Mrs. Stockwood, that your Nicholas baint the best dancer in the world, but he be a real gentleman."

Florence waited for her to go, then stood up indignantly.

"Really! So embarrassing!" she cried. "A common waitress!"

Misterton shook his head sheepishly.

"Now calm down, Mrs. Stockwood. Baint the end of the world."

"Have the horses ready for eight in the morning. I thought we might have had a pleasant conversation, but you've ruined it. I don't feel at all well now."

She left quickly before Maggie could return with the cake.

"Mrs. Stockwood coming back?" she asked, putting down her silver tray.

Misterton shook his head.

"Seems she changed her mind, which be her right, a woman of her means. Might be an idea to take the tea back."

Maggie looked at him, and guessed they had had words.

"What room you in?" she ventured.

"Me? Like every other man: my kennel."

"You upset her?"

"Don't take much."

"Come out with me tonight? You'd like that."

"I would, but I can't. Got to see an angel in the morning."

Maggie shook her head.

"Can't do with a man who talks in riddles. Pity. We could have helped each other out."

Misterton watched her leave, recalled the sensation of her pillowy hip against him, and sighed deeply.

In the morning, he left Lyme Regis in deathly silence. Florence did not even notice that he took the coach via the graveyard.

"Now you can fly, my angel!" he said aloud. "And, one day, when I know my letters, I'll read your name, and you can join my family, now there be a space for one more."

"What did you say?" asked Florence.

"Nothing. I just be wondering how long it takes to sail to Australia."

"I'm sure I have no idea."

In the stone-mason's yard, the mason nodded earnestly, and said, "Of course, I'm sure. Said his wife had jumped to her death at West Bay. Said the child had gone to Australia. Palfreyman be his name. Lives at Palfreyman Manor."

"Palfreyman?"

"Palfreyman."

"No other?"

"Palfreyman."

James Chideock looked puzzled.

"Thank you, Robin. I'm grateful to you for letting me know."

"Where'd he get the idea that you'd taken the child to Australia, which be a bit of a long way?"

Chideock shrugged, left, and, agitated, walked back into Bridport.

Chapter Eight

Zachariah Stockwood checked his pocket-watch, which his father had taken from one of Boney's officers at Waterloo, at the first solemn chime of the grandfather clock. At exactly nine, that morning, he had wound up both treasured time-pieces, and ensured that their hands were in identical positions. Now, at twelve noon, the time when he usually ate his mid-day meal with Victoria, he was pleased to see that his attention to accuracy was yet again rewarded.

As the twelfth chime's eerie note faded, Victoria appeared and announced that the usual fare was ready. She had spent the morning baking rabbit pie, and wondering how many of them she had to make before something exciting came into her life, as Misterton had done.

In the seemingly interminable months following his banishment, Victoria had waited for the letter he had promised, but her faith in him had been misplaced. Such had been her conviction that he would let her know when and how they would be reunited, that she tried to be the perfect daughter. She made no criticism of her father's authoritarian manner, believing it would be only a matter of time before she could escape it for ever. Yet as the months slouched, one after another, as children reluctant to come in at the end of a fine, summer's day, she began to believe that her liberation would never come.

"Three more of them bunnies a-hanging in the pantry. Need

using up," stated Stockwood, prodding the pie's crust, to release eruptions of steam.

Victoria sensed he was tense. Usually, he would have thanked her with either a nod of the head, or, more often than not, the words, "Big bugger, that one."

"All right, father. You can have rabbit pie three times a day if you like."

She waited to be invited to sit, nervous that he had not made the powerful eye contact that would confirm she could join him at the table.

"Wilfred says they're everywhere. Can't live on rabbit all our lives, though."

Stockwood looked at her across the table to see if she understood his request for variety.

"George can pick us a lamb, then."

"Wasn't complaining. Just saying."

She watched him set about cutting a piece of pie for himself. He did it purposefully, and dropped it on his plate, intent on devouring her efforts as quickly as possible, as Megan did when thrown a bloody bone bulging marrow from both ends. With his thumb, he deliberately pushed the pie dish towards her. She met his gaze, and did not care that she was clanging her spoon loudly on her plate as she shook off the food sticking to it.

Then, unexpectedly, as a pheasant flapping into the air from the crops when frightened by a fox, he sat bolt upright, and asked, "All that other done with now, then?"

Her brow furrowed. Another riddle for her to make sense of. What was it he was not brave enough to name?

"All what?"

"You know. Him as dallied with you so's you didn't know dawn from dusk."

She was tempted to persist with feigning ignorance of his meaning, but that would have provoked him. There had already been too many thumped tables, too much moralising, silences as quiet as an interred coffin.

"Nicholas? You mean Nicholas?"

"Misterton. Him as nearly stole you from under my nose."

"Yes. You needn't worry. I expected once to hear from him, but there has been nothing. You were right, father. I must live the rest of my life a lonely, bitter woman."

"You be here tomorrow, and put on a bit of lamb and potatoes, maybe even a honey pudding. Best knives and forks, and polish up a glass or two. No dust in the bottom, mind!"

Victoria could not help smiling at his change of mood.

"Why all the fuss? Glasses not been out in years."

"Fuss? No fuss, girl. Just put on something decent. Look you presentable. You be pretty if you make an effort."

"Why?" she laughed. "You ashamed of me?"

"There's someone as I'd like to introduce to you."

"Who?"

She leaned forward at her father's teasing.

"A man who is coming to make you a wife! Baint that what you want, after all? Now, eat your pie afore it be cold as winter."

Out in the milking parlour, where cows steamed like frost melting in the sun, Mabel emptied her bucket carefully into the churn.

"I loves the froth of the milk. All them little bubbles," she marvelled.

"Only be tiddy bubbles. Not much to get all giddy about," said Edna.

"And why not? What *you* get giddy about? Baint you happy here any more? Were a time you sang to the cows all day."

"'Taint the same now there's just two of us. Edith bint one to gossip like you and me, but she filled a gap or two. 'Twas cruel of Farmer Stockwood to let her go on account of that fling with Nicholas. Did Miss. Victoria a favour, be my judgement."

Then both milkmaids heard an unnatural coughing. It was

Wilfred, silhouetted in the barn doorway, hat in hand, feeding the brim nervously through his fingertips.

"Won't be a moment," Mabel said quietly.

Edna buried her head into the ruby cow's flank. She knew what Mabel was going to say, that it would be painful to Wilfred, but had agreed it would be for the best.

"You decided?" asked Wilfred in a strangled voice.

Mabel nodded, then shook her head, her eyes as brown and big as chestnuts.

"I can't."

"Why not?"

Wilfred had found his proper voice.

"Because I don't love you."

"That be telling me, that."

He turned and plodded into the barn. How would he tell George that she had refused him, after he had brought her flowers from the hedgerow, blackberries in a bucket?

George watched Wilfred's hopeless gait and horse-shoe shoulders.

It's as I thought, George sang inside. It's me she's chosen. I'll make her a summer bride after I've grown my words in spring, and they'll blossom into a spray of meadow flowers, all bright and colourful.

Edith trudged away from the ship in Weymouth. Bound for France, its sails unfurled, sagging like bed sheets on a washing line, on a still day, *The Sweet Maria* was ready to be towed out a mile to catch the breeze.

The Captain had listened to Edith's begging to let her work her passage to Cherbourg, but he had shaken his head. She was no older than his own daughter, and he had sensed an urgency in her voice that aroused his suspicion. No money, no companion. No place to stay in France. He could not take her.

So she went back into town. Under the iron arcade roof stretching along the sea-front, men eyed her, sometimes bade her good-day, mistook her for a prostitute. Smells of food cooking drifted tantalisingly from hotel kitchens. She asked for work, was prepared to scrub floors, clean stinking chamber pots, do anything. But she had no references, had run away from her last employer, and did not want to let anyone know where she had been, what her real name was. She became Nelly Sturminster. Edith had died. To survive, Nelly must work to earn money, buy food, pay for accommodation. But no one wanted to help except the depraved men who prowled the arcade. They were no better than Wareham.

Edith was cold and tired. The previous night, she had refused the offer of a warm bed at a Women's Charity hostel. The woman had seen her sheltering, out of the wind, in an alley, and had promised her sanctuary, and to teach her to sew, so that she would be useful as a maid to a lady, one day.

"In time, you will come to see that the pathway you have chosen is wrong, but that the Lord forgives those who ask his forgiveness," the woman had told her. "Some seek other shores when their life in our house is restored. It is a sort of rebirth. But we have our rules: no alcohol, no men, no tobacco; but prayers are plentiful. Without prayer, we can have no salvation."

"Pathway?" Edith had croaked.

"Yes. The dark one, gloomy as this filthy street, which leads to disease and degradation, at the end of which men line up, ready to buy your body and soul."

"You are mistaken. I be hungry and tired, but I baint what you think."

The woman had taken a card out of her big, black bag, and placed it in Edith's lap.

"Our door, like the Lord's, is always open."

The next morning, not even the scuttling of a rat near her feet, and the lurching of drunken men past the far end of the alley, could persuade Edith to go to the women's hostel. Her dream of London and a post as a maid-companion to a lady lived on. Until it was extinguished, she would try to remain independent.

She knew that she appeared destitute to passers-by, who swerved to avoid her, and looked at her oddly. One gentleman kindly asked if she needed assistance, and he offered a coin, which she refused. Charity was not what she wanted, though her legs barely supported her, so little had she eaten.

"My dear," he said, "if you do not accept my help, the parish has a workhouse not far from here. I fear you may die if you stay on these streets. The wind from the sea does not discriminate. Please, even if it is for a short time only, present yourself at the gate, this morning. I am no great advocate of the institution, but it cannot be worse than life on the streets. Would you allow me to speak on your behalf?"

There was something in the man's voice and appearance she trusted. His pleading eyes showed genuine concern for her.

"Not far, you say?"

"Five minutes. I am no citizen of Weymouth, and am here to take the air and salt water. I live in London, where I have a good friend who supports women in your circumstances. I could ask him to find you a place."

At the mention of London, Edith stood to her full height, and tucked her hair in a pathetic attempt to tidy it, a gesture to convince him that she was a decent human being.

"London? That be where I'm heading."

"But I guess from your accent that you be – *are* – from these parts."

"Sidmouth," she said, knowing that she must not tell anyone, not even a stranger, that she was from Bridport. "Devon," she added when his face suggested he had not heard of it.

"Look, I return tomorrow. Would you let me pay your fare, and introduce you to my friend? You need not fear for your safety. My friend is well known for his work with women who have lapsed."

Indignantly, Edith snapped, "You are very much mistaken if you think I be one of them!"

"Do forgive me. I did not mean to imply that you were. But my friend hates injustice. He recognises that our times are not as kind to women as they ought to be."

"You may say that, but I don't even know your name, or your friend's."

"Again, forgive me. My name is John Forster, and my esteemed friend is Dickens, Charles Dickens. You might have heard of him."

"Never heard of him. What he do?"

"He is a writer, a much loved one."

"Collects women in a house, you say?"

"Saves souls, my dear. Indeed, the nation's very own is in his hands."

Robert Palfreyman awoke refreshed. For several days, he had abstained from drinking wine and brandy with his meals, and had refrained from visiting The King's Arms, and over-indulging himself. With Florence away at Lyme, he had to keep an eye on the domestic staff, and a clear head was essential. His waistline, too, had been a matter of some concern to him, and he resolved to get a grip on personal as well as estate matters.

Though he would have preferred to talk to his stud manager about increasing the fees – there had been many enquiries about his two most productive stallions – he decided he would pay a mid-morning visit to the farm. Misterton's absence had been niggling him. Labourers' demands for higher wages in Dorset was a major topic of conversation among land-owners. Palfreyman hoped Misterton was managing his costs well.

"Since Wareham's death, I've had little appetite for the farm. Seems a good fellow, this Misterton, though he needs to remember that they're not working out of respect for him but for money," he had said to Thomas Melbury, a corn merchant.

"No different from us, then!" Melbury had laughed.

But the price of labour was no laughing matter to Palfreyman. However, workers would come and go, and there would always be a regular supply while there was hunger, he believed.

Misterton had given them instructions before leaving with Florence: clear the last field of turnips, pile them into mounds in the barn, clean the tools and farmhouse, and burn all wood that has no use.

The fields looked abandoned as Palfreyman surveyed them. Dead leaves lay like the discarded epaulettes of fallen soldiers.

"Damn them all! Gone, every single one of them. Where are those pickers?"

He galloped down to the farmhouse, the nostrils of his horse flaring, expelling steam as a dragon. Yellow smoke was belching from the chimney. Palfreyman saw that the broken cartwheel had gone, that the fence round the pigsty had been mended. The farmyard looked different, tidier than when he had last seen it.

"Who the deuce is in there?" he whispered.

He burst through the door to discover a group of men and women sitting round a blazing fire. A woman was stirring turnip soup. There would be meat, that evening, she reminded them. Master Misterton had killed a sheep for them before leaving.

"He be a good man," were the words Palfreyman heard.

"Who are you? Who gave you damned permission to come in here?" he bawled.

Maisie continued to stir the soup slowly. The pot was brimming.

"We be here as Master Misterton's workers, and he told us to stay here, on account of the fact that the barn be full of turnips a-ready to be carted and sold to bring in a fat sum for Master Palfreyman."

Palfreyman faltered, had not expected this. It would not have happened on Wareham's watch. No make-yourself-at-home attitude from him.

"Want some soup?" asked Maisie. "Turnip, see, on account of

there being plenty, though if you returns, this evening, there might be a slice or two of mutton."

Lost for words, Palfreyman rushed over to the barn. The purple and cream jewels amazed him. He had never seen so many. They had settled into the shape of the coastal hills.

"And what are his instructions for you now?" he snapped, back at the house. "He didn't tell you to sit around drinking soup, I'll wager."

"Been filling gaps in fences, cleaning in here for the Master's return. Plough's to be sharpened, later. Tools be already sorted and hung up like pictures. They were left out in all weathers, licked by rain and snow, and rusting in wind and ice. Ewes been separated into their own field. Lambing baint too far away. Tups did their job as if they were at it for the last time, judging by the number of swollen bellies. Fetch a good price at market, I don't doubt," reported Simon.

The others nodded and muttered in agreement. Their interest in the farm disarmed Palfreyman, who strode slowly to the pot, and sniffed the soup. The warmth felt good on his cold face.

"Any salt, pepper? Might perk it up a bit," he suggested.

Smiles surrounded him. He was conscious of them watching him, saw the ladle rising to tempt him, but he raised his palm.

He walked contemplatively towards the door, turned, looked again at the contented gathering, and left.

"Don't know who he be, but he come in like a hurricane, and go out like a whisper. Seem he know about spicing up soup, though," said Maisie, "which be a woman's job more than a man's."

Mrs. Misterton looked dead. Her mouth was open, and her head lolled like a rag doll's on the wing of her favourite chair. Only the sound of her snoring, like the growling and creaking of rope on a ship's timber as it bends to the wind and waves, indicated she was alive.

Emily looked at her, and smiled. There were no obvious signs that Mrs. Misterton had been preparing food, and Emily felt frustrated after a long, hard day at the manor. Still, she reflected, my mother baint young any more; her naps keep her going; and now I must look after her as she did all three of us. Bacon, potatoes, and apples, Emily decided. The long walk home had sharpened her appetite till it was like the carving knife she had applied, that very day, to the whetstone in the kitchen.

She made up the fire from the white ashes, which became rubies when she blew on them. On went the kindling, and two logs, stretched in the hearth like sleeping puppies, were added. The room would soon be full of the smell of salty meat and vegetables.

Emily smiled as she prepared the meal, having something to tell her mother, show her.

Mrs. Misterton awoke with a jump.

"Just went off for two minutes," she apologised, saliva dribbling from the corner of her mouth.

"Nonsense. I've been back an hour, and you were asleep when I got here." And then, unable to contain her excitement any longer, Emily added, "Got something for you, after dinner."

Her mother rubbed her eyes.

"A present?" she yawned.

"Sort of. Though you can't eat or wear it."

"Why both my children so secret, all the time!" Mrs. Misterton declared, shaking her head resignedly.

Emily, the something she had to say breaking its tether like a goat that's been chewing his all day, sat facing her.

"They say Nicholas gone to Lyme with Miss. Palfreyman."

Her mother looked up from her plate.

"Run away with her? My son, you will send me to an early grave with your wild ways!" she cried, clutching her cheeks.

"He be her coachman, that's all, though why him, when he be their farmer, be one beyond us all. They been a-teasing me in the kitchen, saying I'll soon have a sister-in-law."

"And what if it be Providence? Then you and me be rich, girl, and no more slaving, bringing in the wood in winter, and a-stacking up the fire to see us through till the morning."

Mrs. Misterton had put down her fork, and was trembling with excitement, and Emily realised she had made a mistake.

"Now just you squash those silly notions, mother. He be just driving the coach, that's all."

"Then I wish you had never raised my hopes, girl, though I should know myself that rich and poor don't mix. Some serve, and others be served, and that be the way of the world, and we takes our lot as it comes to us, especially we women, who be the bearers of children, and skivvies who go without for the sake of their family."

Emily was just about to debate that belief with her, but did not; there was the matter of what she had to show her.

She went to the bag she carried to and from the manor. Made from an old dress her mother had been on the verge of burning, it hung on the back of the door, where Emily could not fail to see it as she left for work, each morning.

Reverentially, she took out the book, stood before her mother, and turned to the first page. Mrs. Misterton had returned to her winged chair, as was her habit after dinner, to prepare for forty winks.

Emily cleared her throat. Her voice was hesitant, at first, but grew in confidence. The hours spent practising with Florence had not been in vain.

"Then God said, 'Let us make Man in our image, according to our likeness; let them have dominion over the fish of the sea, over the birds of the air, and over the cattle, over all the earth and over every creeping thing that creeps on the earth.' So God created man in his *own* image."

Mrs. Misterton had watched Emily, had listened to the words

which were strange and arresting. Emily closed the book, and smiled. The words had been stones in her mouth when she had firstly repeated them after Florence, but, gradually, they had changed. They were no longer cold and hard, but yielding and sweet, like cherries and plums.

"And can my daughter read now?"

Mrs. Misterton barely had the breath to ask.

"Yes, mother, I can. And write. Your little Emily be a scholar now."

Chapter Nine

The walk to Stinsford had become too painful for Mrs. Misterton. Her hips and knees were rusty hinges. Her stiffness had deformed her body slightly, so that when she lifted her legs, she swung them forward as a tin soldier needing winding up.

"You want our Nicholas make you a stick," suggested Emily. "Plenty of wood up the lane. Only way we going to get you to church be on a horse, which we'd never lift you up on, on account of your weight – and no offence here, mother; we have to be honest – or on a cart, which we don't have, and even if we got one, say borrowed one from the manor, by Nicholas asking Miss. Palfreyman, sweet-talking her with honeyed words, as he does—"

"Emily, don't fuss so, girl. My days of wriggling on a hard, slippery pew are over, as much as I enjoy the orchestra playing the wrong notes, and the vicar a-wobbling his eyes at old Mr. Hardy. No, the Lord will forgive me, but the next time I goes through those church doors, the vicar will tell his congregation that Man has but a short time to live, and then is cut down. Can't remember the rest, but you know the bit I mean."

"Oh, mother, please don't talk like that. You're not that old."

Mrs. Misterton went down slowly onto her knees, and began to sweep the ashes from the grate. Nicholas was coming for his dinner.

"Not as young as I was, and that be a fact."

"You be able to get up if I go now? You want me to nip down and ask Jemima if you can go with them?"

Mrs. Misterton shook her head.

"Need the place tidy for when he comes. He don't want to get here and find his home all shut up, as if we'd abandoned it. He was born under this roof, though the thatch be a bit mossy in places, and grew up in it, till his father sent him packing. But he is now come back, or, at least, lives nearby. That door be always open to him, food be always on the table, and as long as the good Lord wills it, *I* be here."

Emily tied her bonnet and cloak.

"Mother, won't you ever tell me why father sent him away?"

Her mother pulled herself to her feet by holding onto the chair.

"You be right about that stick, girl. Knees are a-cracking, and my bones got toothache. I'll speak to him when he gets here. Maybe put me a fancy knob on, like gentlemen have, now he rub shoulders with lords and ladies. Aren't you best be off?"

By the time he arrived, the flag-stones shone like a pond in sunlight, and the meat and vegetables were simmering patiently in the pot. On the table was a tying of snowdrops, their heads bowed bashfully as a maid listening to her sweetheart's poem. The room looked and smelt like home.

He arrived before Emily. There was no knocking at the door. His mother had scolded him for it, the day he had returned, when his time was more than up. "No need," she had explained. "It's your home." Now she saw him walking leisurely up to the door. There was something different about him, but she did not learn what till he had entered and said, "Mother."

Then she saw what he had done to himself.

"Your face be as bare as a baby's backside! You shaved your beard? I don't recognise you, you so handsome. You look ten years younger. Why you done it? Mixing with all those gentlemen, I expect. Unless you 'suaded by Miss. Florence, now you her favourite."

Misterton hung his bag on the back of the door, on top of

Emily's, and sat at the table; he would not be provoked by her teasing.

"Weather warming up, see. Don't want the blackbirds nesting in it, this time of year. Getting like our thatch: a bit unruly and in need of a raking and a-scissoring. So I buys a cut-throat, and before I know where I am, I sees myself a-changing, and a smile a-creeping up on me, and the more I scrape, the brighter the smile, till all my hair be gone, and I'm laughing like I'm being tickled under my armpits. I look, and I'm me, but not me. More a new one, one to kiss, I expect."

His mother took her cue, and kissed him resoundingly on both cheeks.

"It tingles my lips!" she cried, laughing. "And you smell like honeysuckle. Sweet, like a lady. She been freshing you up?"

"Soap from Lyme. Got a present for you when Emily returns."

"Gone to church. She got something to tell you, maybe even show you. That girl be her own mistress, these days."

Emily entered, humming a hymn they had sung. Her brother had his back to her. Their mother had to hide her face, so that Emily would not see her grinning.

"Master Tom be working on a church. You'd like that, wouldn't you, Nicholas? Up and down the spire like a little church mouse!" Emily teased.

She approached the table, saw his face, and squealed. Her hand cupped her mouth. In front of her sat her new brother, cheeks shining like a glazed vase. He laughed. His wavy hair had not been cut for years, and he reminded her of someone.

"A man shave his face, once in a while, and his sister scream as if she'd seen a ghost!"

"Nicholas, you be an angel, you so glowing. Like one of the Lord's disciples. There be a man in the painting, in Stinsford church, just like you."

"I gone up in the world, then, if you be right," he quipped.

It was Judas, though she could not name him.

They were all in a good mood. They ate, talking between mouthfuls. In the old days, when Mr. Misterton had said Grace, they did not talk, except to excuse themselves from the table. The food had always tasted good, but the atmosphere used to have the tartness of young gooseberries.

Misterton fetched his bag, unbuckled the flap, and took out two small boxes.

"Not much, but from Lyme. Never been before."

They opened their presents. Emily had a small, silver brooch, and her mother a gold thimble.

"Oh, it's lovely!" cried Emily. "I shall wear it all the time, even at work, if Miss. Palfreyman don't object."

Misterton's lips tightened.

His mother eased the thimble on and rotated it, and it fitted perfectly.

"Sticks a treat," she said quietly. "Not had a present since . . . "

She sniffled. The memory of her husband giving her a hand mirror and hairbrush, which he had picked up at Dorchester market, was too much.

Embarrassed, Misterton looked down at his bag, and placed it on the table.

Emily put her arm around her mother's shoulder, and kissed the top of her head. White hairs now outnumbered black.

"Fits just right," said Misterton, to change the mood. He had not considered the purchases sentimental. He had paid little for them. The irresistible urge to choose gifts had rooted him to the table on which odds and ends were in a tray. The handing over of money had made him feel richer. He could not wait till he had the chance to give again. Anything, it could be: help, his labour, money, his best wishes. His greatest gift would be as much time as he could spare to someone who wanted to talk to him.

"My sewing box be upstairs," his mother said.

Misterton leapt to his feet to fetch it.

"Let me go," offered Emily.

Both wanted to escape their mother.

"Stay where you are, girl. I'm not helpless," said Misterton.

Misterton and Emily watched her limp up the stairs. Emily whispered into Misterton's ear, and he nodded. Now he had a chance to give again.

He rolled up his sleeves, and went outside. He knew the axe was ready; he had sharpened it on his last visit. The toolbox made by his father was in the outbuilding. The tools his father had used to make furniture were wrapped in wool, to keep out the damp. He had been a good furniture-maker, had made a living from tables, chairs, dressers. The cottage had been paid for with the money earned from sawing, planing, sanding, joining, carving, and varnishing. And it was never an item of furniture he fashioned but a work of art, an expression of himself, his imagination.

Axe resting on his shoulder, Misterton escaped into the woods. He knew what he was looking for: a piece of wood the right length and thickness. A few shafts he thought might be suitable were rejected, and then he found the one, a sapling. He gripped its base, and stepped back. One chop was enough, and he used his knife to strip its shoots. In time, it would dry, but the weather was not yet warm enough, so he would take it back to the farm, dry it in his hearth, till he could find a top, a small sprig from an antler, perhaps, or an intricate carving detailed enough to be a hand-grip.

Then he searched for an identical one with which she could make do, to stop her falling over, crashing down the stairs. There it was. Perfect. One in each hand, he tested their strength by leaning on them, one at a time. They would steady her. She would not like what they signified, but they would keep her upright to get about, give her confidence.

One he dropped on the grass at the back of the cottage till he left; the other he gave her on his return from the wood. She accepted it graciously. A second present from her son in one day she interpreted as him saying something important to her; the thimble and stick were an expression of gratitude, love.

"Your mother be wobbly, I know. 'Tis a sign of my years, and so this stick will be by my side, always. Thank you."

Misterton could not speak, looked at Emily, and went upstairs to his room for a quick sleep. Soon, his mother looked dead again in her chair. Only Emily stayed awake.

She washed the plates and knives and forks. When her brother awoke, she would show him that she had learned to read, that Miss. Florence had been generous with her time so that she could learn her letters, add them to each other to make meaning. Now she felt more powerful, that she could communicate in a different way, over longer distances, if she wanted. She could decipher the meaning of others, and read stories and poems, even challenge new ideas and knowledge. The wages she earned were nothing compared with her tuition. Miss. Florence, she knew, had set her free.

Emily loved the cottage when it was quiet, bar, of course, the snoring of her brother and mother. Her mother's was sporadic, lighter than her brother's, which was like a big, oak door opening slowly.

Eventually, Emily could bear no longer the anticipation, and went to awaken him. She was nervous, unsure how he would react. The passage from the Old Testament had been her original choice, but then she had found a more interesting text, more thought-provoking. It was one to which she was sure Misterton would respond.

"Be you awake, sleepy head?" she whispered.

"No."

"Then I'll just tickle your nose till you be so."

She lowered her hair with one hand so that it dangled in his face, as sensuous as a feather, light as a fly.

"Can't you let a man rest his eyes?" he complained, allowing her to continue. The recent removal of his beard had made his skin pleasurably sensitive.

"Not till he listens to me properly."

Behind her back, she gripped her text with a moist hand. Her heartbeat was at odds with her calm exterior. She was astonished at her own audacity. There be a risk in all we do. If he blows, why, 'tis not the end of the world, she reasoned.

He sat up and swung his legs over the edge of the bed. Yawning, he stretched, rubbed his eyes, and said, "Better be worth it."

"Oh, you'll want to hear what I've got to say, Nicholas: I can read. Miss. Florence taught me. And I can write. I can be a teacher, one day, I reckon. Bookshop in Dorchester, so I'm going to make up for lost time. Miss. Florence says I can use the library when I'm not doing for her and Master Robert. I can learn things now, be somebody."

"You already be somebody beout books. Fields, heath, and woods be my classroom."

"Want me to teach you to read and write, Nicholas?"

"No good to me when I'm sowing seed, or slitting a lamb's throat."

"Maybe one day."

"Perhaps," he reluctantly conceded. "When I'm old and hoary, and legs be twigs."

"You want to hear me?"

He was not fully awake, could not focus his eyes on her.

"I be listening, girl. Won't let me rest till you've shown off."

She cleared her throat in mock-preparation. It was now or never. He had been looking for sticks in the woods. The sheet of paper had fallen from his bag. White on a slate floor. She had picked it up. Curiosity, combined with her newly acquired ability to read, had made her unfold and read it. The handwriting was distinctive, recognisable. She had seen it before, many times. The letter had trembled in her hands. Its contents had been unexpected, called into question her own position at the manor. Nicholas needed to be challenged, so she began.

> *What I am doing is wrong, I know, but sometimes we all do things we should not. We cannot help it, and that is a fact. Please come to my room tonight. It ill becomes someone in my position to ask you, but I want you to, and I know you want to. I cannot bear to see you as a farmer or a coachman. It can never be so at the manor, but here I am yours. I do not love you. I feel I can never love any man, but that is always expected of me, to love a man when he says I should. I know you will never make any claim upon me, as others do. But you have a secret, and so do I. We are well matched.*
> *Florence.*
>
> *Post scriptum.*
> *Please destroy this note.*

Emily read it flatly, having been tempted to read it melodramatically, and it took a few seconds for Misterton to realise that the letter had been meant for him. Eyes down, he listened to it all, petrified.

"Where you get that from?" he asked, puzzled.

Emily had expected a stronger reaction, anger that she had confronted him with it, but there was only an expression as bleak as a November Dorset sky.

"Found it on the floor. Must have fallen out your bag. Opened it. No idea it was yours, at the time. Read it. Read everything I get my hands on. What's going on, Nicholas?"

"Nothing," he said. "Found it on my bed in Lyme. Must have shoved it in my bag. You shouldn't go reading my letters."

"What will I say to her? This changes things. I'll look at her, and she'll know that I know. My face will look different. Bound to."

Misterton sighed testily.

"No idea what it said," he insisted.

"Why you keep it, then? You must have known."

He stood up, momentarily going giddy.

"You forgetting: I can't read."

Downstairs, his mother watched him, helplessly, pick up his bag and coat, and leave. The other stick remained in the grass.

"Where you going in such a hurry?" she called weakly.

The letter now in her pocket, Emily went to the window, watched him escape. How many times had he tightened those shoulders, not looked back, as he had walked away?

"It's all right, mother. Just one of his moods, that's all."

"You fallen out? What about his cake?"

"What cake?"

"One I baked for him. Special one for today."

"Special?"

"You don't remember, he don't remember, but these things matter to a mother. It be his birthday today. Wanted it to be a surprise."

"He already had one, mother, one to remember today by."

Chapter Ten

Emily washed the pots almost mournfully, bent over the sink as if at prayer. The candlesticks, which she usually rubbed till she could see her face distorted in their curvature, she merely wiped, removing dust but failing to make them gleam. She resented this kind of work, now that she could read and write. It was a waste of time when there were novels and poetry to read. Jemima had shown her a poem Tom had wrought in sounds and rhythm, and she wanted to compose one herself, intertwine her thoughts and emotions, and bind them with fresh words picked from the glades of nature, books, people, experiences. Her poem would be a Christmas wreath: a circle of holly freckled with bright red berries, her ideas the sharp spikes of the leaves. No one would forget her poems after reading them.

"My daughter's a-going off to train to be a teacher," Jemima had told her. "My children ought to have heads as big as the moon they so many books inside them. Stuff em full of tales, and there be no room for evil, be my thinking."

"The trouble is, if I leave, mother will be on her own, what with our Nicholas up at the farm, all the time. He loved his work with Mr. Hardy, but he be a farmer now. Doing a good job, by the talk of downstairs. Master Palfreyman don't seem to have any complaints. Nicholas is not one, see, for a woman's work. If I go, mother'll be stuck there, in our cottage, like an old owl huddled in a tree-trunk, a-blinking, just waiting for sleep to come."

Jemima had smiled and laid her hand on Emily's arm, and squeezed.

"You must go, Emily. Go and don't look back. Can't grow up beout breaking your parents' hearts. Tom not gone yet, but I got to cut him loose, one day. Don't want him to shrivel like a fallen leaf. Let me tell you, girl, that he baint like the other Hardy men. They hammer and bang, and that be their purpose in life, excepting for a bit of fiddling in church, but my Tom, see, will break my heart for the bleak soul of another woman. Yet he will also open the eyes and ears of others with his words. There are songs in them, girl. Architect be his living now, but he so many stories in his head he must tell, he won't have the room to let others live with him. There be a price for everything, and if he marries, his wife'll wither away in a corner, covered in the dust of his neglect."

Since she had read Florence's note to Nicholas, Emily had avoided eye contact with her. The other girls in the house noticed that Emily was withdrawn, and teased her, suspected that her listlessness and taciturnity were the symptoms of unrequited love. Emily, however, explained her conduct as the beginnings of a seasonal indisposition.

"You mean women's curse?" laughed Josie. "You swallowed a book, girl?"

The others joined in, and Emily dashed out of the kitchen, and collided with Florence.

"Goodness, Emily, what is the matter?" she cried, defending herself with both hands raised.

"Just not right, that's all," sobbed Emily.

In her pocket, the note was pressed in place by a screwed up handkerchief.

"Come with me, then, and calm down in the library. I'll have a word with Cook, and then I must see Master Robert about various matters."

Florence reached to take her hand, but Emily stiffened, as she did when she came across an adder on the heath.

"Thank 'ee."

Emily looked at all the books lining the walls. So much to read, so much time wasted, she reflected. Can all those words fit inside my head?

"Compose yourself, and return when you're ready. Cook will put an end to this nonsense. If Master Robert comes in, simply explain that I put you in here."

"Thank you, Miss. Florence."

Later, Palfreyman was waiting for his sister in his usual chair, by the fire. Emily had been assigned cleaning duties elsewhere by Cook. Palfreyman puffed feverishly on his cigar.

"Come and sit down," he said.

Florence detected a tension in his instruction. Transfixed by the devilish faces in the coals and faggots, he did not look at her immediately. She swam through the sweet fug floating above the hearth, and coughed exaggeratedly.

"I wish you wouldn't smoke those repulsive things!" she protested. "They reek of cow dung."

Palfreyman threw his cigar into the fire, sat up, and turned to her.

"I shall be away for the next few weeks," he informed her.

She lowered her eyes. That again. Time after time, he went, and tried, and failed. On his return, he would be unsettled and ill-tempered till he had mingled again with his friends in The King's Arms, had resumed his ribald gossiping, exchanged peccadilloes, drunk so much wine and brandy that his speech was pocked with curses.

"Bath?"

He nodded.

"It's expected of me."

"The season must be well under way now."

She avoided antagonising him. Maybe there *was* a suitable partner for him there. He danced well. His material circumstances were favourable enough to attract a few admirers. Yet he had always come home disappointed.

"Won't you come?"

"How can I? What will happen here if I go, too?"

He stared into the fire, unblinking, like a lizard. There were things he had to say, wounds he was likely to inflict. She recognised his preparation, the stillness, as he gathered his words and nailed them into sentences as prickly as hawthorn.

"Hinton's a good man. He's the talk of the county now you've turned him down. Have you no consideration for his feelings?"

"He's a fool, Robert. Why do you always introduce me to bores, or fat land-owners too full of their self-importance?"

Palfreyman tapped his fingernails irritably on the arm of his chair.

"It makes me look stupid, Florence. You're not getting any younger, you know. He has two thousand acres."

"Don't give me that, Robert, please," she spat. "If I marry, it'll be because I've met someone I love and respect, a man of impeccable manners and dignity. Hinton's acres mean nothing to me."

Palfreyman smiled. His boxes were packed and piled in the hall. Coombs would take him, mid-morning, to catch the coach in Dorchester. An overnight stop at an inn, and he would arrive early evening in Bath, the next day.

"All right, dear sister. Have it your own way."

He delved into his jacket pocket, and took out a piece of paper. Florence watched him peruse it, before handing it to her.

"What is it?"

"I don't know. I was hoping you'd tell me."

He watched her eyes follow the writing.

She shook her head and returned it.

"No idea. Ten pounds for an angel's wings seems excessive. I thought even the poorest could enter the kingdom of Heaven."

"But what this man is saying is that *I* ordered them in Bridport. Look, my name is on it."

He flashed the sheet to her.

"And you didn't order them?"

"Don't be absurd. I don't know anyone by the name of Herries who is buried in a graveyard in Bridport."

Standing up, Florence declared, "But why would anyone claim to be you? They must have been convincing in their deception."

Palfreyman gestured to her to sit down again.

"Did you read the *post scriptum*?"

She shook her head.

"It's a bill for you, not me."

"Then I'll read it to you. It says, 'I trust you had a pleasant stay in Lyme with your sister.'"

She screwed up her face, perplexed.

"But you haven't been to Lyme with me."

"Precisely, but you have been there with Misterton."

She remembered they had stopped in Bridport. Misterton had rested the horses. There had been time for her to browse in the shops, take refreshment. They had not been together all the time. It was possible. He was no Hinton, no acre-gatherer.

"That is true. I have, but he had no motive to do such a thing. Speak to him. Put it to him, but you'll risk his ire, Robert, if you're wrong. What will you do?"

He squirmed in his seat. His face barely disguised his relish of her discomfort.

"No, Florence, I will put nothing to him today, but there is something else I want to show you." He took out of his coat a second piece of paper, which he unfolded ceremoniously, as if it were a piece of incriminating evidence that would send a defendant to the gallows. He waved it, as a flag, celebrating his discovery of it. "Perhaps, you can explain this, then." And he read it to her.

At once, she recognised her invitation to Misterton, felt her cheeks burn with shame. Palfreyman acted out her message. His spare hand clutched his heart, beckoned an imaginary lover to him, and Florence was helpless, tormented by the melodrama of his cry from the heart.

He finished.

"How did you come by it?" she asked timidly, her voice barely a whisper.

"Why, here, on this table!" he shouted. "You were careless leaving it here. Did you not miss it?"

She shook her head.

"The last time I saw it was when I left it on his pillow in Lyme." The truth might be her best defence, she felt.

"Well, someone must have left it here."

The contents had firstly puzzled, then disgusted him. He dismissed her claim that somehow she was the victim of suitors' and society's odious expectations. He found her overture lascivious. It would reflect badly on the family name if the note fell into the wrong hands. His reputation would be ruined. Much would be lost if word of his sister's indiscretion arrived ahead of him, and poisoned the ear of Major Wells and his wife.

It had to be Misterton, she decided. He had secreted the note into the library as an act of perversity, revenge, even, for what he saw as an attempt to establish him as a rich woman's creature. The bill and the note were his work.

"I shall deal with this when you've gone."

"Florence, this is a serious matter. Your . . . sexual adventure with Misterton – I assume it is him – compromises both of us. He must go, and you must dismiss him. Clearly, he has a lack of respect for us. I promoted him to Farm Manager, and did not imagine that you wanted him for other purposes. But things are going to change around here, when I return. In the meantime, you must reconsider your attitude towards Hinton. He has a big house to run, and wants an heir. He is not unattractive. Indeed, Ingrid Quantock is known to—"

"Do not speak of that man as a husband to me! He is a philistine, as are almost all your friends and associates. They drink, hunt, have no manners. They do not want a wife but a timid little woman who will wait dutifully indoors, sewing, painting, or receiving visits from other women in the same situation. That will not do for me at all, Robert."

He stood up, clenched his fists, then tried to compose himself.

"I had hoped to set things out a little more clearly after Bath, but I see I must enlighten you now lest your conduct benight my happiness. It is, indeed, the height of the season there. The tearooms, the dances, attract many, alleviating the rural boredom, which is the disease from which you and I have felt, at times, terminally ill. It has been almost a year since you went. Rabbett looked after the house for us. Then you were so pestered that not even the company of other young women could amuse you. Yet I, Florence, met a charming young lady, whose attitude to me since has been encouraging. Indeed, we have exchanged letters, and I shall be seeking Major Wells' and his good lady wife's permission to ask Rose if she will consent to be my wife."

Florence swayed, then steadied herself. This moment should have been a happy one. How careless she had been in Lyme! She had followed her heart, could have led Misterton by the hand to her room instead of writing. And now she had angered her brother, when she should have been hugging him.

"Then I am sorry, Robert, for all this. I swear I don't know how this came to be here. I'll go to the farm as soon as you have gone. I have not yet met your intended wife, Rose, but I wish you every happiness, and hope that you each are worthy of the other. I shall have a sister, will I not? I've always wanted one. Not that I've been lonely with you as a brother. It's just that a sister will be company when you are out. Is she pretty?"

Palfreyman paced up and down. Life had to change. There was no easy way to tell her.

"Florence, Rose will be no sister to you. She will reside here as my wife."

He hoped that Florence would realise what he meant, but she did not.

"No sister? Do I have to earn that right, as a penance for my mistake with this?"

She held up the note, on the verge of tears.

He shook his head.

"No, it's not that you are unworthy of being a sister. It's just that we will be living here as man and wife. The estate passed to me on father's death. It would be hard for there to be two mistresses here, unreasonable of me to ask Rose to accommodate you. I wish to avoid conflict, not invite it."

"*Accommodate?*"

A knock came on the door. It was Coombs. The boxes were secure. It was time to set off for the coach in Dorchester.

"I'll be along," Palfreyman told him. Coombs withdrew. "During my absence, I'd be grateful if you could give further consideration to Hinton's offer. If you still find life with him unthinkable, then I shall, of course, help you to find a house elsewhere. You receive a handsome, annual allowance, which would maintain you somewhere substantial. I would have preferred this to have waited, but I cannot risk my hopes being dashed on the rocks of your hedonism. I suggest you destroy that note before it destroys us."

He slammed the door behind him, leaving her trembling. The manor would no longer be her home. Rose would accept him. He was handsome, charming, witty, though had bad habits, which a wife taken a few years later would find difficult to eradicate.

Florence had to see Misterton. The stonemason's bill and the note needed his explanation.

On her way down the corridor, she met Emily on her way back to the library. Emily concocted an excuse: she had finished the bedrooms, and was anxious to know what to do next.

"Go back to the kitchen. I am going to the farm to see Nicholas about the repairs to the seed drill. Master Robert will be away for a few days."

Emily saw the note in Florence's hand, heard her strangled voice. It had happened so quickly. Palfreyman had entered the library, seen Emily reading *Gulliver's Travels* at the table. Her chance had come quickly. She had pushed the note away from her. He had found it, had read it, and had held his sister to account. Emily did not want to lose Nicholas to satisfy the whim of her mistress.

"Was his birthday yesterday. Please to let him know, Miss. Florence, if you would be so kind, that it was so, and that if he care to come to the cottage, there be a cake a-waiting for him."

"There *is* a cake waiting for him!" corrected Florence.

Emily curtseyed and returned to the kitchen.

Misterton was kneeling. Pushing the whetstone along the blade, he smoothed the snags caused by stones as the plough, pulled inexorably by the Clydesdale, had collided with them. The soil, bitten by the curve of the iron, had rolled over, become shining tubes of pink and gold. The horse's fringe and fetlocks had billowed like banners, and the beast had pulled and nodded, had led Simon up and down the furrows. Simon had felt the shudder and tremble of the handles as he had plodded and kept the line as straight as a birch. The furrows had converged to a point.

In the barn, Melbury had stacked the sacks of seed ordered by Palfreyman.

"Next year, you will deal with Misterton. A year under his belt, and he'll know what he's doing," Palfreyman had said.

"Same fields as last year?" Melbury had checked.

"Yes. The same. A year hence, and a few pounds more investment, and I'll have the most productive farm in Dorset. He's as strong as a Clydesdale."

After the plough, Misterton would check the seed drill. His plan was to build a forge, turn two men into a blacksmith and farrier. Then he would buy more cows, collect a few more maids to milk them. Wareham had wasted opportunities; Palfreyman had let him.

Florence flogged her horse to the farm, jumped down, and stood over him. Her shadow stretched in front of him. Forward slid the whetstone. Rhythm was everything. Neither a shadow nor its owner would spoil the precision.

"I'd like a word," she announced stiffly.

Rasp. Rasp. Blow. Wipe. Rasp. Rasp.

"I'm listening."

Angry that he did not stand to speak, she dropped the stonemason's bill. Still he continued.

"The bill is dated the day we stopped in Bridport. An angel grew new wings, and Robert was sent the bill. Was Alice Herries your wife, your lover, or your daughter?"

She would claim his attention somehow; he worked for her, and was not her equal, in her eyes.

The paper had settled face up. He had not forgotten what he had done, nor regretted it. Her brother had not called the doctor to Maisie. It would have cost less than wings.

"I know nothing about it," he declared. "No wife, no lover."

"Daughter, then?"

"Don't like owing anybody anything. My father used to say he'd have us all go beout rather than owe a penny."

He looked up at her, and she picked up the bill.

"And this? Your father have an opinion on things like this?"

Misterton took the paper she was offering. If he betrayed Emily, defending himself, then she would be dismissed, and he would protest till he went, too. There would be no money coming in. It would kill their mother.

"What is it?"

"You don't recognise it?"

He shook his head.

"Can't read. Write, neither."

"I left it on your pillow in Lyme Regis. You must have brought it back. Master Robert found it in the library. Are you saying you did not leave it there?"

He nodded.

"I got work to do. Seed drill needs doing. Seed all ready to sow. Been here all day. Not been near the house."

Exasperated, she mounted her horse, and stroked it.

"You might not be able to read and write, but you understood what it said. Hotel staff don't leave notes on pillows."

He had resumed the sharpening of his plough-blade.

"Don't stay in hotels. Can't read. Write, neither."

Florence called over her shoulder, "By the way, it was your birthday yesterday," and spurred her horse into action.

He looked down at his hands. His birthday. He was a person, after all. When had he last been aware of his birthday? Ruth.

Emily opened the cottage door. Her mother smelt her daughter's misery: marrowbone and night dew. Emily hung up her cloak and bag on the door. Plates and pots looked lonely on the table. A chair scraped, sent a screech skittering across the flagstones.

"What be the matter, girl?" Mrs. Misterton asked.

Emily sat down, and put her fat purse on the table.

"That be that, mother. I'm done with the manor. I'm going to train to be a teacher, or maybe become a governess, now I can read and write."

"Nicholas?"

Emily looked away.

"I'll take him his cake tomorrow."

"You parted with Miss. Palfreyman?"

"What be for supper, mother? Whatever it be, let us take it with that cider that been sitting on the shelf since last Easter."

So her mother locked the door, and they ate, and drank the cider, and soon the cottage, once the words had drifted upstairs, was filled with two competing rhythms of snoring: the rapid tapping of a woodpecker on lime-washed walls; and the fragmented whistling of the wind as it squeezes in through the door-frame. In the air, the sweet, heady fumes of apples.

Chapter Eleven

In the early sun, the dew glistened as if millions of diamonds had been scattered on the grass in front of the farmhouse. The moon was just fading sleepily. Megan cocked her leg against the hedge, and slunk back to the kitchen, in which Victoria was frying eggs she had collected earlier. Then into the pan went the bacon, and Megan's nose twitched. Zachariah followed her, and slung her, by the scruff of the neck, outside, knowing she would wait till Victoria was distracted, then stealthily snatch the uncooked slices, and eat them in three convulsive bites and a swallow.

"He'll be here at twelve. He knows we're not church people, and baint himself, but that don't worry you none, do it?"

Victoria slid the blade under the spitting egg, and winced when the fat pricked her.

"Don't matter to me one way or the other, but it don't feel right, father, fixing this up. And what if I don't like the look of him?"

Zachariah examined his daughter's hand, and she shyly turned her face away. This was an unusually tender action for him, one that took him, too, by surprise. Then, ashamed that she could see the black rims of his nails, he released her hand.

"Fixing up? I be no match-maker, me. But a father has to say something when a young fellow like Gabriel Ilminster asks if he may pay a visit. With my permission, of course. Me and his father go back to the summer when lightning forked his roof, and lit a bonfire they could see in France. Put him up till he was back on his feet, did your mother and me. So he's no stranger, is Gabriel, though you've not seen how he's growed into an oak."

Breakfast was ready. Zachariah burst his egg with his crust of bread, which he dabbed in a sprinkling of salt. Then he folded and stabbed a flap of bacon, and closed his eyes as he chewed.

"Well, I aint promising to marry him," she made clear. "Can't make these things happen if it aint Providence. Different with tups and ewes, but we're humans."

Zachariah opened his eyes, laughed heartily, and licked his salty, greasy lips.

"Why, don't you think I don't know that, girl, me being a farmer?"

"I shall be polite, as is my duty to any guest, but that be my only promise."

"You may show him the farm, take a stroll down the lane, but no further."

"You want to come with us?" she teased. "You want to walk between us?"

"That won't be necessary." Then he realised she was jesting. "Now run along and get the meat in the oven. Young Gabriel got an appetite, judging by his size."

Zachariah went to see the milkmaids. Jobs needed doing early. The place had to look tidy.

Raised voices could be heard. He was tempted to stand and listen, but the conflict was so heated that he went in and saw two men, two women, shouting at each other, tears in one woman's eyes. Their explanation was a winding country lane, its bends sharp, and opening, now and then, onto a straight bit, which soon twisted again, so that it was impossible to see the place to which it eventually led.

"If my cows dry up because of this argumenting, then you'll all be to blame, and I'll have to pack you off somewhere. Now, men, go cut me some logs for the grates. The pile's shrunk to a twig or two. And you two, go to your milking, which be what you're paid for."

Of all days! thought Zachariah. Done with squabbling at Gifford's.

Gabriel Ilminster arrived, looking like a Bridport Quaker outside the Friends' Meeting House. He had washed and brushed his beard, so that the curls hung like sprained springs from his face.

When she saw him, Victoria gasped.

He's got red hair! All our children would be goblins, she thought.

She tried to suppress a smirk, and he noticed. His trousers, though of good quality material, were short, and his jacket was too tight around the shoulders. Must be borrowed, she decided. His father's, perhaps.

"I be pleased to make your acquaintance, Miss. Victoria," he stammered, frozen by the fear of mixing up the words he had been practising since sunrise. They stepped awkwardly from his mouth, giving the impression of a speech impediment, which did not escape the notice of Zachariah, whose eyes widened in disbelief.

He asked after Gabriel's parents, who were well, on the whole, though his father's gout had left him with a limp as severe and painful as a soldier's sustained in any corner of the British Empire; and his mother was in tolerable health, though she could no longer bear Dorset winters, which jammed her joints, leaving her, too, with a gait reminiscent of a sailor stepping on *terra firma* again after a long voyage from India.

What is this family which you would have me marry into? she wondered, with a glance at her father. They are horseshoes from the waist down, and walk as if tiptoeing through mud. Zachariah saw and understood, having been himself taken aback by the rather alarming report on the state of health of his old friends. And Gabriel, in his ill-fitting clothes, looked like a scarecrow overstuffed with straw. In his working attire, he had looked at ease, handsome, even, when Zachariah had last seen him.

Gabriel began to relax after a pot of cider, and took the seat, at the table, facing Victoria. Zachariah sat at the head, and carved the meat, releasing eddies of steam. Eager to eat, Gabriel touched his knife and fork. Victoria watched his fascination with the ritual of serving. She and her father received so few guests, that they wanted to make a good impression.

"I'll give you three slices, Gabriel, what with you being a big-boned young fellow."

"Father!" protested Victoria. "It's not polite to comment on people's build."

"Oh, baint no harm in what I say, eh, Gabriel?"

"Oh no, sir, not at all. In fact, I've always been big-boned, even when I was a baby!"

And that made Victoria laugh.

A silence, bar the clanging of cutlery on plates, settled. Gabriel ate with relish, wielding his knife like a soldier his sabre.

Then came a timid knock on the door. Victoria alone heard it. Might be Mabel come to say they were off to Bridport. They usually borrowed the cart, and one of the men drove. George was best with the reins; Wilfred had once been thrown from a horse, and had lost confidence.

"Sit you down, girl. The pots can wait," ordered Zachariah.

"The door, father. Probably be George and them a-gallivanting somewhere. Their afternoon off."

"Mind they be back for milking, evening."

Victoria opened the door. The young woman smiled broadly. Her hat did not quite sit correctly, and did not match her coat.

"Something smell good," she said. "Lamb if my nose don't trick me. Know that smell anywhere."

"What is it you want?"

"Nothing. Not a-begging nor a-borrowing, which what most volk might be thinking when a strange woman turn up on a Sunday. Came today on account of me having the money to take a ride to Bridport. Never been before. Good a place as any. Heard a man say he's heading Pilsdon way, so I ask him if he be going past Farmer Stockwood's Farm, and he says yes, so here I be."

Victoria found the explanation of the woman's presence amusing, though hoped a few more details might follow.

"And have you come to see one of the girls in the parlour?"

"Oh no. I've come to see Farmer Stockwood. Said to call and see him, one day. You baint Mrs. Stockwood, though. She's much taller."

"I'm *Miss*. Stockwood, Farmer Stockwood's daughter."

"Then you're not like either your father or mother, who did not look too pleased, last time I saw them."

Victoria was puzzled. The woman sounded convincing. Occasionally, an itinerant person or two, a journeyman, would call and ask if there was work, or if they could have a drink of water, but this visitor was not one of them.

"That must have been a long time ago."

"Not that long ago, deary. 'Twas in Lyme, where I was a-waiting upon them."

"I'm sure you be mistaken. My father hasn't been to Lyme, and my mother been dead these last five years."

"Who be that?" called Zachariah, concerned that his daughter had been absent from the table longer than good manners dictate.

"This lady has called to see you. Says she knows mother, too."

Zachariah could see that Victoria was unnerved. The woman was a stranger to him, too.

Maggie looked at him, and shook her head.

"Why, if you be Nicholas Stockwood, then you changed since you danced me and put your arm round my waist!"

"Danced? I don't know you from the next woman. My name baint Nicholas, either. Called Zachariah by my mother at birth, and don't intend changing it."

Maggie put her hand on her hips, and sighed deeply. Her day

had been long after an early start. She had asked for a ride to the farm, and was now as frustrated as the other two.

"Man who said he was Farmer Stockwood at Gifford's Farm definitely went by the name of Nicholas. Tall, strong, wavy, black hair. Taught him to dance. Stayed at the hotel where I works. Lady with him. Guessed she was his wife, but can't be sure any more. Nicholas, he be, not Zachariah."

Victoria felt her skin prickle. If it was him, he had not forgotten her. This woman, his wife, he had been with: who was she? It had to be him. The deception – humour, he would deem it – was a message to her, a sign that he was not too far away. Yet she also knew her father would be embarrassed, humiliated by this woman turning up on his doorstep. Misterton's revenge for his dismissal was cruel. Yet, perversely, Victoria was intrigued. Gabriel Ilminster could never interest her as Misterton did.

"Then you've had a wasted journey, Miss. No one going by the name of Nicholas here. You been taken for a ride, be my view. My mother's buried up the hill."

"And I never seen you before," added Zachariah.

"Then this be truly a mess. Good man, he seemed. Held back a bit, when most men would have . . . Well, I'm sorry you've had this disturbance, and I won't trouble you no more. Left something behind, he did. Came to give it to him."

Maggie smiled weakly, and started the long walk down the track.

Victoria shut the door, and bolted it.

"Don't look at me like that, father," she said, lowering her voice. "I've seen neither hide nor hair of him since he left, and I don't like this kind of thing any more than you do."

"If I sees him around Gifford's Farm, I'll shoot him as dead as any other vermin. Now do you see what he's like?"

Back at the table, Gabriel knew that the interruption to the meal had been unexpected. Zachariah's hand trembled, and too many thoughts were jostling in her head for Victoria to appear normal.

"I'm sorry about that, Gabriel," said Zachariah.

"Something bad happened? I'll go, then. I understand."

Victoria looked up, shrugged off the distraction, seeing that Gabriel was capable of sensitivity, empathy, tact.

"No, don't go. Let me show you the farm. 'Twas nothing at the door but a gypsy girl a-cursing us for not giving her money."

"Yes, let her go, and if she returns, she'll feel the sharpness of Megan's teeth!"

"And when we get back, we got apple cake and cream," promised Victoria. "You like that?"

Gabriel nodded and offered his arm.

"That be a bitter-sweet temptation, for to rush through the walk to get to the pudding seem a crime, when the longer we take, the more we can talk ourselves into better acquaintance."

Zachariah looked up, and saw his daughter blush.

"You run along. Don't want an old man a-slowing you down. Though, daughter, my own, you'd make your father the happiest man alive if you'd cut him another slice of lamb, and scrape a bit of gravy onto it before you go. I expect you'd manage another, Gabriel?"

Gabriel nodded.

"That is, if it baint any trouble."

"None whatsoever," said Victoria.

To pass the time on the long walk back to Bridport, Maggie sighed and made up a song:

> "He baint be a truthful,
> a straight-talking man,
> but he danced with his sweetheart
> till he from the room ran,
> and they're ne'er now so youthful
> but always apart."

Then she heard the harmony of happy voices behind her.

"You going to Briddy?" asked Mabel, as the cart slowed alongside her.

"Yes. Is it far? My feet are rubbed skinless in these boots."

"Let me help you up," offered George. "You familiar, these parts?"

"Come to bring a man something he lost, but seems he don't live here. No such man as Nicholas Stockwood 'cording to the proper farmer's daughter."

"Who says there was such a one?" asked Mabel.

"Why, he did! Pity he aint the farmer. Got something belong him he'd be glad of. Now he'll have to wait for it."

"What be that?"

"Where you all from?"

"Gifford's Farm. Work for Zachariah Stockwood. Sourpuss bugger, he be."

"And do *you* know a man called Nicholas?"

The others looked at each other, and Mabel told her the truth.

"He used to work here. Never got on with old Zachariah, though."

"You be seeing him again? He be coming this way again, you reckon?"

"Doubt it," said George. " Not the type."

"But if he does, you tell him to come see Maggie in Lyme. Tell him she got what he lost. Tell him I'll keep it till he comes."

"What is it?" asked Mabel.

"Something I bet he wishes he'd taken better care of."

All the way into Bridport, they sat in near-silence. All, in their own way, missed Misterton. His absence in their life was as wide as Chesil Beach, as painful as its crunching stones underfoot.

Chapter Twelve

The clock clucked slowly, as if trying to restrain time's career, out of respect for James Chideock, who sat in his leather, winged chair, his head resting in his right hand. He dared not look at the door lest it open.

On his desk, various papers lay parallel to each other, organised, recently read carefully. The signature's strokes were thin, weak. Underneath it were inky smudges of an unsteady hand.

The oil lamp's frail light cast sad shadows. On the walls, books were gathered like relatives, standing shoulder to shoulder, awaiting the latest bulletin on a gravely ill member of the family.

In a nearby park, a nurse held a young child's hand, and pointed out the birds, the child then imitating her. From her bag, the nurse brought out some stale bread, which she broke and gave to the child to throw. Suddenly, they were both surrounded by flapping, hysterical blackbirds and starlings, and the child grabbed the nurse's coat, frightened. The nurse picked her up, hugged her, and said, "Never mind, my precious. Birdies won't hurt you."

Chideock fought back tears, and banged his fist frustratedly on his desk.

"Damn!" he cried in anguish. "Damn it all!"

Then his hand relaxed; it was useless, he knew, to rail against death. His sigh was long, and relieved him.

Then the door opened.

"It's time," said the doctor. "You'd better come quickly."

His wife was staring at the ceiling. Chideock rushed to her, believing he was too late, then saw her eyes flicker towards him, and she swallowed.

"Would you like some water?"

Her eyelids closed and opened, and she mouthed no.

The doctor hung back by the door, and turned away, as he always did at these moments.

"My darling," Chideock whispered in her ear. "My Myrtle."

She nodded, ever so slightly, acknowledging his final declaration of eternal love. In recent days, she had been refusing the liquid which took away all pain, all consciousness of the real world. Again, she tried to speak, but had not the energy. He bent down to hold her, and put his ear close to her mouth.

"Miranda," she whispered.

He withdrew a little to reply, and saw her eyes pleading with him.

"I'll look after her, my darling, and she will grow into a beautiful lady, just like her mother."

Myrtle's eyelids fluttered, froze. Her staring at the pillow made him turn to the doctor, who approached her, held her wrist, put his ear to her mouth, and declared, "She's gone, sir. She suffers no more. No more pain. I'll leave you alone for a few minutes."

Chideock felt the doctor's hand rest momentarily on his shoulder. The doctor shut the door behind him, and Chideock turned to his wife. The life had already fled from her, but her cheek felt warm against his lips; her fingers did not intertwine with his, as they used to.

"Are you really gone, my love?" he asked, his voice sounding strangely unlike his own. Then, a few seconds later, he added, "One day we will be together again for ever, and, in the meantime, you live on in my memory as the young, beautiful girl with daisies chained and threaded through her hair. Though death has robbed you of your life, he has given you eternal youth. I will be but a shrivelled apple, in years to come, but you will still be a bough of pink and white blossom, my darling. You are for ever young."

He heard the front door open and close. There were faint voices, and, after a while, footsteps on the stairs.

"Sir?" croaked the nurse.

Chideock went to the door, but was careful to screen the bed from her view. He slipped through the gap, noticed the fresher air on the landing. On his return, he must open the window, let out the vile odour of death, the reek of water in which chrysanthemums had wilted.

"Your mistress has passed away, Dorothy. Is Miranda downstairs?"

Dorothy started to cry.

"Yes, Mr. Chideock, sir."

"Then I must go and tell her at once."

"Oh, sir, I'm so sorry. Mrs. Chideock'll go to Heaven, sir. You mark my words, she will."

"Of that, I have no doubt. No doubt at all."

Miranda said nothing when he told her that her mother had gone to Jesus, just allowed him to clutch her to him.

"We saw some birds in the park," she said. "We gave them some bread."

"Did you, dear? Would you like to go to the kitchen? I'll ask Dorothy to give you a drink."

Miranda reached the door, turned, and asked, "Shall I take one up to mother?"

It was a warm evening. Hazy gnats irritated Emily, followed her. She wafted them, her hand slicing through them as if they were spectral.

Outside the park gates, she heard whistling, wheels, and snorting, so turned. It was her brother. He stopped the horse, and asked, "You want me to take you home? Look."

In his hand, he brandished a silver button. He looked pleased with himself.

"A button, you show me? You try to make friends with a fancy button?"

"For mother's other stick. Come on. I'll take you home. You moved the stick from back the cottage? Left it till I found something different."

"Not touched it. What you going to do if it's not there? Walk out again till you've calmed down? You can't keep running away, Nicholas. You don't have to go. We both been worried."

He hung his head, offered his hand, and lifted her up onto the cart.

"Same as a sack of seed," he teased. "Or more, even."

"Now just you mind your manners!" she warned.

"Button just the right size to sit on top of the stick. Finish it off nicely. We got any glue left from father? Stuck his furniture well enough. Pretty engraving."

Emily rubbed it on her dress till it came up shining.

"Silver, be my judgement," she said. "Off a sojer's jacket, perhaps."

His mother looked at him warily as he ducked on entering.

"Mother," he said, sheepishly.

"Wondering when we'd see you gain," she said. "Smelt food?"

All he wanted was to live that day, not return to another, more painful one. He turned and went out again to fix the button on the other stick.

"Don't go, Nicholas," she called. "You only just come."

"He's gone to do a job, mother. Give him half an hour, then let us eat. Light the fire in his room. He's staying tonight," said Emily. "Your precious son be staying."

Misterton dried the stick on his jacket, and opened his father's toolbox. He sawed the end of the stick so that it was flat and slightly bigger than the button. Carefully, he applied the black, pungent glue, and pressed the button into the stick, hard, and held it there for five minutes. Then he returned to the house for dinner.

They ate. Misterton made an effort. The women exchanged glances, his good humour surprising them. Normally, they had to prise news out of him, maybe even chisel it, as a collector a fossil from a rock on Charmouth beach. Now he was free with it: Palfreyman had been gone three weeks; seed shoots were showing like green velvet; and Maisie was so well mended that she banged and nailed like the men.

When Mrs. Misterton accepted the stick, she looked puzzled.

"Don't need a stick, sitting down," she grumbled. "Done on my feet for the day."

"Look again, mother. The end. See what it be," urged Emily.

Her mother squinted comically.

"'Taint that hard to see!" laughed Misterton. "Silver, that be."

"Engraved with an M," added Emily. "See. M be for Mary, or Misterton."

Again, her mother looked hard, even brought the end right up to her nose.

"An M?"

"Well, baint an upside down W!" said Emily.

"Why, so it is! And so it is."

"It's a letter," emphasised Emily.

"I know. Your father wrote it when he signed to buy the house. Baint any other letter he knew as well as that one. Never needed any more than tolerable, what with his hands being like a wizard's with wood. Good job he learned it or we wouldn't be living here now."

"You like it, mother, the stick? You know, the fact that it be an M, like father's name?" asked Emily.

Then her mother understood. She had not forgotten it.

"Misterton. Your father's name." She looked into an imaginary distance. "What happened to him, girl?"

Emily looked at her brother.

"He died, mother," she said.

"What of?"

"Only the Lord be certain. But look, mother: an M. 'Twas Nicholas' idea."

"Thank you," she said quietly. "Best make a fire in your room, Jacob."

When her mother had gone, Emily said, "Now look what you done, Nicholas. Poor mother. But why you really here tonight? Could have come any time for that. And how come you know that button be an M?"

He shrugged.

"Didn't. No idea. Don't know any letters, but that's why I be here tonight, not being able to wait a sigh longer. Letters aint going to blow into my head by magic. Not even Conjuror Sayer can give me letters, on account of him never catching any himself. He has the knowledge, though, and we all be different. Can't have everything in this life, it seem."

"Brother of mine, you talk in such riddles!"

"Letters, Emily. I want the letters. If I see and keep them, then I won't be Nicholas Misterton any more. Will you teach me read and write, sister, my own? You got all the letters, and I have none."

She hugged him tightly, smelt faintly the farmyard on him.

"But you *be* Nicholas Misterton. Why you want to change who you be? You be Jacob's son."

He held her at arm's length.

"One day you will find out. But will you help me now? A late birthday present which cost you nothing but time?"

"Yes, Nicholas Misterton. I will. And you're right. Emily of yore be but a ghost. She don't live here any more."

"Then give me the letters, while mother is asleep."

Soon they began, these two new people, and Misterton felt more powerful than muscles could ever be. He need never arm-wrestle again.

*

"Some prefer white marble, some black. Whatever takes your fancy, I suppose. Stone be damned expensive, though. That's why it don't do to set to chipping away too early in the morning, when your hand's a-shaking, and you aint quite woken up. Take it from me: a headstone done proper's a work of art. Volk appreciate the words. Shame you got to die to get one!"

His new apprentice, a boy of fourteen, listened attentively. Early starts and boys of that age are deadly enemies. Christian had worked at an undertaker's but had tired of being praised for his pallor, which was the natural consequence of taking little food, exercise, and air. All he did was stride slowly and lugubriously in front of the horse-drawn hearse. He had also been a grave-digger, for a day only, finding that he had not the strength or stamina to dig to the required dimensions, and that so dangerous was the employment that, halfway down, the soil once gave way and nearly buried him before his time. And so, when he saw the sign advertising the apprenticeship as a stonemason, he applied within, deeming it safe and relatively undemanding.

His first lesson was interrupted by the entrance into the yard of an old man wearing a coat too long in the sleeve, and a hat too tall for his shortness. When he removed the hat to introduce himself, he revealed eyes so bloodshot, and skin so wrinkled, that the stonemason wondered whether he had come to order his own memorial.

"Good morning to you, sir," began the stonemason. "May I be of assistance in any way?"

"It be my sincere hope so, as I been a'mighty puzzled for some time. Days when I think the Lord has spoken and done a miracle. Others when I think my eyes be a-tricking me. God willing, someone do know about it, and can explain it, because I be blowed if I can."

The apprentice looked at his master for a lucid translation, but was disappointed at his lack of comprehension.

"You in mourning for a loved one, sir? I meet many volk who

think they sees their dear and departed. 'Tis natural enough, and will, in time, ease down a bit. You after a headstone? If so, you come to the right place."

The old man shook his head, and smiled.

"No, no. Don't need a headstone. At least, not for a year or two, despite my sixty-odd years a-weighing me down. No, I can't complain. I be in tolerable heath. 'Scaped the 'sumption and cholera, though my legs be too wobbly for the regiment now. Once upon a time, they gave old Boney a run for their money at Waterloo."

"You at Waterloo? You fought the French?"

The old man scratched his head.

"Think so. Got a medal somewhere."

The stonemason ended this digression, and returned to the reason for the man's visit.

"So why you here, then, sir?"

The old man's eyes lit up, more in alarm than joy.

"Wings, sir!" he cried. "My daughter, Alice, well, she had only one, on account of the other breaking off in a bad frost. She went too early, be my opinion, even though the doctor said it was God's decision. Too young, I said, and God be cruel if he takes young children like that. So I orders an angel a-fluttering her wings above her poor little body in that cold grave. The other day, though, I sees a miracle: the angel be white again – well, perhaps, grey, my eyes not being so good any more – and has two wings. And what I want to ask is: be that your doing or the Lord's?"

"That be my work, sir, on account of a request made by a gentleman who thought she ought to have *two* wings. He paid – or, at least, *will* pay – the sum required. I hope you baint upset, sir, as I had no record of the original commission, and was unable to contact you."

The old man breathed a sigh of relief.

"Oh no. I just be glad I know what happened. When you get to my age, your mind plays tricks. Would you mind telling me again the man's name so I can thank him personally for what he done?"

"Robert Palfreyman. Lives over Dorchester way."

The old man nodded and left.

Soon, when the apprentice had been set to practising a straight line on a piece of surplus stone, James Chideock entered the yard. His wife's burial had taken place, the previous week. The stonemason visited the registry weekly, and knew whom to expect.

"I be sorry that the good Lord took your beloved wife, but she be in a better place now," he opened. "A far better place."

Chideock did not share the man's confidence in this, but confined his reply to the purpose of the visit.

"I'd like a headstone for her. I've written down the words for the inscription."

The stonemason read them, and said, "Very fitting. Very fitting, indeed."

"Not too small but not too big. The one next to my wife's grave is quite small."

"I shall pay a visit today, see what room there be. When it done, I shan't anchor it for a few weeks, just to let the soil settle down, or the stone topple over. The movement, you see. Where in the graveyard shall I find it?"

"Next to Ruth Abbas, the young woman, you recall, who jumped from the cliff. Somehow it was Providence that my wife's was the only plot remaining."

"Then I be out of business soon, though there do be a field behind the church."

"It is the only place left, as I said before. Good-day to you."

When Chideock had left, the stonemason said to his apprentice, "Now there goes a man with the weight of the world on his shoulders."

Chapter Thirteen

The Home was surrounded by fields but connected to London by omnibus. Forster had rarely discussed Dickens' plans for it with him, though knew what it meant to him. Only once had Forster been there, with Dickens, and now, as he knocked nervously on the door, he wondered whether the matron on duty would remember him. That visit had been during the early days, when the interior was being equipped for the first cohort of fallen women. Dickens avoided describing to him the Home's work after it opened; he preferred to talk to him about his own stories.

"Madam, I call here unannounced with this young woman, Nelly Sturminster, whom I found in dire straits, on my travels. My dear friend, Dickens, the advocate of all suffering women, would find no reason to refuse her admission. Indeed, he would thank me for bringing her here, as she has a desire to escape her current circumstances. You may recall my brief visit with him, some time ago. There can be no better place for Nelly than here."

"Mr. Dickens aint 'ere, and Miss. Coutts is out on 'er charity work," Matron pronounced flatly. "My time 'ere is nearly done for the day."

"Then Miss. Coutts must be praised for that, but let not her absence deter you from providing for Nelly, however pressing your need to leave. I shall write to Mr. Dickens immediately to acquaint him with the liberty I have taken. I shall, of course, mention, in glowing terms, your generosity of spirit in helping Nelly in her hour of need."

Matron assessed Nelly: no trouble-causer, tired, eyes soft yet proud.

"She can come in, but it aint regular with Miss. Coutts and Mr. Dickens not being here."

Forster was about to thank her, but Edith pre-empted him.

"It's a long way from home, and I be a-trembling with it all, but I thank you for letting me stay. I won't be any bother."

Matron glanced at Forster, who said, "I'm sure you'll soon make an acquaintance or two here, Nelly. Isn't that right, Matron? It's a friendly place, I'm told."

Matron nodded ironically.

"There are some to be friends with, and others to avoid, them being a bit rougher than you. You're expected to work hard, especially in the laundry, where it's wet and tiring. You any good with a needle?"

"Tolerable," answered Edith. "Had to be."

"What you been in your time?"

"Milkmaid, mostly."

"Not too many cows round here for milking," laughed Matron, "though there's grass enough."

Forster began to feel superfluous.

"I leave you in excellent hands, Nelly. I shall enquire after you in a few days."

Matron led her up some stairs to a room. At the top, Matron said, "You in this one with Polly and Tilly. Then you be Tilly, Polly, and Nelly. Oh my word, but I'll wonder at Miss. Coutts' face when she hears that!" Then she opened the door without knocking.

"What you doing coming in here without knocking?" protested Tilly, a tall, slim girl with sores round her mouth. "Miss. Coutts says we got to show respect to each other!"

"You're not up to anything you shouldn't be, are you? Besides, I'm done for the day, and, if I'm late, my old man won't get his stew on time, and then there'll be trouble."

"Well, we pity him being married to a fat-arsed old cow like you!" joined in Polly. "He wants a proper woman like Tilly!"

"You wait till I sees Miss. Coutts! You'll be back on the streets if you say much more," warned Matron. "Tart!"

"You saw her come in without knocking, didn't you, gal? You heard how she spoke to us, didn't you?"

Edith had expected sanctuary, not bickering or being asked to take sides.

"Leave you to get to know these two young ladies, then, Nelly. Don't forget to snuff the lamps, ladies. You want a wash, Nelly, there's a jug on the table. We'll sort you an apron in the morning. There's night attire in the drawer. The front door is locked at all times. The new matron comes on duty any minute. Show Nelly the ropes, ladies. Remember how you felt when you first came here, poor feckless whores that you were."

Matron left swiftly.

Polly and Tilly gesticulated, cheered, and laughed.

Edith sat on the edge of the bed, one of three again, as she had been in the milking parlour, at Gifford's Farm. What she would not have given to be in the barn with Misterton, or in his bed in his cottage, on the heath!

Above the beds hung crucifixes. Edith looked at the three suffering Christs, and felt depressed.

"Cow, that Matron," Polly told her. "Thinks she owns the place."

"You don't look like one of us," remarked Tilly. "Had enough of the streets?"

"Mr. Forster brought me here. Said the Home help me get back on my feet."

"That's the trouble with gals like us: always on our backs and never on our feet. Anyway, who's Mr. Forster? A do-gooder? You get men like that. Pay for you till they want a change, and then bring you here. Makes things all right then, see? And then they go home when they've dropped us off here. All nice and tidy, eh, Tilly?"

"For them," grunted Tilly.

Edith shook her head.

"No, Mr. Forster's not like that. He's a good man."

"Must be the only one, then. He queer or pay you for it?"

"For what?"

The two others looked at each other, and guffawed.

"For your virtue. You know, your mouth, your hand, your fanny." Edith frowned, only guessing what was meant. "What? You mean you aint one of us? Never had the pox? Never—"

"Shut up!" shouted Edith. "What do you take me for?"

Her raised voice took them aback. They had not expected such force, believing her to be weak.

"All right, gal. No harm meant. You're in the wrong place, then. Your Mr. Forster got it all wrong. You see, we're Mr. Dickens' fallen women, and he wants to save us. Hunts for women like us, he does, just like a good Christian. What he don't realise is that it takes more than a prayer, a hot meal, and a sympathetic ear. He's a man, deary, same as your Mr. Forster, and they only after one thing, and the sooner you learn that, the better."

Polly threw Edith a nightgown from the drawer.

"Thank 'ee," said Edith, taking comfort in her Dorset sounds, which contrasted with their nasal, wide-vowelled accent.

"Don't worry, gal. We'll turn our backs so's you can get changed," said Tilly. "Matron'll pop her head in, in a mo', and check the lights are out."

Edith prepared for bed quickly. There was clean attire and sheets to enjoy. She saw out of the corner of her eye the others undress. For a few seconds, they stood, naked, whispering, but not about her. Then they put on their nightgowns. Polly whispered to Tilly, and Edith heard her say, "Yes, doll. When Matron's been and gone."

"Good girls," whispered Matron, when she discovered their room in darkness. "You're all good girls tonight."

That's what my mother used to say when I was a little girl, remembered Edith.

The key turned in the lock. Edith heard one of the girls get out of bed, a whispering of clothes.

"Hurry up, Till, gal, and don't put your cold feet on me," said Polly.

Edith fell asleep to the gagged giggling of her room-mates.

When she awoke, she felt a hand trying to stifle her cries. She grabbed it, fearing for her life, and lashed out with both hands.

"Quiet, gal, or you'll wake the whole Home up!" hissed Polly. "You had a bad dream, that's all. Screaming your head off like a lunatic, you were. 'S'all right now. 'S'only a nightmare. 'Taint real."

Edith sat up. Polly was a voice in the dark, then a gentle stroke on her arm.

He grabbed her wrists, forced her down onto the straw. His hand pressed on her mouth, stifling her screams. She smelt the cider, which scorched her as he tried to kiss her. Her pleas to stop were muffled to a murmur of bumble bees. Up went her dress, then down, she pulled it, her body beginning to arch in its attempts to throw him off. She heard them before she felt her undergarments rip. Then, against her flesh, hot with the writhing to repel him, she felt the coldness of the knife. As he ripped, so did she, as she had seen Stockwood do to an occasional pig to be smoked on Gifford's Farm. He butted her as he fell, and she pushed and rolled him off her. Wareham convulsed, his own knife, which had slipped from his pocket, still rooting in his bowels.

Polly held Edith to her.

"There, gal. Just a dream, that's all."

Instinctively, Edith hugged her tightly, felt Polly's flesh warmed by Tilly.

"You weren't half shouting," said Tilly. "Top of your voice."

"You want two minutes with me?" asked Polly.

Edith was shuddering. Her tears had splashed onto Polly's breasts. Tilly turned away, and pulled the blanket up to her chin. Slowly, Polly calmed Edith, and fell asleep, cuddling Edith like the doll she had had, as a child.

The sky above the Home was as dark and menacing as the Thames. The rain gushed and gurgled in the gutters, and black, faceless figures leaned into their journey, backs bent, hastening to their destination. John Forster peered out of the window. Next to him stood Nelly, keeping him in her sight. His kindness in taking her there had been well meant, but had resulted in further misery for her. The other women had been suspicious of her, had teased her for her Dorset accent till she had rounded on them, and accused them of harassing her. She had made up her mind: she would return to Dorset.

"Nelly, it's not too late to change your mind. In time, as Mr. Dickens so rightly said, you would be of great assistance to the women who pass through these doors. Help them to change their lives. You can read and write. Almost all who stay here cannot. All around us are shame, poverty, and neglect. Our Ragged Schools bulge with boys and girls who never wash, know nothing about the world. You could teach them, Nelly. Why don't you stay?"

Edith shook her head.

"Not one for living in big houses with lots of others, Mr. Forster, especially folk who ask me questions all the time. Why you come all this way? How much you earn? What you do for the gentlemen that we can't? And that Mr. Dickens, sir, well, I know he's been poorly, but he being a famous man don't give him the key to lock me up and turn me into someone he thinks I ought to be."

Forster laughed. How he wished Dickens could hear her disparagement, argue with her! Why, she would end up a character in his next number!

"Have you read any of his stories, my dear? They are full of compassion for the displaced and disadvantaged in society. He ill-deserves criticism for his energetic efforts to provide shelter, occupation, and training for, as he would term it, fallen women."

"But I'm not a fallen woman, sir, and never will be. I was willing for you to bring me to London. 'Tis where I wanted to be. You know, be a maid or companion to a lady, but the time baint right. Every night, I thank the Lord that you helped me, but now I must return and right some wrongs."

Forster looked at his pocket-watch. The rain must delay them no longer. The cab would not be long.

"Tell me, Nelly. Which part of Dorset do you come from?"

"Why, Sturminster, sir! Why else you think I be called Nelly Sturminster?"

She laughed, and Forster joined in.

"I'll let Dickens down lightly."

"As you wish, sir."

Forster handed over a purse.

"This should enable you to meet a month's expenses if you live modestly."

In Edith's hands, it felt heavy, and her heart quickened at its possibilities.

"Thank 'ee, sir. I'll pay you back, one day. If not in coins, in time here. I promise."

"You're a good girl, Nelly. Write to me at this address."

She read the words on the paper, which she folded and slipped inside the purse.

"I will, sir, and I pray the world will be a better place when I do."

"Your cab is here. Goodbye, Nelly Sturminster."

He squeezed her hand, and walked her to the cab. Her face was a white rose petal blown onto the black, wet window. Goodbye, she mouthed.

Miss. Coutts poured him a cup of hot chocolate.

"Your protégée has fled our cosy, little nest, then," she remarked. "Shepherd's Bush won't be the same without her strange expressions."

"Yes. You know, this house is not for everyone. Oh, I know it transforms the lives of many, but Nelly is different. I made a mistake. You know, she chided Dickens for his charity. Yes, I can hardly believe it myself. Dickens, of all people!"

"It's not charity we offer, Mr. Forster, but hope. Without hope, we cannot live. It's what sustains us."

There was a pause in which he leaned forward to take a slice of cake from the tray.

"Miss. Coutts, may I ask you a question?" he said, at the end of his first mouthful.

"You may, indeed, though perhaps you ought to save it for Charles, whom I saw just pass the window."

"Have I missed the poor child?" gasped Dickens. "I had hoped to be here sooner, but my letter to George Eliot took longer than expected, and I had to catch the post. Nelly? She was that rare plant which promises to flower in even the stoniest ground. Troubled, yes, I have no doubt, but not beyond salvation."

"Tea? A slice of cake?" offered Miss. Coutts.

"Temptress! Forster, I promised to buy you a chop, and I shall. Shall we say five?"

"We shall, though I would be grateful if you could address a question I have."

Miss. Coutts smiled and said, "I saw its enormity knitted in his brow, and thought, therefore, it one which you might address."

"I shall endeavour my best to answer it."

"Do people in Dorset take the name of their place of birth?"

Dickens thought at length, and shook his head.

"Forster, I have absolutely no idea, though imagine: Oliver Twist, by Charles Portsmouth. What do you think, eh?"

Now I know the answer, realised Forster. Clever girl, our Nelly

Chapter Fourteen

The young man slouched against the wall in the morning sun. Already, the stone was warm on his back. His hat was on his right knee, and he was chewing a piece of bread. The light flashed on his wavy, black hair, which flopped onto his brow. His skin was golden from working outdoors, fixing broken fences, shepherding, walking from job to job. He examined his hands: knuckles knotted, and palms padded with calluses caused by gripping tools to cut and shape wood so that it would become a chair, table, or box. That is what he did best: make objects to use or please the eye.

At Canonicorum, he had made three boxes for a widow.

"For my apples and plums when they drop," she had explained. "No way of storing them proper, see? You made a good job. See you call again, October time. Perhaps need more of 'em, amount of buzzing bees been a-doing. Such a great darting from nest to trees! You got a name?"

But all the young man had said was, "I'll call later in the year. You sure you haven't given me too much?"

"Too much? Grinder sharpens my knives asks for more, and he makes nothing 'cept a few sparks. No. These boxes'll still be here when they nail me into a bigger one."

Her money bought him bread, and there would be plenty left for meat and cider.

As people passed, they blocked then revealed the sun, which

dazzled him so that he had to look up or down the street. People hummed and gathered gossip. Misterton heard laughter, then a drum. All he could see were legs in front of him, so he stood up, his bag of tools wedged between his feet.

"What be all this?" he asked a man in a shepherd's smock.

"You baint be from Bridport, 'tis plain!" replied the shepherd. "Why, 'tis midsummer's day, and this be the festibities to mark the occasion. There be dancing and music, and, if I'm correct in memory – and that be in doubt today on account of me festibating late, last night – a hog roast and cider to go with it! 'Tis wondrous you've stumbled across us, and 'tis said that once you've danced in this street, your feet return you here wherever you try to take 'em. Why, 'tis merely a fable, some say, but more like 'tis true, 'cause I be one of 'em to testify so!"

Misterton smiled. A cheer arose as musicians appeared at the top of the street. They were fluffed with coloured feathers, like chickens, and led by a drum. The applause took up its rhythm, and the procession made its way towards the Mayor, whose gold chain caught the sunlight, setting him ablaze.

Misterton licked his dry lips, as he listened to the Mayor's speech.

Bucky Doo, Misterton laughed to himself. 'Tis a strange name for a gathering-place, but so be everything if you baint have bumped into it before.

He sniffed: smoke, sweat, animals, cider, straw.

On the twelfth chime of the bell – each of the previous eleven accompanied by the drummer – a line of maidens in white walked into the road, and formed a circle, holding hands. Their hair was embroidered with daisies and buttercups, and they floated, now tiptoeing to the right, now to the left, before separating into stars of four, creating a constellation of angels.

Misterton watched them intently, his eyes resting on one with long, black hair, and dark eyes. She did not smile, as the others, but wore the mask of a saint, looking up to Heaven self-consciously, illuminated in a sacred book. He followed her graceful movements, her bows and soaring hands keeping time with the drum.

Soon, she was in front of him, and saw him looking at her. He smiled and nodded, and though her next movement took her away, she glanced over her shoulder at him. Throughout the dance, their eyes continued to meet, and Misterton's heart drummed a quicker beat.

Two more dances followed before the music stopped. Misterton managed to manoeuvre himself closer to the front, and stood in the space where she had trodden. Another girl grabbed her hand to pull her towards a table on which there was a jug of water. Misterton could barely disguise his alarm. There was no mistaking the dancer's message in her eyes, and he stepped towards her. She broke free of her friend's hand, and stood alone, waiting.

"A man has told me that if you dance in this street, your feet will bring you back here wherever you try to go," he began.

"Then you be a stranger in Bridport, not to know that."

"My feet will always bring me back to this spot, even though I haven't danced here."

She feigned puzzlement.

"And why be that?"

"Because 'tis the place where I first saw you. 'Tis a holy place now, and every day from now be a pilgrimage here."

"You talk in riddles, but 'tis also poetry to my ears."

"'Tis worship."

"Baint right to worship so when you don't even know me."

"'Tis worship and what do please God, for I have never see such an angel as you."

"Your tongue has practised these words before, 'tis plain."

"Never! I be snatched by your dancing and eyes of blackberries, and 'tis they that make me say these wondrous things. I be bewitched."

"You going to burn me at the stake? You'll have me skimmitied afore I fish me a husband, and I shall have to find me another place to live afore the summer's flit."

"Ruth," called one of the other dancers. "'Tis time for the Solstice Reel."

"I must go," Ruth told him, hesitating.

"Then dance and weave your spell again, but tell me how many chimes must sing afore you walk with me towards the bay?"

"Three, but you shall not meet me here. By the Friends' Meeting House, yonder."

And by the end of this day, he resolved, I shall make you my wife.

Down the road stiffly strode a giant, and children screamed. He wore a tall hat, and his lips and cheeks were rouged. He stopped to talk to his audience, wobbling on his stilts as they caught a cobble.

The Mayor had provided refreshments from the public coffers, and he inched through the crowd proudly, receiving their gratitude with a regal nod, a shake of the hand, till he felt like the important person he had always wanted to be.

Misterton watched the Solstice Reel, saw the girls' arms reach up, make suns, and then dip into an imaginary sea. Out came the stars, all a-twinkle, with a fluttering of their fingers, high above their heads. And Misterton watched Ruth, till he felt he would faint.

To recover his senses, he took some cider, and sat out of view of the dancers. Not even the cider lit his appetite; instead he fidgeted, listened for three clangs of the bell, not wanting to miss them.

His long wait was broken when the shepherd to whom he had spoken earlier sat next to him on the wooden seat.

"Don't mind if I sits and rests awhile, do 'ee?" he asked. "Why, 'tis the young fellow I spoke to, baint it?"

"The same. 'Tis too hot to stand."

"The days grow shorter now," he said, resting his crook on the floor. "We must pack all of them into a smaller space, which be just like our lives. Every day be like that, with fewer to squeeze in our makings and our dancing, though my feet too gone to dance, being as heavy as a cow's, and almost as smelly, me being out in the fields with the sheep, most the time."

"Yet the days be tolerable long yet a-while, time enough to feast and settle to sunsets. Besides, you baint ancient yet!" laughed Misterton, the cider beginning to glow in his limbs.

"But my meaning be we do much to remind us that all we will soon see be wind and rain, and mud, and shut doors. Weight drops off trees, and we back by our hearths. No, this day be the longest so that we may know they soon be shorter, and that be fact."

Misterton nodded. The girl, the chimes, their walk, today, as the next day there will be less light, and the one after, even less.

"Then I drink to you, wise man," he laughed. "I have learned that I must not put something off."

"You must drink alone, though 'tis sad. I wish 'twere not the case, but my brain a-rattles still, and, for all my years and hoary hair, I have not mastered the art of stopping the cider when my tongue misbehaves. 'Tis a blessing and a curse for us men, who be weak, and it leads us by the nose to ruin and misery if we don't master it."

The shepherd picked up his crook after a few minutes' rest, and shook Misterton's hand.

"Take care, wise man," said Misterton.

"Not wise but old. Seen the Solstice come and go nigh on sixty times."

With that, he walked back up the street, his crook clicking on the cobbles.

Two o'clock came and went, and Misterton moved towards the Friends' Meeting House. There were fewer people that far down the street, and he felt conspicuous, leaning against the wall. Close to three, she appeared, still in her white dress, the flowers still in her hair, like diamonds and topaz in a crown.

Misterton held out his hands to her, but she put hers behind her, out of reach.

"'Tis only two I've heard!" she protested. "Three be tarrying."

"Would you deny me a few extra moments on this the day when time begins to squeeze into a smaller glass?"

Again, he offered his hands.

"Only if you can guess my name."

"Then 'tis Angela if anything."

"Why so Angela? Is there one other with my likeness?"

"There cannot be one only, for your face be saintly and lights up the dark aisles and corners of all the churches in England."

"Your words be like the gushing stream yonder, but are so musical that I might start a-dancing to them if you say them enough!"

She giggled, and gave him her hands, and he pressed them to his lips.

"Will we walk to the bay?"

She shook her head, and took back her hands.

"'Tis true I be more saint than sinner, though I be no more an Angela than an angel. I be Ruth. What they call 'ee?"

"Nicholas Misterton."

"Why, 'tis pretty, and tinkles on the tongue like a jester's bells."

The walk to the bay was tiring in the heat, and they were glad to accept the offer of a ride on a passing cart.

"Come," she ordered, running towards the path to the cliff-top.

"Up there? 'Tis far," hesitated Misterton, "and a ladder to the sky."

"'Tis a place I love."

"Then one I love, too."

At the top, the breeze soothed them. Ruth's hair flapped and fell. The amber edge of the cliff was a giant's stride, a twirling of four dancers, away. Ruth looked out at the sea, which had melted into the sky, so hot was the blue-grey haze.

Misterton dropped his bag on the floor, and his iron tools clanged.

"You be a journeyman?" she guessed.

"Carpenter. Make things, mend things. 'Tis nothing to recommend me, I know, but 'tis what my father taught me, and all I can do, though tolerable."

She took his hands, and stroked their roughness. Her own had been marked by labour, but were balm on his. He held his breath, and she looked up at him, saw the spell her caresses had cast.

"Ruth, this be my first kiss of a girl," he said.

"Then 'tis well I've waited all these years for it."

She tasted the juice of apples on his lips, and he salt on hers.

"But Bea and Connie both must be bridesmaids as 'twill cause wrangling and upset enough to fill Lyme Bay if I choose one over the other, but 'tis the cost of their dresses that be the sinking sand, on account of me not having any money," explained Ruth. "And where we going to live, what with you a-tramping all over Dorset, seeking out work like a ferret in a rabbit hole? I'll always be by your side, Nicholas, but my legs be as short as a sheep's, and if I wear 'em out too soon, how I run around after you, a-washing and a-cooking?"

Misterton laughed. She made their poverty sound like a shower instead of a biblical deluge, and he kissed her for it.

"Then Bea and Connie must be in church as equals, and as for your legs, though they be short, they be right for your body, and almost as if I'd carved them perfect to mount at a sacred altar."

She kissed him, and stroked his cheeks.

"Dear Nicholas, how I do love thee! And when we are wed, we shall each keep the other warm in winter, and say our vows again each Solstice day."

"And why so, my Ruth?"

"Promise you'll never leave me, Nicholas."

"I will stay with you till the sea is dried to a salt bed, till the sun is snuffed like a candle by God himself, tired of his works."

She put her fingertip on his lips, gently.

"But the wait for that be long, and we live but a short time, and then be cut down."

Nicholas said, "I will make furniture in an empty building. I will not drag you round the lanes of Dorset till you are worn out, like your shoes. We will marry, and live in Bridport."

"That is what I want," whispered Ruth, resting her head against his chest.

"I, too, my love. We shall be wed as soon as the vicar allows, and you be dressed accordingly. And I shall enquire for a house that'll fit us well."

"I have no parents to come, Nicholas," she remembered.

"Nor I. We be twinned in that."

"Buried afore their time."

Nicholas hugged her, and said nothing.

He found them a house on the road to West Bay, had enough time to locate logs, and bang them into a bed. Other furniture followed: a table, two chairs, drawers. The space he begged, once used for storage, was free bar the promise of a dresser for the owner. In time, Misterton could sell his woodwork all over Dorset.

A few people stopped, on their way into Bridport, to see them come out of the church. Misterton had asked Ruth if all three could wear the same white dresses worn when dancing on Midsummer's Day. But the buttercups and daisies had long since withered.

They drank cider, and ate bread and blue vinney. Bea and Connie had embroidered a table-cloth with names and the date, to commemorate the wedding.

When the bridesmaids left, sighing and giggling in equal measure, the happy couple walked to West Bay.

"Come," Ruth ordered, offering her hand.

The blue vinney soon slowed them.

"I baint in the right attire for climbing mountains."

She led him to the exact spot where they had kissed for the first time. She had noticed, on that occasion, that they had stood by a slab of stone.

"Now kiss me again, my Nicholas."

Again, the sweetness of cider and salt from the cheese mixed on their lips.

"You be Mrs. Misterton now."

"'Tis like a cricket in the grass to say it," she laughed. "And 'tis the same when you say Nicholas Misterton! I want to keep my name, Nicholas. I be the last to wear it."

"Then wear it, as mine feels like a coat that don't fit me, betimes."

"You'll never leave me, will you, Nicholas?"

"Never. Why you ask such a silly question on your wedding day?"

"Because if you do, I shall jump off this cliff at this very spot," she warned.

Chapter Fifteen

Palfreyman rushed home after only two weeks, rather than the four he had anticipated, in Bath. The chance to ask for the hand in marriage of Rose Wells had come sooner than expected, and she had accepted him without hesitation. Palfreyman had felt that there was no point in delaying the happy event, so had begged forgiveness for an early departure, and it had been granted in the knowledge that there was much to organise: the vicar, rooms for the bride and her entourage, and, of course, the search for a new home for Florence.

"But will not people speculate about the shortness of the engagement?" had wondered his bride-to-be. "I wouldn't wish to be portrayed as, well – there is no other phrase for it – a gold-digger."

"Dearest, let them think what they will. You will soon win over the charming folk of Dorset. They are largely good-natured, but can get above themselves when they've a mind, having an acute sense of what they perceive as injustice. Quite a bit different to the people you've been used to in Bath."

"And your sister: will she turn against me when I become mistress of the manor? She has enjoyed living there for so long."

"She understands perfectly well the need to move to her own house. Besides, it would never work. She has become, well, rather eccentric of late. Nothing too strange, you understand."

"I'm sure you shouldn't be telling me this, Robert."

"Then I shall say no more. I shall write, confirming the arrangements, which must be my priority."

And he had returned, in a most business-like frame of mind. At his desk, he made lists, ruthlessly: wines, menus, people to see. Stinsford church was out of the question. The vicar, of course, would be disappointed, displeased, even, but the church was not big enough to seat all the guests. Dorchester would be better, but less romantic. Yes, Dorchester.

He summoned Florence as if she had been a servant. There was no affectionate kiss. She tried smiling, but he would not be melted. He had important matters to address.

"I trust you've been well during my absence," he began.

"Apart from a sniffle," she replied laconically.

"And the house? The estate?"

"Life has continued as normal in the house, though I cannot speak for the estate, it being *your* responsibility. And soon I doubt even the house will be mine to care for."

Palfreyman sighed wearily. Florence could be difficult, he knew, and he suspected she was edging towards being so.

"I'll come straight to the point, seeing as you have directed me there in your inimitable style. I made you aware of my visit to Bath, and my early return must not raise your hopes that I failed in my mission. Rose has accepted me. There will be no lengthy engagement. They are nearly always a matter of form. I hope you and I will remain on good terms, that you will, indeed, come to know her as a friend, too. I do not ask you to adore her immediately. It will take time, but you must understand that our marriage will make her mistress of Palfreyman Manor and the estate, and that, by removing to another house, you will retain the status and authority that being mistress of your own home confers."

"Then congratulations, Robert, though do not believe that such a short acquaintance can ever be a good foundation for a happy marriage. A half-year's engagement, as is the custom, would enable you both to nurture your love for each other."

Palfreyman could see in her expression sincere alarm, and he felt uncomfortable, backed into a corner.

"I fear your concern is based very much on limited experience, unless you count your ridiculous attempt to bed Misterton in Lyme!"

Before she had chance to protest, there was a knock at the door. Palfreyman knew it was Coombs.

"Come!"

"There is a man in the hall says he would like a word, sir. I asked if he had an appointment, and he said no, but that you would want to see him as it was about an unpaid bill."

Palfreyman was well served by Coombs, but irritated by the mien of over-done gravitas he wore whenever things did not go quite right.

"Did he give his name?"

"He did, sir. Robin somebody or other. A stonemason from Bridport. Apparently, he—"

"Yes, yes, Coombs. Show him in."

Robin entered. Back in his yard in Bridport, his apprentice was working on his first proper job: a headstone for a man suspected of dying of cholera, though that diagnosis had been made by his friends at his wake, after much cider, when a liver ailment would have been closer to the mark.

"'Tis about the angel's wings, sir, done in good faith, though you don't look a tiddy bit like the man who gave me the commission. The roundabout way is the only way for me to explain myself in this matter. 'Pears he, *you*, did not like to see an angel with only one wing, so he asks me to help her fly again by mending her. 'Ten pounds be the cost,' I says. 'Send the bill to me at Palfreyman Manor,' he says. 'My word as Robert Palfreyman be as good as payment,' he assures me. Now I baint one to doubt my betters, but actual payment be much more useful to me than the promise of it. 'Tis now a few weeks since Robert Palfreyman was sent the bill, but I habn't received no payment. Though what be worrying me like old age be the distinct impression that you're not actually the man who said he was you, travelling to Lyme with his sister. I hope all that makes sense."

"Strangely, it does, though I had forgotten all about it during my absence. The man who claimed to be me is, in fact, my farmer, who drove the coach to Lyme. He is nothing more than a scoundrel, and he will pay for his nimble footwork. Still, I suspect you will not be remotely interested in the whys and wherefores, so here is your ten pounds, which I shall deduct from his wages."

Palfreyman went over to his box, and took out the money.

"Thank 'ee, sir, and may I say that if ever you need a headstone, then think of Robin of Bridport. That's me, sir. Good day to 'ee, sir."

Robin was about to leave but Palfreyman stopped him.

"I hope that I shall not be in need of one for a good few years, but I'd be grateful if you could confirm my man as the one who deceived us both. Coombs, ride over to the farm, and fetch Misterton."

Coombs bowed and left.

Robin was anxious to extricate himself from the situation, having now the ten pounds in his pocket, but Palfreyman was adamant he should stay.

Florence recognised the signs that her brother's fury was growing. She herself had put him in this antagonistic mood, and now he was riled enough to make Misterton pay for his folly.

"Robert, this is not a matter for this poor man. Let him go. His journey is long. Why delay him further?" she pleaded.

"Because if Misterton is the man who stole my name, then he has lost my confidence in him. Come, sir. I'll have you brought some food. Florence, will you ask Cook to bring in some pie? You'll take pie, sir? And brandy? To fortify you for the journey back to Bridport?"

Florence saw that he would not be moved on the matter, and fetched the food herself.

Robin was grateful for the brandy, but was unsettled by Palfreyman's pacing up and down the room.

"The gentleman concerned—" Robin began, but Palfreyman would hear none of it.

"Gentleman? He's no gentleman. He's a scoundrel, and he'll be made to pay once we're sure we've got the right man."

"Don't want to get anybody in trouble."

Palfreyman refilled Robin's glass.

"He's got himself into trouble, which is a pity, as he's made a good show on the farm."

"Seemed a good enough man to me, though he looked ridiculous in his coachman's red. Not a good fit, if I remembers correctly, and not the right colour for him, though I be no fair judge of clothes, as you can probably tell. Seemed so concerned, so tender 'bout this poor, broken angel."

"Pray, don't go on about him so. He deserves to be shot for his insolence."

Robin gulped the second glass of brandy, which fired his courage.

"Well, don't 'ee forget, sir. Robin of Bridport's your man for a headstone."

The pie, when it came, was gratefully consumed. Florence stayed, wanted to be there when Misterton faced her brother; she feared that Robert would do his worst. For though Misterton had humiliated her, he had been the only man who had ever interested her.

"My compliments to the cook. Now if I'm not mistaken, there be pigeon and pheasant and rabbit – or be it hare? – and bacon in that pie, and I'll be a tree stump if that baint bone jelly a-holding them together in that pastry."

Palfreyman let Robin talk freely, while he himself rehearsed his words for Misterton, who came quickly. Coombs had conveyed to him extreme urgency.

Misterton did not recognise Robin. Florence's eyes were wide open, a warning, but Misterton looked through her.

"Is this the man?" asked Palfreyman. "Take your time."

Robin looked long and hard, and almost shook his head.

"'Tis difficult. The man who ordered the statue was as red as the devil himself."

"Come, man, use your imagination. It's not that hard," snapped Palfreyman.

"Now, that's never been my strong point, on account of me being a stonemason. I have to chisel, not imagine. Folk pay me for my fancy letters in marble."

Misterton then remembered Florence's visit with the bill, when he had been in the field.

"Leave him be. It's not his fault."

"You said the bill had nothing to do with you," reminded Florence.

Robin looked from one to the other. He was two brandies and a wedge of game pie to the good, but could not fathom what was going on.

"I said that to you, though it baint true."

"For God's sake, man, why—"

"Robert!" protested Florence.

"Did I do it, you were going to say? Why did I give your name for the bill? 'Tis plain and not a secret. Before I came, Maisie was sick so bad she could have gone, was just a milking away from her last breath. You were told how bad she was, but you let her go beout a doctor. So when I sees that poor little angel beout a wing, I want to help her, see. Angels have two wings. They can't fly in Heaven beout two. And you could help that angel, help her fly off or watch over the poor soul buried in that grave beneath her. You done a good job there, helping an angel. You owed that to Maisie."

Halfway through this peroration, Robin began to nod in agreement.

"Why, 'tis only just. No amount of gold buys the kingdom of Heaven," he declared.

"You deceived this man, took my name in vain, and must be punished. You've done a much better job than Wareham, but I cannot trust you, and, therefore, you must leave. There will be a deduction of ten pounds from what is owing you. I want you off the farm by the end of the day."

"You would dismiss him for ten pounds, Robert? No, you cannot do that!" cried Florence.

"I can, and have. By the end of the day, he must be gone."

"You treat me worse than Wareham. I never did what he did. He got what he deserved, but I don't deserve this. This aint as bad as what he did."

"And what do you mean?"

Realising he had said too much, Misterton turned to leave, and Robin followed.

"You did a good job, that angel," he told Robin. "You looking for an apprentice? Turn my hand to most things."

"Got one. That Robert Palfreyman be bad."

"He should have called a doctor. She could have died."

Back at the farmyard, he collected a few things, crammed them into his bags and pockets.

"Got to go," he told the others. "End of day."

"Why?" asked Simon. "What you done?"

"Long story."

"What we going to do?"

Misterton shrugged.

"Don't know. You all done a good job. He's no argument with you."

He took Maisie aside, held her gently by the wrist.

"Come with me to my mother's," he offered. "She needs help now she be old and cracked. I cannot leave you. 'Twill come out to her and my sister in good time."

She nodded and put on her coat, and they started the long walk back to the heath.

Chapter Sixteen

The early months of their marriage were strawberry jam and clotted cream, and he worked hard. What he was good at was making furniture, which Ruth sold on market days, being more persuasive than him. Flashing her eyes drew a few orders, which cheered him up, but he knew he would never make the fine objects, trimmed with beading and scrolls, rich people bought for their beautiful houses.

"Not got the money to buy the best wood, see. I scavenge from the countryside where I can, but I don't chop down or steal oak from the estates. I baint a thief," he explained when she asked him why he was not more ambitious. "'Tis lack of money mainly, but 'twould be strange to carve like a master, when I be more of a 'prentice axeman! Father taught me basic, not master."

"But the tin be empty, Nicholas. Everyone be sitting on your chairs in Bridport, and eating off your tables, yet the tin be as empty as the sky."

Her accusations made him shrink. His words in his defence were dandelion clocks.

"I could look for other work. Never been work-idle, a-wandering, but I swore I'd never drag you off down the by-ways. We'll make do, though I'm ashamed that the tin be empty, for 'tis my job to make sure it rattles, and when you say 'tis empty as the sky, the blame lays me low for days."

"Then we must work out a better way, for my tiddy job like the weather, right now."

The strawberry jam was soon gone, and what was left of the clotted cream turned slowly rancid. The house felt cold, the grate was bare. Some days, he vowed to end the sawing and hammering, was frustrated that Ruth returned from the market empty-handed.

In bed, one night, he said, "Let us leave Bridport. There baint luck for the likes of us here no more. 'Tis like a friend who passes us by with his nose in the air."

Her back to him, she choked on the words, "'Tis our home. We need to think. You make a cider press?"

"Tolerable, probably."

"Then do it, and we can squash them little apples till they all a-mosh, and juice runs into tubs. Most folk got a tree or two, and leave their fruit to rot brown on the floor so's wasps at 'em."

"But that be but one season. There be three others."

"Then we think. You ever fish?"

He shook his head in the dark.

"No sea where I grew up. Heath my sea. Rabbits, hares, and pheasants my fish."

"You scared of the sea?"

"Don't know."

"You want to find out? Might get casual work, down West Bay."

"Might drown."

"Might earn money."

He went knocking on doors, after that, asking if anyone needed a job doing. Choosing his houses carefully, so that he would not waste time on folk as poor as himself, he showed them a child's chair, which he strapped to his back, as an example of his craftsmanship. He picked up one or two orders, that way, but eventually he ran out of houses.

In West Bay, he watched the boats from the shore. He chose fine days to go, to build up confidence, convincing himself that fishermen would not put to sea in angry weather. One day, he watched a man row in and drag his boat up the sand, till it rested. The fisherman worked methodically, lifted a big box from his boat. Near the cliff stood his wife, left hand on her hip, knife in her right, a basket at her feet. In the vicinity, gulls hovered and loitered expectantly. Misterton watched how she left some fish whole, but gutted others, throwing heads and tails away. There is nothing left of this man's work, Misterton saw. When I finish working, there is an object, pleasant to the eye, which will last years. Fish be eaten soon, but I be a creator.

"You need a man?" he called.

The fisherman looked up. It took him time to focus, his mind still at sea. There were feelings in him he could never describe. The pact he made with the movement of the water was renewed, each trip, and he was thankful, once again, that the jostling waves had not broken their word. When the box was full, he always returned to shore, never greedy.

"Boat not big enough for two," he called. "You fished before?"

"Carpenter. You need anything doing?"

"Man who made this might, but he lives at Beer, which be miles westward. Always need boats."

Misterton felt a chance of regular money float away, like flotsam.

"Know anyone need a man?"

The fisherman shook his head.

"The sea's a graveyard for a carpenter."

When Misterton told Ruth that he could not fish, she humphed, then hugged him, thinking better of it.

"Rent be due, Thursday. We shall have to go to a lender if money don't turn up," she told him. "Landlord likes his rent on time."

"That be a fast road to the debtors' prison."

"Some say 'tis better than the workhouse."

"I will find the money today," he reassured her.

And he did, and enough food for the rest of the week.

"Where you get it?" she asked.

"Sold two boxes with lids. Carved their names for free."

He pressed the money into her hand. His smile did not fit together convincingly.

"What name they go by?" His eyes told her. She fought back tears, but her eyes glistened. "Don't you do that again, Nicholas."

"What?"

"Lie to me."

He went out, into the hills, where he sat and composed himself enough to return to his yard.

He brought back for her a little box, which she accepted with sadness.

"Oh, Nicolas! 'Tis beautiful, though I have nothing but buttons to put in it."

He set to thinking. If only she had something valuable to put in it, the box would be useful. Every market day, people looked at his chairs and boxes, felt them, sat on them, commented on how well they were made, but did not buy them, so he decided to try other things: shepherds' crooks, walking sticks for wobbly legs, name-plates for houses, arches for climbing plants, made-to-measure picture-frames. For a week or two, he sold, then people lifted, looked, and moved on again.

In a rush of enthusiasm, he went to the church in which they had been married, and copied the images on the vicar's lectern, with the view of trying to carve them so that he could specialise in churches. There were many features to admire, maybe to add to. With samples in his bag, he went to see the vicar.

"I copied these," said Misterton, showing two different leaves and an eagle, both varnished.

The vicar traced their lines with his fingertips.

"They are very good, Nicholas. You have a steady hand."

"Maybe the church could have more of these. I could do them. You see what you need, and I'll do them."

The vicar looked into his eyes, knew how poor people were, was used to them knocking on the door of the vicarage.

There was nothing in the church that needed repairing. Its history should not be tampered with to put food on a man's table, the vicar decided.

"I'll bear you in mind. At the moment, the wood is in good condition. Admittedly, a few pews creak, but that's all," he said, handing back the samples. "You have a talent, Nicholas. I shall recommend you wherever I go."

"Thank 'ee, vicar," said Misterton, and left.

They went for long walks, till it became too cold, or the light vanished, so that they could use candles sparingly. Their spirits lifted when they stopped to talk to others, and they felt included in life again. They locked their door at night, snuffed the candle, and there were only the low tones of their voices, like the moaning of wind in the eaves, and the warmth of their sheets, that stopped the bedroom feeling like a crypt.

He edged towards her, curled his arm round her, but she wanted to go to sleep, so that the next day would come quickly and banish the darkness, for if she saw daylight, there was hope their circumstances would improve.

One day, with a spare coin or two jangling in his pocket, he went to an inn. He felt the warmth of the fire, and of the nods and smiles as heads turned to see who had joined them. He had been passing, and the door had opened. From beyond the man who was leaving had drifted the murmur of conversation, and the sweet smell of ale. On impulse, he had entered. A penny or two, he had calculated, would not be missed. Besides, he might find more work here.

"Good evening," greeted the landlord. "What can I pour you?"

"'Tis cider for me," said Misterton.

"A wise man who drinks it, and he be wiser afterwards!"

This warm welcome made Misterton glad to have not gone straight home from his walk. He had left Ruth darning socks.

"Do we know you?" called one of the men by the fire.

The orange flames lit up the man's glossy cheeks.

"Nicholas, I'm known as," Misterton replied.

"Then, Nicholas, draw up a chair. 'Tis not often we get anyone new here. I be Obediah."

"And I Zachariah."

"Samson."

"And Jude."

They all shook hands with Misterton, and asked him so many questions that they soon discovered how little money he had to keep Ruth.

"'Tis a pretty name, Ruth," remarked Jude. "Jewish if I be right."

"Not as pretty as her face, which played magic on me at Bucky Doo, last Solstice."

"Then you still in love, young fellow?" asked Obediah, winking to the others. "You still sweethearts?"

Samson picked up the glasses to take them to be refilled, but Misterton held on to his.

"Though 'tis kind, 'tis difficult, as I cannot pay my way."

"Neither can we. Oh, we know the times. They be the workhouse, the begging-bowl, or the hangman's noose, but a man needs a drink when his pride be threshed like corn," opined Obediah.

"You ever work on a farm?" asked Zachariah.

"No, but I'll work anywhere. Carpentry don't pay a living in a place like Bridport. Every market day's the same. I can carve fine things, though I don't have the money to buy the oak. Oak be the choosing of the rich folk, be what I hear."

Zachariah rocked back in his chair, and ran his eyes over Misterton's muscles. He might do, up at Gifford's.

"You got muscles like boulders. Last the day like my Megan, and I'll give you work on my farm, come the summer. Set on temporary, July onwards. Gifford's Farm, up Pilsdon way, near Shave Cross. Stockwood, ask for, come the time."

Misterton nodded. He would do that if things had not improved.

"This one be on me," insisted Samson, "on account of your company, which be welcome, so fresh it is. Add all our years, and be too many to count. We be in the autumn of our lives, so a bit of spring be a change."

"Then thank 'ee, all of 'ee, and 'tis promised that 'ere the end of the year, Nicholas Misterton will have repaid his debt to you all."

Zachariah Stockwood nodded, the only one to refrain from buying him a drink.

Misterton left with empty pockets. Having been unaware of the passing of time, he found himself in the street with several hours of absence from home to explain. He felt suffused with the spirit of friendship offered by his new acquaintances, and made his unsteady way home, tipping his hat to this passer-by, grunting, "'Night" to that.

Ruth had waited up for him. He never came in this late; never went to an inn. The likelihood of him lying dead in a ditch was slim, she knew, but she was worried and angry, and when the loud knock came, she rushed to the door.

"Where have you been, Nicholas? I've been a-fretting, all evening!"

He bent forward to kiss her, and she smelt the cider on him.

"You stink!" she cried, stepping back. "Where you been?"

"Rope-maker's Rest. Been with my friends, who bought me a drink."

"How you pay your way?"

"Friends be friends."

She went up to bed, relieved, yet angry that he had not bothered to let her know where he was. It would have taken only two minutes.

She put on her nightgown in the dark, and settled at the edge of the bed.

Misterton could not undress himself properly. His feet became tangled in his trousers, and he fell over.

"Daft bugger!" he laughed loudly, kicking the air wildly to extricate his feet.

"Nicholas, the neighbours'll hear you!"

"'Taint every day my trousers won't let go. How many times you known me a tumbler?"

His tone was sharper, a response to her anger at him.

"Never married a tumbler or a fool!" she spat.

Somehow, Misterton managed to climb into bed, and the room fell still.

"Where you gone over there for?" he asked, reaching to touch her.

She recoiled as if stung by a wasp.

"Don't you dare touch me when you been drinking!"

"Then when must I touch 'ee? Never, these days, it seem. I be your husband."

"Then be he, but not a nuisance."

He wriggled across to her, and kissed her on the back of her head.

"Might be work, come the long days."

He could not remember the name of the farmer who offered him work.

"Where?"

"Farm."

"Which?"

"One not far."

"You so drunk, your memory be muddled as an old man's."

He pulled her to him, and her warmth aroused him.

"No, Nicholas. 'Tis late, and you be sodden with cider."

"You my wife. 'Tis your duty."

He was too heavy for her, and it was too late to argue. The last time they had raised their voices, their neighbour had banged on the wall with a shoe.

"No, please. I don't want to!" she protested.

He did not take long, could not even remember going to sleep on top of her, or her exertions rolling him off. She sobbed into her pillow, and resolved to see Connie and Bea in the morning.

When Misterton awoke, he was sick in the chamberpot. Ruth had gone out early. The house was in mourning. It had changed. Things he had lovingly made did not talk to him; he was an intruder. Head in hands, he recalled Ruth's struggles, the knee brought up suddenly to stop him, and her cry when he violated her.

He dressed, left, and never went back while she was alive.

Bea rocked her; Connie stroked her hair.

"I can't tell you. 'Tis too horrible!"

"Drunk as a Lord, you say?" said Bea.

"Men!" exclaimed Connie. "They be selfish, all on 'em."

"Maybe I should have told him," sighed Ruth. "Then he might not have gone to the inn and drowned himself in cider. 'Tis my fault."

"Don't you go blaming yourself, girl. Told him what?"

Ruth swallowed.

"That I missed my time two full moons and a sickle."

Chapter Seventeen

On the way back to Higher Bockhampton, Misterton and Maisie took frequent rests as, though her cheeks were fuschias, her strength had not fully returned, following her illness. She linked her arm with his, gaining support, and reassurance that she would be looked after.

The question, when it came, was expected, and Misterton was ready with an answer. He would not lie, after what had passed between them. During her convalescence, he had watched over her, fed her, talked to her, wiped her face so gently that she knew he cared for her. So openly had he helped her, that the others had accepted him as a saviour. And when she was almost better, capable of walking, and had, once again, flesh on her bones, she had gone to his bed, so that he knew she cared for him.

"What did you do wrong?" she asked.

"Nothing."

"Then why must you leave?"

"I mended a broken angel in Bridport, and pretended I was Palfreyman, so that the stonemason would send him the bill."

Maisie giggled.

"'Tis so?"

"'Tis so and just. We must all pay, Maisie, for our sins."

"And what he done wrong, pray, to make 'ee trick him so?"

"You could have died. You needed a doctor, but he wouldn't pay for one."

"Masters be like that, Nicholas. Don't you know?"

"'Twas his responsibility whether he liked it or not."

Maisie giggled again, and squeezed his arm, when she realised what his ruse meant.

"And you did that for me?" she gasped.

"There will come a time when our masters be cut down, too. We are all born and die. Palfreyman and his like need reminding."

Soon they were passing the Hardys' cottage. Jemima was gathering herbs, sniffing them, and putting them in her basket.

"Mrs. Hardy," acknowledged Misterton, raising his hat.

Jemima looked up, still crouching.

"Nicholas," she replied. "You back?"

"Yes. Farm not worked out. Well, the farm be fine, but 'tis the master and I lock horns too much."

"I'm sorry to hear that. I'll tell Thomas when he returns. Here. You give your mother these."

Jemima took the herbs to the gate, and smiled at Maisie.

"This be Maisie," introduced Misterton. "She come with me from the farm."

"Pleased to meet you," said Jemima.

"'Tis a beautiful garden, all colours and scents."

Jemima held the basket under Maisie's nose.

"They go well in clothes drawers, though best to hang them up to dry," advised Jemima. "Go well in a stew."

Maisie took them from her.

Jemima watched them up the lane, and smiled.

"They be like a bride's posy," she chuckled.

Maisie began to feel nervous, once the lane became heath. She knew that Misterton would have to explain again. He had described his mother, told Maisie how she waddled like a duck, now that her legs had shrunk so much that she needed a stick, one with a silver button on, to help her move.

"She sleeps a lot, and Emily says she talks to father, who been dead and gone, these last few years," explained Misterton.

"What will you tell her and Emily about me?" asked Maisie.

"The truth: that you be my love."

"No, Nicholas, no! That will surely turn her against me. 'Tis the way with mothers and sons."

"But she baint a simpleton. Her words be no weathervane to what she means, but she knows that if I bring a woman home, then 'tis sure she aint a stranger to me."

Emily was not yet home. Mrs. Misterton was peeling potatoes on the table.

"Nicholas? You home?"

"Yes, mother. My room still empty?"

His mother looked at Maisie.

"'Taint my strongest point, girl, names, but you be Edith, if I remembers correctly. You better?"

"I be Maisie, Mrs. Misterton, and I be much better now, thank 'ee."

Misterton looked at Maisie, who put the error down to what he had said about his mother's memory.

"Maisie be my girl, mother."

"Your wife? You two married?"

"No, mother. Maisie my girl, and we be wanting to stay a while. No work at the farm now, so we'll stay, and Maisie can lend a hand, so's you can rest."

"Well, I don't know when things will blow in any more, but I'm glad they do, 'specially at the quiet of the day, when thoughts pester me."

"Thoughts, mother?"

"Yes, Nicholas. You'll know what thoughts when you as saggy as me, though it don't bear painting them with words when we got guests. Come sit down, Edith. Your legs be as wobbly as mine, coming all that way from Dorchester."

Maisie looked at Misterton for guidance.

"Emily don't know we're come. She back soon?"

"When the shadows slip in, usually."

Emily was getting ready to leave when Cook beckoned to her. Confidentially, Cook said, "Miss. Palfreyman would like to see you upstairs before you go. 'Taint you done wrong, girl, so don't go a-fretting."

Emily picked up her coat, and did as requested.

Florence looked pale. Since her brother had returned from Bath, and had begun preparations for his wedding, she had withdrawn from her staff, giving instructions to only a few when necessary.

"Emily, I'll come straight to the point. It has been an unspoken fact that, since I knew you were Nicholas' brother, I have taken a special interest in you. You had a desire to read and write, and how I have marvelled at your progress! Now, though, I choose you as the first member of staff to know that I shall be leaving Palfreyman Manor. I am, of course, delighted that my brother is to marry, but it puts me in a position where I must find myself a different place to live."

Emily heard the tremulousness of Florence's voice, and knew that her departure was unwanted. Rumours had been exchanged in the kitchen, and Cook had crushed them. The news that Palfreyman was to marry had been well received, on the whole, by the staff, but it had been followed by wild speculation about his wife-to-be.

"After all these years, Miss? 'Tis a shame. You'll be missed, especially by me. I know you will say it be nothing, but you changed my life with books and a pen."

Florence swallowed.

"Well, you are kind to say so, but I'm hoping we may not be so easily parted. I'll need a house-keeper. I am to buy Monksbury Manor, and would like you to come with me. There is, of course, your mother to consider, but she could come with you, have her own apartment. What do you say, Emily?"

Florence looked at Emily's down-turned eyes, and knew the answer. Emily gave a little cough, and began what she had been rehearsing, and intended delivering on her last day.

"'Tis wondrous kind, but my mother be a beam in our cottage, which would split and crash down beout her. Why, she married and raised a son and daughter in it! And she talks to it. I've heard her. 'Twould most like kill her to leave, though there be another reason why I cannot go with you: I, too, am leaving, to become a teacher. You taught me to read and write, and now I want to help others. Had a letter, see, to train, so I be off to Bath, next week."

It was now Florence's turn to look down at the floor. Her future would be elsewhere, and without the girl for whom she had high hopes.

"Then you must fly, Emily. You will make an excellent teacher. And does your brother know? He will miss you."

Emily shook her head.

"Not yet, though 'tis pressing. I wrote a letter of acceptance, and have received my instructions. Separation will hurt mother. She lost father, and Nicholas, on and off, and now me. All my life, I've looked after her, and now I must go, and hurt her, most probably."

"We all have our hearts broken, Emily, and there's very little we can do. Will you write and let me know your news, once you've settled in? I shall inform Robert, this evening."

"Thank 'ee, Miss."

Spontaneously, Florence embraced her.

"Goodbye, Emily."

"'Bye, Miss."

When Emily arrived home, she froze. Nicholas, and a woman. Maisie curtseyed, embarrassing Misterton.

"Tongue gone to sleep, girl? You be late," said Mrs. Misterton.

"Home again," said Misterton. "Back and forwards, me. Off I go, all at once, then back I come. I'm on a piece of string that this place keep a-winding in, and letting out."

Maisie had brought nothing from the farm. Emily looked at her mended clothes. Firstly, Edith, now this woman, who was smiling in attire as patched as the fields.

"This be—" began Mrs. Misterton.

"Maisie," jumped in Misterton. "We come to stay, Emily, on account of me having no job at the farm any more."

"And I've come with him," added Maisie, "if that be all right with you."

"First time I seed your tongue idle, girl. What you got to say?" prompted Mrs. Misterton.

Emily went to her room, brought down a letter, and handed it to her brother, who read it.

"You tell her, Nicholas, for I can't, though it be Providence you a-spun back here, me going, next week."

Maisie took a step backwards, not wishing to intrude into the family's upheaval.

"Maisie be my girl, Emily. From the farm."

Emily looked at her and laughed happily, not expecting such openness.

"Then you come at the right time, Maisie. Nicholas Misterton be like the tide, back and forth, but he needs a bank like Chesil, to catch and keep a bit of him, when he goes too far!"

"Don't know about saving him, but he saved me."

"Edith been ill, but better now," informed Mrs. Misterton.

It was awkward, eating with a stranger. They avoided talking about Emily's plans, which sat at the table as an invisible guest. There was plenty of clattering of cutlery and pots, and Emily winced.

"I got a bit put by, till you find work again," she offered, when her mother had gone outside, for a breath of air.

Maisie turned away, began to tidy pots near the sink, to allow a private conversation.

"You need all you got. Got a tiddy bit." Misterton nodded towards Maisie. "She got nothing 'cept me."

Emily went over to Maisie.

"You go in my bed tonight, and I'll take Nicholas'. Come me going, Monday, he can have it back."

"Thank 'ee."

"Won't take everything, Monday. Got one or two things might fit you, you can have, if you come light."

"Upped and came as we be. No place for fine wardrobes on the farm," explained Misterton.

"You going to try Mr. Hardy again?"

"Wife going to mention she seen me again. Depends on his jobs. Maisie can do in the house, help mother cope."

"Don't want to get in the way, though."

There was extra in Emily's money, on her last day. Florence insisted she take it; there would be, no doubt, unforeseen expenditure. Emily handed over her address in Bath, though reluctantly. She intended the fresh start to mean a clean break from all but her family, but Florence wanted to let her know about Monksbury, give her the option of returning if she did not, after all, like teaching. The parting, when it came, was tearful for Florence.

"Send me news, if you do not object, of your brother, from time to time. It was none of my doing, his dismissal," she made clear.

"'Tis past remembrance, on his part," said Emily.

Florence looked hurt by this, even though that had not been Emily's intention.

"What will he do?"

"What he will. That be his way. He can make furniture, turn his hand to most things, but when he sees wrong, 'tis like a weed he must pull out the ground."

On the morning of her departure, Emily kissed her mother, and walked down to the Hardys' cottage. Thomas was waiting in the lane, up on the cart.

"Ready?" he asked her.

She turned to Misterton.

"Write you safe," he instructed.

"Let me know how you all are, from time to time."

"Thank 'ee," Misterton said to Thomas.

Emily kissed her brother on his cheek.

Thomas looked away.

Jemima stepped back from the window.

Misterton turned back up the lane, wondering how he would explain to his mother that Emily had left home.

"Bath? Where be that? That be a holy place? Your father once took me to see the cathedral if 'tis the same. Big one, 'twas. Not as pretty as Stinsford. Like a block of stone had fallen from the sky. Or be that Wells? Went up Glastonbury hill, and, the next day, my body ached in the squeeze of a fever."

"You remember all that, mother?"

"And more. At the top of the hill, your father pointed to the countryside - 'twas like we were up in the clouds – and said to me, 'See all this?' And I nods, my eyesight a lot better than it be today. And he says, ''Tis one of God's paintings, missing only a face, these centuries, to set against the background, but now it got one: you, dearest.' Then he stoops down on one knee, and says, 'God, I would like to buy this masterpiece, and pay for it with all my heart and soul.' Then he asks me to marry him, and after all that romancing, I says, 'Yes.'"

"And you remember all that?"

But she did not answer. Instead she went up to Emily's room.

Maisie was wearing a blue dress Emily had given her. In the corner, she was sewing, reinforcing a split seam in her old dress, which Misterton had urged her to throw away, but which she had kept. She had held words back, that morning, knowing that Misterton needed to think about others that needed speaking. Her eyes did not stray from her stitches.

"She gone. What mother just said, I never knowed. So much more locked away, probably, in that little head of hers. Never knowed father was a poet like that. He always used words like a hammer on me."

Maisie did not look up. Misterton could see that she was thinking about something, that each stitch was a barely disguised, deliberate step to a question.

"Your face be full of things you want to say," he remarked. Calmly, she put down her sewing, and looked up at him. Usually, she smiled when she saw how he loved her. "'Tis like cream gone off."

"Nicholas, there is something I been a-fretting over since that first day, and now I must let it speak."

"No point bottling it, girl."

Maisie breathed out slowly.

"Why did you not tell me that Edith had been here after she killed Wareham?"

Chapter Eighteen

The young boy followed his father silently, a deferential distance between them, to a clearing in the scrub. The day before, Jacob had scooped slices with his swinging spade, leaving a circle. Nicholas had scraped with his rake the tufts and sods into mounds. Jacob had wiped the tears of sweat from his brow, and muttered to his son, "That'll do." Nicholas had not responded, had merely returned to the cottage, knowing that he must be patient.

Nicholas now looked up into his father's eyes, as a dog into his master's when it wants feeding. Jacob nodded towards the trees.

"Small, dropped bits first. Put them there in the circle," he instructed, "so's they be to hand."

"And then will you light the fire?" Nicholas asked excitedly.

"The kindling's to get it born, and it'll soon die beout a branch or two to go on the top. When they catch, we get big flames."

Nicholas ran off; it was a chance to please his father, express regret for what he had said to his mother, and for which his father had strapped him till he had screamed.

Axe resting on his shoulder like a soldier's rifle, Jacob gave him a wide berth. Knowing which branches would yield and blaze the best, he worked quickly. Thud. Thud. Thud. Crack. He stacked the sections, gathered them in his arm as he had done Nicholas to thrash him, and strode back to the circle, where his son and the kindling were waiting.

Surprising himself, Jacob acknowledged Nicholas' efforts with a nod.

"Like this," Jacob said. "First, grass, then the twigs."

"How will it set to burn?"

"With this."

The tinderbox lay grey and lifeless in his hand.

"Can I do it?"

"You must, but first, build more kindling, and stuff the gaps with dry grass. It's like making a chair, only with grass and wood. It looks easy, but it baint."

Nicholas watched and did his bit, but overly gently with the grass, irritating his father.

"Bold," ordered Jacob. "Won't get anywhere like that."

Soon, Nicholas mastered the art, began to itch for the tinderbox. Jacob stood back to appraise their work. It was time. He showed Nicholas the flint, explained how the sparks came into existence. Nicholas practised, and when perfection was achieved, he crouched.

"The grass, remember. Then blow gently till it takes. There'll be orange, a little crackling, like a walnut splitting, and a wisp of smoke. It's then you whisper to it, till the flames get confident, and you cuddle it with more kindling, but don't smother it, or stray too close, or you'll singe your hair."

Nicholas followed his father's instructions, and the fire began to click. He waited for a sign that his father was pleased, and when it came – no word, just his habitual nod – Nicholas whooped and started running round the fire, leaping ecstatically, eyes fixed on it, lest it expire.

Jacob let him run wild, then stretched out his arm, and caught him.

"Heed it, or you'll let it go out with your stupidity. You've only litten it. Now you must feed it, and raise it, as your mother and me have you. 'Tis only a tiddy thing, just now, and you must leather it, if necessary, make it eat its food, or it will not grow. You must control it, boy. Only then can you sit and warm yourself. Fires are dangerous, 'less you guard 'em."

Nicholas relaxed in the grip.

"Let me go, father."

"When I say. Come you a man, you do as you like. Till then, I must tell you how 'tis, or I baint a proper father."

Nicholas obeyed his father's commands, and poked a log into the heart of the heat.

"Why are we building a fire?" asked Nicholas. "'Tis not cold, though 'tis the tip of the day."

"Don't you know? Can't you feel why?"

Nicholas looked at his father staring through flames like ragged flags.

"'Tis powerful hot."

"Hutch closer."

Nicholas loved a dare, and wanted to show he was not afraid. He inched forwards, till he was nearly licked by the flames, stung by a spark. He jumped back, the heat too fierce, and melting the landscape.

"I'll burn, closer. 'Tis scorching me."

"Then you now know 'tis foolish to do what can harm you."

With that, Jacob stood up and started to walk back to his cottage, leaving his son torn between following him and minding the fire.

"Where you going, father?"

"Keep the fire alive till I return," replied Jacob, not looking back.

The big logs lashed out, making it harder to feed. The heat fended Nicholas off, so that he had to throw on more wood, instead of placing it.

Soon, he would run out. Off he darted to the trees, and he trod on a stiff squirrel. He knelt. It had not decomposed. He prodded it, to check it was not alive, and picked it up by its brush. The flies abandoned their meal in a black cloud.

His father had not returned. It would not be long. The squirrel was dead. What did it matter?

Nicholas' arm was a pendulum, each swing a plucking-up of courage, till he released it into the air, and watched it land in the fire's heart. Nicholas listened for the squirrel's squeal, and watched it burn to nothing. Other creatures followed: worms, an eyeless bird, an adder. He saw that they all burned the same. Then anything on which he could lay his hands: ferns, toadstools, berries. All disappeared.

He was desperate to maintain the height of the flames. He did not want his father to see that he had failed, that he had let him down. There would be no strapping, but there would be shame. He grabbed everything, even the sods of turf, which began to dampen it. Where was the squirrel now?

His father returned. Nicholas saw him walking purposefully. The fire survived, just. Nicholas assessed it, was unsure what his father would say.

"There be no more wood," explained Nicholas. "I looked."

"And why is that?"

On the floor lay the axe, and Nicholas had missed the invitation to use it. If only he had seen it, he would have wielded it, brought branches crashing to the floor!

"I wasn't sure . . . the axe . . . "

"You did not think to do as I had done?"

Nicholas hung his head. The squirrel had diverted him, set him wondering.

"I wasn't sure."

"'Keep the fire alive till I return,' I said."

"'Tis alive. See. I have not let it out. Stand near, and it will burn you. I have not let it out."

Jacob nodded.

"'Tis true it lives, but more feebly than before. The flames are tired, too friendly. And do you know why, Nicholas?"

Nicholas looked at the fire. The sun was setting, the gnats swarming like a sandstorm.

"No, father."

"Because you have fed it vermin, not wood. Learn this, Nicholas: that you must accept wisdom when it is offered, and not go your own way."

"Will you strap me, father?"

"No, son, but you must obey me, or you will never learn, and will always have to suffer the consequences. Do not merely listen, but accept that I have discovered things before you. Now, come in. Your mother has tea ready."

Nicholas was glad to be in the cottage, where his mother could make him feel like a son again. Emily was at the table, on which her mother had placed bread, blue vinney, and soup. Nicholas' face was camouflaged with black smudges from the fire. His mother glanced at him, then at her husband, who had been silent, tense, since he had come in, and given his daughter crumbs for answers.

"What's gone off?" asked Mrs. Misterton. "He been bad or something?"

Jacob looked at Nicholas, who was now at the table, next to Emily.

"Nothing," he answered. "Least, what's not been put right."

Mrs. Misterton scowled.

"You been up a chimney, boy?" she asked Nicholas. "You a sweep!"

He shook his head self-pitifully.

"Been making the fire with father."

"Tell her what you made it with," ordered Jacob.

Mrs. Misterton busied herself with the food, pushed the cheese towards her husband, and placed soup carefully in front of Emily.

"Let us eat and put the fire behind us," she pleaded.

"When his food's finished, he's to snuff the flames, and be off to bed."

It was as if Nicholas had left the room. His father's eyes roved everywhere but on him. The cheese stuck in Nicholas' throat; the soup stank of decay. All he wanted to do was to find a different place to be.

He began to smother the fire. As well as digging and throwing soil, he searched for the squirrel. Perhaps, it had escaped. Otherwise, he had murdered it.

From a distance, his father watched him.

"Is it done?" asked Jacob, coming to inspect. "Don't want it to rear again."

Nicholas nodded.

"'Tis covered up."

They went back to the cottage, separately. There was light enough for Nicholas to amuse himself. In the outbuilding, he listened for his father's voice. Through the window laced with cobwebs, he saw Emily holding their mother's hand. The lesson was the names of flowers. The tools were asleep in the oily box his father had made. There was order to the place. His father knew where to put his hands on what he wanted.

The plane was first. It was an important tool, one his father used regularly. Nicholas hid it up his shirt, backed outside, and leapt over the fence. In case his father had seen him, he ran at full speed. It had to be far enough away to deter a thorough search. The undergrowth, where he stopped, panting, was thick with brambles. He slid the plane under it, and stepped back to check that it looked undisturbed.

On his return, he picked some mushrooms, which he stuffed inside his shirt. His mother would be pleased. He often gathered some for her, when asked. It was easy work, something to keep his father off his back, an alibi. They always smelt sweet, sizzling in butter with wild chives.

He was about to climb back over the fence. His father, unaware that Nicholas was in the vicinity, was walking towards his place of work. There was little for Jacob to do, no progress to be made. For a moment, Nicholas wondered whether he should shout to him, let him know that he had picked enough to fill a pan. Jacob loved his workshop, had even decided to install a stove, so that he could work in cold weather. Then Nicholas gasped: he had forgotten to lock the door. His father would notice. Quickly, Nicholas threw away the key.

His mother sniffed the mushrooms scattered on the table, and looked at him. Usually, she had to ask him to pick them. Emily began to count them, but stopped at five.

"You been busy," observed Mrs. Misterton. "Like spinning tops, most of 'em."

"There's more than five," said Emily.

"Where be father?" asked Nicholas.

Mrs. Misterton sniffed, wiped her hands on her dress, and knew something was not right. He was bound to have seen his father.

"Up the path. One or two bits to do."

Nicholas knew she knew. It was impossible for him to be nonchalant. Never before had he brought her mushrooms, unasked. She left them where they had rolled, and he knew they had not convinced her.

Emily felt awkward, wriggled in her seat, and wished her mother would do something with them, those white, earthy accusations. She looked at Nicholas, who dared not move from his seat.

"We got mushrooms?" asked Emily.

Silently, her mother placed them, one by one, on a plate.

The door opened.

"Nicholas, I want to show you something," ordered his father.

Nicholas avoided looking him in the eye.

Mrs. Misterton turned her back on them, began to slice the mushrooms, and put them in the pan. On slid a curl of butter, a tickling of chopped chives.

"Will you be long?" she asked, unable to face her husband.

"Not long."

Nicholas followed him.

Emily watched her brother, who was tethered to her father.

"That boy!" sighed Mrs. Misterton. "'Tis hard to be a mother, girl."

Emily swung her legs under the table, and dared not look up.

When Jacob returned, the mushrooms had shrunk, had sweetened the air. His wife had fetched in the logs for the night.

"You ready?" she asked Jacob.

"Need to eat."

Emily pleaded with him, and he kissed her forehead. His wife brushed his hair with her lips. Eyes still stinging from the smoke from the fire, he chewed the mushrooms, shoved them against a ripping of bread with his knife. Emily smiled when he winked at her.

In the pan were the brown mushrooms she had saved for Nicholas.

When the silence had stretched to breaking, she asked, "Will he be long?"

Jacob sat back in his chair.

"'Till he be as clear as the sky with me. My plane and key be gone. The door was open, and the key had walked. Don't add up, to me. A magpie come? A jackdaw? I know 'tis 'cause he hates me, and 'tis so with sons and fathers, betimes. 'Tis nature. But the truth, my love, is the north star, which guides the shepherds and furze-cutters. 'Till he tell the truth, be wise, he will take the wrong path and be lost."

Mrs. Misterton sighed, wiped a tail of hair from her eyes with the back of her hand.

Emily shuffled in her seat.

"Nicholas' mushrooms will go wrong," she pointed out.

They all stared at the pan.

Mrs. Misterton went to the window, and looked up towards the workshop.

"You use the spare key?" she asked.

"Can't use the one I hides in the tree. That gone."

"When he come out?" asked his wife, now tearful.

"When he own up, and tells me where he hidden the key and plane. Now pass me those mushrooms a-withering in the pan. No point a-wasting 'em."

Chapter Nineteen

Mabel had been bending two lengths of willow round her head so that, when tied, they sat comfortably on it. They were wrapped round each other, like strands of rope, but not tautly, leaving spaces in which she intended to place flowers, making a crown of colour, on her wedding day. She would be George's queen.

Zachariah had granted them two days off, and had grumbled to Victoria. It meant extra work for him, though it was the fact that he had not been invited to the wedding that rankled.

"Oh, father. Don't 'ee go on so. 'Tis Mabel's day," scolded Victoria. "And we must buy her something for their life together."

"Well, don't 'ee go mad with the money, which be as rare as rain, this summer. Lost too many lambs in spring, and prices are as poor as peasants."

"I shall buy her a thing or two for her trousseau, which shall be pretty enough to please George, too, if they hang on her right, which she has the figure for. Or do you have a different idea?"

Zachariah shook his head in mock-disgust.

"'Taint for me to say, though it don't become you to go a-telling your father the ways of women."

Victoria laughed.

"Why, your cheeks be berries!" she teased. "'Tis false modesty, as we all know, with men."

Mabel had wanted to invite Victoria, but thought that the master's presence would darken her day.

"We don't have to have him there," explained George. "The day will shine, and the walls will be warm till late. Why ruin it by inviting a man who never has a good word to say to us?"

"Because he's our master and pays us. But you be right, my dear. 'Tis our day, and I'll love you till my last breath, which, God willing, will be when these hairs of mine be grey and stiff as wire."

A bride's veil of early mist covered the valley, on their wedding day. Edna, Mabel, Wilfred, and George took the cart to the church in the village of Marshwood. The view back across the vale mesmerised them as, by the time they arrived, the mist had lifted, and the hills and fields looked as if they had been polished by the light.

Wilfred had long since overcome his hurt at Mabel choosing George. In time, he had come to realise that it was possible to see beyond her attractions to her foibles, which might, he suspected, develop into more alarming defects. No, he was pleased to see George the winner, if any man or woman could be deemed to be a winner before they have had time to become better acquainted.

Mabel's wedding dress had been handed down to her by her mother, who had guessed that her daughter would be the same size as herself when she, too, had been married. And when Mabel emerged from the women's sleeping quarters, all in blue silk, and crowned with pink carnations, poppies, and forget-me-nots, her groom gasped.

"'Tis a vision of an angel and not of this life," he said.

"Your words be as welcome, my love, as this day, which be the beginning of a new life for us."

Edna wiped the tears from her eyes and said, "Mabel, he's right. You are an angel, and, George, take 'ee good care of her, and watch you don't clip her wings so much that she don't fly as before. Angels baint angels 'less they able to spread their wings, from time to time. We all need wings, only some of us aint growed 'em yet, though our time be said to come, one day. Everyone have a time to fly, and this be yours, girl."

The vicar was at the church door, ready to receive them. His thin face and long, pointed nose gave him the appearance of a crow. The light streamed through the windows, painting the pews and stone red with the blood of Christ.

Mabel's mother's wedding ring fitted – just. The only bridesmaid, Edna, glanced at Wilfred, who smiled and offered his arm, which she took.

Outside the church, Edna took from the cart a bag of red rose petals, which she had plucked, that morning, and with which she showered George and Mabel.

"Your carriage awaits, Ma'am," invited Wilfred.

The vicar watched them disappear down the lane. He felt the warm hand of the sun on his back. An unusually intense calmness possessed him. The simplicity of the wedding party's presentation had affected him. Above him, a buzzard was sailing in the sky.

"Let no man put asunder," he repeated wistfully.

Then he locked the church door, and went to the vicarage for lunch.

At Gifford's Farm, there were refreshments: cider, and sandwiches they had covered up to prevent flies helping themselves. The men lifted the table out onto the grass, watched by a variety of animals, which had quietly gathered to greet the newly married couple.

Nervously, Zachariah said to Victoria, "Ready? They're sat. You got the cake?"

"'Tis all here, with the juice of the berries a-marbling the yellow. I'm not Victoria Stockwood if this baint the best cake I ever made. Smells so sweet we've to watch for wasps, who'll find cake and cider as difficult to ignore as us."

When the wedding party saw them approaching, their conversation faded. Victoria smiled weakly, sensing their apprehension, and holding aloft their gift of the cake.

"'Tis a cake," whispered Mabel excitedly. "Miss. Victoria brought us a wedding cake, as sure as you're my husband."

Zachariah had smartened himself up so much that he felt odd, a caricature, as if he had volunteered for the role of himself in a play. Behind him slunk Megan, expecting a crumb or two.

"'Tis such a God-given fire of a day that I've baked you this cake in it, for your wedding. I hope you'll be happy, and that you'll be blessed further, one day."

George looked at Mabel, puzzled.

"Thank 'ee, Miss. Victoria, and 'tis kind to wish us well, though George got to get used to me yet afore we gets to hearing the bleat of a tiddy one."

"Children, George," whispered Wilfred, "case you missed the point."

Victoria placed her gift on the table.

"'Tis kind of you," echoed George. "Will you join us?"

Victoria turned to her father, who stepped forward and nodded.

"I hope you'll both be as happy as Victoria's mother and I were, till the Lord sent for her," he began.

"That be a long time ago," reminded Victoria, not wishing to dampen the spirits of the gathering.

"'Tis only yesterday, but no matter. We were married in the same church as you, only the vicar were a more well fed man, and not the scarecrow we have now. The old tenant farmer – a man as suited to farming as a sailor – let me move into the cottage down the lane. As you know, 'tis the dwelling of spiders and bluebottles and—"

"Father, why you going all round Dorset to get to the bottom of the pathway?"

"Hush, girl. 'Tis only my way of saying things. No matter. Anyway, I can't have you, George, or Mabel, an honest, married woman, living under the same roof as Wilfred and Edna. It baint right, so I'm giving you the key to the cottage, and with a bucket of water, and a brush, and a tolerable airing, you gets yourself off to a pretty start. 'Taint a palace, even though you look a princess with those flowers a-threaded in your hair, but we were happy as lambs in it, and so bill you be. Chimbey'll need—"

"Father!" interrupted Victoria. "Give 'em the key!"

With trembling hand, Zachariah gave the key to George, and shook his hand. Mabel offered her cheek, which Zachariah kissed, and everyone laughed loudly when a carnation poked him in the eye.

"Thank 'ee, master," began George. "We'd be glad to accept, but it leave these two short of company, even though they know each other well."

"I'd rather sleep in the field than make Edna feel awkward. What say you?" asked Wilfred. "You bear be under the same roof as just me?"

"'Twill be strange, at first, but it baint the talk of Dorset for a man and a woman to share a roof, in these circumstances."

"Then, we won't dwell on such tiddy matters," summarised Zachariah. "And now I must go do the jobs others have escaped from, for a couple of days!"

They all laughed, and then the Stockwoods withdrew.

All afternoon, the other four were making the cottage habitable again.

"'Tis tolerable clean," said Mabel. "'Twill do for now."

Edna cried again, and walked back up the lane.

Outside the farmhouse, a horse was tethered to a fence. Victoria answered the door. It was Gabriel, who had ridden hard, and was slightly breathless. He ran his hand over his hair, to make himself more presentable.

"Gabriel? Is there something wrong? Your face be burning."

"Yes. I mean, no. I mean . . . Victoria, there is something I have to say to you, but not here. May we go somewhere else?"

And so they walked, till they had slipped out of view of the farmhouse. Only the birds and Wilfred could see them.

*

Robert Palfreyman tried his best not to appear to push his sister into Monksbury Manor, but she removed thence with undignified haste, which invited disapprobation. Her goodbyes were brief, her staff torn between their allegiance to their master and their urge to follow her to Monksbury.

"'Tis better we stay put," advised Cook, when Florence had tried to lure a few of her favourites away. "We be like part of the building, solid and reliable. Been here years, some of us. And who's to say Master Robert's wife won't treat us kindly?"

The kitchen girls, heads hung on their breasts like sleeping pigeons, were inclined to agree.

Improvements were made to Palfreyman Manor at almost the rate God created the Earth and populated it with beasts and Adam and Eve. This effort served to persuade Florence that her tenure was over. There was no fuss. Her furniture and other possessions were boxed and transported to Monksbury. Her brother had lent her two maids for a week, which, he pointed out, would be ample time to appoint her own staff. Indeed, though he was greatly preoccupied with more important matters, he would make enquiries among his friends and staff at The King's Arms, in Dorchester.

Robert himself made clear to the vicar their requirements: extensive and joyous ringing of the bells, three hymns that everyone would know, even if they could not read the words in the book, and little preaching. This last was very important as there would be a few young children present. He apologised to the vicar for this indulgence – he, personally, wanted no children there, but Rose had insisted – and hoped that his curtailment of any preaching would restrict the children's boredom. The vicar's eyes bulged and almost popped out at this, but the prestige of hosting such a wedding in his parish, and the money he would receive, were more than enough to persuade his eyes to stay put. Indeed, the sum Robert offered prompted the vicar to invite him to, "Fill the church to the rafters with the little cherubs if you like."

Florence used the servants borrowed from her former home to good effect, and soon the rooms, cold as an ice-house, even in August, became habitable again. When the day of the wedding arrived, she was most glad that she was not suffering the anxiety pervading the corridors of her former home. Word arrived that Master Robert was not himself, that his temper had been unleashed, in unacceptable measure, on almost everyone.

"'Taint that he wants this just so, or that. 'Tis like someone – and we all know who it be, and that be natural in an engagement – has wivven a wand, and cast a spell on him, and turned him into an ogre from a fairytale. That's what they be saying. Word is, his head'll explode if he don't let the steam out," reported Cook to Florence, who could not help giggling.

"Poor Robert. He does get all worked up about things."

Florence was determined not to be pushed out of the church as well as her home, and had a dress made which would not place the bride in her shadow, but would undoubtedly invite interesting comparisons.

Florence made her presence known to her brother on her arrival at the church. He looked ghastly, told her he had not slept a wink.

"There's a big crowd outside. Not the whole of Dorchester, be reassured, and a few you would rather see outside than in, but enough to create quite an atmosphere of excitement and expectation," she told him, his embrace reminding her that their years together still meant much to him. "Your side of the church is almost full, but Rose's family and friends are conspicuous by their absence."

"Their coaches cannot be far away, I expect, though she will be late. It's eleven now, and the vicar comes to take his place."

Florence placed her arm on his.

"Let him wait. You're paying him enough, aren't you?"

Robert muttered into Thomas Hardy's ear, and the Stinsford church orchestra, who had looked forward to playing in grander surroundings, shuffled their music sheets again, igniting speculation, the flames of which swept down the pews like a heath fire.

Thomas Hardy just had time to whisper to his son, Tom, before they played their first piece for the second time.

"When the moon be a moulding blue vinney, there be something afoot, 'tis certain. I said to your mother, last night, 'There be veins and sores all over the moon's yellow.' And she replied, 'That be a sign, truly.' I been to more weddings than there be tatties in my garden, and if this one don't go wrong, then I'm not Thomas Hardy, builder and fiddler and sometime master of the reel."

"Well, father, I've read that marriage is not a coat that keeps everyone warm, and though you and mother have kept well wrapped up, over the years, I imagine it starts with a button popping off, then a hem dropping, and so on, till the marriage leaves them both naked and a-shivering in the frosty air," replied Tom.

"'Tis true, Tom. And you tell it almost like a poet instead of a tolerable architect."

The vicar strode purposefully down the aisle towards a stranger who had beckoned to him. The vicar read the note the man gave him. Meanwhile, the congregation, struck by the vicar's pace, turned and ceased speaking. One by one, the fiddlers gave up their bowing.

The man left, and the vicar returned to the front, where he spoke quietly to Palfreyman. Florence saw her brother stagger, then compose himself.

"What is it?" she asked, stepping forward.

Palfreyman handed her the note, and rushed out of the church, leaving the vicar to explain to the congregation.

"No more merry tunes," ordered Thomas Hardy. "The blue vinney moon, 'twas, as I knew 'twould be."

"Providence, father. People paint their future, but 'tis beyond some to frame and hang it. Blue vinney moons or no, there'll be no wedding here today," added Tom.

The crowd misunderstood Palfreyman's appearance, and cheered, but he shouted, "What are you all staring at, you idiots? There is no wedding. It's all been a mistake. Now, let me pass."

He started to push his way through but came up against a man, who stood his ground.

"You should have sent for the doctor, and this be another reminder, master, though, this time, 'tis someone else apart from me delivers it. And I've come all this way to wish you and your bride a long and happy marriage! Well, now 'tis all broke, I can return to Maisie, and tell her you baint married after all," Misterton said quietly.

"Get out of my way or I'll have you flogged!"

Misterton smiled and let him pass. The cheers had become jeers. Florence had seen the confrontation, but before she could reach him, Misterton had disappeared into the crowd.

Back at Monksbury, she saw a young woman walking up to the door. The coach slowed, and the woman allowed it to pass. Florence glanced at her visitor, who smiled faintly.

The woman had made an effort with her appearance, and waited, at a respectful distance, to be invited forward.

"Do I know you? Your face is familiar, and yet I cannot fix it to a time and place. It must have been at Palfreyman Manor. On the farm, perhaps?"

"No, madam. Never been there before. Came about the job I hears about at The King's Arms. It aint gone has it? Just my luck!"

"I'm sorry, but this is an awkward time to see you. Do I detect a London accent?"

"Lord save me! Make me stick out, does it?"

Florence smiled; the woman's easy manner was light relief after the awful scenes in Dorchester.

"A little. People round here talk differently. The job, you say? Any experience?"

"I'll say! The lot: kitchen, waiting, ironing, washing."

"All right. References?"

"The best, written no less than by Mr. Charles Dickens himself!" Florence laughed.

"Then I might be able to offer you something. Now, do you have a name?"

"Just the one me mother gave me, but it's as good as any."

"Well?"

Polly and Tilly have got me this far, but it don't pay to wear them out, thought the woman.

"Sturminster, madam. I'm Nelly Sturminster."

Chapter Twenty

Misterton read the letter to himself, pleased that he had made good progress with his letters, and hoping that Emily, too, would be happy. Maisie busied herself with pointless jobs at the table to show she was not eavesdropping on private, family matters. Mrs. Misterton looked up at him, expecting him to convey its contents. It was still her house. Letters without explanation, and read silently under her nose, unsettled her.

"Who be that from?" she asked bluntly.

"Your daughter, Emily. She be settled in tolerable, and learning the children, who baint all angels, on account of their age. Still, 'tis well she crams their letters into their heads afore they get to my age. She'll send you some money at the end of the month."

Mrs. Misterton sniffed and took a swipe at him.

"Just as well with you not bringing in. You sniffing for work? 'Taint going to come a-knocking at the door. You got your father's way with wood. Bound to be something that way in Dorchester. You got the tools in the box a-lying as idle as you."

Maisie shot her a withering glance, though did not approve of Misterton's indolence, which had grown on him like lichen. She had always seen him as an active farmer, knew nothing about his father's tuition. Nor had she liked him ridiculing Robert Palfreyman, whose humiliation he had described in imaginative detail, and with excessive relish.

"He left me with barely enough breath in my body to strip a dandelion clock, 'tis true, but he must have had a heart to have proposed to his true love, and though 'tis cleft like an axed log, it don't mean he don't hurt. Money don't stop you having a sweetheart, so you should show charity, Nicholas," she had told him.

"And what charity he showed you when your breath a whisper?"

"That be the point, Nicholas. We be better than that. No money, but open hearts and a good mind towards others."

So, he felt outnumbered by the women, put in his place. And now he would be kept by his sister's money. Yet how could he tell them that he knew how it would go again with wood? Some pieces would sell, then it would all dry up like grass in an endless August, as it had done in Bridport, when Ruth had been alive, when he had first received a woman's rebuke for failing to bring money into the house.

He looked at Maisie, who was now as pretty as hawthorn blossom, and had never asked anything of him, had followed him without question. She will change towards me, one day, as Ruth did, he said to himself. Ruth pushed me further away from her, till I ran. And Maisie and her friends will soon forget what I did for them, and I will become a husk again.

He read the second letter outside. Woodpigeons and blackbirds replaced with notes of hope the censure of the women. When he had read the letter three times, to be sure of its message, he went for a walk in the woods, where the sun had not yet dried the morning's dew.

On his return, he sat Maisie down and held her hands.

"See these?"

"Feel their softness, too. Used to be rough. Fingers a-been like long pine cones to touch when you've been a-scrabbling in the soil, digging up turnips."

Misterton fixed her eyes, tightened his hold. Seeing this intimacy, and reminded of dead scenes from her own past, his mother slunk outside.

"And they will again be rough as father's rasp. There be a chance of work in Briddy. Thought once of being a stonemason, but he already got an apprentice. Rope-maker's there, though, and rope be always needed, to hang thieves and murderers, and to keep boats and ships at sea, and tied to the harbour wall. Can only ask. Heard they might be taking on, so I'll be gone in a day or two."

Maisie said, "But Emily's gone. Your mother."

"Stay with her, Maisie. Now her memory wanders like a chicken in a coop, she needs someone here."

"But if you make ropes in Briddy, will I not come with you?"

Misterton felt her hands slacken in his, relax in disappointment.

"You must stay here, and I will return in a few days."

Maisie withdrew.

"I will stay here when you go to see, but I won't leave you, Nicholas. Not now. Not now we so far down the lane together. I will be with you in Briddy, 'less the Lord says different, as he sometimes do when we aint paying heed. If you become a rope-maker, you must provide for your mother some other way."

"Let us see," concluded Misterton, frowning.

He waited on the fringe of Dorchester to find someone to take him to Bridport. In his pocket was a coin or two in case he needed to pay his way.

"Climb up," invited a man.

In the back of his cart were small items of furniture: chairs, a coalscuttle, a carpet, an oil lamp, a painting of a soldier.

"Obliged."

"Market day, tomorrow, see. Hope to make a penny or two from these."

Misterton looked back at the cargo.

"You trade for a living?"

"No. Mother died, the other day. Needs clearing out, she do. Sat on these chairs myself for years. No, she needs a-clearing from top to bottom. She been a squirrel. House full of stuff. You don't need a tub, do you?"

"No."

"That been my mother, a-hoarding till the walls began to bow outwards like an old man's legs."

All the way to Bridport, he described the extent of his mother's storage of worthless items, taking Misterton on a tour of the house, room by room, acquainting him with every nook and cranny.

That night, Misterton slept in a field, and saved the coins to buy breakfast.

He read the letter again. The clock in Bridport said he had time before his rendez-vous. West Bay Road, on which Ruth used to sell his furniture, was lined with people shouting their wares. There, on that spot, in the middle of Bucky Doo, she had danced herself into his life, their marriage, their misery, her premature death.

He waited by Ruth's grave. Someone had recently placed fresh flowers in the pot, which obscured the words on her headstone. Eleven rang in the town, and a man traced Misterton's footprints. Misterton had heard the gate clang shut; the man had wanted him to be aware of his presence.

"Nicholas Misterton?" he asked.

Misterton turned.

"James Chideock?"

"The very same."

They shook hands solemnly, befitting the occasion.

"Mr. Misterton, I would invite you elsewhere to give you information you deserved to have a long time ago, but this very place is so much a part of our shared history that no other place suffices."

Misterton looked at Ruth's grave, the flowers a stranger had left. Somehow, they seemed out of place to him, a futile gesture, even.

"Seems someone been a-looking after my wife's grave," he remarked. "A few petals more than I've ever brung her."

"Then you can confirm that you are, indeed, the husband of

Ruth Abbas? I make no judgement, I assure you, of an estrangement between a man and his wife, but it is important to ascertain that it was you who placed the notice in the newspaper, enquiring about the whereabouts of the child of the woman who met her death at West Bay, and to which I replied, saying that she had been adopted, and that her new family had emigrated to Australia, to start a new life."

"'Tis so."

"May I ask, then, what prompted you, after such a long time after your wife's death, to try and find out about the child?"

"First, I only knows she be dead when I leaves Gifford and comes back to Briddy. Then I learns that folk be saying she jumped off the cliff and left a child. No one knew the tiddiest bit about what happened to the child, which be mine, by law, I reckon, me being sure it baint anyone else's."

"Mr. Misterton, please don't be offended by my next question, but how can you be sure you are the father? I ask this to prepare the path for what I have to tell you."

All Misterton's memories could not stay his alone if he wanted to meet his daughter. The truth had to be told: Ruth had rejected him as a man, and he had failed to take home money; his marriage had crumbled like sandstone between fingertips.

"And I was not growed up as I be today," he concluded. "But Ruth be my wife, and she would not have forsaken me as I did her."

"And she did not tell you she was with child?"

"Not in words, but in her fear and coldness, which I only just come to read. They say it do strange things to a woman, so that she don't want to be touched."

Chideock dropped his head, moved by this honesty and humility, and now satisfied that Misterton had a genuine claim on the child.

"Forgive me. There will be no further interrogation, but a little was necessary, as you will soon see. And now it is my turn to complete the child's history, from the moment it was left on the cliff-top, following your wife . . . being found at the bottom of it."

Chideock stepped towards his own wife's grave, and beckoned him closer.

"You see, my wife is buried next to yours, and by no accident. But let me start by saying that the circumstances surrounding Ruth's death provoked much speculation. To this day, the town believes that your wife jumped, her being in such a miserable state. She saw, they say, that the only way to give her daughter a good life was to ensure that she would be looked after by people in more favourable circumstances."

Misterton shook his head.

"She had her cloudy days, but no storms to speak of. Loved those cliffs. I can't believe she would have jumped from them."

Then he remembered her words on their wedding day, her threat to jump if he ever left her, and he covered his face with his hands, to hide his shame and guilt.

"We shall never know, but I acquaint you with the common opinion as it prevailed at that time. No more, no less. It was a miracle that a man eventually found the little girl, and raised the alarm. By that time, a fossil-hunter had found your wife at the foot of the cliff."

Misterton knelt by Ruth's grave, hat in hand. She was so young, he remembered. Had he not run away from her, she might have been alive still. Below that soil, she was in her coffin, no longer in the bloom of youth. If he were responsible for that, he had to make amends to her and their daughter.

"'Twas kind to put these flowers here," he sighed, "which be more than I ever done."

"*I* put them there, in remembrance of what joy Ruth's death inadvertently brought into our lives. Being unable to bear a child of her own, as sometimes befalls a woman, as God wills, my wife expressed the wish to adopt the little girl, who was being looked after at the orphanage. Being a man of means, I was able to make a donation to the charitable works of that institution, and the little girl became ours. My wife doted on her, as did I. She never wanted for anything."

Misterton looked up.

"You talk as if this is all in the past. Does the girl live still? Or is this a way of leading me to worse news?"

Chideock shook his head quickly.

"She lives, and is called Miranda. When my wife was taken from me, I fell apart, neglected my work. I own the rope-making factory in Bridport. Her Majesty's navy needs rope when *they* say, not when I decide to put in an appearance and crack the whip. You see, I lack my wife's touch with Miranda. It's different with a man. A nurse, Dorothy, looks after her, and is more of a mother to her than I am a father. And at the back of my mind always is the lie I told you, and which I kept from my wife. I told you the child and her adoptive parents had gone to Australia so that any fire of hope you had would be quickly doused. I could not risk my wife being destroyed by the reappearance of her natural father."

Misterton had no heart for castigating him; his own sins balanced Chideock's.

"And why now? Does she know about me?"

Chideock shook his head.

"No. The death of her mother is almost impossible for her to understand. The gain of her natural father might compound her perplexity. Remember, she is but six years old."

"Now that I know all this, 'tis like I'm so full up with surprise that I think I'm groggled with cider. My head be a-turning like a cart wheel, and I can't hold steady, at the moment." Misterton scratched his head. "Now it be off your chest, what is to do?"

Chideock took a deep breath.

"I must – *we* must – do the right thing. As much as it would pain me, I must offer to return her to you, her rightful father, for I deceived you. In years to come, she might never forgive me my deception if I continue to keep you a secret, and she found out. There have been enough secrets. I understand your life as it is now may prevent you from looking after her. Have you a new wife, children of your own?"

Misterton shook his head.

"Conjuror Sayer once said . . ."

"Conjuror Sayer?"

"'Tis no one and nothing but a fancy. Got no wife nor a tiddy one. Only Maisie, who lives with my mother and me. My sister Emily gone to be a teacher."

"And you have a trade?"

"Make tolerable furniture. Father taught me. Did farming tolerable, too, for the Palfreymans, but I'm looking for work. These hands be made for it."

He spread his hands before Chideock, then showed him the other side.

"Reckon they could make rope?"

"Reckon."

"Come and see me, then. I may have something for you."

There followed a silence. While the digression of a possible job making rope had been welcome, the real subject of their meeting returned.

"A daughter for me be a loss for you. She don't know me none."

"You're her real father. You must think about what I've said. The lie is making me ill. It dangles above me like a hangman's noose. Every knock at the door I think is you come to accuse me of a terrible wrong-doing. In all this, we must do the right thing."

"I'll go talk with Maisie. I can't keep this a secret. It will write itself in my face, in every mouthful of food I chew too slowly. My voice will crack till I tell. This I know, for I have tried to face folk with a false smile, and they know 'tis a mask. 'Taint easy to look at folk in the street when you done such bad wrong that all you want to do is mend it."

They shook hands.

"When will we meet again?" pressed Chideock.

"This day, when seven sleepless nights have passed."

"So be it."

They parted, Chideock to resume his duties at the factory, Misterton to spend the pennies in his pocket. He trembled as he ate and drank, sat upright. At last, he knew the truth about Miranda, and that he had to do the right thing.

Back at the cottage, Maisie was rooting for herbs in the dry earth. Wild garlic was in the air. Mrs. Misterton was dozing in her chair, which Maisie had dragged into the sun for her. Maisie looked up when she sensed Misterton behind her.

"You scared me!" she cried, puckering her lips.

"Your hands be all soily," he pointed out, pecking her.

His mother had not heard him.

"Glad you back. You got any work?"

"Might have. Might have rope-maker's hands in Briddy."

"Then you best forget that, as we must stay here where we have a roof over our heads that don't cost us. 'Tis our home now, and we must grow our roots here."

She closed her eyes, and invited another kiss.

Misterton smiled and granted her wish.

"Mother asleep?" he asked mischievously, seeing the cottage door was open. "She dozing long?"

"There be none of that!" she made clear.

"'Tis only fair. I been away a few days."

"Fairness be a cobweb of a reason. Anyway, there be something you must know."

"There be fried tatties for tea? And a tiddy bird all boiled up in cider?"

"No."

"Palfreyman gone shot himself?"

"No, and that be wicked!"

"Then don't be such a goblin, and tell me."

Maisie turned and checked that Mrs. Misterton was still asleep. Then she placed her flat palms lovingly below her ribs, looked down, then up at Misterton.

"You see anything?"

"Maisie?"

She nodded.

"Yes, Nicholas, my boy. 'Tis so. Good job Emily gone. We're going to need her room now - for a tiddy one!"

Chapter Twenty-One

Nicholas watched for shadows: of trees, the cottage, people. Sometimes, they crept up on him, in the garden, stealthily, as an intruder, and before he knew it, they were there on the floor, growing taller as it got later, when the birds had quietened, and all that could be heard were distant sheep and the snorting of heath-croppers.

If he worked hard, learned to use a new tool, improved his skills with familiar ones, he might be rewarded with an extra foot of shadow, but never a yard. So he took to wandering on the heath, even dared to follow the forbidden path to Conjuror Sayer's house, and into the woods. When his father called, he pretended not to hear. He could judge, after his father's tone became more formal, when it was time to come in. Often, his mother yelled, knowing his father was busy, timing it so that Nicholas could have a precious half-hour more. Yet he was wary of taking advantage of her.

Once, he had been setting traps for rabbits, as his father had instructed. Nicholas had never been squeamish about releasing them from the iron teeth and wire nooses, and skinning them.

"Don't be afraid. 'Taint alive no more, so you won't hurt it. Down the belly from under the head. Then you peels it off like this, see. Comes off with a good stretch and pull. Don't forget the head."

His father had worked quickly and confidently. The rabbit had become dinner in seconds. Then it was Nicholas' turn.

"Here?" he had asked, plucking up courage.

His father had covered his hand and helped him to push the blade in and down its belly.

"Don't 'ee fuss so. Now the skin."

Nicholas had begun tentatively, then had savagely ripped off the fur.

"That be it. Now your mother takes over."

The day he knew for sure he should not steal time came when he entered the cottage, and saw his family eating. He had picked up, in the garden, the enticing aroma of soup and meat. No one looked at him. His mother had not agreed with her husband.

"Boy got to eat," she had protested.

"He got to learn, first. He tread on rules, he lose direction, as a gull a-shoved by the wind. Words bounce off him, so he must learn by doing, or not doing. 'Tis a lesson."

"Where my dinner?" asked Nicholas.

"Thought you weren't hungry. Your mother called three times, but you never came. Thought you off your food," explained his father.

"'Tis true, Nicholas," confirmed Emily, who had extra on her plate. "She kept shouting you."

"I did call you. Three times."

She said this to show her husband solidarity, though her conviction was weak as a spider's thread.

"But I'm hungry."

"Don't whine so, Nicholas. You sit or go to bed now."

Better *she* say it than her husband, who would rant and rave and strap him.

"'Tis still light. I can't sleep."

"Close your eyes, and then it be dark," advised Emily, demonstrating the remedy herself. "See, the room be black with a few stars."

Nicholas scowled.

"But I'm not tired."

"Then you should be," snapped his father, who had heard enough. "You not tired, you not worked hard enough in the outhouse."

"I did all you asked."

"When you only twelve, you come when we shout. Now go to bed. Learn from it. When we call, 'tis time to eat. Then and not when *you* decide. And now you be twelve, you learn the rules, 'cause beout 'em, we be nothing but wild animals."

In the following days, Nicholas trudged in when called, worked silently at what his father gave him, but muttered oaths when alone in the outhouse. This was his way of arguing for more freedom, when his father could not contradict him.

And there was no longer the chance to play with the boys on the Maurwood estate.

"Might as well learn to make things as sit in a classroom. Can't read nor write anyway. Just stares at the book. Won't even try, teacher says. It be a foreign tongue to him. Don't know why. Something in that boy's head that be different in a world where we all have to do the same for a tiddy bit," said his father.

"We not all the same. He'll change," said his wife. "Nicholas be different, 'tis certain, but it don't do to wring the life out of him as you would a pigeon."

On Sunday mornings, Nicholas was regularly ill, made himself vomit so that he would not have to go to Stinsford church. From an early age, he used to pretend to follow the words in his hymn book, and had learned them quickly by listening, so that others would think he could read. He fidgeted on the polished pews, slipped forward so that he nearly fell off, causing his mother to grab his hand, quell his sprouting boredom.

He watched the vicar, who seemed to be sitting on the winged lectern's back, held his breath to preserve the silence during prayer, marvelled at the rhythms of speech, until his eyes roved to the stained glass windows. How had the colours got there? He guessed that the end of a rainbow might have splashed onto the pictures. Maybe that was God's painting palette when he created the Earth.

Thomas Hardy and his orchestra striking up a tune broke the monotony, especially when there was an errant note or two, or a squeak. Giggles bubbled up inside him till he had to bite his tongue to prevent them escaping. He watched a fiddler doze off and have to be dug in the ribs to wake up. Once, Thomas Hardy winked to him when a wrong note ruined a crescendo, and caused the vicar to turn abruptly to the culprit and glare witheringly.

The worst time was when Nicholas closed his eyes and put his hands together. Why did he have to pray for forgiveness for his sins? Sin seemed so small a word for a big wrong. And when did something that went wrong become a sin? If he knew that, he could avoid it, and the subsequent prayers required for absolution. All these people were sinners, too; he was not that different, after all.

So the sickness came at the right time, and his father had just the medicine.

"You be sick again, Nicholas? Your mother must be a-poisoning you, Saturdays," he said.

Nicholas shrugged.

"'Tis the same feeling, though it baint poisoning."

"Then 'tis church. 'Tis the gospel, then, that don't agree with you betimes. 'Tis so?"

"Say the truth, Nicholas. 'Tis better to tell it, or it shouts itself, sooner or later," encouraged his mother.

"I don't like it."

"But you must go. We all go. 'Tis the way of things. You know the Lord's Prayer you say, every night? You been taught it. 'Tis no different."

"Nicholas said he never says his prayers before he goes to sleep," revealed Emily, not understanding that she should not have let it slip, though it was the truth.

"Do so!"

"Not so!"

"Say the Lord's Prayer now so's I know you aint forgot it," ordered his father.

Nicholas glared at Emily, and turned his back on his father.

"Nicholas!" begged his mother.

"Don't like the Lord's Prayer. 'Tis all wrong. The words be like pebbles, all a-grinding my teeth, and filling my mouth so that I can't get any of my own words out. And the church be all wrong, 'cepting Mr. Hardy and his instruments, who be funny and make me laugh, on account of 'em sounding like mice come in from the fields."

Mrs. Misterton escaped the ensuing silence by lighting the oil lamp for Emily, who knew that she would soon have to go to bed. From an early age, she had been haunted by the sounds on the heath. Horses munching grass were monsters trying to break into the house and eat her up. Owlets screeching like cats made her yell for her mother to comfort her. Only the oil lamp eased her anxiety, providing light so that she could see she was safe.

"Time you went to bed beout the lamp, girl," said her father. "No ghosts in this house."

"She only a child, Jacob. She don't see the world like us."

Nicholas still loitered, hoping his father would relent and allow him food, grant him more time, perhaps till it became dark, at least until twilight, when black bats scythed the sky, attacked the cottage, and swerved away just short of it.

"How can you tell they be bats and not swallows?" Nicholas had once asked his father.

"Same time, each night. Jagged wings and no beak. Main thing be regular time."

"They bite?"

"Say they go for your neck, so's they can suck all your blood."

Emily went to her father, and offered the top of her head. He kissed her. She hesitated for more, then went to her mother.

"Don't 'ee bother 'bout the lamp. 'Tis Naughty Nick 'ere who put the words in my mouth. Go to sleep before I comes up, and the angels might leave you something."

"Like what? A kitten?"

Her father could not think of anything to hand that might please her, so said, "Sweet dreams."

Disappointed, Emily said to Nicholas, "'Night, Naughty Nick."

Nicholas' eyes narrowed threateningly, and he muttered.

His father turned to him, and said, "You, too. Up."

"But I be older, father. Emily younger than me."

"You want to sleep outside 'stead?"

Nicholas remembered: scything bats biting his neck and sucking his blood, the sky turning inky. But he could not back down.

"I be older than her."

"You disobey me, and you'll go in the outhouse. Which you want?"

Muffled voices drifted from upstairs: Mrs. Misterton singing quietly, and Emily joining in, as she did, every night.

"Outhouse."

"Follow me, then," his father calmly invited.

At a leisurely pace, he led Nicholas to the bedroom in the garden. Nicholas entered, and refused to look at his father, who locked the door, and returned to the cottage.

Mrs. Misterton came down and said, "She so tired she went off, so I nipped the wick. Where be Nicholas?"

"Gone to bed."

"Never heard him come up. Must be starving."

"Got to learn. Wanted to sleep in the outhouse, so I locks him in."

"You locks him?"

"Gave him a choice."

"Jacob, what sort of father be you to lock up your own son? 'Tis cruel. I didn't carry him to see him locked up by his father."

Fists clenched, she rushed to free him, but Jacob blocked her.

"Leave him. We must break his will, or, one day, somebody else'll lock him up. He must learn to come to meet us."

"He's only twelve, Jacob."

"Soon, he be working. You too soft, and 'tis that which feeds his stubbornness."

"You his father, and you do that to him!"

She pushed by him, but he stopped her with, "I'll go. Forgiveness be mightier than anger."

"He must eat, too."

"I've made my point. Let him eat, then."

Nicholas was propped up against the wall, arms wrapped round his knees. The key turning startled him. His father was a silhouette in the doorway. Nicholas checked beyond him for bats.

"If you've slept well, your dinner be a-waiting."

Nicholas did not move, was surprised by his father's conciliatory tone.

"Are the bats out?"

His father looked over his shoulder.

"Hurry up. We'll miss 'em. I be sorry, Nicholas."

Nicholas stood up and followed him.

Mrs. Misterton put a plate of food onto the table.

Her husband winked to her, and she smiled with relief.

"Don't bolt your food, mind," she told Nicholas.

Jacob crouched to feed the fire, his back to them, giving them privacy to heal themselves.

He has not won, he told himself. There can be no winners when father and son be two rams a-butting each other.

Then Emily shouted, "Mother, I want the light!"

The next day, Jacob rose early. He was working in Dorchester. His tool bag was slung over his shoulder, and he set off, the rising sun a welcome companion. He liked to work off the heath; it made his return to it special. It always felt as if he had been absent a long time, and he missed its tranquility, but he looked forward to his conversation with men, when he learned what had been happening in the world.

Nicholas slept late. His mother looked at him, and he knew there were things she wanted to say, but to which he did not want to listen.

"A few jobs to do today. Mushroom basket, there. Then kindling. Sun been up long before you, so it should be dry. Fetch a faggot or two for this evening, as the night still pinches, though 'tis warm, during the day."

He was glad to be outside. Four rabbits had been snared, and their eyes bulged.

"Here!" He held up the rabbits, his trophy. "You want 'em skinning yet?"

"Yes, and I'll pot 'em, though do it outside. Don't want spilt blood of any kind in this house."

Slash. Creak. Rip. Skin and blood became grease, and oozed through his fingers. There was plenty of meat. His mother would think well of him, now that he had provided.

"Where be father?" he asked.

"Dorchester. Big job on."

He ran outside, and fetched the small axe for the kindling and faggots. The mushrooms could wait. Fistfuls of dry grass made a nest. So wildly had he snatched it from the ground, that he had invisible cuts, which irritated him. If only he could kill the bats, he would be happy. He could not see them, but he knew they were there, in the trees, like the owls.

The tinderbox was kept by the fireplace. When he went for it, Emily was up, at the table. She would see him, ask him questions, and his mother would hear.

"I just saw a kitten outside, a tiddy one with long whiskers," he told her quietly.

She was outside long enough for him to pick up the tinderbox, and place it in the mushroom basket.

"Can't see it," she moaned, on her return.

Nicholas went outside, and called, "You just scared it off," which made her cry.

The fire soon took. Firstly, little glows of orange, then a crack or two, followed by eels of smoke. The pages of the Bible curled and disappeared. He remembered his father's instructions on the heath: next, the kindling; finally, the logs. Nicholas had been well taught.

He went exploring, over Conjuror Sayer's way, the forbidden land.

"You must never go over yonder," his father had warned.

"Why not?"

"'Tis a bad place."

That was enough to intrigue Nicholas. Over the brow of the hill he hurried, not daring to look back at the black plume of smoke. There was Conjuror Sayer's cottage, hiding at the bottom, only its thatch visible, like a haystack.

Jacob was building additional shelves for the bookshop.

"You sell many in a day?" he asked.

The bookseller smiled.

"A tolerable living, though I'd be a rich man if more people learned to read."

"Couldn't get words inside my boy's head, teacher said. Some reason, Nicholas shuts the door on 'em, like he's saving the space for something else."

"You read?"

"Tolerable."

"Borrow any book you like. No charge."

"Thank you. 'Tis kind. No book 'cept the Bible at home."

The bookseller nodded.

"'Tis the one to have."

It would take another day to finish the shelves: a final coat of varnish would do.

"Heard it be hiring day, next week. Time Nicholas was a-working."

"Next Wednesday, market day, I believe. Does he have your skills?"

"Tolerable."

"Then he would be wasted on a farm."

Jacob smiled awkwardly, and threw himself into his work.

At the end of the day, he walked up the lane, sniffed the acrid air. When she saw him, Mrs. Misterton ran towards him. Her eyes were black, smudged circles. Emily stayed back, leaning against the doorframe, as commanded.

"Oh, Jacob!" cried Mrs. Misterton. "Your outhouse be gone."

He looked over at the smouldering stumps.

"What happened?" he gasped.

"I was cobwebbing, upstairs. 'Twas not till I opens a window that I hears a roaring like the devil, and a-spitting and a-cracking. I looks in the garden, and there I sees your outhouse a-sitting in the middle of the bonfire like 'tis 5th November."

"Where be Nicholas?"

"Gone!" she cried, before crumbling to her knees. "Gone only the Lord knows where."

Chapter Twenty-Two

Maggie sat down on the edge of the Cobb, just above the boats chained to it. The tide was in. In the background, the white houses and hotels were napping, tired after gorging on guests. Trees frothed, and, up the coast, the golden cliffs glowed, as if lit from inside by an oil lamp. This scene always made her tranquil, at the end of a long day on her feet, waiting on guests in The Bay Hotel. It was an antidote to their surliness and bad manners.

As usual, she recalled the man with wavy, black hair, and how he had held her as she taught him how to dance. That he had not tried to force himself upon her, at the end of the night, had only served to make him more attractive to her. His dishonesty about his name and occupation she interpreted as humour. It made her smile to remember how she had turned up at Gifford's Farm, only to discover that his ruse had been designed to humiliate Farmer Stockwood. She did not mind that she had been the agent; rather, in a life she preferred to be less dull, she was excited to find so inventive a man.

Since she had left Mabel, Edna, Wilfred, and George in Bridport, on their day off, there had been nothing to break the monotony of her life. Men had leered at her, and a few had treated her respectfully, but none had made her feel as Misterton had. She still possessed what he had left in his bedroom. It was her only link with him; frustratingly, she did not know where he was, so she could not return it.

She dangled her legs, her heels bouncing off the harbour walls, as a child might. Then hope filled her as the tide the harbour.

"Why didn't I think of it before? 'Twill be here, 'tis certain!" she cried aloud.

It was Friday, but Monday would not do. She had to return to the hotel immediately.

The night receptionist was already behind his desk. She had seen him before, but did not know him. He liked working at night, to avoid the long, lonely hours at home. She preferred the day so she could dance, if the chance came, in the evening. He looked efficient, not a man to do anyone a favour, not even a fellow member of staff. Maggie was still wearing her uniform, and would be recognisable, she hoped. But her plan relied on him granting her access to the guest book. There was a good chance that Misterton and his fellow traveller would have registered in the previous one, and she was not sure that it was kept behind the desk.

It would be impossible to lure the receptionist from his position, it being his responsibility to stay and ensure that guests paid their bills before leaving. What she needed, therefore, was a convincing reason for her to look at the book.

"I be Maggie. I works here, as 'ee can tell by my uniform."

She bobbed, an impromptu gesture half-way between a curtsey and a nod, and he smiled at her deference.

"Pleased to meet you, Maggie. My job don't bring me into much contact with maids. Guests, all the time, but maids, no, 'cept as they flap by like magpies across the vestibule," he said, his humour lost on Maggie.

"Magpies?"

"Your uniform. Magpies are black and white," he explained.

Keep him sweet, girl. Laugh. Make him feel clever. He's got the guest book right in front of him.

"Oh, magpies!" she cried. "'Ee be a true jester with your black and white."

But don't overdo it.

He looked pleased with her response, thought about telling her a funny story he had heard, a good one, but better to save it for another time.

"Glad you liked it. Not everyone appreciates my sense of humour."

Maggie forced a smile, then seized the moment.

"Can I confide in you?"

"I'm the font of discretion, I assure you."

"A few months ago, we had a guest staying said that if ever I needed a job, I could always rely on her. I didn't do much out of the ordinary for her, but she appreciated what I did. Fact be, I don't know her name or where she lives. All I knows is she be kind, and, well, says I be just the sort she looking for. It aint that I don't like it here. I do. 'Tis just that I need a change. The thing be—"

"Which room she in?"

While he disappeared below the counter to find the guest book, Maggie smiled; her plan was working.

"The coachman be in room three, as I recall. They be registered together, probably. She be rich, I could tell."

"A few months ago, you say?" he asked, placing two guest books on the counter. "Was it before or after Christmas they come?"

"After."

"You look through here, and I'll do the old one. You read?"

"Tolerable."

"Hope you don't mind me asking. Three . . . three . . . three. We're looking for . . . Now the thing is, she probably signed for him, he being below her in rank, so to speak."

"So we're looking for two guests, same handwriting, one in room three."

Maggie was dreading someone interrupting their search, so she read as quickly as possible, but it was the receptionist who found them.

215

"This might be them: Florence Palfreyman, Palfreyman Manor, Palfreyman Estate, near Dorchester, went in room thirty-four; Nicholas Misterton, of same address, went in room three. Sound right?"

"'Tis them!"

She remembered Stockwood revealing Misterton's name. Now she could return what he had left in his room, see him again.

"I'll write it down on this piece of paper, but don't lose it. I hope you find she's still a-wanting you. I'll be sorry to see you go, now that I've just met you."

Maggie took the paper from him, saw something in his eyes that surprised her.

"Thank 'ee. 'Tis kind."

"Name's Edward, Edward Frome. At your service, Maggie."

Then, knowing that she would add herself to all the other women he had helped, and then be sucked away from him by the under-current of Providence, he adopted a more professional pose.

She offered her hand. He scanned the vestibule; it was empty, so he took her hand, leaned forward to kiss it, but changed his mind, resulting in him stooping into a clumsy bow.

"See you again, Edward."

"Yes."

She could see that he had heard that promise so many times that she added, "No, really. Won't get the job anyway."

Outside, she calmed herself. At last, she had an address; she would take the coach to Dorchester, in the morning.

The item she wished to return slept safely in her bag. She had enough money to pay for a room, for Saturday night, assuming a vacancy. Not all establishments welcomed lone women.

She arrived just after lunchtime. A band was playing in the street, and she stopped to listen, before asking the way to Palfreyman Manor. The woman she asked turned round and pointed the way.

"'Tis a stretch of a walk for a woman with a bag. My husband and I on the cart, but we baint a-going back till the sun yawn. You welcome to wait."

"'Tis kind as summer of you, but I got to see someone at the manor. Works for Miss. Palfreyman."

"'Twas a shame her brother's bride changed her mind. They say he be a man as broke as Corfe Castle. Still, 'tis the way of things, betimes. Love grows like a cherry on a tree, all sweet and shining, then, if it don't get picked and enjoyed, it rots, goes sour and shrivels. Girl must have had a good reason."

"'Tis poetry, that. Lovely, like a lesson from the Bible."

"Don't mean to preach. And poetry? Not me, though my son, Tom, have words which, sewn together, be a beautiful tapestry to hang in your soul."

"Thank 'ee for the offer, but I must go now. Time a-slipping away fast today, though the band slowed it down a tiddy bit."

"'Tis true. Their notes be letters, a-spelling joy."

"I must start the long walk. Sometimes, your feet master you, and you can't argue when they don't drag you places."

"Passing through Higher Bockhampton, stop off. We be the last cottage on the right, top of the lane."

"Thank you . . . ?"

"Jemima, Jemima Hardy."

"Maggie."

After an hour, Maggie's feet began to ache, so she sat down on the side of the road to rest.

Soon, a coach stopped, and the man looked down.

"You all right, Miss?"

"Just resting. Feet complaining, near a-yelling at me."

"You going far?"

"Palfreyman Manor."

"Going there myself. You after the job in the kitchen? Can't fill it since the girl got notions and took off to be a teacher."

"Yes."

"Then let me help you up. Don't make sense a-walking."

Coombs helped her up.

"That be kind. A-looking for Miss. Florence Palfreyman."

"Then you won't find her at the manor, for she a-upped and offed to Monksbury on account of her brother wanting to settle his new bride in as mistress, but 'tis all crumbled, as master be left high and dry at the altar. Miss. Florence needn't have gone, after all."

"Where be Monksbury? Not far, I hope."

"'Tis the same stride from here as the manor."

"Then I must step down and walk to Monksbury, if you would kindly point me in the right direction."

Coombs shook his head.

"'Twould wear your legs to stumps. I have time yet to take you and be back to do the master's bidding, when he wakes up. 'Tis his habit to sleep on, on account of his late nights with his gentlemen friends at The King's Arms."

Maggie accepted the offer, and Coombs turned towards Tolpuddle.

"Best not go up the drive case she tell the master I brung you. 'Twould dip him in a rage so he'd make my life a misery."

Maggie climbed down, and offered him a coin.

"My word, no, Miss. Mr. Coombs won't take a penny. 'Twas a pleasure to have your company, on account of me not seeing many ladies to talk to."

First, Edward, now Coombs. Why, I be quite popular! she thought.

Edith opened the door.

"I be Maggie, come to see Miss. Palfreyman."

Edith assessed her carefully: little money, but takes as much care with her appearance as she can.

"She expecting you?"

"No, though she might be able to help me, but I'm not here a-begging, please to tell her. I work in The Bay Hotel, Lyme Regis. Tell her the name, which she knows."

Soon Florence came. Edith waited a few paces behind her, out of the light, in hearing distance.

"Yes?" began Florence.

"I be Maggie, and I come to ask you if you know where I can find Nicholas Misterton."

Florence's face twitched just enough to give herself away.

"No. I've never heard of him."

When Edith heard the name, she started, and stepped forward to get a better view of the visitor. Had Maggie filled the space in his life she herself had once occupied? she wondered.

"Baint true, Miss. Palfreyman, I know. 'Ee were with him in The Bay Hotel, in Lyme Regis. He was your coachman, and I thought he was your husband, and I never knew he wasn't, or I wouldn't have danced with him, but then it turns out he weren't your husband, or Mr. Stockwood from Gifford's Farm, and 'twas all his jest, and—"

Stockwood. Gifford's Farm. Edith's heart boomed as loudly as the sea pounding the Cobb, she felt. So, he was still himself: not quite as you see him, but masquerading, enticing yet another woman into his irresistible web, as a spider a fly.

"Edith, can you see this woman to the gate, please?"

"Certainly, Miss. Palfreyman."

"Why you a-lying?" asked Maggie, her voice cracking in disbelief.

Florence retreated from the door, and Edith stepped outside.

"Come with me, Maggie," she whispered, taking her arm. "You and I have more in common than you think, for I know Nicholas myself, and know where he bide, and, if you like, I can take you there, for we both need to talk to him."

"You?" gasped Maggie. "I have something belonging him, and I know Miss. Palfreyman do know him."

"'Tis true. Meet me at Higher Bockhampton, tomorrow. 'Tis Sunday, my day off, and if it be Providence, we shall both see him, according to our needs."

"But I have nowhere to stay round here, and Dorchester be a deathly distance."

Edith bit her bottom lip, as she always did when trying to solve a problem. Then she had an idea. There was an old folly in the grounds. One could sit in it, and look down to the lake.

"I could leave this gate open. Come back just before dark, and follow the wall till you see a stone building with a dome. Inside, I shall leave a blanket to keep you warm, though 'tis mild at night, and you might squeeze onto the wooden bench with a beetle or two. No one'll disturb you, but you must creep out the gates when shapes return, in the morning. I shall meet you at the end of the lane, where the signpost point."

Maggie had come all that way, and would not be deterred.

"'Tis kind of you. How you know Nicholas?"

Seeing no point in lying, she said, "At Gifford. I was a milkmaid once, and he was a farm labourer."

"Well, wondrous strange! All this space in the world, and we all a-split our own ways, only to find we got to come back to each other. Why 'tis so be a mystery."

With that, she thanked Edith and slipped through the gate.

Florence stayed out of sight for the rest of the day, and Edith made no mention of Maggie or Misterton. In the garden temple, Edith left some wine, bread, cheese, and cold meat. In a note, she reminded Maggie not to leave any sign that she had been there; Florence had expressed the wish to clean and repair the temple so that she could enjoy the soothing view of the lake, and she might pay a visit.

"'Tis far?" asked Maggie, the next morning.

"We'll be there when the sun be at his tallest. The day be full of bees and butterflies."

"'Tis like a dance, but I need to be back in Lyme before the moon, for, in the morning, I be a-serving tea and bacon to guests."

"Then it be a grand reason to bring you a-looking for a man who—"

But Edith strangled her sentence; Misterton had given her sanctuary as well as secured her dismissal at Gifford's Farm.

Jemima heard women's voices in the lane, and their words were watered with laughter. She went to the gate to see who it was. Few strangers passed. The odd furze-cutter descending from the heath bade good-day; otherwise, only Misterton came that way.

"You be the girl at the band in Dorchester?" asked Jemima.

Maggie looked hard, and recognised her.

"Yes. The day be a perfect rhyme again."

"'Tis a rhyme and a picture. You time for a rest?"

Edith took charge, felt that their visit should not be interrupted.

"'Tis kind, though I think we must continue our journey, or your return to Lyme, Maggie, will be so delayed, you may not make the breakfast service, and 'twill surely steep you in a pan of trouble."

Maggie agreed.

"Perhaps, another day. Your son have a purpose for his pen today!"

"We just back from church. Tom and the others are inside."

Maggie and Edith smiled and moved on. Soon their destination was in front of them.

"Let us go together, for my legs be a-wobbling from the walk, and my heart be afeard, for I don't know if he will greet me with the face I remember, or slam the door in mine."

Mrs. Misterton saw them approaching. Maisie was resting her eyes, in a chair, and Nicholas was lying on his bed. The cottage was warm and peaceful, had made them all sleepy and lethargic. Only a bluebottle, buzzing angrily, and flying frantically to escape, disturbed the silence.

Edith thought Mrs. Misterton changed: a little more hunched, eyes more yellow, the lids sagging and raw.

"You remember me, Mrs. Misterton? I be Edith, Nicholas' friend. You and Emily nursed me when the world nearly done with me. And this be Maggie, another friend. She come to bring Nicholas something."

Maisie woke up, heard the tail-end of Edith's interruption, but kept her eyes shut, and resumed breathing the rhythm of sleep.

"'Tis something he left in Lyme."

"Lyme?"

Mrs. Misterton looked at Edith. Something in Edith's bearing, her blond hair, reminded her of a time when Nicholas gave up his bed for someone.

"You once sick?"

"Yes. And you let me stay till I was better. And this be Maggie."

"You sick, too?" asked Mrs. Misterton. "That why you come?"

Upstairs, Nicholas stirred. Voices. Visitors. He sat up and listened.

"I aint sick, no. Just brought Nicholas something."

"Emily at the manor today?" asked Edith.

Mrs. Misterton held her head in her hands.

"Don't know. Just don't know. She gone to church?"

Edith looked at Maggie, then at Mrs. Misterton, whose head was empty, except for a few names, without faces, gathering dust.

Nicholas slumped down the stairs. Half his face was creased from lying on it. He came into view. Maggie smiled. Misterton did not remember her.

"Nicholas, your mother . . . " began Edith.

"You go and sit, mother. These ladies have come to see me."

"What time Emily back?"

"Just go and sit."

He led her gently by the elbow to her chair.

"You remember me?" asked Maggie.

He shook his head. Maggie sighed. Had everyone in the house lost their memory?

"Can't say I do."

"I be Maggie. We skipped a few reels in Lyme when you were Miss. Palfreyman's coachman."

Maisie calculated. She could not remember, either. Something be in the air in this country. Or perhaps it was when I was sick, when the clock stuttered. Her eyes stayed shut; there were things to listen to.

Misterton recalled his visit, the dance, her openness to him, even his lie about his name, his job. He fixed his mind on the details, had to; she would not have traced him to his cottage to castigate him for a tiddy lie.

"'Twas a night when I had four feet, which seemed to go in the wrong order, if I remembers correctly."

"You did tolerable. But I was a-cleaning your room when I notices something. I picks it up, and looks at it. The letters on it be so tiddy, I has to screw up my eyes to read, and then I knows it belongs to 'ee."

She delved into her bag. The ring was safe in a small box she used for buttons and odds and ends.

Maisie's curiosity then prompted her to end her pretence, and go over and see what it was.

Maggie handed it over.

Edith looked at Maisie, remembered her from the farm. Wareham had danced round Maisie, too, only Maisie had smeared herself with cow dung, peed herself to ward him off.

Misterton looked at it in the palm of his hand.

"Nicholas?" said Maisie.

"There. See? 'Tis your wedding ring! And there be your names engraved in tiddy letters: *Nicholas* and *Ruth*. So you be Ruth?"

"No, not I. I be Maisie. Nicholas, who be Ruth?"

"Ruth be my wife."

Maisie gasped.

"And where she be?"

"In her coffin, in a Bridport graveyard."

Edith put both hands to her face.

"At Gifford's Farm, were you . . . ?"

"Yes," he admitted. "'Twas so."

"What time Emily back from church?" called Mrs. Misterton. But no one could speak, except the bluebottle, which raged against the window-pane.

Maggie was first, now keen to escape. The last time she had seen him, he had been clean-shaven, but now he looked dishevelled.

"I shall wait by the cottage down the lane. I brought the ring in good faith," she stated, as if trying to clear her name.

"I'll come with you, Maggie. 'Tis only fair you explain to Maisie, Nicholas, though I shall come back, another time, for there is something I have to say, though it be a fact that I've been made a fool of, and I'm not the only one."

When they had gone, Maisie said, "Why didn't you tell me? I would have understood, but you buried your past with her so deep, you make it seem like 'twas a sin she died."

"She died after I left her. 'Twas for the best, I left. I was younger then."

"And Edith?"

He hung his head in reply.

"And what more must I know? Were there any tiddy ones?"

"'Tis a sorry tale I must tell."

Maisie listened.

"And Miranda will come and live with us? Here?"

He nodded.

"Then you better start earning, Nicholas. 'Tis not a-ranting you need now but a job to feed your family, which seem to be swelling by the day."

Edith said goodbye to Maggie, and returned to Monksbury. She could not help replaying scenes from Gifford's Farm in her mind, on the way. She might have forgiven him if Ruth had been dead, but he had left her alive, only to take his pleasure from two women, in the straw. She and Victoria had been terribly used.

When she arrived at the door, she saw a suitcase. She rapped the lion's head three times, and Florence came.

"There be a suitcase," said Edith.

"Yes. It contains your possessions."

"Mine?"

"Yes. Yours. You must leave, Edith. I thought I could trust you."

"Why, so you can, Miss. Palfreyman!"

"I think not."

"You can trust me with your life!"

Florence then took the note Edith had left for Maggie, in the folly, from her pocket, and passed it to her.

"My life would, I fear, be in grave danger if I did. I found this. It is your handwriting. You disobeyed me, and you must now leave."

With that, she closed the door behind her.

Chapter Twenty-Three

Ruth went to the oak chest Misterton had made. On that day, each year since he had walked out and not returned, she opened it, releasing memories of their time together, as a child frees butterflies from a net, and took out the white dress in which she had bewitched and married him. It was the summer fair in Bridport, and the eager sun had jumped out of bed, and was the first to arrive in Bucky Doo. She held the dress against herself, took a step or two, imitating the moves she had made on the day she had met Misterton. They had walked to West Bay, had kissed on the cliff-top. How could she then have known that his idea of eternity was different from hers? Maybe if I wear it today, she thought, parade in it at Bucky Doo, he will see me from afar, and be won by me again, for I would have him back as my husband and the father of our little girl without the tiddiest doubt. But I be older now, and my feet be heavy as headstones.

Miranda toddled towards her, and put the dress in her mouth.
"Are you hungry, my daughter?"
Ruth picked her up, kissed her, and began to sway, soothing her with a lullabye.

Miranda drank milk, and ate bread. There was not much money for food. The landlord had taken no pity on Ruth when Misterton had left. The rent had to be paid on time, he had insisted. So she had sold a few items Misterton had made. It was the way of things, she reflected, that they had attracted buyers now, but not when he was there with her.

And when there was nothing else to sell, she had presented herself at the workhouse. Connie and Bea had begged her not to go, but she had had no alternative. She had submitted herself at the gate, stood in the queue at the entrance. What little she had – the chest, a few personal items – she had left in her house. She had listened to the rules read to her by a monotonous matron in a grey dress, who had concluded Ruth's induction with, "All paupers who have the itch be separated, and if you aint got it now, you soon will have if you mix with them from other parishes, as this be a Union workhouse. And 'ee best make sure the tiddy one pipe down, or 'ee'll be out again."

The noises, claustrophobia, smells, the threat of catching the itch, steeped her into such a marsh of misery so quickly that she knew she must leave. Death itself would be preferable to such an absence of friendship and freedom. Outside, she would hand Miranda over to someone in the desperate hope that they would care for her.

Bea and Connie found work at Chideock's, the rope-maker. He needed two cleaners, and they convinced him that he would be able to eat his dinner off the factory's floorboards if he hired them. And it was Bea who suggested that she and Connie live with Ruth and Miranda, so that Miranda would not grow up without her mother. Chideock could not have known that the wages he paid would keep a roof over the little girl he and his wife would eventually adopt. Luckily, Ruth's landlord had not let her house to anyone else, so Ruth took Miranda home, leaving only her name in the workhouse's register.

"How blessed are we to have two such friends!" wept Ruth. "You have saved us."

"Don't 'ee thank us, girl. We must all thank Mr. Chideock, as 'twas he gave Connie and me our freedom as well as you and Miranda."

"But I can't pay you anything, and Miranda be too tiddy for me to leave her and go out to work."

"Her smiles be our payment. What say you, Bea?" said Connie.

"Her smiles be treasure!" agreed Bea.

"And you two are God's best angels," said Ruth.

The summer fair at Bucky Doo, and what it meant to her, galvanised her.

"The day be dazzling, and 'tis a waste to sit in the shadows and mope. Though our spirits be as worn as the wick in the lamp, we must sing and mingle, as beout this day, you, my tiddy one, would not be here."

The dancers moved down the street, and wove their tapestry, their movements stitches in an intricate pattern. Youths quaffed cider, and lined the road, sharing views on which girls were the prettiest, and the heady fumes made them more desirable, so that even the plainest looked beautiful, and the plumpest, svelte. Ruth searched for her husband in the crowd, her hopes raised at the sight of dark, wavy hair, and then dashed when the face did not match, and she shuddered when she could not spot him. She held Miranda tightly, smothered her in kisses, as if in haste to use them up.

She put Miranda down, and let her walk a few paces. Some women looked at them, and Ruth knew they were talking about her, speculating on the reason her husband had left her. Insult me, she cried inside, but not my child. She is as innocent as a lamb. But the tongues clucked like hens in a strut, and Ruth moved further along the road to West Bay, till she was halfway down it, where she felt the urge to continue to the sea.

A cart stopped, and a man and a woman helped them up.

"'Tis all a bother in Bucky Doo," complained the man.

"Once a year aint asking much," remarked his wife. "The only music I gets to hear be the sea, which 'as few instruments: stone, sound, and water, by my reckoning, and though it be a daily tune, 'tis much of the same."

"Once a year be a blessing and a curse," opined Ruth.

"Your daughter be an angel. What name she have?" asked the man.

"Miranda."

"Miranda? Why, 'tis a name above the common crowd. I'll wager she won't be a Briddy lass for long, a-jingling a name like that!"

At West Bay, Ruth carried Miranda in her climb up the steep path to the cliff-top. In the sun, Ruth quickly became breathless, but, with several rests, when she looked down onto the harbour, she made it to the top.

"'Tis more blowy up here, my sweetheart, so hold my hand, and don't go near the edge. Keep your bonnet on, too. The sun's kiss be fiery today, and your face'll pink-up if you don't shade it."

Soon, they were sitting in the spot where Misterton had first promised her the rest of his life. Miranda settled in Ruth's shadow. Faint voices drifted up from the beach. It sounded as if a game were being played, and there was splashing in the sea. A dog was barking wildly, as if being teased.

"And now I'm going to tell you why this place be sacred, my cherub. Well, 'twas the day of Briddy summer fair, and your father watched me dance in Bucky Doo. He brought me up here, and, by the time we caught our breath, we said that we would love each other for ever more, and 'tis still so, on my part. But your father went away, one day, beout a word, and didn't come back. The problem be, that he went beout knowing he had a tiddy girl, and when he gets to know he got a Miranda, he'll come a-running back so fast he'll be as wheezy as I am now. 'Tis certain. And in the chimes between now and then, we shall live with Bea and Connie."

From the beach came loud cheering, followed by a song:
"Let us all dance on the beach by the sea,
and twirl in the light, gently bend at the knee,
and holding the hand of the one that 'ee love,
ask her to marry, and pray she'll agree."

The singer was a woman, accompanied by the rhythmical clapping of her friends.

"'Tis a pretty air, Miranda. Listen. She sings of love."

Ruth started to clap, too, even took Miranda's hands to help her join in. Another verse, in which the girl declined the offer to marry, and Ruth was seized by the urge to go to the edge of the cliff to see the enchantress.

"Stay there, girl. 'Tis a merry group, though the song have a sad face."

She remembered her steps in Bucky Doo. Lightly, she danced towards the voice, the sun making her squint.

"And when you have danced on the beach by the sea,

and twirled in the light, gently bent at the knee,

you will weep at the loss of the one that 'ee love,

and smile at the thought that at least you are free."

Ruth could not quite see the group on the beach, so she inched forward, as a blind woman in an unfamiliar place. Over her shoulder, she could see that Miranda was content.

Below Ruth, the siren was greeted by rapturous applause. Ruth felt the passion of the sun on her face, then the sea's cooling breeze. In the sky, gulls, too, danced, the turbulent air their partner. They flapped back to the cliff-face, rested on ledges, nooks where the wind had eroded the sandstone.

"So free!" Ruth marvelled. "So light."

The man's voice drew her as far as she could go. A fiddle accompanied him, his voice strong and jaunty.

"The ship set sail, and 'twas bound for Spanish treasure.

Up the masts climbed the men, with no time for idle leisure.

'When we all come back, we'll be rich for ever more,

and we'll tap a cask of brandy, and we'll pour ourselves a measure.'"

Again, the audience began to clap to the rhythm. Ruth bent forward the upper part of her body, daring to move her feet no further. It was then that she joined the gulls in the sky, though they could only watch her tumble, like an acrobat, through the air, silently, the soil and sandstone, on which she had been standing, falling, too, after holding firm for millions of years. She flew with fossils of vertebrae and sharks' teeth.

She landed at the feet of the merry-makers and fossil-collectors, the lumps of rock continuing to follow her, for a second or two. The women screamed, the men gasped, the quest for Spanish gold ended, and they all took steps backwards towards the sea, for their own safety. Even the hysteria of the gulls ceased, and there was silence. The party looked up to the cliff-top. There was no one, but they saw where the cliff had splintered, on the very spot she had been standing.

A man went to her, and listened for breathing.

"She gone. Just a child, by the look of her."

"She jump?" one woman whispered to another. "On a day like this?"

"'Less the cliff give way, as it do regular."

Along the length of the cliff, at its foot, boulders and blocks of sandstone were a fragmented testimony to the cliff's weakness and the relentless assault of the sea.

"No way of telling, though 'tis a place which make folk jump. 'Tis a certain way of ending your life."

Out of sight, above them, Miranda was still sitting, wondering where her mother had gone. She became anxious, and started to cry. A man, walking along the path, blinked when he saw her; there seemed to be no one with her.

"What be a tiddy one like you doing all alone in such a dangerous place?" he whispered to himself. "Hello?" he called loudly, and on his third shout, received an answer from below.

He picked up Miranda, and carried her down the slope, onto the beach. Men were kneeling, as if praying, around Ruth.

"Can't leave her here. Tide be in, a few songs hence. We must take it in turns to carry her. She look light as a robin."

Miranda and Ruth were reunited where the path met the beach. People strolling round the harbour came closer to see what had happened, clinging to the tragedy like barnacles.

One man said to his wife, "Why, 'tis the girl and her tiddy one we brung here in the cart!"

"Oh, don't say she gone, her time of life! That poor baby no mother now."

By the time they had laid Ruth on the grass, and the police arrived, the general conclusion was that she had jumped to her death, that her original intention had been to take the child with her, but that she had changed her mind, at the last minute, prompted, no doubt, by the Lord, who had called her to his side, when she could bear her suffering no more.

The man who had found Miranda did not leave his name, and resumed his coastal walk.

"In all my years a-walking, I aint seen such a sorry sight, and that child's face will live with me for the rest of my days," he said.

Bea and Connie were still in Bucky Doo when the undertaker was sent for. The fair was at its liveliest just as the news broke, and it smothered the high spirits. When Ruth and Miranda did not return home, Bea and Connie feared the worst. The undertaker let them see the body; they might be able to identify her, though he warned that she had sustained disfiguring injuries.

"Jumped from the cliff, they say, so her face be cut and bruised, and the blood be got off as best we could, though 'tis difficult. She swollen where her bones be snapped."

They approached the bed. The sheet had been pulled up to her shoulders, sparing her friends the sight of her broken body. Her eyes stared upwards, her lips slightly apart.

Bea hugged Connie.

"'Tis her, and yet 'taint. Poor darling Ruth!" Bea wept.

Connie was a statue.

"She never jumped. 'Twas that husband of hers pushed her, in a manner of speaking."

"No, Connie. She must have slipped. She loved Miranda. And now all the child got be us."

The undertaker coughed quietly.

"I hate to intrude on your grief, which be greater than you can bear, with it all fresh as morning dew, but if it be your friend, and you knows her name, then I beg you to report it to the police, as it needs to be recorded in the parish registry."

"Do you know what's happened to the child? 'Twas hers," said Connie.

"Well, unless there be a father who can keep her, she be an orphan, and there be a swollen tribe of 'em in Bridport, on account of the 'sumption, which picks us off cruelly and beout warning. I bury 'em all, you see, and good job there be an orphanage, which be maintained by a benefactor, or the poor mites would be on the streets, a-wandering like ghosts."

"There be a father, 'tis certain, though he long gone and nowhere to be seen. We all she got."

"Then try the orphanage, where the police will have left her. She almost certainly there, as she be too young for the parish poor-house."

"She aint going back there!" declared Connie.

"I shall leave you a few seconds longer, then ask you to leave. There are preparations I must make, ointments and—"

"Pray, do not describe what you do to rob death of its shame!" cried Bea. "We will go now to find Miranda, who be living, God a-willing, unlike her poor mother. When be the funeral?"

"In due course. Certainly, by the end of the week. The details will be displayed on the public noticeboard. As you know her, I ask if you have sufficient funds and a wish for a headstone. These matters take a little time to organise, on account of the stonemason having no apprentice, at the moment. If there be no one who can pay, then the bill will be sent to the parish, though as it will be a pauper's burial, there will be no headstone, and she be in a pauper's plot. If she be a suicide, then she might not get a place in the churchyard."

"We have no money, though 'twould break my heart to see her buried without a 'scription. We shall find the money, though 'twill be just a few words," Connie decided.

"Just let me know what you want."

Bea and Connie then went to the orphanage to find Miranda, whom they hugged and showered with kisses.

"No point in explaining," said Connie. "She too young. Let's get her home."

The matron, however, shook her head.

"I'm afraid you won't be able to take her. You are not a legal guardian. In time, you may apply to adopt her, but, for the moment, she must remain here, at the parish's behest."

"But we're all she knows, poor mite! Her mother gone, and now us," protested Bea.

"You may, of course, come to visit her as often as you wish, though I be bound to let you know that there be enquiries for children by childless couples, some of 'em making grand donations."

"We aint rich, 'tis true, but we love her so much."

"I'm sure you do," said the matron.

Back home, Bea and Connie touched Ruth's hairbrush and nightgown.

"What we do with all this? Can't leave it lying around. 'Twould make us think she coming back, and she aint," pointed out Connie.

"All her things must go in the chest, and that be the only thing he ever gave her," said Bea.

"'Cepting Miranda and a wedding ring."

The next day, Connie went to the undertaker, and told him to instruct the stonemason to inscribe the words she said. She could not write them, and she asked the undertaker to read back what he had written.

234

"But, Connie, we aint got enough. Where we get that sort of money?" said Bea.

Connie hugged her.

"She got to have a stone, and that's all the there and back of it."

The next three nights, Connie returned with Bea from Chideock's factory, and after visiting Miranda, Connie rouged her lips and cheeks, tidied up her hair, and left the house.

Chideock had heard of Ruth's death, and Miranda being cared for by the parish.

"And how old is the child?" he asked.

"She just toddling," said Bea, "but only with a hand."

Chideock sat in his office, in deep thought, then put on his hat and coat, and left.

"I will be gone for a couple of hours," he told his foreman. "See the men stay at it."

Bea said to Connie, "You not out again, be you? Where you go?"

"Ask no questions, tell no lies, but 'tis the last time. 'Tis the funeral tomorrow, so I won't be as late as last night."

Connie turned left at the clock. It was still light, and she hoped she would not be recognised by any of the men at the rope factory. She walked slowly along the bank of the stream, till she caught the eye of a man coming in the opposition direction. They exchanged a few words, and she shook her head emphatically. She was out of practice, but had not forgotten the rules.

"You be awful dear for just your hand," he complained. "Should be mouth for all that!"

"'Tis that or nothing, and the money gone up, since last night, on account of my rent being due."

He grudgingly handed over the sum demanded.

"That bush over there," she pointed, " and quick. 'Tis the last night I come, and there still be a lot of work to do before the blues come a-snooping."

And the man did as he was told.

Chapter Twenty-Four

The words refused to make sentences when Misterton expelled them from his mouth. They were short and sullen, like a schoolboy's when he is asked to account for his bad behaviour. Slowly, as Misterton's explanation gathered momentum and clarity, he felt better, as when he had looked after her at the farm.

"'Tis all?" asked Maisie. "Say now."

"'Tis all I know."

Maisie screwed up her face; his answer was shy and needed prodding.

"That be not the same as, 'Yes, dear Maisie, that be all.' '*Tis all I know*,' be foggy as the fields, mornings."

"Can't tell you 'bout something I don't know," he argued.

Maisie humphed.

"And you never seen this child? Never knowed about her?"

He shook his head.

"Said so more times than turnips at Palfreyman Farm! You not think of anything else?"

Maisie felt she had a right to the upper hand. Mrs. Misterton had gone outside. There were important matters to discuss, some practical, others emotional. An invisible child was now in the room with them; and Ruth's ghost would always be a face at the window. When he looked as bilious as a storm cloud, Maisie knew that Ruth had been talking to him, now sharing their daughter with him, as she had been unable to do in Bridport.

"You fallen into a clump of nettles? This all new to me. Thought there would be three of us, and ends up four! What I do? Sit here and say 'tis fine?"

"'Tis life. We don't hold hands with Providence, we might as well throw ourselves off a cliff-top, and then we be at an end, just fossils in a graveyard."

Maisie returned to her basket of questions.

"Miranda got used to her house. She already lost two mothers, and now she going to lose the man she thinks is her father. 'Tis almost cruel to snatch her from Bridport. And how we going to manage?"

"Got ideas," quickly came back Misterton.

"Give me one, then, Nicholas, that taste like honey. My mouth full of sour."

"There be work at the rope factory in Briddy. We can live there."

"'Twill always have a ghost. And this cottage, our home, your mother?"

"Sell it."

"Can't sell your mother. It's all she ever known. That baint honey, Nicholas, but pickling vinegar."

Misterton then roused himself, realised his passivity was only increasing the severity of the brow-beating.

"You want honey? I give you hives of it. Palfreyman be in a bog, up on the farm. Fields be a-lazing on account of no one working them. We been two rams a-butting each other, but I be different now. I want to go to Dorchester, see, and the road be flooded, so I waits nowadays. Once, I'd a-swum through it rather than wait. Sometimes, you can't walk down the path; you must go round the edge of the field to get where you a-going."

Maisie thought hard. She had nearly died on the farm. Misterton had taken her away. There was no security on the estate. A man had died there.

"That be rancid pork dripping," she said. "Make furniture instead."

"'Tis what my father done!" he snapped, then added, "Besides, I lack his way. There be no magic in my hands. Time was when I wanted to carve scrolls and leaves for the church, but my leaves withered, and the scrolls would not curl proper."

"Then we lost our way, Nicholas."

"There be honey soon."

"Good job it keep, then."

Her questions continued to buzz like bluebottles. In two days' time, he would have to give his answer to James Chideock, and he could not let Miranda down twice, whatever the impact upon her, in the short term.

Mrs. Misterton did not return. Nicholas went looking for her. She could not have gone far; her legs would not take her. Coming briskly up the lane was Thomas, in his work attire. His face was showery.

"Glad I sees you," he called.

Then let us hope there be work for me, he thought.

"I'm looking for mother. She been too long."

Thomas looked at the floor, then up at Misterton.

"She be with Jemima. Nicholas, there be something wrong. She think you're still gone, that your father be home from Dorchester soon."

"She be old, Thomas. Can't lock her up, all day. She don't know time any more, which be a blessing, these days."

Thomas placed his hands on Misterton's shoulder.

"'Tis the curse of old age, and no medicine, no whortleberry or elderflower juice, can put things back in the right order. She lost bits of time, I reckon. Called Jemima Emily. You come and get her now?"

"Yes. I be sorry. She lost Emily, see, though she jumbled before Emily went."

Jemima's eyes misted as he helped his mother out of her chair.

"Goodnight, Mrs. Misterton," said Jemima.

Mrs. Misterton did not reply.

The walk up the lane was slow.

"Joints need oiling, mother?" said Misterton.

But she did not answer.

"Glad you back," welcomed Maisie. "We been worried."

Mrs. Misterton sat in her chair, and fell asleep.

The day of his departure came, and Maisie asked, "You bringing her back today? We aint ready for her. And your mother. How we going to tell her about Miranda?"

"Won't understand anyway." He put on his hat, and slung his bag across his shoulder. "She be fine with her food. She got that, she be fine. 'Tis all we can do. Have to hold hands with Providence. Miranda be my daughter, and the path must be found for her to come from her home to ours. Mr. Chideock don't yet know what I be a-going to say. Then 'tis our job to prepare the path."

"How you going to do that?"

"Don't know. Never done it before."

In Bridport, Chideock was already at his factory, in his office. He was expecting Misterton, but had said nothing to Miranda. There was no point; Misterton had not yet indicated that he wanted to claim the daughter he had not known he had. Chideock and his wife had adopted her, but Misterton's name was on the birth certificate, which Chideock had brought in with him, that morning, as proof, in case it was requested.

Both men shook hands nervously, felt the enormity of their business. Chideock loved Miranda, but did not wish her to find out, later in life, maybe from Misterton himself, that he had withheld the existence and identity of her real father. Miranda had a right to know and live with him.

There was, of course, the obligation to ensure that she would not be removing to an environment in which she might suffer disadvantage. Chideock knew that Misterton had no work, and, therefore, no income. However, if Misterton were not too proud to agree, Chideock would provide an annual allowance. Miranda would never find out. Instead, in time, she would forget her early years.

Sometimes, he heard his dead wife screaming, "No, James. Don't do this!" but she had not known the circumstances. Chideock could not, was his final decision, live with his lie.

"So, have you spoken with your . . . "

"Maisie? Yes, and I have come to say that I be Miranda's true father, though some might say I have no right to her, but I swear I would never have left if I'd known Ruth was with child."

Chideock knew from the sincerity of his tone that he was telling the truth.

"Then first you must see this. It shows what your wife wanted."

Misterton read the birth certificate. There it was: father - Nicholas Misterton. He now understood Ruth's withdrawal from him, her uncertainty, her fear, maybe.

"I been a fool."

"We are human, all of us."

"'Tis the curse of Nicholas Misterton. But what if she don't want to go?"

"We must introduce her to you and Maisie, slowly, perhaps take her to your house, and when the time is right, we will tell her."

"Maisie be expecting, so Miranda will have a brother or sister. I will work soon. Maisie don't want to leave the heath."

"Then I will make an offer to you, which I hope you'll accept. I would like to give Miranda an annual allowance. She must never know where it comes from. There will be hard times when—"

"'Tis kind, but 'twould be like you there with us, in the cottage. She can only have one father. 'Tis hard."

Chideock was momentarily stung, then realised that he must let go, as painful as that would be.

"I understand."

"'Tis kind."

"Then I shall bring her to see you at your house. A few visits may be necessary to reassure you. You and Maisie will be able to get to know her gradually."

"But what if, after all her comings and goings, she still don't want to come? 'Tis a scene I dread."

"We must do the right thing."

"But the right thing to one baint to another."

"A child of her age cannot know the difference between right and wrong, in this case. We must be strong. If you let me know how to find your cottage, I will bring her on Saturday. She has a nurse, who is close to her, and who does not yet know of the circumstances. I expect much criticism from her, though she will not be privy to the full facts of the case. She will find alternative employment; I shall write her a good reference."

Chideock stood up. Someone had knocked during the meeting. There was always a problem to address.

He did not want to become too close to Misterton. Once Miranda had left, that it was clear she would be safe, and have a good chance of happiness in her new home, there would be no further contact.

"It be best if I meet you in Dorchester. Ask for The King's Arms, and I will meet you outside. 'Tis but a pleasant ride from there to the heath, which sits a-top Higher Bockhampton."

"Shall we say twelve o'clock?"

"Twelve. 'Tis a pretty place, the heath, in summer, all tangled with bloom and wild flowers. There be heath-croppers, too. And not forgetting mother, who all confused, though 'tis nothing that don't afflict us all, when the time comes. My sister, Emily, be training to be a teacher, up Bath way. The cottage be plain but clean, and a place to smile in."

"The King's Arms at twelve, then."

They shook hands, and Misterton left.

*

Edith's words made him think of Victoria Stockwood, from time to time. All the signs were there, she had said. A fullness of face, a roundness of body; women saw these things. And Mabel and Edna had commented on them, too, apparently. Yet he had been sent away, the barrel of a gun waving him goodbye, on a journey to find work elsewhere.

He decided to find out if Edith's insinuation that Victoria had been carrying his child had any substance. Maisie's questions had prickled him, and he was sure that if she discovered that Victoria, too, had had a child by him, it would damage Maisie's love for him. She would wonder whether there were more revelations to come. And what would he do for his child? He could offer money, but should he not claim him or her as he had done Miranda? An allowance was what Chideock had offered to her, and what he himself had turned down due to pride. To know would be enough, and to acknowledge to Victoria that he was now mature enough to return, even staring down the barrel of a gun.

He was not prepared for the landscape to look different. Sheep grazed in fields once golden with corn. The cottage down the track now had a vegetable garden, and washing was waving to him from a line between two trees. There was Mabel, sitting in a chair, eyes shut, the sun on her face.

He looked at her, wondered why she was not up in the barn. The cottage had been unoccupied during his time there.

"Cows a-milked, then?" he called, hat over his eyes.

Mabel recognised the voice, though it lacked a face.

"'Tis you, Nicholas? You back?"

She shielded her eyes.

"'Tis me, Mabel, blown in on the wind."

He went up to her, as if to kiss her, and she was panicked into explaining that she was now married to George.

"Only been gone two minutes. Thought you might have been mine, one day," he teased.

"That be your way, Nicholas. Edith gone now."

She did not regret her reference to his dangling Edith and Victoria, two puppets, on strings, to make them dance to his tune.

"That be a lot of dreams ago."

"Why you back, then?"

"Not come to cause trouble."

"You after work?"

"Not here."

"What you been a-doing with your life, then, Nicholas?"

It was time to go. The question begged an answer as long as the lane.

"'Tis a tale which wriggle through Marshwood, down to Briddy, Lyme, and round the lanes to Bockhampton. 'Twould weary your legs."

He touched his hat, and set off up the hill to the farmhouse. Stockwood was in a field, up towards Pilsdon. Victoria was in the kitchen, preparing a stew for the evening. Megan heard him, and creaked round the corner of the lane. She barked at him loudly enough to alert Victoria, but quietened when he called to her.

"Your legs be like mother's, though I think you remember me better than she do."

Megan sniffed him, allowed him to play with her ears, as he used to.

The door opened, and Victoria stepped outside. The crouching man stood up, and she froze.

"Look all you like, but yes, 'tis me."

"Nicholas?"

"You not forgotten my name, then."

And then he noticed, how she held her hands, how they rested on her bulge, as if drawing his eyes towards it.

"You should not be here. You said you'd write, and now 'tis too late. If father comes, he will shoot you."

"'Tis true I did not write, but 'twasn't my fault. I never had my letters then. They were will o' the wisps. Never got to know 'em, growing up. How could I write?"

"You could have sent me a message, even if 'twas you had changed your mind, and wanted Edith."

He hung his head, would not insult her with an apology. That was not why he had come.

"Heard you might have made me a father, after I was sent a-packing," he put to her. "Come to be a father, one way or another, if 'tis so."

Victoria threw her head back, and laughed loudly, fetching Megan back to see what the fuss was about.

"Oh, Nicholas, you make me laugh! No, you baint the father of no child of mine, and I thank the Lord for that, for you be a year or two late, if 'twas so. You lost the tick of time? 'Tis not yesterday father shooed you."

"Wanted to see, put things right."

She laughed again so loudly that Gabriel opened the window to see what had dragged him from his afternoon sleep.

"What be the matter? I cannot rest with all this shrieking."

Misterton looked up at him, then at Victoria, who smiled.

"'Tis only the ciderman come to see if we want him to press our apples when autumn knock 'em to the ground. 'Tis a funny story he told me, though he knows I shall not be wanting his services on account of you being here, my husband, who can do what he do anyway."

Again, Misterton looked at Gabriel, pulled his hat over his eyes to hide embarrassment and hurt, and set off down the track, watched by Megan, who scratched herself, and returned to sentry duty in the shade.

Edna emerged from the milking parlour, and remembered his gait, the steady pace. Wilfred saw her looking.

"Wonder what he want," he said.

Upstairs, Gabriel resumed his afternoon nap. Victoria went

inside, and sat down. She trembled, not expecting all that, his overdue concern, his audacity. And though he was too late, she could not help recalling their parting at Shave Cross, where he had promised that he would find work, and write to her. So full of hope she had been that the discovery that Edith had betrayed her by talking to her father had hit her hard.

She could hear the steady rhythm of Gabriel's snoring. Closing her eyes, she tried to shut out the haunting images of their lovemaking, but was startled when she heard the double report of a shotgun. She rushed outside. At the top of the track stood her father.

"Father, what is it?" she cried.

He turned and looked at her accusingly.

"I told him," he said. "I told him what I'd do, and I be a man of my word."

Chapter Twenty-Five

Misterton grappled with the numbers. There were three bedrooms: one for his mother, one for Maisie and himself, and one for Miranda. When the baby is born, he thought, it will have to sleep with its sister, and if Emily turns up, she will have to sleep with mother. 'Tis a bigger house we need!

There were only two days till Miranda paid her first visit. Misterton dressed the garden, scrubbed the floor, swept the fire-grate, brushed cobwebs from the beams on the ceiling. Maisie tired quickly, suffered sickness, and helped when she could. Gradually, the house began to look different, almost too tidy. Mrs. Misterton watched her son transform it. The beds were made with clean sheets, and the pillows were aired. Maisie smiled at his suggestions of fresh flowers. And Mrs. Misterton tutted when she thought Emily late home.

"The house be a palace. 'Taint what Miranda used to, but 'twill do and more. Don't be ashamed of what we got, Nicholas. She got to blend in with us, be a heath girl," pointed out Maisie.

"Mr. Chideock will judge us," he warned. "'Tis nature."

"She *your* girl. A speck of dust, here and there, won't change that."

"*Our* girl," corrected Misterton.

He put on his coat. His clothes were clean, his appearance impressive.

"You going somewhere?"

"The farm. Thomas no regular work. Got to tether me a job by Saturday. Swallowed my pride like a pot of cider. Did a good job there, once, remember. Farm needs me again. My words will be ointment to his sores."

And he left. Firstly, he would go to the farmhouse, see if anyone he knew was still there, look at the land. Then he would go to the manor, and speak to Palfreyman. Farm manager. That's what he wanted to be again. A proper one. Not a Wareham.

The fields had grown into meadows. There were no sheep, no cows. The land looked abandoned, like a lost domain, isolated, as if consumption had wiped out all living creatures, except the birds, and flowers.

The last time he had seen the farmyard, Maisie had taken his arm, and they had been watched by Simon Beer, Katy Cerne, and William Seaton, who had taken orders from him, been paid, sheltered, fed by him. They had watched him weigh up day-labourers, and give them work. He had shouted at no one, and they had copied his respect.

He found the farmyard just as he had left it: everything in its place. The barn door was shut. Chickens stared at him. There was no smoke coming from the chimney. It was early autumn, too warm to need a fire, except for cooking. He listened at the door, thought he caught movement at the window. Then he knocked: three single raps. The door opened.

"Master?" said Simon.

"Simon?"

"'Tis me."

"Your beard be a fox's brush! No razor?"

Misterton's cheerful voice drew the others to the door.

"'Tis the master!" cried Katy.

"So it be," added William. "And so it be."

They all agreed that it was, indeed, the man who had set them on, saved Maisie, given them hope.

Misterton laughed, and took off his hat.

"Now you all satisfied 'tis me, aint you going to invite me in and tell me what there been happening while I been gone? The fields be as sad as a new widow."

They stood back, allowed him in to survey the room.

"We kept it as it was, the house," pointed out Simon.

"Case you came back," said Katy.

"You staying?" asked William.

"Hope so. That be if Palfreyman have me back."

"He don't come, these days," said Simon. "Like he's dead. His sister gone, his bride gone. He gone to seed like a thistle, and the farm a-wasting. After you gone, we stays here, but he never come. We be living off meat and milk and turnips. Eggs, too. But we don't work. Like he forgotten we're here. So we just stays, a-waiting."

"But we aint coffin-dwellers," said Katy. "Least, not yet. How be Maisie?" William looked at her as if to suggest that Maisie's absence might be a sensitive matter, and Katy put her hand to her mouth, and added, "'Taint that I be a-prying, master. I be sorry if I shouldn't have asked."

"She be fine. She having a tiddy one, soon."

And Katy burst into tears.

"Oh, master! 'Tis wondrous news."

Simon swallowed hard.

"Truly, master. Maisie Poole was almost taken, till you saved her, and now she almost a mother. 'Tis truly wondrous."

They sat at the table. There was no cider to offer, just soup, which they all ate silently, not even daring to contemplate the possibility that Palfreyman might not want Misterton back.

Eventually, Simon asked, "'Ee and Maisie coming back to live here if he have 'ee?"

Misterton had anticipated that question.

"Aint licked his boots yet."

The others could see that if he and Maisie brought their child, there would not be enough room. Misterton thought that the others would have to sleep in the barn again. It would need to be adapted, made more habitable than the last time they were in it.

"Farm need sorting," said William. "Fields aint been combed for ages."

Misterton wiped his mouth and stood up.

"I must go."

"You had your fill, master?" asked Katy.

"Left a bit of room for humble pie."

They waved him off, and shut the door.

"Master be the man to raise the farm," said William.

"Whatever he done before upset Palfreyman," reminded Simon.

"Palfreyman a fool, 'tis certain," said William.

"'Twas probably why his bride never came," suggested Katy.

Coombs went to inform Palfreyman that Misterton wanted to see him. Palfreyman had been sleeping deeply, on his chaise longue, and was now looking round the room to see where he was.

"What the deuce does he want?" he yawned.

"Don't know. He seems—"

"Tell him to go away! He's no right coming here after what he did, the scoundrel!"

"Very well, sir."

"And tell him that if I see him lurking round the estate again, I'll shoot him!"

Coombs relayed the message. Misterton winced; the wounds in his buttocks from Stockwood's welcome had still not healed properly.

"I'm afraid you called when he be suffering," said Coombs.

"We all a-suffering. Whole of Dorset be a-suffering," pointed out Misterton.

"He be a-suffering from a bad head on account of last night. I'd call at a better time, though 'tis hard to know when that be, him drinking to forget. You hear what happen in church?"

Misterton nodded.

"She be wise."

"Rumour been drifting in the kitchen that Miss. Rose got a letter telling her of his drinking habit, which he wear around Dorset like a cape."

"And where be Miss. Florence? She coming back now?"

Coombs shrugged.

"The rumours blow in from east, then west, though I pays the weathervane no heed, as 'tis certain others will float in from north and south, too. She still at Monksbury."

The next day, Misterton went to see her. He had made up his mind to ask her to speak, on his behalf, to Robert, and to acquaint her with the degradation of the farm. She knew that Misterton had been a good farm manager, though he suspected that his appeal might be shot down like a pheasant flushed from the woods. He had not gone to her room in the hotel in Lyme Regis; Emily, her protégée, had deserted her to go to Bath; and he had masqueraded as Palfreyman himself, and incurred a bill for the repair of a headstone. The odds were not favourable.

Used to the grandeur of Palfreyman Manor, he was not at all intimidated by Monksbury. Instead, he found its modest size and grounds more appealing.

He waited, hat in hand. The servants on loan from her brother for a short while had returned to their former home, and Edith, of course, had been dismissed for clandestinely colluding with Maggie. Florence was on her own, and rather liked the restorative tranquility her new circumstances brought.

Misterton licked his lips nervously as she opened the door. She looked more rested than the last time he had seen her, and flashed him a half-haughty, half-conciliatory look.

"I beg your pardon, Miss. Palfreyman, for disturbing you, but there is something I must tell you, and a favour to ask," he began.

"I am surprised, but I have been surprised often of late. I had not expected to see you again. Nor had I anticipated the arrival of a woman wanting to know your whereabouts. Imagine my consternation when Edith, who promised to be an excellent maid and possible companion, installed this . . . associate of yours in my folly overnight. Edith clearly knew where you were, and I did not. Had I known, I would not have disclosed where you lived without knowing the visitor's motives. I had, though, no alternative but to dismiss Edith. I felt betrayed, and betrayal is something I experienced when it was made clear to me that I had to leave Palfreyman Manor, my home since I was a child."

Her anger had gathered momentum, each clause in her response adding more force to her conviction.

"That be what I came to tell you, and on the back of that, I come to help Master Palfreyman, if he can forget my being wrong towards him, on account of him not sending for a doctor when Maisie's angel came to fetch her."

Florence shook her head.

"I don't understand a word you say. You talk in riddles."

"'Tis the curse of Nicholas Misterton, so I'll sing it as plain as I can. Maisie be having a baby. She lives with mother and me, now Emily in Bath. When I was sent a-packing, Maisie came with me, as she grown as close to me as this ivy to your wall. Truth be, I already been a-married, and have a child, Miranda, though I never knew, on account of me a-upping. 'Tis a tale as long and pebbly as Chesil. Now Miranda will come and live with us, but I need a job, or there be too many mouths to feed. A few labourers still be there, a-wasting their time, in the farmhouse, with nowhere to go. I could go back, set them to again." Florence had been enjoying a book prior to answering the door. She had deliberately not visited Robert. He had not replied to her letters. For too long she had borne the strain of watching him waste his life. At Monksbury, she had begun to take pleasure in her own solitude, found time for her own inclinations, instead of organising servants, maintaining a house her brother owned but neglected. And now that Misterton had confirmed her worst fears, and offered an end to the farm's decline, she saw no reason to make matters worse by sending him away.

"There is some merit to your proposal, which would serve us all well. I'll tell you what I will do: I will pay your wages if you restore the farm to its former state, as it was when you were in charge. Do what is necessary. Robert spoke so highly of you that he confined his previous involvement to ensuring that you had all that you needed. He was confident you would make him a handsome profit. Your predecessor was unsuitable. I warned Robert, but he thought Wareham would be a harsh task-master, the sort other land-owners urged him to hire. There had been agitation among the farm-workers all over Dorset. They were being paid a pittance, and Wareham squeezed every drop of life out of his. I despised him."

"He got his reward in the end, though. Had it coming."

She looked at him oddly.

"Whatever he did, he didn't deserve to lose his life, which is precious. It is a sin to take a life."

He thought of Edith, pictured Wareham pinning her to the ground, his grinning, till she stabbed him in self-defence.

"They ever catch him?" asked Misterton.

"The police spoke to everyone. The problem is that day-labourers come and go. Wareham kept no record of whom he hired. It was a shambles till you came."

"And then I was sent on my way."

"But you will resume your duties on the basis I propose?"

"'Tis kind to forgive me, and I say yes."

Florence smiled, almost laughed.

"Kind, yes. But forgive you? No, Mr. Misterton. I will never forgive you, though you were right. It was an obsession born of my position in the house, and which embarrasses me still. But living at Monksbury has helped me to escape the confinement of the other place. I am mistress here, but I was the woman who gave instructions to the servants there. Robert made the big decisions. If my brother comes to the farm, tell him you are there on my instruction, and ask him to see me. Come to me if you need money. I trust you. Keep good accounts, and show them to me, once a week. There are some things I cannot help Robert with, but I see no reason why I, too, should neglect the farm. Who knows? Maybe, one day, I shall be a proper mistress when he has drunk himself to death."

Misterton hung his head. She had drawn a line under the past. Maisie and he would stay in the cottage. Simon, Katie and William would remain in the farmhouse. Simon could build up the animal stock again, and William could keep the woods, shoot pheasants. Katie could run the house, collect the eggs. And he himself could oversee it all, order seed and equipment, keep accounts, pay the bills, visit Florence.

"'Tis kind of you," he said, swallowing hard. "'Tis wondrous kind."

He could not wait to return to the farm, and tell the others that he would again be their master. He began to plan. Katy was the only woman, and her privacy was limited. The barn was not a suitable place for itinerant labourers. One of the outbuildings must be converted. Then there were rams to bring to the ewes. The two fields adjacent to the farmhouse would be jumping with lambs in the spring.

He knocked on the door, and found his workers in a sombre mood. Even when he was telling them about Florence's plan, no smile lit their faces.

"And 'tis like I come and you all have a hangman's rope round your necks. What crime you committed? Come Simon. You have words a-plenty, enough to fill a book or two. Find some that explain why your faces be death-masks."

Simon looked at the others, and they nodded.

"'Twas while you been gone. Master Palfreyman, he been here a-ranting in drink. Smell it on him the moment he bursts through the door, a-screaming at us to go, and slashing the air with his riding crop so that it whistle."

Misterton noticed William's hand on his face, and moved it to reveal a red welter where the whip had stung him.

"He did that?" croaked Misterton.

"He comes for me like a madman, and then William steps between us, and he took the whipping instead," explained Katy.

Misterton's lips and hands curled in anger.

"He'll suffer for this!" he promised. "He must be threshed like corn at harvest-time. He no better than Wareham."

Misterton rushed out the house.

"Don't, master, please! 'Twas the drink in him," begged Simon.

Misterton occasionally broke into a run. Up his sleeve was a riding crop he had picked up from the barn. Palfreyman would know what William had felt.

By the time Misterton reached the manor's gates, he was sweating profusely, and he wiped his sleeve across his forehead. It was important, he felt, to appear calm. He would say that he bore a message from Florence. If Palfreyman were still drunk, the very mention of the name Misterton would be enough to incite him.

Misterton could see through the gates that a coach and two were outside the front entrance. They did not belong to Palfreyman. A visitor might thwart his plan. Then the door opened, and out stepped a man in black tails. He had a pointed, white beard, and in his hand was a large, black bag.

Coombs emerged after him. The two men exchanged words, and the coach moved towards the gates. Misterton hid behind a tree, even suppressed a sneeze as the coach rattled past. Coombs began to close the gates, and Misterton made his presence known.

"Be the master in the mood to see me? I have business with him, and though he baint expecting me, he'll put down his glass and attend. 'Tis Nicholas Misterton, and I be 'ere to make him an offer."

Coombs looked at him in surprise.

"You on the farm after Wareham? You the man make a go of it?"

"That be a season or two ago."

"'Tis true he sent you a-packing?"

"'Tis true his heart be a fossil."

"You can't see him," said Coombs decisively, shutting the gate. "He won't talk to nobody today."

"You aint going to ask him?"

Coombs shook his head.

"Could do, but I'd be a-waiting for an answer till the sun and stars be snuffed by the pinched fingers of the Lord himself."

"And why be that?"

The whip up his sleeve stiffened his arm, made it look injured, unnatural.

"Well, the sketch of it be that Bosun, his hound, went a-riding with him, and came back, all a-panting, on his own. 'Tis unusual, that, as the dog be the master's shadow. I hears Bosun's deep, loud bark. I goes to stable Roman, thinking the master be back, but he aint there. Bosun be all agitated, worse than when he want a-feeding. He then runs off out the grounds, and I follows him. I be out of breath afore I sees Roman a-munching grass. I looks about me, but the master be nowhere. Then Bosun stands at the top of a pit, and calls me over with a howl which freezes the hairs on my neck. There, at the bottom, lies the master, all cut, bruised, and a-bleeding."

"Be there a bottle in his hand? I doubt it not."

"Bottle or no bottle, he baint have been able to drink."

"Then 'tis a thing as rare as his kindness," said Misterton.

"No more will he drink, for the master been thrown by Roman, by the looks of it."

"His bones been broken?"

"Whipped Roman too many times, be my judgement. Roman stronger than him, see. The doctor a-been, and 'tis certain: the master be gone, and it be my task to go to Monksbury to give Miss. Palfreyman the bad news."

Misterton let the riding crop slip from his sleeve.

"Then 'tis Providence," he declared, " and what do please God."

Chapter Twenty-Six

Dorothy gently closed the study door behind her, as if not wishing to awaken a sleeping child. Earlier, Chideock had asked to see her, and she had seen in his face that the matter on which he wished to speak was no ordinary one.

"Do come in and sit down, Dorothy," he invited, avoiding eye contact.

His writing desk separated them, and he fiddled nervously with his pen.

Miranda was playing with her doll's house. Usually, she would have been within calling distance of her nurse.

"Thank you. Miranda's safe, upstairs."

Decisively, Chideock put down his pen, drew a deep breath, and began.

"What I have to say will take you by surprise, but there is no way of avoiding it. As you know, Miranda was adopted by Myrtle and I, following the death of Miranda's mother. To me, Miranda has always been *my* child; having her from a very young age made that easier to believe. Ruth Abbas, however, was married, and when her husband left her, he was unaware that she was expecting a baby. And this is where it gets difficult, Dorothy, and circumstances prevent me from withholding from you information which will change the course of all our lives."

Dorothy frowned. In his voice, she detected a tremulousness she had heard only in the days following Myrtle's death, when grief shook him so hard that his knife and fork rattled on his plate.

"Whatever it is, if I must know, then please tell me. It obviously distresses you."

"A long time ago, there was an announcement in the paper, requesting information about Miranda's whereabouts. Fearful that its author was her real father, I replied anonymously, saying that she had emigrated to Australia with her adoptive parents. I lied because I did not want us to lose her, and have her world turned upside down. Whatever his reason for leaving his wife, Miranda is his daughter, and my deception, I have decided, must end. In years to come, Miranda would not thank me for deceiving her, too, if her father ever found her. Therefore, I have made contact with him, and he has expressed a wish to get to know her, with the view to her going to live with him, permanently."

Dorothy quickly worked out the implications for herself. Since Myrtle's death, she had become close to Miranda, who had clung to her. Dorothy had tried to maintain a professional distance, but, at times, it had been impossible. Now her services might not be needed, soon, and the prospect of separation from the child she had come to love threw her into a panic.

"Oh, Mr. Chideock, please don't do it! This is her home. She has suffered much since she came into the world, and now she will lose you!" she protested. "It would be cruel!"

Suddenly wounded by this accusation, he snatched the pen from the desk, and stabbed it into its surface, bending the nib, and breaking the pen in half. Dorothy recoiled; she had never seen him so angry.

"Cruel? *Cruel*? You talk to me of *cruelty*? Is it not cruel to deprive her of her real father? He left his wife, not his daughter. He did not know about the child."

Dorothy hung her head.

"Forgive me, Mr. Chideock, for speaking from the heart. I want only what is best for Miranda, but I have spoken out of place."

Chideock was trembling, making visible attempts to calm himself, control the volume of his voice, which had risen.

"It is I who must apologise. I have agonised over this. I have had to consider the morality of my lie, just as I have had to accept that Myrtle is dead. I have a factory to run. That responsibility limits the time I can spend with Miranda. And then there are . . . but I will not burden you with that."

"Please, open your heart, Mr. Chideock, if it helps you to see that Miranda's place is with you."

The surge of anger, which had overwhelmed him, a few moments before, almost returned. He was not used to being challenged like this.

"There have been times when I, too, have thought that, but be aware that it was my wife's desire alone which led to Miranda's adoption. I tried hard to convince her that it was the Lord's wish that we should be childless, but she persisted in trying to persuade me otherwise. Eventually, I relented, and, in time, grew to love Miranda, but none of us owns anyone else, and her real father now wishes to get to know her. In all honesty, my circumstances are likely to change. I have found living alone depressing. I want the warmth of a woman's companionship." Here, Dorothy hung her head in embarrassment. "Making and selling rope cannot be my only fulfilment. I'm sorry if my candour distresses you, but it is *Myrtle*'s life which has ended, not mine."

Dorothy stiffened, summoned the courage to advance the conclusion to which the meeting was leading.

"I understand. I shall leave whenever you wish. You've made your position clear."

"We leave early for Dorchester, in the morning. Miranda will need to look her best. We will stay overnight in a hotel, so please pack additional clothes for her."

"I will pack her case, but refuse to go with you. It would be tantamount to condoning your decision. I would be glad if you could advise me when I am to leave, so that I can make arrangements."

"I was hoping you would stay till the matter had been concluded."

"Matter? You call Miranda a *matter*? I had a different opinion of you, Mr. Chideock. It is best if I leave now."

Chideock opened his drawer, and took out an envelope, which he slid across his desk. So, he was prepared for this, she thought.

"I have paid you your wages, and an additional sum reflecting your dedication to Miranda. There is also a letter of recommendation which should secure you a position elsewhere, in the very near future."

Dorothy took the envelope, and left the room.

Chideock went to his sideboard, and poured himself a large brandy, which he attacked. He wanted rid of the acidic taste of opposition. How could the nurse possibly know what it felt like to be him, to know there was another man with a greater right to Miranda than him?

Back at his desk, he took out from a drawer a copy of her birth certificate, and the certificate of adoption issued by the parish. And that was all there was to prove her connection with both men: two pieces of paper.

Misterton rose early on the Saturday. His sleep had been as thin as gossamer. Maisie spoke to him, and he would not look at her as he replied, not wanting her to see the fear of the unknown in his eyes.

"'Tis a day to remember," she told him. "You look like you just seen a ghost."

"She will look like Ruth, who be a ghost. If Miranda knows already who I be, then her eyes will haunt me for leaving her mother. If not, then we must knead our time together till it rise and taste good."

"She be too young to know such things. 'Twill flow as smoothly as the Frome," Maisie reassured.

"But the river bursts and floods when 'tis swollen and angry," he pointed out. "People sometimes swept away in the rush of it."

"My cake clogged with cream. She will like that."

Maisie went to the table, on which sat the cake.

"'Tis true. Mother made cakes I stole afore Emily and father neared 'em!"

"Be happy for this day, Nicholas, as 'twill be one you won't forget, this side of the grave."

"You be a fine one, be all your talk of the grave."

Mrs. Misterton went outside, calling, "Cake smell good. Cut me a piece for when I gets back."

They watched her walk to the fence, and stroke the pony, which stood still for her. Her hand traced the muscular hills and vales of its haunches.

"Put the cake away for Mr. Chideock and Miranda. Mother won't remember it been on the table. Don't want creatures a-jabbing their noses in the cream. 'Tis warm enough for thunder flies, which stick to everything like whiskers," advised Misterton.

When Mrs. Misterton returned, she said, "Old soldier would stand there all day if I carried on a-patting him. What you two done with the cake? You not saved any for that poor, little girl a-coming?"

Misterton looked at Maisie in disbelief at her remembering what she had been told.

"What little girl?" tested Maisie.

"That Emily. Love her cake, little Emily do."

And Misterton could not bear the disappointment, so set off early for Dorchester, leaving Maisie to explain that they would soon be having visitors.

Misterton thought about watching The King's Arms from a distance, so that he could see his daughter before she saw him. Ruth lived on through Miranda. If Miranda resembled her mother, then he would have Ruth back with him, be reunited with her.

In the hour before they were due to arrive, he went into the bookshop. The bell clanged loudly, surprising him; he did not recall there being one above the door. Silence settled like particles of dust. The rattle of carts' wheels, and the bawling of commerce, were locked outside. The owner was sitting at the back of the shop, his ledger in front of him. He followed his forefinger with the aid of spectacles clinging to the end of his shining nose, down which they slipped whenever he leaned forward.

"Good day to 'ee," called Misterton.

"Good day to you, too, sir," replied the book-seller.

"Father's shelves be still up, after all these years?"

The book-seller eased his spectacles up his nose. The last time he had seen Jacob Misterton, Jacob had been in his work clothes, and the shop had been filled with banging and sawdust.

"They are. They are, indeed! They are the finest shelves in Dorchester. Their extra depth takes the weight off the feet of the largest tomes. They are shelves *par excellence. Par excellence!*"

Misterton's hat was at home. His usual companion, it was in a chest, out of sight, considered too battered, too time-degraded, by Maisie. Fiddling with its curling brim comforted him, led him up the rungs to his opening sentences to people, and now he felt bare and tongue-tied.

"Good. Er, good."

After a few seconds, in which Misterton let his eyes rove over his father's work, the book-seller asked, "You looking for anything in particular?"

"You have a book for a young child?"

"Probably. Child read like a good one?"

Misterton had no idea. He assumed so, having a nurse all to herself.

"Expect so."

The book-seller licked his lips, loved to show his knowledge, so went over to a shelf, and began pointing.

"Ghosts a-haunting country houses; giants a-roaming the countryside; dragons a-breathing smoke and fire. Boy or girl?"

"Girl."

Then Misterton remembered his last visit to Conjuror Sayer. Seek a boy, not a girl, Misterton had been told. Conjuror Sayer's knowledge had been wrong because he was now old, like Mrs. Misterton. That was the reason; had to be, concluded Misterton. Percival might have told him a lie.

"Girls got imagination, too," said the book-seller. "They read more quickly, though women don't buy as much as men, who like stories in ships and in strange lands, where people wear unusual clothes, and speak in weird tongues."

"And what do girls like?"

The book-seller scratched his head.

"Love stories, mostly. They more interested in feelings than fights, though Mr. Charles Dickens puts his arms round both men and women, and leads 'em alike down murky streets in London. His stories are full of characters as grotesque as any in fairyland. His giants and monsters be human."

Misterton chose a book with drawings of exotic birds, animals, and flowers.

"Not sure I want to frighten her with this first book. This look good. How much?"

"Take it. If 'tis for a child, then 'tis free as the air."

Misterton tried to force a coin or two on him, but the book-seller would not take them.

"Then 'tis kind."

The book-seller wrapped it in brown paper, and tied it neatly with string.

"I hope she enjoys it. And the child's name?"

"Miranda."

"Shakespeare! The daughter of Prospero, a wizard. She will grow up with a head full of spells."

Misterton left, happy that Ruth had chosen that name, one to turn heads, make someone listen.

He decided to wait up the hill, watch The King's Arms from a doorway. In his hand was the gift. A book would show Chideock that he valued reading, Miranda that he wanted her to have knowledge, as well as spells.

A woman walked past, and glanced at him. She took a more deliberate look, and Misterton averted his gaze.

"I know you from somewhere?" she asked.

"Doubt it. I don't talk to women I don't know."

The woman put her forefinger to her lips as she thought.

"Now don't you go getting all like that with me. I aint that sort of woman. Now let me see. Yes, I knows, though 'tis a birthday or two since I last sold you frumenty, at the fair. If I remembers right, you broke that fellow's arm in the wrestling. And you never did come in and see me in The King's Arms!"

A different place, a different time. All that concerned him now was that Chideock should not see him talking to a woman who sold frumenty.

"I remember the day well. Your frumenty be good."

"Make you some more?"

He smiled at her invitation and wink.

"'Tis wondrous kind, but my Maisie make it for me, these days."

"Then she be a lucky girl."

"I'll tell her."

The woman continued up the hill, and did not turn round. She had welcomed him from his exile, had offered him something, and denied him nothing. And she had remembered him, after all that time, long before he knew Maisie, and discovered that his father would now never hear the apology he had vowed he would make.

Maisie had fretted, that morning.

"Nicholas, what will she call me? I baint her mother, so mother sound like a crow. Maisie be my name, but she be just a child to call me that," she had said.

"Maisie be a buttercup; mother be just a word of six letters. There be crowds of mothers, but not Maisies. When she taste your cake, she'll be your shadow, a-tugging at your dress till you bake another. I shall say you be Maisie. 'Tis enough, at the moment. Fill her basket with too many eggs, and some will break, 'tis certain."

Maisie had looked at him doubtfully, but his kiss on her forehead had made the matter less important

She had put out clean clothes for Mrs. Misterton.

"Baint be Sunday already?" Mrs. Misterton had cried. "Where do time run?"

"Saturday today, not Sunday. Visitors be a-coming, like I told you. Miranda. Remember?"

But Mrs. Misterton had taken the dress up to her room, and put it back in the chest. That was her church dress. She was not going to wear it on a Friday for anyone, she had muttered.

Misterton walked down to The King's Arms. Chideock would be expecting to see him waiting for them. Misterton looked up and down the hill for a man, a child, and possibly a woman, the nurse, if Chideock had decided to bring her. The clock struck twelve, and Misterton took a deep breath. There was no sign of a child, and that was what he wanted to see.

Then there was a tap on his shoulder. It was Chideock, his face creased. Black bags sagged under his eyes. He must have come out of The King's Arms, deduced Misterton. The handshake was uninspired, hesitant.

"I been a-watching for you up-a-hill, down," opened Misterton.

"I just had a drink."

Misterton sensed something wrong, smelt it as he always did on the land, when a storm was brewing, or a lamb went missing. Iron, gunpowder, and camphor, all mixing in the air.

"Where be Miranda? She inside? Got a present for her. 'Tis only tiddy, but pretty."

Chideock hung his head, and swallowed.

"I'm afraid I've not brought her."

"You changed your mind? After all you said? Or she didn't want come? 'Tis that?"

Chideock had started to shake his head after the first question.

"No, none of those things. I wish it were. But the fact is, Miranda has gone."

"Gone?" gasped Misterton. "'Tis certain?"

"Not dead, no. Disappeared, taken by her nurse, who could not bear the separation. The police are looking for her. I'm sorry."

Misterton shook his head.

"And there be a cake, too, which Maisie baked."

"They will find her, and maybe have, already. Dorothy loves her, and no harm will come to her. Dorothy's mind is but temporarily disturbed."

Misterton started to run down the hill.

"Where you going?" called Chideock.

But Misterton did not reply; it was important to see Conjuror Sayer as soon as possible.

Chapter Twenty-Seven

When Edith said goodbye to Maggie, following their visit to see Misterton, she knew that she must see him again soon. Her willingness to help Maggie trace him and return his wedding ring had cost Edith her job at Monksbury. If only Maggie had not left the note in the temple! she wished. On such trivial oversights does fate rely to bestow happiness, or inflict misery.

Edith had money to last her a week or two, but no more. The little room she took in Dorchester was pleasant enough, overlooked a square with grass and a seat or two, where she might sit and enjoy the flowers. She was still intent on addressing the matter on which she had made up her mind in London. Misterton had once offered her a refuge when she had fled from the farm, to avoid arrest, following Wareham's death, and had nursed her back to tolerable health, as he had Maisie, later. In Edith's hour of need, he had been there for her, and he had, therefore, to be the first to know of her decision.

That he had been married when she had loved him, at Gifford's Farm, and that he had been selfishly taking advantage of Victoria, mattered little to her now. Somehow, even though he lived with Maisie, she felt an affinity with him. Maisie would understand.

On the Saturday Misterton discovered that Miranda had been abducted by her nurse, Edith rose early. Determined to make the most of the fine weather, which showed no sign of changing, though the leaves had begun to curl and gather in crispy clumps, she walked into Dorchester. She felt strangely uplifted by the thought that soon she would be rid of the secret which, though kept as tight as the door to an airless catacomb, had lived with her since she had taken a life to save her own.

After feeding birds from a seat – they had flapped frenziedly round her feet – she strolled through the town. The light set fire to the golden stone of the buildings. She placed her hands on the walls; already they were retaining the sun's heat. In the clear sky, the moon shyly offered half its face, as if posing for a portrait to be hung in the Dorchester Museum.

It was as good a day as any, she decided, to go and see Misterton. She had all day to walk to Bockhampton and back. The corn was cut, the stooks had been stacked into gently swelling mounds, like smaller coastal hills. The hedgerows drooped with the weight of blackberries. Sheep gathered in the shade of trees and hedges, and mist indolently stayed in bed in the lower fields.

Edith reached the fringe of the town, when she heard the sound of fearful wheezing. She turned to see a man running desperately, his neck straining with urgency. Anxious to be safe, she stood aside, close to the hedge, to let him pass, and as he did so, she saw it was Misterton.

"Nicholas?"

His wild eyes met hers, and he stopped, his breathing robbing him of normal speech.

"Edith," he gasped. "You."

He bent forward, hands on knees, as if offering himself for a game of leapfrog. She laid her hands on his shoulders, to comfort him.

"'Tis all right, Nicholas. Whatever it be, 'twill be all right."

With her other arm, she raised him into an upright position, and drew him to her. She felt his heart pounding in her ears, his chest rising and falling like bellows squeezed by a blacksmith determined to revive his furnace.

Gradually, his heaving subsided, and he drew back to look at her.

"She disappeared, Edith."

"Who, Nicholas? Who disappeared?"

"Miranda, my daughter. What you doing, going down this road?"

"To see you, Nicholas. To see you."

She put her arm in his, and he realised the futility of running.

"Why you want to see me?"

"There be something I got to tell you, dear, and there be no one else, you being the only one who cared for me." Misterton stopped. His tears fell silently. Edith clutched his arm more tightly, seeing how big the splashes onto the floor were. "'Tis all right, Nicholas. Things work out, in the end. Tide always come in, and the sun always rise and set. Things we can change, things we can't."

He nodded, wiped his face on his sleeve.

"'Tis certain. You got something to say, say it now. 'Twill take my mind off things."

"Oh, I doubt it, Nicholas. I doubt it very much."

Misterton stopped.

"Well, if 'tis passing strange for me, then let us sit in this field, while you tell me. My legs wobble like I grown old, and my face burns."

He helped her over the stile, and they sat on a dry carpet of straw. Outstretched on it, his breathing was slowing, and Edith lay down beside him, and rested her head on his chest. His right arm pulled her closer, till he felt the warmth of her breath.

"Tell me, Nicholas. Who be Miranda, and where she gone?"

"Then you tell me afterwards what brings you back to me, to tell me things."

"I will."

So Misterton began, and Edith listened, smelling him, as she used to do in the loft at Gifford's Farm. When he had finished, he took back his arm, now dead with the weight of her head, and shook it like a wet coat. Soon the tingling stopped, and Edith began.

At the end of what she had to say, there was silence, bar the occasional complaint of a sheep. Misterton contemplated her intention, and told her she should go with him to the cottage, to be with Maisie.

"'Tis for the best. I have to help to find Miranda, and Maisie need someone to talk to, what with mother being blown about like washing in the wind, and Maisie having a tiddy one to grow."

"'Tis wondrous kind, but where will I sleep?"

"In Miranda's room," he came back quickly. "She won't be needing it for a while."

Back at the cottage, Maisie listened to Misterton's account of what had happened to Miranda. Mrs. Misterton slowly hummed a tune she was making up, and peeled potatoes.

"Then we best eat a slice of my cake, which be a-sitting and a-waiting in vain," she sighed. "Don't want the cream to sour."

Edith was hungry, took a slice willingly, ate hungrily. Maisie watched her, examined Misterton's explanation of why she had come. He had said she was seeking work, though Maisie wondered how Edith had come to know he was again the Farm Manager. How odd that their paths should meet!

"Bump into each other, then?" said Maisie. "You worried 'bout Wareham? Mouths all been shut; no one knowed a thing when they asked."

The last bit of Edith's slice stopped in the air.

"Not any more," replied Edith, at last.

Misterton watched the women, squirmed in his chair.

"Edith staying tonight, maybe the night after, then be going to the farm. I'm off for an hour, to think. My head be all boggy. The day been clappety."

"What you doing 'bout Miranda?" asked Maisie.

"Pray she be found safe. Need to find her."

Irritated by Maisie's attitude, he set off onto the heath, bound for Conjuror Sayer's cottage. On his way, Misterton kicked the heather, stunned a bee with a swipe of his hand.

The old man peeped out of the window, his eyes blood-shot and yellow. He had slept through the afternoon, and was now exhausted. On his table, the jug for special juice was empty. He rubbed his eyes, which were not ready to focus. As he yawned, he showed rotting stumps of teeth.

"'Tis Nicholas Misterton. You remember me?"

Conjuror Sayer opened the door. Misterton followed him, and looked for the bird.

"Percival gone?"

The old man had to think.

"Been gone ages. What you want?"

"Knowledge, though knowledge that baint mouldy. Last time, you said a boy, when 'twas a girl. Don't want mould again, not at that price, but 'tis burning me, and I must know where she is." The old man wrapped his scarf around Misterton's eyes. "Don't trick me, old man," threatened Misterton. "'Tis my daughter I need to find. Say if you know; let me go if you don't have the knowledge."

"Sure 'twas a boy," muttered the Conjuror, filling his jug with ale. Into it, he poured a vial of dark liquid, and mixed it with his crooked, yellow finger, which he licked.

"'Twas a girl!" shouted Misterton. "A girl!"

"Percival baint here to answer. Drink."

Misterton drank greedily. The opium changed the shape of furniture, made objects lurch drunkenly, gave them sounds and colours. Bright lights ringed the room. Water rushed, lifted and dropped. Conjuror Sayer finished the jug, and cursed.

"Too much! Oh, far too much!"

Misterton's eyes shut. He was elsewhere: up a mountain, in a river, in a dark, misshapen house, but he could hear, hear the Conjuror's knowledge come tip-toeing out of his mouth.

"In a room. The sea grabs at the wide wall, clouts, and spits at it. A woman. A girl. The girl cries, and the woman rocks her in her arms till she sleeps."

"The girl has dark hair?"

"'Tis black."

"Her name?"

Conjuror Sayer shook his head; the woman had not named her.

The opium rushed through Misterton's body, but he did not miss the Conjuror saying the name of the hotel in Lyme Regis, the one in which he had stayed with Florence Palfreyman.

At that moment, Maggie was knocking on their door. Dorothy peered into the corridor, through the crack she protected. On the tray was tea, hot chocolate, cake. Miranda had complained of being hungry, wondered where her father was, moped.

"He's given us some money to go on holiday. Look. Here it is. Tomorrow, we're going to go on a boat to France. That will be nice. He's very busy, at the moment. And you'll be able to learn French. You've learned some already, haven't you? *Je m'appelle Miranda.* Say it, dear. *Je m'appelle Miranda.*"

But Miranda was enjoying her cake, and inspecting what was left after each bite, in case some of it disappeared inexplicably while she was chewing.

Dorothy was watching her. Already she felt guilty at what she had done: merely replaced one separation from Chideock with another. But it was too late. The plan to take her to France, for just long enough to make him see sense, miss her, must go ahead.

Down in the vestibule, Maggie was still thinking about how she had been asked to leave the tray outside, in the corridor, instead of taking it into the room. She knew there was a child; she had seen her when they had arrived to register.

"Penny for them," said Edward Frome, behind his desk. "I hope you're not thinking of cancelling our dinner engagement, this evening."

"No. My face be a wet Sunday on account of that lady in twenty-four. I had to leave the tray outside, and she kept the door shut, so I had to squint to see the little girl. 'Twas like the woman wanted to keep her a secret, when most mothers would want to show off such a pretty face."

"Don't fret so, or *your* pretty face'll be furrowed as a field, afore the Good Lord cuts you down and harvests you. I go off duty now. Don't like thinking you baint happy."

She smiled weakly, and went back to the kitchen, and it was there that she decided that, when she collected the empty tray, she would enquire about the little girl.

The tray had been left outside the door, so Maggie knocked. There was no reply. On the tray, on the floor, one plate had been licked clean. Perhaps, they are asleep, or have gone for a walk, she supposed. She took out her skeleton key, when she was sure that it was safe to enter. The wardrobe was empty. They had gone.

Down at the desk, she asked the new receptionist if they had paid their bill.

"Yes, about fifteen minutes ago. Said they had a change of plan, when I asked if everything was to their satisfaction."

"Can I look at the book, please?"

The receptionist turned it round, and pointed to the last entry. Reading was not Maggie's strong point.

"Lavinia and Elizabeth Montrose, they be," he said. "Funny woman. Didn't want her change. In a bit of a rush, if you asks me."

"Say where they going?"

"No. Just grabs the child's hand, and strides out as if she late for something."

Maggie took off her white apron, and threw it across the counter.

"Don't ask!" she said.

Then she ran into the street. They could not have gone far. Maggie's instinct was to search for them, sure that the names in the guestbook were false.

When Misterton awoke, Conjuror Sayer was sitting at the table, fiddling with odds and ends in a box. Slowly, the parts of the room started to fit together, till it was whole again.

"I must go," croaked Misterton.

"'Twas definitely a boy, last time. Split yolk for a boy. Cleared it up. And now 'tis a hotel in Lyme."

Misterton arranged money abstractedly on the table. The Conjuror stared at it, eyes bulging.

"Thank you," said Misterton, shaking himself from his stupor.

He thought of Edith, and her plan, and now he was being pulled in opposite directions. Firstly, he would send a message to Chideock. He had heard of the telegraph, that it could send messages down a wire. That would be the quickest way. And if Conjuror Sayer were wrong again, then he would kill him. Afterwards, he would need to return to Dorchester.

The telegram was sent to Chideock, but it was the next day before he and the police arrived at the hotel. Maggie's description of the woman and child confirmed that it was, indeed, Dorothy and Miranda.

"Looked up-a-hill, down, for them, but they blown away like thistle flock. 'Twas passing strange."

"And so did I," added the receptionist. "While her mother, or whomsoever she be, was paying the bill, the tiddy one kept a-reciting, '*Je m'appelle Miranda,*' which be French, if I baint mistaken."

On their way out, the policeman asked Chideock, "Girl know French, then?"

Chideock shook his head.

"Not to my knowledge, no."

"And her nurse?"

Chideock recalled Dorothy saying that she had learned some French from her father, who travelled often to France, on cargo ships."

"It's possible."

"Then we best go down the harbour, see what we can see."

The Queen's Consort should have left, that morning, but a few hands had turned up late, enfeebled in body and mind by drinking too much wine and brandy, in the town. The Captain had a mind to sack them, but knew that he would find few experienced replacements.

The Captain had ensured that travellers had paid their passage, and were settled in their cabins. The police stated their business, asked if he had the woman and child on board.

"No woman and child on this ship. 'Taint my job to tell a woman her place, me being a bachelor, and determined so a one by Providence, but a ship baint a place for such ones, as 'tis a man's province, and ever will be, be my opinion, which be the only one that count, me being Captain, who have the say-so."

"You mind if we have a look round?"

"Not at all, though I'd be glad if you policemen would turn a blind eye to all the goods for which we aint yet paid a loading tax, on account of this ship being so many hands short that I been too busy to pay the harbour master his dues."

The police assured him that they had more pressing matters, and that it was more a matter for the Revenue than them. Their search, however, proved fruitless. Chideock cursed Misterton. The telegram had raised hopes, put them all on the scent, only to see them dashed on the rocky outcrop of despair.

They visited all the hotels and guesthouses, but none had taken in a woman and a young girl.

"How did this man know that they had been to a hotel here?" asked one of the officers.

"No idea," confessed Chideock. "He's Miranda's father. I shall have to go and see him. It's quite extraordinary. He lives on the other side of Dorchester."

"Then I suggest he knows more than we think. This is a most unusual case. I think we ourselves should pay this Misterton a visit."

Saddened and frustrated that they had been close to finding Dorothy and Miranda, Chideock returned to Bridport. He locked the door behind him. The factory would have to wait till the next day.

The first brandy made him cough, hungry. There was a little bacon, an egg or two. On the wall was a portrait of Myrtle. She was smiling at him, reminding him of happier times. How she would have ranted at me, he thought, if she knew that I had lost our daughter!

He ate his food quickly, and went upstairs to rest. At the end of the landing was Miranda's room, to which he was drawn, his mind swimming in a sea of brandy-induced sentimentality.

He opened the door slowly, feeling he had no longer the right to intrude. The doll's house was by the window. He walked towards it, looked through the front door, heard her speaking to him:

"Father. Where have you been? Dorothy has gone, and I'm hungry."

Chapter Twenty-Eight

He began to climb the tree by running at it, and grabbing the branch which had grown horizontally. As he pulled himself up, he swung his right leg over it, as if mounting a horse, giving him enough points of contact to wriggle into an upright position. The easier route would have been up the trunk, using knots as foot and hand holds, but he was bored, wanted a different challenge, to pit himself against Nature.

His father watched him, admired his strength and agility. Nicholas was now taller than him, and there had been a subtle, mutual display of pride when they had stood back to back, and seen how Nicholas had overtaken him.

"Well, 't'as happened, as is normal, and let us hope that 'ee use thy height and strength well in thy work," Jacob had said.

Nicholas had smiled, had waited for that day, when he had surpassed his father for the first time in his life.

Higher up the tree climbed Nicholas, stopping only to pluck a pear, and bite into its hard, speckled flesh. He heard it crunch, took one more bite before throwing the core at a squirrel, which was jumping across the undergrowth. When he reached the top of the tree, he returned to the branch, and leapt to the ground. He had learned to soften his landing by bending his knees and rolling, but, this time, he lost control, exposing his bare hands and arms to a crown of nettles. The welters were painful, so he grabbed a leaf, and rubbed them rapidly, as if summoning a shine on his leather boots.

He looked around for something else to do, ripped up a spear with pink feathers from the ground, and launched it into the air. It flew high and long. Once he had perfected his technique, he aimed at targets: trees, birds, butterflies.

He sprinted at bushes, and leapt over them. Then he tried doing it with his eyes shut. The first time, he was anxious, which stiffened his limbs; the second, he mastered it. He ran and ran, hurdling everything in his path. More than a match for Nature, he did forward rolls in the soft grass, loved the sensation of the Earth being upside down.

And then it returned: his dissatisfaction with their patch of the heath. Up the hill and beyond was the forbidden kingdom. What danger was so great that he must avoid it, he who was now taller than his father? The warning had been clear enough. It was a bad place. A conjuror lived there. Nicholas had pressed his father to tell him what a conjuror did, but his father's reluctance to divulge the truth made him curious.

Nicholas had asked friends, who invented stories: a conjuror was the incarnation of an evil spirit; someone who ate children; a magician with a spell to change people into birds. And how do you become a conjuror? he had asked. You can't become one, they had told him; you have to be born one.

Nicholas ignored his father's warning. To see a conjuror perform his magic was what Nicholas wanted, *needed* to do. To know about everything was only natural. How could he defeat evil unless he recognised it?

In Conjuror Sayer's garden, beyond the rotting, wooden fence, there were no flowers or vegetables. The heath had seized a grip; the paling might as well not have been there. All the way up to the door grew knots of grass and weeds. There was no path from the gate. It was as if no one ever walked there. Maybe there was another entrance at the rear.

Nicholas stood at the gate, disappointed, even thought the house abandoned, so lifeless it looked. Then he heard the rattling of an upstairs window being opened. A man leaned out, and gruffly called to him, "You want something?"

The man's hair stuck out at odd angles, like a clump of dry grass, and his eyes bulged, as if something were pushing them out of their sockets. His cheeks were sunken, his neck as thin and gristly as a chicken's.

"Do a conjuror live here? They say so, and that he can cook spells, which is why I be here: to see if 'tis true."

"I be Conjuror Sayer. Who be you?"

"Nicholas Misterton. You baint have seen me before, though I live on the heath, and my father stops me a-coming, on account of him saying there be bad things here."

"And how many times he been, to know 'tis idle gossip and superstition?"

Nicholas shrugged.

"Then you do spells and magic?"

"I got the knowledge, see things others can't. That be all the bad I do, and 'tis why I be here like a hermit, till a body comes for help, and we be like the last left on Earth, we so few, nowadays."

"Why don't folk come as before?"

"The church forbid it. When I die, I will rot in these clothes, and them who find me will see my skeleton. There be no stairway to Heaven for me."

Nicholas felt the grievance in Conjuror Sayer's words and tone, he himself knowing the pain of disapproval, when it had been applied with a strap.

"Nor for I. 'Tis something I hate, church-going."

Conjuror Sayer waited, then said, "Wait a minute."

Nicholas went into the house, when the conjuror beckoned him.

"I don't disturbs you?"

"No. Sit yourself down, you got a minute or two."

When his eyes adjusted to the darkness, Nicholas saw how Conjuror Sayer lived. In a basket, on the table, were eggs. On a shelf stood little bottles of green, purple, and yellow liquid. Hanging up by the chimney were two unplucked pheasants. Next to the eggs was a book, and a pen and ink. There was a strange smell, coming, guessed Nicholas, from the pot on the fire.

Conjuror Sayer nudged a chair towards him, saw him sniff.

"'Tis the garlic in the pan. Smells a-wild, but good for guts. I put the pretty, white flowers, which be like white suns, in everything, and 'tis said it keeps the vampire bats away. You seen 'em, nights, these parts? They flocks in great clouds from the woods. Keep your neck a-covered, Nicholas. 'Tis often thought they suck your blood by biting your vein here." He pointed to his own, which looked drained of all its blood already.

"How you see to get the knowledge? You born with the eyes for it?"

"Not everyone do it, and I needs a little help myself."

He nodded to the small bottle on the shelf.

"You see the future?"

"Oh, more than that, Nicholas. Much more than that. The past as well, how 'tis broken up and scattered like seed in the field to grow a future. Our life, see, be never complete, just bits which come from all places to make the present, which get rearranged, betimes."

"Can *I* see the past and future?"

"Maybe, maybe not. Folks come, but the art, for 'tis certain it be an art, and not the work of the devil, be dying out in Dorset, slaughtered by the church and science."

"Will you show me the knowledge?"

"I will, but you must pay me, as 'tis my trade, as your father's is making furniture. When the times been good, folk have been a-straggling up the hill, and the pennies jingled in that there chest. Now I lives on the last of it. Yes, Nicholas, that be why my neck be ringed, just a pipe of gristle."

"How you know my father be a carpenter? You know him?"

"I be a conjuror, and knows everything."

He chuckled, and so did Nicholas, who felt in his pocket.

"I got no money."

"Then pay me next time you come."

Nicholas nodded, excited and anxious. If my father could see me now! he thought. Why, he would take down the strap from its hook, though I would stop the leathering, on account of me being stronger than him now.

The conjuror poured beer into a jug, and added the opium from a bottle on the shelf. He sipped to taste, and added elderflower juice.

"And what do that?" asked Nicholas.

"Give me the knowledge."

"And me?"

The conjuror smiled.

"'Twill smash up the world, and let you see it as it could be. 'Tis nothing to worry about, as they pour it down the mouths of wounded soldiers whiles they cuts off their shredded legs. 'Twill take away all your pain, and put things together so the world be different, for a while, better."

The elderflower came first, then the opium cut through the sweetness.

"'Tis best if you lie down on the couch. I be here in my chair."

Nicholas lay on his back, but then Conjuror Sayer turned him on his side, so that he would not swallow his tongue.

"My head be funny," cried Nicholas, but his panic lasted only a second or two.

Conjuror Sayer settled into his chair, and closed his eyes.

Doors opened and shut. Nicholas' arm grew and lost its bones, and he dragged it across the floor. A monster bit chunks out of his body, but no sound came from his lips as he appealed to it to stop. Whoosh! he went, into the sea, which spilled down the hill, engulfing his family's cottage. He tried to grasp things, but he tumbled helplessly through the air, heading for a mountain.

He looked round the room. Conjuror Sayer was in his rocking chair, looking at him with bleary eyes. The lids were drooping, the red flesh, on their reverse, shining.

"So you back, then?" welcomed the conjuror.

Nicholas examined his arm. It was its normal length, had bones again.

"What was all that?" he croaked.

"The knowledge."

"And what it tell you?"

The conjuror rubbed his nose, scratched his stubbly chin.

"That you must go away before you can return, that you must do wrong before you can apologise, and that you must live enough years before you grown up. Now drink this water, go home, and the next time I see you, you will pay me."

Jacob returned from Dorchester. He had completed a settle for The King's Arms, carved a small oak tree, his signature, on the back, and had been paid. Some of the money would buy food, half would go into the rainy day box, which he kept under the floorboards, and the rest would go into the Glastonbury teapot, so called as it kept savings which would pay for a trip to Glastonbury Tor, as a commemoration of the day he proposed marriage and was accepted.

He placed the bag on the table, and loosened his bootlaces. Emily came to kiss him.

"'Tis payday, father?" she asked.

He could not help smiling.

"A grand one," he replied, nodding at his bag. "Fetch me the teapot, dear, and there shall be a penny for you, as well as several for Glastonbury. The date be only a few full moons away now."

Emily went to the dresser, and brought the pewter teapot.

"'Tis light today, father," she said.

Jacob frowned. Usually, he heard the coins jangling. He lifted the lid, and there was nothing inside.

"You been in the Glastonbury teapot?" he called to his wife.

"Now why would I do that, dear?"

She came over, held the teapot upside down, screwed up her face.

"Disappeared," she stated flatly. "'Tis passing strange."

Jacob, too, shook it, even looked inside again.

"Emily?" she asked.

She shrugged.

All that money; all those long hours of work; all the imagined gasps and joy of standing at the top of the tor, and saying that his wife was beautiful, that he would love her until God extinguished the sun and the stars. All gone.

Nicholas. But why?

Jacob walked up the hill and over the brow. Nicholas came into view, unsteady in his gait. I warned him not to go, told him since he was a young boy to stay away from the conjuror, and he has disobeyed me. Been coming, though, as sure as a mist slips down the heath. Been a good father, thought I'd taught him right from wrong. Can forgive him no faith, but not this, not this stealing of his mother's memories, as 'tis exactly that: what we once had, and must cling to. Need to remember what good has been, case we blunted by the days.

Jacob watched him stagger, trip once, from behind a tree. Oh, my son! he cried within. What have you done? Why have you thrown it all away? And now there is no turning back, no apology which can change things. It is all spoiled. And if 'tis Providence, then you must go.

"Nicholas?" he said, stepping out in front of him.

Nicholas rubbed his eyes, blinked.

"Father."

"You been yonder?"

Nicholas' eyes were red, as if he had been upwind of a bonfire. He hung his head. Sentences had not returned. Excuses were still in pieces, mere words tumbling in his head. His mouth shaped to speak, but closed.

Jacob turned and set off home. Nicholas followed, his pockets lighter.

He went straight to his room, avoiding his mother's and sister's stares.

"What's happened?" asked Mrs. Misterton.

"Nothing."

Jacob made sure that money was transferred from the rainy day box. His wife must not know that their son had stolen their special time.

Emily sensed something wrong. The atmosphere oppressed her, and her spontaneity was checked. She leaned against her father, irritating him. As he pushed her away gently, he said, "Don't. Stand on your own two feet."

Mrs. Misterton wanted to know what Nicholas had done, and did not want to go to bed depressed.

"What has happened?" she said again. "Why is Nicholas avoiding us?"

"Do not speak of him, dear, as 'twill set me alight. He has done wrong, and 'tis once too often. He must go in the morning. These rooms are too small for him now. He has climbed every tree. Our part of the heath appeals to him no longer, and the urge to breach my boundaries has been too great for him. I will go and tell him now."

"No!" she cried. "He will change, in time."

"But only by seeing the error of his ways, for how do we know that the inky toadstool be poison if we do not taste it?"

Emily was listening.

"Please don't send Nicholas away, father. He is my brother, and I will miss him."

She went to her mother, who enclosed her in her arms. They comforted each other, listened to the slow, heavy footsteps on the stairs. Jacob's words were few; none came from Nicholas.

When Jacob returned, he said, "It is done. If it could have been any other way . . ."

"Where did he been?" asked Mrs. Misterton, when Emily had gone to bed.

"The conjuror's."

"I thought so," she whispered, hanging her head.

In the morning, early, as he thought that if Nicholas were going, he ought to go at first light, so that the lesson began immediately, Jacob opened the bedroom door. There was Nicholas, in his clothes; he had slept in them. He started at the creak of the door, and felt nauseous at the memory of what his father had told him.

"It is time. Go now. Do not speak to your mother or sister. Go."

Nicholas hauled himself onto his feet, could not see the tears in his father's eyes.

In the next room, Mrs. Misterton was listening, knew that Nicholas was leaving. She wanted to run after him, drag him back, make him apologise, but knew that he would transgress again, in time. She buried her head in the pillow, and sobbed. But young men leave home at his age anyway, she reflected. Perhaps, it is time, after all. 'Tis Providence.

Nicholas said nothing, asked for no food, did not wish to protract the parting. Without rancour or show of defiance, he left, closing the door quietly.

Down to the lane he strode, it mattering not where he was heading. The Hardys were all inside. Dorchester, first. He needed to find work, earn money, to eat. The sun was up. Some things change, some things don't.

He had not handed over all the Glastonbury money to Conjuror Sayer. Desperate to acquire more knowledge, Nicholas had paid for the first time, and had had his world smashed into fragments a second, for a penny or two more.

"What can you tell me, conjuror?" Nicholas had asked.

"Seek the dancer with black hair, for she is the last of her name."

"But where shall I find her?"

"Make your way westward, and there, at the summer solstice, she shall find you, but beware, Nicholas, for if she perish, her name be wiped out for ever."

Westward take me round the Earth and back, mused Nicholas, as he entered Dorchester. Solstice be an age away, and I must wait till then? Ah well, if 'tis true what the conjuror said, then I will pass my days preparing.

Dorchester was yawning, rubbing its eyes, and scratching its head. Slowly, it rose to face the day, as Nicholas had been forced to do. He picked a quiet place to pee, then set about finding somewhere to eat breakfast. A dancer, with black hair, and the last of her name, he laughed. She sound an angel, though I baint sure which way be west. I must find out proper, as I always wanted to see an angel.

Chapter Twenty-Nine

Late autumn, and early winter reminded it that its lease had all but expired. It was time to pack its bags and go, shortly. The quilt of decaying leaves was now covered in frost, and Florence lit all the fires at Monksbury, to make the place more welcoming to the prospective buyers who were viewing, later, that morning. Looking at the pale blue sky, in which the moon was slowly saying goodbye, as a reveller leaving a protracted celebration, Florence knew that the day would be fine, that few rooms would remain in darkness, and, in those that would, she would light lamps. That is what she missed, at Palfreyman Manor: the way light lingered late, seemingly lengthening the day.

The visitor arrived at the exact time stipulated in the letter sent to him. By his side was a younger woman, tall, like him, wearing clothes chosen to perfection. She stood closely to him, yet not touching, and smiled, but not extravagantly; the man was the protagonist.

"I see you are on time!" said Florence, cocking her ear to the chimes of the clock in the hall.

"It is an obsession of mine," he admitted. "May I present Miss. Trenthide? I will be glad of her opinion. In fact, she will be judge and jury."

Florence looked at the woman who wielded such immense power. Then it is to *her* attention I must draw the house's merits, thought Florence.

Monksbury needed no exaggerated encomium, its beauty and practicality clearly manifested in the exquisite detail of the exterior, and the ideal proportions of the rooms, of which there were enough to satisfy the requirements of a family, its servants, and guests. In brief, it had everything for which one could wish, a fact which had persuaded Florence to buy it, in the first place. Yet she could not resist an emphasis on this, and dwelling on that, and the couple interpreted this as a love of the house, rather than a too obvious effort to sell it.

Florence could not fail to observe the contrast between the man's and woman's reactions. He echoed Florence's enthusiasm, while she remained neutral in her responses, always looking at the rooms from different perspectives.

Florence offered to make them some tea, but the woman declined. It was clear that she would not be distracted from her appraisal of Monksbury's suitability. Florence concluded the tour of the house in a similarly business-like manner.

"There is nothing more to see inside. The grounds themselves are attractive and easily maintained. There is a delightful Greek temple, which I have found a wonderful refuge. Please feel free to stroll at your leisure. I do not wish to rush your deliberations, but my notary has advised me that there has been a great deal of interest in Monksbury, and that he has received a number of requests to view. My expectation is that the house will be sold sooner rather than later."

"Thank you, Miss. Palfreyman. Monksbury is a fine manor, and very much suits our purpose," said the man, glancing at the woman, who said nothing.

"I wish I were not in the position where I have to choose. However much I have enjoyed living here, albeit for a short time, my allegiance is to Palfreyman Manor. Though it retains still an air of sadness at the death of my brother, it will, I am sure, remind me again of my early years, and many happy moments. I am the last of my family. Have you children yourselves?"

Florence could hardly believe she had posed such a personal question. At last, she had provoked the woman, who turned instinctively to the man. He stared back at her, till he felt obliged to answer.

"No. We have no children, at the moment."

Florence looked from one to the other, had noticed the woman's unspoken request for the man to manage the situation. So, you are not married, Florence guessed, but might be, one day.

"They are a mixed blessing, I hear!" remarked Florence, attempting to dispel any embarrassment.

"Well, Miss. Palfreyman, we shall discuss matters, and write to your notary, who practises in Dorchester, if my memory serves me correctly. You can expect to hear from us, in the very near future. Thank you for your time. Good day."

Florence smiled, and the woman moved her lips a little, as if contemplating doing likewise, but decided it was of no consequence whether she did or not.

The visitors moved towards the coach and two waiting for them.

"I'm sorry," called Florence, "but I'm afraid I've forgotten your name."

The man turned, and said, "Chideock. James Chideock."

And the woman carried on walking, silently.

Back at Palfreyman Manor, Florence wrote to her notary, and asked Coombs to deliver it personally, once she had opened other letters. One, in particular, delighted her, and she felt she should write immediately with an answer to the question to which the author's preamble had led. Coombs would post that in Dorchester.

So off he went, glad to escape the clucking hens in the kitchen, as he thought of Cook and her assistants. He could take as little or as much time as he liked. Receiving his orders from Miss. Florence, and not from Master Robert, had reduced his workload considerably. It was now a pleasure rather than a duty to work at the manor.

The notary was pleased to see him. James Chideock and his silent woman had not returned home but had driven directly to the notary's office, and had let him know their decision. Coombs and the notary exchanged letters, and Coombs was pleased to leave sooner than expected, as he deemed the notary a rather serious, he might even say lugubrious, man in need of decent company and a pot of cider, now and again.

Florence read his missive, and smiled. So much, all in one day! she reflected. I think I shall treat myself to a glass of sherry, this evening.

She sat in her chair. She really must remove Robert's from the room; it reminded her too much of his drunken bouts, when it would be the place in which he would sleep off his excesses.

A little exercise would be just the thing, at that moment. It had been a long time since she had ridden on the estate, so she decided to go to the farm, see what progress Misterton was making.

She had only reached the boundary of the first field when she saw him coming towards her.

"Good day to 'ee," he said, removing his hat.

"You anticipate my intention. I was just coming to see you."

"And me you, on account of Edith, who gone and done something best not to have, but 'tis done, and we all must face it, and do something about it."

"You're still talking in riddles, Nicholas."

"'Tis a curse not even my father could strap out of me."

Florence dismounted, and Nicholas told her all that had happened.

"Then we must go immediately!" exclaimed Florence.

"No, not now. Tomorrow. There be time enough, and Maisie be as big as a sack of turnips. The tiddy one could come a-screaming, any day. Besides, we need to sit on an idea I have, but it won't hatch beout you helping me a-warm it."

"Maisie need a doctor?"

"Only once, she needed one, and your brother left her like a lamb just popped out all wrong, and waiting for an angel to lift it up and lay it on a soft cloud in Heaven."

"Nicholas, I baint my brother. He long gone, afore his time, but gone true. Don't know where, don't know how, but he a-taken. And 'tis certain I be more angel than debil," she said.

Misterton was amazed. So perfect was her Dorset, that there was no trace of mockery. And how she had waited for the right moment, when she could show him that she did not live with her ears closed, that she was not governed by her brother's view of the world!

"Well, Miss. Florence, you sound a spickle like Mabel!" he laughed.

"Who be Mabel?"

"A milkmaid, Pilsdon way."

"'Tis an honest job, though hard for a girl with palms as smooth as butter."

She showed them to him, and he took them in his, pretending to examine them with an expert eye.

"Fingers be long, and the nails be clean as the first flakes of winter, but they be tolerable warm, which a cow like, when 'tis dark and freezing, and the droplets of milk left in the pail be pearls."

"Then I got the job? Please say 'tis so, Nicholas!" she begged.

"'Tis certain."

And he drew her towards him, wrapped his arms round her, as if the day were bitterly cold, and he was saving her life, as he had done Maisie's. He lay his cheek on her hair, smelt the mixture of perfume and hay. She stayed there, like a stook he could lift with that grip only, and he inadvertently rasped her forehead with his whiskers.

"Then we must save Edith. No Palfreyman will again leave a woman to within a tiddy peck of her life."

"'Tis natural, this?" he asked.

"It be as natural as if we'd always been a-clamped together. 'Tis passing wondrous."

The first thing Emily heard was screaming. She was tired after her journey. The one case she carried was cumbersome, so she could not run to the cottage. Instead she waddled, as if one leg were longer than the other. Her feet were heavy with disappointment, her heart saddened by what she felt was failure.

She pushed the door open, leaving her case outside. At the table sat Miranda, hands over her ears, her eyes turned upwards, indicating the source of the noise.

Emily ran upstairs to find her mother staring blankly at Maisie.

"Baby a-coming?" cried Emily, rushing to take Maisie's hand.

"'Tis a big one, and not a tiddy!" yelled Maisie. "Awkward, too, like its father."

Emily could see the baby's head.

"Edith?" said Mrs. Misterton. "You better now?"

There was no time to explain. The cry which reverberated across the land petrified the heath-croppers, sent crows flapping and hopping in the gorse and grass.

"Maisie, girl, 'tis a boy, with a mop as black and wavy as a moonless sea."

Miranda took her hands from her ears. Her former home had been quiet; this one was full of noise, of people unlike others.

And Conjuror Sayer sat upright, ripped from his drowsiness by the reassurance of the birth, which confirmed that he still had the knowledge, had never lost it, despite what Misterton had insinuated.

"Said 'twas a boy, and so it be!"

The key rattled in the door, and the policeman brought Edith a cup of hot chocolate. He walked steadily, not wanting to spill it.

"Carefuls, my dear, as 'tis passing hot. You hungry?"

She smiled weakly, shook her head. There did not seem any point to eating, which had become a mere mechanical movement.

"Just thirsty."

The policeman turned to go, but stopped at the door.

"Hopes you don't mind me saying, but you baint the normal sort of person we has in here, not the screaming and a-pleading their innocence type at all."

"No," was all she could say.

"Fetch you a man of the cloth? Bit of comfort in his words?"

"No, thank you. 'Twas God who sent me here, in the first place. Told me what I had to do."

The policeman stood in the doorway, almost reluctant to lock her in again. He looked at her blond hair covering her shoulders. She baint have the strength to lift a knife, let alone end a man's life with it.

At night, the cries of deranged prisoners sometimes woke her. There had been times when she had been fleeing from place to place, when Wareham's face, eyes bulging and unfocused, would wake her up, strip her of hope, but since her decision to confess what had happened, she had slept without his leering visage before her, a blessing bestowed, she knew, by God.

One morning, she awoke to the sound of the cell door being unlocked. Bound to be another pointless breakfast, was her first thought. Her usual warder stood respectfully in the doorway. She saw that he carried no bowl of gruel, no tin mug of hot chocolate. It felt late. She must have dozed off at first light, though there was little of it, there being just a tiny window so high up that no view of the outside world was possible. All she heard was banging, clanging, rattling, howling, shouting, snarling.

"You slept the sleep of the righteous?" said the warder.

Edith did not understand the meaning of righteous, or his cheerfulness in such a forbidding environment.

"'Tis hard to sleep."

"They cries the cry of the hopeless, the near-dead. Their hearts be bled of charity. Some been locked up time after time. Others preparing to meet the hangman and his noose. Buys it from a rope-maker in Bridport. Special thickness, a weave so fancy it fit under the fattest chin. Not hairy, so's it don't irritate the neck. Considerate he be, the hangman."

His casual talk of death angered Edith, and she snapped at him.

"Have some compassion, sir, as 'tis certain that my head will go through his noose, and that I will swing in front of a crowd who will gasp when the trap-door opens, and then they will cheer at my death. Speak not of my end, as 'twill come soon enough."

The warder shook his head. It was time to state his purpose in visiting her without her usual, meagre breakfast.

"And may your end, when the good Lord decree it, be in the next century and not this, which seems, at times, to march too quickly for prisoners in such circumstances as yours."

"Tease me not, sir. I cannot bear it."

"I tease 'ee not. Up you comes, and out you goes."

He jerked his thumb into the corridor behind him, as he stepped outside.

"Oh, too cruel, sir! 'Tis time? And yet no judge have yet condemned me. I have had no chance to explain to one why I did it. And that be the scourge of our times, when a man try to take advantage of a woman as if she be a whore, and she don't get to say a thing, as she won't be believed, on account of the way everyone be and think."

"'Tis certain."

"May I begs one last prayer before I go? Never been to church, but he spoken to me once, told me the right thing to do was tell the truth, and he will comfort me."

"Now, dear, that baint a wish I can grant, on account of this cell being required for a greater sinner than 'ee."

"There be no greater sinner. 'Taint possible."

"Possible? 'Tis possible as you baint no longer a sinner. At least, not in the eyes of the law of this land."

"You mock me still?"

"Nay, dear. You're free to go. Now, if you don't minds, I got a man chopped up his wife into tiddy pieces coming in whose neck fits the hangman's noose perfectly."

Chapter Thirty

"We went on holiday, father," said Miranda. "But we didn't do much."

Chideock hugged her, worked out, after a quick look inside Dorothy's room, that Dorothy had opened the front door, let Miranda in, and disappeared.

"Did Dorothy come in with you?"

"No. She kissed me."

"Did she say anything to you?"

"She was crying."

Chideock let the police know that Miranda was safe, and they said that they would continue to search for the nurse, who had caused a great deal of distress, and wasted a lot of busy people's time.

In the following days, Chideock took Miranda to the factory with him. She stayed in his office, most of the time, but occasionally went with him onto the shop-floor, and became, for the workers, the highlight of their monotonous day. Soon, she herself became bored, and Chideock found it difficult to transact business in his customary way. In the past, he used to slip out, give himself space to think, but dare not now leave her in someone else's care.

Daisy Trenthide came to him in the evenings, when Miranda was in bed. Then they would spend time alone, talk of the day when she would no longer be the woman who came in the night and was gone by daybreak. Miranda must never know of her existence. Two many women had already come into, and gone from, Miranda's life already.

"And when do you think she will go to live with her father?" Daisy asked. "This state of affairs cannot continue. It is not good for her or us. You said you would sell this house, once she had gone, that it was too full of ghosts and bad memories."

Chideock took her hand.

"Dearest Daisy, you have been so patient, but I think I have found the perfect place for us: a manor house, a mile or two outside Dorchester. For some time, I have been thinking of selling the factory. We could start a new life at Monksbury."

"Dorchester? Selling the factory. A man needs an income, James. How will you pass your days?"

"That is something I will contemplate at a future date. You know that I love you, and we shall be comfortably off. When Miranda is rightfully restored to her father, we will be married, and I think that Monksbury Manor will be the perfect home."

Something was troubling Daisy, who knew that Misterton lived at Higher Bockhampton, near Dorchester. Monskbury could not be far from him.

"James, you need to be absolutely honest with me. Do you think that, by living near Miranda, you are letting her go? The temptation to see her would be too great. If you really are sure that she should return to Misterton—"

"Daisy," he interrupted, "he is her father. Myrtle and I did not steal her, but looked after her, till he came for her. I always suspected that would happen, one day. Monksbury is not near Bockhampton. It is nearer than Bridport, yes, but it is at a distance which would prevent a chance encounter."

Daisy nodded.

"Then tell Miranda the truth today. It will be strange for her, but the sooner she goes to Bockhampton, the better."

"I shall send a message to Nicholas today, then, saying we are ready."

When the time came, Chideock was more relaxed than he thought he would be. He had become resigned to a life without Miranda. Indeed, Myrtle's death had forced him to recognise that he had not spent enough time with Miranda, that she was more Myrtle's daughter than his. She had usually been in bed when he had left and returned. He could not have coped without Dorothy.

"Please, sit down, dear. There is something I have to tell you. A long time ago, when your mother was alive – do you remember her?" he began. Miranda shrugged, a movement suggesting uncertainty. "Yes, well, it was a long time ago. Let's try this a different way. Once upon a time, your real mother died, and your real father, a man called Nicholas, had gone away, and was not able to look after you. But Nicholas has come back, and he wants you to go and live with him. That will be nice for you, won't it?"

A shadow of confusion crossed her face, and then she said, "Yes, but won't you be lonely without me?"

The tears came, but he stood up quickly, wiped his eyes so that she would not see them. And when she left the room, the worst was over. There was no turning back.

At The King's Arms, Chideock saw her resemblance to Misterton. Miranda was holding her doll. Down the road, Thomas was waiting on his cart, as a favour, whistling a tune they were to play at a party, Tolpuddle way.

Misterton lifted her up. He had to touch her immediately, make a physical connection.

"'Tis Ruth all over," he marvelled. "Eyes and hair, and smell. 'Tis the smell bring her back to me."

Miranda looked at him.

"Are you my father?" she asked.

"I be your father, yes."

"I have informed the registrar of the circumstances, and he has amended the register of adoptions," interrupted Chideock, anxious to part quickly, to manage the pain.

"Thank 'ee, Mr. Chideock," said Misterton, perching Miranda on one arm, and shaking Chideock's hand with the other. "'Tis curious how things turn out, betimes. And I will write to 'ee, from time to time, to let 'ee know that she be well, and a-growing into a fine girl. You be as honest as a man can be, and, one day, I will pay you back for it."

Chideock blinked, swallowed, and returned to Bridport, where Daisy was waiting to hear that they could now make plans for the rest of their life.

"Well, 'tis passing strange how things do turn out," remarked Thomas. "'Twill get Jemima all a-brooding, what when Maisie's baby a-come, too."

"Passing strange, 'tis certain. This be Mr. Hardy, Miranda, a neighbour, down the lane. Say hello to him."

"Do you have chickens?" she asked.

"Chickens, yes, though we 'as a crafty, old fox come a-padding, betimes, in the night, and takes one for his supper. Feathers all over be his signature. Still, 'tis Nature."

"There be chickens, up the lane, be us, too, girl. You can collect the eggs, be your job, now mother too creaky and wobbly to bend."

Soon, the jolting of the cart, and the length of the morning, sent her to sleep on Misterton's knee. He breathed in deeply. She was there, in the air, in his nose: Ruth, who lived on through Miranda. Then he knew, when he saw how perfect, beautiful, Miranda was, that Ruth had not jumped at West Bay.

"No, girl," he muttered. "'Twas Providence and not her own will took my Ruth, and returned you to me. And soon there will be another tiddy one."

"Here we be," said Thomas.

"Thank 'ee, Thomas," said Misterton, when the cart stopped in the lane. In his arms, Miranda began to stir.

Jemima came to the gate. In her hand was a bunch of flowers tied with straw.

"These are for Maisie, and 'tis hoped she be fine," she said.

Miranda woke up, and rubbed her eyes, and Jemima smiled at her.

"This be Miranda, my daughter," Misterton said. "Say hello to Mrs. Hardy."

Miranda turned to Thomas, and said, "Has the fox gone now?"

Thomas laughed, and replied, "No feathers, so I expects he full up some other ways!"

Misterton carried her case, and Miranda walked by his side, up onto the heath. Maisie had come outside to greet them.

"And now we be a proper family," she said.

Miranda looked at her, how she rested her hands on the baby inside her.

"Miranda, this be Maisie, my . . . Maisie. Maisie, this be Miranda, our daughter."

Maisie burst into tears.

"Don't mind me a spickle, girl, as it be nearly my time, and a woman sets to a-crying when she happy or sad when she this big."

"Are there any chickens?" asked Miranda.

"Chickens a-plenty. Take a look, girl. This be all yours."

Misterton turned a full circle, pointing to his kingdom.

"Can I stroke them?"

"There be the garden, the heath, the wood, and the creatures," he said proudly. "They be all ours, yours."

"Of course you can, my dear, but first you come inside, meet granmer, who be awake now."

Maisie glanced at Misterton.

"Mother, this be Miranda, come to live with us, just like I told you."

Mrs. Misterton looked at Miranda through narrowed eyes. Lately, she had begun to squint to focus, even close one eye, occasionally, to obtain a clear image. It often gave her the appearance of meanness, and Miranda looked to Maisie for protection.

"It's all right, girl. Granmer don't see so well, these days, and that be why her eyes be skinny as a cat's. Go to her. She won't bite or scratch like one," explained Maisie, giving her a nudge in the back.

Mrs. Misterton took a step forward, stretched out her arms to Miranda, who looked to Maisie for confirmation that it was safe.

"'Tis your Granmer Misterton," added Misterton. "She bake cakes, don't you, mother, dear?"

"You like cake, girl?" asked Maisie.

Outside, crows cawed in a black, cacophonous cloud. Miranda's eyes flickered to the open door, and returned to her grandmother, who took hold of her granddaughter's cheeks.

"Nicholas," she whispered.

"'Tis Miranda, mother, my daughter, from Bridport, come to live with us."

"Nicholas," warned Maisie, anxious that Miranda might be scared by Mrs. Misterton's confusion.

"'Tis you, Nicholas. That be how you looked when you were as tiddy as Miranda. She got your waves. Girl, you like your father, and 'tis like I have a son, all over again."

Mrs. Misterton kissed Miranda's forehead.

"Where's Dorothy?" asked Miranda.

The golden buildings held up their faces to the sinking sun, and had a pinkish hue. Shadows lengthened, and the air became cooler. By the water, gnats swarmed. Emily sat on a seat in the park, in a circus, a grand wheel of high houses, in which curtains had been shut early to keep out the sunlight, and protect the rooms. And that is how Emily felt: excluded. I have tried, she told herself. How I have tried to belong here!

In her room, at the college where she had been training, her case containing her clothes and books was packed. Her tutor had tried to persuade her to give it more time.

"It takes years to be convincing," he had told her. "Give it more time."

But she had tired of her pupils' superciliousness, their open mockery of her Dorset accent, of which she had only become aware when she had noticed its absence in her pupils.

"But there be no point. It's what I wanted, but can't have, on account of Bath being so different."

Her tutor had shaken his head.

"You must not give up," he had urged. "In time, you will make a good teacher."

Then it was Emily's turn to shake her head.

"I've made up my mind, and when 'tis set, 'tis granite. All the time I been here, I been a-hiding my tongue, borrowing others' words, yours, even, and they don't fit like mine. Bath's words be iron, straight, and in lines, whereas mine come a-spilling out my mouth like a waterfall. And all the time I been here, the flow been a-getting weaker, till it don't splash the same. And the children won't listen, on account of them believing I be common, like I blown in like a weird, winged insect from the deserts of northern Africa. You see, my heart will shrivel like the skin of a missed windfall apple if I lose my voice, which be a stranger here."

There was silence, and her tutor rubbed his forehead for a few seconds.

"I understand, but that is precisely why you must stay. There will always be a place for someone like you."

"'Tis kind to say, but I must go home to my family, who be having a baby soon."

As she sat in the park, she forced herself to examine again her feelings. People passed her, ignored her, looked ahead. All that stone, she mused. Big blocks of it, made to fit into a whole. All that vision of neo-classical grandeur, order, rules. No thatches, no whitewash on walls. 'Tis passing strange.

She rose to go back to her room. The sky flushed pink and grey. She had an early start, the next day. Had Florence received her letter? There had been no reply. Before leaving for Bath, Florence had reassured her that she would welcome her back, any time. Emily knew that she had to earn money, was an extra mouth to feed.

In the morning, at first light, Emily boarded the coach. She would stay overnight, at an inn. During her time in Bath, she had secured some additional hours of teaching, and had saved money. There was enough to feed her family for a few weeks, but no more, so she prayed Florence would keep her word.

In his study, her tutor made notes. He was preparing to write to the Dean of the college. There were important things that needed saying. He had never noticed that he sounded the same as his colleagues. In Bath, their sentences were all considered, rigidly grammatical, balanced, controlled. The girl is extraordinary, he wrote, and we have let her go, probably will never see her like again. It was a privilege today to hear her speak as she is inclined. I suspect she is one of only a few remaining who connect with the past through their language. Remarkable. Quite remarkable.

Chapter Thirty-One

"We have much to do today," said Florence, "and nothing more important than going to the police station. Coombs has been instructed to have the coach ready."

Misterton had set his workers tasks to keep them busy till midday. Then there would be an important meeting, he informed them. That provoked speculation, when he had gone; meetings, unheard of during Wareham's time, meant change for the better, under Misterton.

Coombs clicked the two horses into motion, and Florence and Misterton sat together, shoulders almost touching. They could hear Coombs singing softly, contrasting with the solemnity of the interior.

"Her trial be next week," said Misterton.

"And she is resigned?"

"'Twas a yoke far heavier than she ever shouldered on the farm. She be free of guilt and torment now."

The coach stopped outside the police station.

"Let me deliver the explanation. You are a good man, Nicholas, honest and true, but my position may carry more weight."

"And I can say what Maisie seen, paint Wareham a devil's portrait."

"If they ask, Nicholas, but only if they ask," she stipulated.

The Sergeant on the desk looked up. Florence's attire and bearing instantly made an impression; and Misterton stood just behind her, by her shoulder, so that he was seen to support her.

"Good day to 'ee," said the Sergeant.

"I have come to make a statement about the death of my former Farm Manager, Christopher Wareham. He has long since been buried, but I believe you have in custody a former worker, Edith Charmouth, a woman who has recently confessed to killing him, in self-defence. Her trial, I understand, is next week."

"And your statement: do it affect the charge against the woman in question?"

"It does, indeed, and should secure her liberty, this very day."

The Sergeant said, "Well, that remains to be seen. And who be you, if I may make so bold?"

"My name is Miss. Florence Palfreyman, owner of Palfreyman Manor and its estate."

"Then you'd better come this way, Miss. Palfreyman. 'Taint every day we has a lady comes through those doors. More often than not, there be drunks, thieves, and men and women so depraved it baint for the eyes and ears of a lady."

He lifted the counter, and beckoned to her.

"And this is Nicholas Misterton, my current Farm Manager. Please, may he be allowed through?"

"I'm sure he be fine, but 'twill be a matter for my superiors, on account of me being a mere mortal, in this station."

The clock on the waiting room wall ticked loudly. There was just one window. The seconds dragged their feet. Fifteen minutes passed before two men entered, a sheaf of papers in the hand of the one with the bushy, red beard. The other, a tall, slim colleague, sat and picked up a pen, which he dipped in ink, ready to write.

"Now, Miss. Charmouth has made a statement, confessing to sticking a knife into Christopher Wareham. She says he attacked her, and attempted to molest her." Here, he took a few seconds to sift through Edith's statement. "'Fearing dreadful for my life and reputation, I grabs his knife, and, as he pressed himself on top of me, and pulls my dress up, I sticks the knife in him, and he rolls off me, a-groaning. I did not stay at the farm, but ran away. I confess what I did to bleed myself of the guilt of knowing I killed him.'"

The officer let the confession sink in. Misterton recalled Edith's words when she had turned up at the cottage, and they were now the gist of her written statement.

"Were you present when she signed this?" asked Florence. "She has signed and dated it, I assume?"

The officer prickled, and scrutinised the document. It seemed an eternity before he was able to answer.

"Firstly, I baint a-been present, and I regret to say that no other officer of the Dorsetshire Constabulary has indicated his witness, either. Most irregular, as this document be the only evidence against her in court."

The first stirrings of optimism could be seen in Florence's and Misterton's faces, which the scribe noticed.

"'Tis regular for this to happen? A signature be a sign of . . . " but Misterton could not recall his former master's use of the word *authentication*, which Robert had once explained in the context of accepting deliveries and placing orders.

Remember what I said about letting me do the talking! reminded Florence's stern glance.

"It be obligatory. 'Twon't stand up as high as even a milestone in court, though that be for the judge to decide. Now, what puzzle me be that, a-flicking through these here papers, some of them writ by folk on your estate, including your brother, there is none signed by you. 'Tis an offence to withhold vital evidence. And why now, after this time, do you come here and offer us your version of the truth?"

The ticking appeared to be counting down to success or failure. Florence had prepared herself for awkward questions, had imagined the police's dismay that the case had to be reopened, after Edith's confession. It meant extra work for them, when they were busy with fresher cases.

"May I tell you what really happened, from the beginning?"

The scribe sat poised with pen, and his colleague said, "Please do. A woman's life may depend upon it, but I remind you that what you be about to say will have to be put to my superiors. These be most unusual circumstances."

"Wareham had seemed, initially, a competent Farm Manager."

"Please, Miss. Palfreyman, don't 'ee stray into the realm of misty vaguery. Keep to the facts, as you see 'em."

"Robert, my brother, appointed him, having seen two good character references from other tenant farmers, for whom Wareham had worked in a supervisory capacity. The first time I saw him, I knew I would not like him. He looked at me in a suggestive manner, even though he knew I had the power to dismiss him.

I told Robert of my concerns, and he thought I exaggerated, though he observed, and remarked upon, Wareham's brusque manner with the labourers. Robert even warned him, following a complaint from a girl who did not stay long enough to be abused a second time, that he should restrain himself."

The officer began to show signs of frustration: fiddling with his beard, tapping his fingers on the desk, exhaling loudly.

"Miss. Palfreyman, can you refer *directly* to the events concerning the death of Wareham?"

"Certainly, though I think it important that we establish what sort of a person he was," countered Florence.

"We are not in a court of law," he reminded her. "At least, not yet."

"Well, the first I knew of his death was when my brother informed me, and told me he had sent Coombs to alert the police. They came, interviewed the workers, who said nothing, and would not reveal who had been working, that day. Robert said he'd found Wareham in the barn."

"That still leaves us with Edith Charmouth's recent confession. And we have no statement from her from the original investigation."

"I'm coming to that."

Misterton sat uncomfortably, felt she was no closer to securing Edith's release.

"Please, do, and be quick about it, Miss. Palfreyman. 'Tis like waiting for the first cuckoo in spring!"

"My brother had gone over to the farm with the intention of speaking to Wareham on one or two matters. He was told that Wareham was in the barn. When Robert entered, he heard muffled cries. Wareham was on top of her, muttering threats. She managed to push him off, and ran towards Robert. There was blood on her. Wareham ran after her. Robert grabbed him, saw that there was a bad cut on his arm. They fought. Robert could smell the drink on Wareham's breath, had himself been drinking, as was his habit. They fell to the floor. There was a bitter struggle. Wareham thrust the knife at him, but Robert grabbed it, and plunged it into him, fearful for his own life. Robert urged Edith to quickly leave, told her not to say anything, that he would deal with it."

"But why does she still believe *she* was responsible?"

"She had deflected the knife, and he had cut himself. It was dark. She was confused. Her life was being threatened. His blood was on her. She panicked. But it was not she who killed Wareham. It was my brother."

"And when did he tell you all this?"

"Months ago. He felt it was a risk to tell the truth. He did not want to hang for such a man. In those circumstances, why should anyone hang when they have just saved an innocent woman from a fiend? What sister would betray her brother?"

"Then we must apprehend your brother, Miss. Palfreyman. Immediately."

"That will be impossible, sir."

"And why is that?"

"My brother is dead."

On the way back to Palfreyman Manor, Florence said to Edith, "I would like to offer you a position on the estate. I shall be leaving Monksbury shortly. I have a buyer for it, and though I dismissed you in unfortunate circumstances" – here, she looked meaningfully at Misterton – "you were an excellent worker."

"I don't know what to say. I've gone two steps from the trapdoor and a-swinging to having a job! 'Taint usual, 'tis certain. I still don't know why I been released, when 'tis plain I killed him."

That was what Misterton and Florence had not discussed: how they would explain their presence at the police station, how they knew she was being released.

"Officer said you put me down as next of kin in his book, and he sends out a scarecrow in a uniform, to let me know that they dropping the charges as if they were coals a-brought up in a bucket from fiery Hell itself!"

Misterton's imagery caused Edith to open her eyes and mouth wide. Florence bit her tongue to stop herself laughing.

"And he came to me, seeing as it all happened on the estate."

"But why be I let off?" asked Edith.

Come on, Nicholas, boy. Time to talk in riddles. If ever a curse were useful, 'tis now.

"Well, afore Wareham comes to the farm, he been a-wandering from place to place, doing a tolerable job. But he a bad one, and turns out he been a-stealing from here and there, and a-scuttling away like a rat, afterwards. 'Tis all in a sunny morning and rainy afternoon, far as men go, these parts, but then he do something in Devon sent him hiding for weeks. It be so bad, he don't show his face."

"Tell the girl what he did, and put her out her misery!" ordered Florence.

"Well, Devon tells Cornwall, Somerset, and Dorset, sends 'em all a good likeness of him. A reward so sweet offered, 'twas only a matter of time he got caught, or so they thought."

"But what did he do?" asked Edith.

"Seems he a-wilded up on opium, breaks into a church, and smashes the offtry box into tiddy pieces. Then he find there baint a farthing in it, so he sets fire to the pews. The flames so hot and high, our Lord Jesus on the cross a-melted in the window frames. Church be as charred as a spent gorse fire. Prishners locked out. They never caught him, but the police said 'twas blasphemy, and he would have swung anyway, so 'twas justice. Should've stoned him, as in the Bible days. You free now, Edith. 'Tis so and just."

"'Tis wondrous so," added Florence, covering Edith's hands with hers.

"How'd they know 'twas Wareham the fire-raiser been a-knifed?" persisted Edith.

Misterton had to think quickly, explain convincingly.

"The Lord know everything."

The meeting began late. Simon, Katy, and William sat nervously, waiting for Misterton to arrive. Simon was chewing his split fingernails, Katy was mending an apron she had snagged on a nail, and William was reading the Bible, a habit which pleased and annoyed the others in equal measure. They liked him to read the story of turning water into wine, and feeding the five thousand, as it seemed a solution to Dorset's rural poverty, but disliked him showing off his knowledge of the testament.

"'Tis like Sunday morning, all the time," complained Simon.

"But the farmhouse feel empty without the Word a-wafting away the cobwebs, and blessing Katy's oven. The Word live here now. 'Tis in our togetherness, and up the chimbley, even."

This last contention made the others laugh.

"'Taint the matter whether we believe in the Word or not. 'Tis the thought of it covered in soot and pigeon paint make me smile," explained Simon.

"Don't take a spickle of notice of him. 'Twould not be us and here beout your nose in the gospel," reassured Katy.

"Thank 'ee, Katy. And may He bless your suet pudding tonight, which I hopes you've a mind to do, on account of it filling me up just right, and a-smelling and a-tasting like beout compare."

"Thank 'ee," said Katy. "And if 'tis a poplar wish, I'll put my mind to it, after the meeting."

They were all surprised to see Florence with Misterton, and stood up for her. It was the first time she had set foot in the farmhouse while they had been living there. She felt humbled by the simple arrangement of the furniture, by the well swept floor, the sense of harmony.

"Thank you for waiting for us. I shan't keep you long. Nicholas, as Farm Manager, will tell you all about the improvements we are going to make. Your work is always hard, more often than not, outdoors, in the cold. That takes a toll on your health. In the past, under the orders of Wareham, and also my brother, you have been mistreated. One of you – Maisie - nearly died for want of a doctor. Only your love and care for her saved her. I will arrange for a doctor, from now on, if you fall ill, and it will be at my expense. I will make available a substantial sum for the renovation of all the farm's buildings, including this. You deserve warm, dry conditions, not only because you are human beings, but because you are loyal to Nicholas, and he is a good man. A *good* man."

Her emphasis on Misterton's goodness made them look at him.

"'Tis kind," he gulped.

"And you must know that you have a job and shelter here for the rest of your days. We will be a new model for farming in Dorset."

Florence held back the tears till the last word. Katy stepped forward, and hugged her.

"Thank 'ee, Miss. Palfreyman. 'Tis wondrous kind. We all will do our best to help 'ee whene'er we can. And tonight I shall cook a suet pudding with lamb and rosemary, to celebrate."

"And now I wants to introduce you to someone who will level you up, as men and women, who been here before, in times worser than what be coming, 'tis certain." Misterton opened the door, and called, "We're ready."

Edith stepped into the house, had looked forward to doing so, though with a little awkwardness, as expected after such a long absence.

"Edith, girl?" whispered Katy.

"Yes, 'tis me, and come to stay for good. That is, if you'll have me."

"Better make a *big* pie, then," advised Simon. "And William can thank the Lord, at the table, that Edith be a-come among us again, as without her, the pie be a tiddy one."

And they all laughed.

Chapter Thirty-Two.

An extra bed was needed, for Emily, who had to share her mother's room, now that Miranda had hers. Misterton threw himself into making one, according to his sister's design. He even measured her, to ensure it was wide enough, in an outbreak of untypical frivolity, and she demanded a personalised headboard, with the names of all her enlarged family carved into it.

"'Tis a task!" Nicholas complained. "Can do an acorn or two, and a tolerable leaf or scroll, but 'tis certain I'll spell the names wrong, like when I was a-learning my words."

"Then write 'em on paper, and copy 'em, first, dear," advised Emily.

"Trouble be, we all a-squashed like sheep in a pen."

"Then you shouldn't a-been such a ram, Nicholas!" she quipped.

"Too late to cut 'em off now!"

"Nicholas Misterton!" she cried, hands on hips, in exaggerated mock-indignation. "I hopes you don't a-fall into that way of talking in front of Miranda and Seth. A fine example, you be! And, by the way: you having your boy a-christened at Stinsford?"

He shrugged.

"Be Maisie you need to talk to about those things."

"But you their father, whether you see it up-a-hill or down. You got your daughter, and a tiddy boy, and soon you'll be at Stinsford to make Maisie a wife, 'less you got other plans you hiding down a rabbit warren. You got responsibilities now."

"'Tis all a Dorset fog to me, and 'twon't clear till one of us stamps our feet."

"Then, knowing you, my brother, I best have a word with Maisie to get her clogs on, though I expect she been a-practising already!"

Miranda sidled up to him, outside, where he was planing a leg of the new bed. She watched the thin shaving of wood curl into a scroll, and fall onto the floor, lightly. In her hand, she held a sheet of paper, on which she had drawn, and Misterton examined it.

"'Tis wondrous, like a house be a thatch a-top, like ours. And this be me, girl? If so, I got the wrong hair, see? 'Taint a-sticking out like spokes on a wheel. 'Tis wavy."

He lifted up a handful of hair, which bounced back into position when he let go.

"It's not our house, and this man is not you."

"Then who be it, girl?"

"I don't know his name, but he lives not far from here, and he wants to talk to you."

"And why be he a-lying down?"

"Because he is dying."

Nicholas dropped his plane, and set off up the hill. Over its brow he marched, purposefully, and down towards Conjuror Sayer's cottage. The door was ajar.

"Conjuror?" he called, peeking inside.

"Up here," came back a feeble voice.

"'Tis Nicholas."

Conjuror Sayer was lying on his bed, breathing heavily. His eyes were empty. There were no vials in the room, just a smell of age, urine, and dust. Everything was still, as if there had been no movement in the room for years.

"You got my message, then?"

His voice was hoarse, as if the words had been grated like nutmeg.

"How?"

"She got the knowledge, Nicholas, just like me."

The conjuror tried to smile, but his face collapsed with the effort.

"'Tis certain?"

"Wondrous so."

"Shall I fetch a doctor?"

The conjuror shook his head, the effort making him more breathless.

"Pass me that tin, there. Quick."

Misterton followed the line of his bent, yellow finger, and brought the tin to the bed. The conjuror opened it, the effort exhausting him. He glanced at the papers inside, replaced the lid, and thrust it towards Misterton.

"Take it, boy. 'Tis all there, all yours, though promise me one thing."

"What be it?"

"That you bury me in Stinsford churchyard, next to your father. There, and no other place. Swear it, Nicholas, swear it!"

The old man tried to sit up, reach for Misterton, to physically force him to obey, but his strength failed him, and he slumped back onto the bed.

"I swear it, conjuror, but why must you rest next my father?"

"Because Sayer only be what folk call me 'cause I say the knowledge. He be my brother, Nicholas, and we be together again, two Mistertons, as is proper."

Maisie, Misterton, Miranda, and Seth sat uneasily in the rectory.

"We have come to ask for baptism for our children," began Maisie. "We baint church-goers, 'tis certain, but we believe in God, don't we, Nicholas?"

Nicholas nodded, fearing God, if he existed, might strike him down if he uttered a falsehood again.

"The Lord God embraces all his flock, young and old, faithful and not so faithful. It is never too late to hear him calling," reminded the rector.

"Then when be best?" asked Maisie, who had warned Misterton not to jeopardise the chance for the children to join the Church.

"Next Sunday? It has been quite a while since we have conferred baptism. There will, of course, be a small charge, as is customary on these occasions."

"We got money," confirmed Misterton.

"Then that is settled."

Maisie beamed, squeezed Miranda's hand, and kissed Seth, who was sleeping contentedly.

"There be one other thing, and 'tis a sad affair, though one best opened up now. 'Tis never a cause for festibating when a man die, whether he be great or small, and 'tis wrong to forget that we all equal in the eyes of God."

"You are, indeed, correct, Nicholas."

"Then I must ask you to allow the burial, in the churchyard, of Conjuror Sayer, who went, yesterday. 'Tis said abroad he danced with the debil, though 'taint true; he just got the knowledge, which be no worse than you or your kind, who got the ear of the Lord."

The rector shook his head, certain of the impossibility of granting permission.

"The man who has died cannot be interred there. He has not repented of his sins. I have no authority in the matter."

"Then that be a pity as, in his papers, he have left a will full of money, case the church roof leak or burn – and I hopes I gets the following words correct – and *for the study of human intuition and supernatural instinct*, so that there be no further misunderstanding of what it mean to have the knowledge."

The rector looked at him in amazement.

"How much is his bequest?"

"He asks that the orchestra have new instruments, when their notes become headstrong, and that the rector be paid a sum to keep a good supply of wine for Easter and other such times, as it is needed."

The rector paused, gave due consideration to the offer, and decided that the memory of a man whose generosity extended to such lengths should not be tarnished by unsubstantiated rumours.

"His beneficence does him great credit, and I think that forgiveness is everything, in these matters."

"Thank 'ee, and to show he be no different to us, I be prepared for him to rest his bones next to my father's, as my father would talk to anyone."

"I'm sure that can be arranged, Nicholas."

"There, then!" said Maisie to Miranda and Seth. "'Tis all settled."

Florence's notary's pen flew over the paper, in extravagant hills and vales, as she spoke.

"As you know, I left Palfreyman Manor at the behest of my deceased brother, who wished to install his prospective wife as mistress. His untimely death allowed me to return, and to sell Monksbury to James Chideock, though I hear that he has not yet moved in. It appears that he has had second thoughts about marriage. She did seem, I recall, a distant, cold woman. Oh, well! I've no doubt he will sell it himself, in due course, unless he moves in on his own."

"It is as you say, Miss. Palfreyman, though you have hardly come here to tell me what I already know."

"And you are correct. I have come to ask you to draw up my last will and testament. It is my sincere hope that it will not be executed for a very long time, but these things are best faced in sound body and mind. I am the last of the Palfreymans, and I am not of the opinion that I will be blessed with children of my own. In fact, the thought of such a prospect quite alarms me!" She chuckled briefly, then resumed her business. "Therefore, in view of my circumstances and wishes, and, of course, a love of the manor and farm, I have come to a decision concerning the choice of the beneficiary of my estate."

The notary looked up.

"It is possible for you to revoke your will at any time, should you so wish."

"Thank you, but I have made up my mind. If I die before the beneficiary becomes twenty-one, then the estate will be managed by a person I will nominate. However, it would not do at all if the expectation of such wealth were to affect the beneficiary adversely. Money can corrupt, change people, prepare the way for sloth and indolence, as was the case with my brother. His judgement was impaired by a life of excesses, and it probably led to his premature death and my alienation."

"A good wife may well have corrected his conduct," ventured the notary, mindful of his wife's close supervision of his own habits. "It is a pity she left him at the altar."

"Not at all!" Florence came back quickly. "Rose Wells did the right thing. She knew all about his drinking, and made the decision not to marry a man with good intentions but set in his bachelor ways."

"She saw them at close quarters?"

"No, but they were described to her in such graphic detail that she could not risk marriage." Florence saw the notary working out what she had implied. "Yes, and you would be correct in the assumption your face suggests. It was I who wrote to Rose Wells, and told her the truth. Marriage would have led to their mutual misery, and the permanent loss of my home."

The notary remained inscrutable. The morality of her actions was of no concern to him.

"I understand. All that I now require are the names of the sole beneficiary, and your nominated trustee."

"Then the person to whom I bequeath everything is Miranda Misterton."

"And the trustee?"

"Nicholas Misterton, her father."

Even if mother know that the conjuror be her brother-in-law, she not remember him, thought Misterton. No point in standing her by a coffin a-lowering into the grave when she don't understand why she there.

So there was just Misterton. Tom and Thomas played a hymn, which the rector sang too loudly, and of which Misterton had a vague recollection from childhood.

The grave, as agreed, was dug next to his father. There would be a headstone, in a few months, when the ground had settled. On it, Misterton would have the stonemason inscribe: Here lies, next to his brother, Conjuror Sayer, who had the Knowledge, and told it. One of Mankind.

The rector said his words solemnly, and asked if Misterton wished to say anything.

"Kept my word, and your papers be with a notary. Don't know why you and father didn't talk, and it don't much matter now. But better you keep each other company, in the hope you bury the hatchet. Miranda got the knowledge, and 'tis wondrous."

The mourners tossed soil into the grave.

"'Bye, father," said Misterton, replacing his hat.

"Nicholas," said the vicar, "shall we see you at two, on Sunday?"

Misterton remembered.

"Two, sharp as a scythe."

"You ever been baptized?"

"Not so's I know. Stopped going to church when I was tiddy. No use asking mother. She won't remember. 'Less you got a book of names . . ."

"Follow me," invited the vicar.

The book he required was in the vicarage. He ran his finger down the pages.

"Going back a few years," reminded Misterton.

"When were you born?"

Misterton scratched his head.

"No idea. 'Twas a long time ago. Mother said 'twas a strange day. Starlings everywhere, she said. And bats a-swarming."

"That doesn't help me, I'm afraid."

The vicar continued searching. Some years, only two or three entries had been made. Eventually, he found what he was looking for.

"Here it is: Nicholas Glastonbury Misterton."

"Glastonbury? I be *Glastonbury*?"

"Did you not know?"

"No idea."

"Does the name have any significance for your parents?"

"Not so's I know."

"Not to worry. The main thing is, you've been christened. You have the protection of the Lord."

"Glastonbury!" exclaimed Misterton. "'Tis nothing I know not a spickle about!"

Then he remembered the teapot, the theft which had sent him into exile.

Chapter Thirty-Three

Florence told Nicholas to take the day before his wedding off. She was going to say, "You only get married once," but then remembered Ruth, Miranda. Nicholas had invited Katy, Edith, Simon, and William, but they said they would look after the farm instead. "'Taint right we a-going when 'tis the master getting wed," Simon had told the others, when they had discussed the possibility that he might invite them. Florence said she would not miss it for anything, and even offered Coombs and a coach, from the top of the lane, which was as far as it could go. Nicholas gratefully accepted as, though Thomas had said he would be pleased to transport them, he realised that he would have to make more than one journey.

"There be our instruments, see, eh, Tom?" pointed out Thomas. "And Maisie don't want our fiddles and bows a-prodding her more than they baint welcome!"

"Father!" protested Tom. "'Tis passing vulgar."

"And don't 'ee fret 'bout young Seth if he begin a-hollering in the church. I'll take him outside for Maisie. Might be all right, though, this time, on account of him not having no holy water a-splashed over his head, and a-blinding him," offered Jemima.

"'Tis Emily who be holding him. Miranda be the bridesmaid," explained Nicholas.

Nicholas stayed out of the way of the women, the day before the wedding. Maisie had made her own and Miranda's dress. Nicholas had seen Maisie's take shape, had admired its simplicity, and had snorted at Emily's reminder that his seeing it before the day would bring bad luck.

"All be Providence, sister. Baint worth the worry," he had told her.

Mrs. Misterton was going to try to squeeze into her own wedding dress, had she not outgrown it, a long time ago.

"'Taint *your* wedding mother," gently reminded Emily. "Now why don't you wear your blue one, with the high collar? 'Tis passing pretty."

"So Nicholas getting married, eh? He seem to do things back to front by abbing children first. Can't remember Miranda being born now. 'Tis an age ago."

"You must sleep early tonight, mother, as I be doing your hair for you, in the morning."

"Emily, I've been a-brushing my hair, all these years, so don't need a body to show me how now."

In the garden, Nicholas raked the soil, which crumbled in his fingers when he thumbed and fingered it. The grass had stopped growing, the clumps now flat. From the sky, a buzzard looked for food on the ground. A heath-cropper came over to the fence, to see what Nicholas was doing.

"Hello, soldier. What be you a-wanting?" said Nicholas, quietly.

The horse's tail flicked and swung at flies.

Miranda came to join him.

"There be cake for tomorrow, father, and apple juice. Emily says there will be a ribbon for my hair."

Why, how she be a-growing! he marvelled. She be more her mother, but a tiddy bit of me be there in the whole picture.

"Come here, girl."

His arms widened into a semi-circular invitation, and Miranda ran into them. He lifted her up, hugged her, and spun her round, till they both became dizzy.

"One more!" she begged, after she had finished staggering, as if drunk.

"Last one."

She squealed, bringing Mrs. Misterton to see what the fuss was about.

"Jacob, don't make Emily sick, as 'tis certain it will if you make a spinning top of her."

"Who be Jacob?" asked Miranda.

Now was the time to tell her, decided Nicholas.

"Sometimes, when you're old, and your hair be hoary, or a-falling out, the world seem different to how it be. Like, your eyes see what once a-been in front of you, but not now, and 'tis like you go back and forward, and you don't match the time on your clock. That be the case with Granmer, but we must not let her know that her memory be a pail with holes in it, as 'twon't mean a thing, as she probably a-gone elsewhere while we telling her."

Miranda listened, subtly pushing herself into her father to encourage him to make her go dizzy again.

"Father, you talk in riddles," she laughed.

"That be my curse, dear, but 'tis me, and how I say what I a-thinking. Words come out and hold hands with any wanting to go a walk."

"Can I talk in riddles, father?"

"I hope so, my dear. 'Twould be wondrous."

That evening, a quiet, missing during the day, settled throughout the house, in the garden, on the rest of the heath. The birds had fled early. Even the owl was respectful; its usual screech was muted to a brief call.

Miranda and Seth were sitting round the table, in the middle of which glowed the oil lamp.

"There be cakes, cold meats, a bird or two, which be cooked already," said Maisie.

"Leave it all till the morning, dear," said Nicholas. "'Tis quiet, and we should keep it so."

"I agree with Nicholas," said Emily. "'Twas not the same in Bath, which hide you in its noise and bustle."

"You back now," said Maisie.

"Going up now," said Mrs. Misterton. "Wedding, tomorrow."

Early, the next day, Nicholas put out the table and chairs, ready for the food when they returned. Maisie looked down at him from the bedroom window. There be the man who saved me, she sighed. The house be ours, the tiddy ones be ours, the day be ours. 'Tis a wondrous life.

Miranda sat still while Emily threaded ribbons into her niece's hair.

"You look like an angel," said Emily, when she had finished.

Miranda ran into the house to look at herself in the mirror.

"You'll wear that mirror out, girl," said Mrs. Misterton.

Nicholas had bought some new clothes, the first in ages, from a shop in Dorchester.

"They be for my wedding, and my Maisie want me tidy in church, but I don't want to add up to a gentleman, on account of me not being one, but a farmer. You got anything tolerable?"

So had begun the tailor's trial, and he sold Nicholas a new pair of trousers, a shirt, and a long coat.

"No hat, sir?"

"Got one as old as me. There be dust on the brambles, so 'taint a day for hats anyway."

"'Tis the custom."

"Not mine."

Thomas collected Mrs. Misterton, Emily, and Seth. On the way, Jemima cuddled Seth, told him a story about elves on the heath. Tom stood on the footplate, holding onto the side of the cart.

"Give us a song, Tom, to set the journey," called Thomas.

"You ever tried singing a song, holding on for dear life?"

"A song, please, Tom, and a merry one, too."

"A C, please, then, father."

Thomas delivered what he thought was a C, though Tom said he was flatter that Timothy Fleet, on Sundays. Tom found his own C, and began.

"O, please be my bride, all pretty and true,
and bake me a cake, cook a panful of stew,
and pledge me your love, daily, anew,
and I'll be your ram, if you'll be my ewe."

Jemima covered Seth's ears.

"Tom Hardy, there be a tiddy one on board!"

Emily and Thomas laughed so much, that Tom began a second verse, the narrative of which developed the last line of the previous one, in a more oblique way.

Coombs took Florence to Stinsford before fetching Nicholas and Maisie, who strolled down to the lane to await the coach.

"'Tis passing strange, this nobody," remarked Maisie.

"'Tis wondrous. Just you and me. Come a long way, girl."

"You saved me, Nicholas."

"Saved each other."

At Gifford's Farm, Victoria looked at her father's feet planted widely apart. Nicholas Gabriel Ilminster was sleeping soundly in his cot. In the barn, Maggie, who had fled the attentions of the receptionist in Lyme to seek a different way of living, and the other milkmaids held their breath, listened to the young master receiving his marching orders, the barrel of Zachariah's gun pointing the direction down the track. Megan never stirred.

"And if I ever sees you up at Gifford again, I'll shoot you!" warned Zachariah.

When he was sure Gabriel had gone, he went over to the barn, and hooked out Maggie with his finger.

"You, too," he said, "and take your fancy Lyme ways with you. This be a farm, not a knocking shop."

Nicholas was frightened by the word *asunder*. It rhymed with *thunder*, had a rumble like it, too. And then it was all over, when Maisie's ring – one her mother had passed down to her – was on, after a bit of pushing and shoving, a little *ouch* from the bride, and the vicar had pronounced them man and wife. When the orchestra began a tune, the zeal of the instrumentalists knew no bounds, and no one threw himself into the playing more than Thomas Hardy, who had oiled his bowing arm joints with a toast to the couple, with the other players, at the back of the church, before the ceremony.

Outside, in the light washed clean for the wedding, Nicholas stood with Maisie's arm in his. Over in the corner, the two brothers Misterton watched quietly. Miranda held her posy self-consciously.

"Come here, girl," called Maisie.

"What shall I do with my flowers?" asked Miranda.

Nicholas looked at Florence, who was standing back from the family, with Coombs.

"Take 'em to the lady, over there, and say they be for her."

Florence expressed great delight at her gift, and bent down to say something to her. Nicholas saw Miranda nod.

The orchestra removed itself from the church, and struck up a jolly tune. The vicar thought the jaunty rhythm rather incongruous with the headstones, felt the music ought to stop, but when Nicholas took him behind a tree to pay him for his services, the vicar's growing concern about the orchestra subsided.

"This is more than is owing," the vicar felt obliged to point out.

"'Tis so, but what you deserve, and what do please God."

"Then you are most kind, Nicholas. And you and Maisie look a picture, an absolute picture."

"Thank 'ee. 'Tis kind."

Eventually, Maisie and Nicholas were helped up into the coach, by Coombs.

"You will come and take a slice of cold meat and a tatty or two?" Maisie asked Florence. "There be cider, or wine, which Nicholas bought in Dorchester."

"'Tis wondrous kind, but I shall make my way home when Coombs returns. 'Tis a family day, and it be right, so."

Nicholas shut the paling gate.

"All in?" he called. "All my family home and dry?"

Nicholas sat down at the table, and the women started to bring out the food. The Hardys would stay for just a short while, not wishing to intrude, and Nicholas had only to ask, if he wanted a splash of music to help the food go down.

When Dorothy turned up at Chideock's house in Bridport, she looked as if she had not slept in ages. Chideock himself had passed sleepless nights, following his decision to separate from Daisy, who would have been, he felt, his prison warder. Monksbury, which was no longer required, was immediately in demand, and he sold it for more than he paid.

Dorothy stepped inside.

"Where have you been? The police are still looking for you."

"I know. I shall give myself up to them today, but I had to see you. I never meant any harm. I love Miranda so much that I had to try to make you see how much you would miss her if she went. But I now deeply regret it. I was foolish. And, of course, I have lost you, too."

Chideock passed her his handkerchief.

"Me?"

"Yes, you. Oh, how could you fail to see what I felt for you? Still feel for you. But all that is past hope now. All gone, and I am tired. So tired."

Chideock managed to catch her before she fell, carried her upstairs to her room, and lay her on the bed.

"Go to sleep now, Dorothy. We shall talk about this when you are better."

The Hardys left, Jemima barely able to prise herself away from Seth. The meat had all gone, and only a few crumbs of cake remained. Soon, there was a sense of the day coming to an end. Plates and pots were taken indoors. There was talk of ordinary things. Nicholas contemplated his return to the farm, the next day. No time must be lost in realising their plan for improving workers' conditions. But that was tomorrow; there were still a few hours of his wedding day to go.

Mrs. Misterton, the elder, had slept, on and off, had held Seth, and given Miranda a hug.

"You all right, mother?" asked Maisie, when they were alone.

"As right as you'd expect, given my age and bones, which a-hurt in the hips and knees so much I'd snap if I bended any."

"You enjoy today?"

"Tolerable."

"Tolerable? Aint you pleased I'm your daughter-in-law, mother?"

"You a good girl, Edith."

Towards the end of the afternoon, the air became cooler. Emily told Miranda a story. In the middle if it, Miranda saw James Chideock and Dorothy, in another place, in clothes different from her father's and Maisie's. Their words had somehow the same meaning, but had different sounds, followed each other in a different order.

"And they all lived happily ever after," said Emily.

Nicholas popped his head in.

"Just seeing out the day, for a minute or two," he said.

He looked at the cottage, from higher up the garden. The house needed to be bigger, and there was space to do it. Conjuror Sayer had earned money, in a different way from his brother, in his *own* way, had spent little, and saved a lot. Thomas would make a good job of it.

As he walked aimlessly in the garden, he looked for the spot on which the outhouse had stood. It had been dark inside, and it had taught him patience and a love of freedom. He had set fire to it, which had taught him the futility of vengeance, and the pain of punishment, had seen his father work there, and he had himself learned to make objects in it.

In the grass, adders slithered. In the woods, birds called to each other, and Nicholas knew the voice of each one, their repertoire. On the grass, evening dew was forming, showing on his shoes. Above his head, a halo of gnats wobbled.

These clothes belong to this day, and I will not wear them again. Today I have more than I did the last time, when there had been just a table in a dark room, on a street, and so far back I wonder if 'twas a mere story I have heard, and not me and Ruth. And me, a-sent away by my father because I went to his brother. 'Twas as big a secret that ever was locked away, what split them, and has died with the conjuror. Now mother so lost, 'twon't ever be known, and 'tis probably best. I be married again, this time to Maisie, and we have a boy, and he will learn that there are things he can do, things he can't.

The heath-croppers bowed their heads, kissed the ground. A fox stopped in the middle-distance, and, when it saw him, stared, and continued on its way.

Nicholas listened. Father and son had taken up their fiddles again, the tune now more contemplative, less frenetic, and the notes were drifting up the hill like smoke from a chimney.

Back in the garden, Maisie was waiting in the doorway, arms folded.

"Thought you might have left me," she said.

"Been in the woods and round about."

"Seth and Miranda both down, mother a-snoring, and Emily a-reading."

"And 'ee?"

"Thinking. Just a-thinking."

"'Ee darned those socks?"

"Yes, and tolerable."

"A good wife, then."

"'Tis certain."

He sat in a chair, and thought of the time when he had no letters, and how Emily had taught him. If only he could put his finger on what made things as they are. Providence, it be, or I aint Nicholas Misterton, he concluded.

He promised one thing: that, one midsummer's day, he would take Miranda to Bucky Doo, when the time was right, would show her the corner round which the dancers had come, and how Ruth had danced her way into his life, so that she could be born. Then he would take her to Ruth's grave, explain how she had fallen accidentally off the cliff, and died. To keep Miranda ignorant of what had happened would be wrong.

And maybe she herself would put on a white dress, twirl, rise and fall on tiptoes, draw eyes to her, grow wings, two of them. Angels need two, just like Alice Herries.